A BLACK ENGLISHMAN

Carolyn Slaughter was born in New Delhi, India, and spent most of her childhood in the Kalahari Desert. She is the author of eight other novels and the memoir *Before the Knife*. She now lives in the United States.

ALSO BY CAROLYN SLAUGHTER

Relations

Columba

Magdalene

Heart of the River

The Banquet

The Innocents

Dreams of the Kalahari

The Widow

Before the Knife: Memories of an African Childhood

A BLACK ENGLISHMAN

Carolyn Slaughter

faber and faber

First published in 2004
by Faber and Faber Limited
3 Queen Square London WCIN 3AU

This paperback edition published in 2005

Published in the United States by Faber and Faber Inc.
an affiliate of Farrar, Straus and Giroux LLC, New York

Designed by Gretchen Achilles
Printed in England by Mackays of Chatham plc

A CIP record for this book
is available from the British Library

ISBN 0–571–22028–2

2 4 6 8 10 9 7 5 3 1

For my grandmother, Anne Webb.
No more sad endings.

Love needs not caste, nor sleep a broken bed.
I went in search of love and lost myself.

—HINDU PROVERB

ACKNOWLEDGMENTS

MY THANKS AND GRATITUDE go to Leita Hamill, Jonathan Galassi, and Betsy Lerner for their invaluable editorial assistance and support throughout the writing of this book. Thanks also to Kemp Battle and Marianne Velmans for their insights and improvements to the text, and to Alexandra Martin for her help in medical matters.

I am indebted to many writers who have been a great source of inspiration and without whom I couldn't have even contemplated writing about India. Some of these are E. M. Forster, George Orwell, Somerset Maugham, Paul Scott, R. K. Narayan, Ruth Prawer Jhabvala, V. S. Naipaul, Salman Rushdie, Arundhati Roy, Jhumpa Lahiri, Charles Allen, Peter Hopkins, Barbara Crossette, Gurcharan Das, Hari Kunzru, Monica Ali, and, of course, Rudyard Kipling.

THIS BOOK IS loosely based on the life of my maternal grandmother, Anne Webb, who went out to India after the Great War. When she was thirty she was placed in an asylum called Ranchi, and she stayed there until India became independent. She was then transferred to a mental hospital in England, where she stayed until her death in 1984. It was here that I first came to know her, having believed up to that point that she was dead.

PART ONE

One

1920

There's no twilight in India. Darkness overtakes with shocking finality. I can't get used to it, but it's something to do with the breathless quality of the country and the sudden way things happen here. There's no time to adjust—no warning. I miss the slow blending of colors as shadows come and go until at last there's just one color, the way it is at home. Here saffron turns to flame and then to gold tinged with blue, and then it goes black. In a moment it's all over, and that startling dip into darkness feels like a reflection of jarring change or even a foreshadowing of something dreadful. Now of course I see that it was my own darkness that came on suddenly, but I didn't know it at the time. If I had, would I have stepped so jauntily up the gangway of that P & O liner and waved goodbye, wearing my new suede gloves the color of pistachios? Would I have chosen any of it if I'd known that darkness can strike like a fist or that a person can drown in it—

and want to? Absolutely. I'd have chosen the whole bang shoot because I thought I could pull off anything then: I was twenty-three and invincible, and I was going out to India, India, India. It was as though that crimson, heart-shaped continent were thrumming with excitement and glamour all for me. And love had come again. So I picked up my skirts and charged at it, not caring how it would end. I was frightfully in love with love; I saw myself running to meet it the way a man stretches up his arms and whirls a woman down from a train and says: Beloved, you're here, now we can begin our exquisite life together.

My mother knew better, but I wasn't listening. As she turned to leave the ship with me on it, she said: You've made your bed now, Isabel, you'll have to lie on it. She had no idea what she was talking about because for her there'd never been any getting used to, putting up with, or making do. She was a thoroughbred; she had her own money, and it was only in marrying dear Pater that she'd taken a step down, which no doubt was why it was particularly galling for her to see me making the same mistake. When I'd told her that I was going to marry Neville, she was against it. It's not his origins, she said. No, don't give me that look; it's not those I object to, though certainly they leave much to be desired. I know the grimy village where his aunt lives, and there are God knows how many Webbs in the villages of Wales. And it's not even that he's been in India too long: his father born there, and Neville too. That's far too long to be away from civilization. And though you will sniff at this, it's not even that he's an noncommissioned officer. No, it's really not that. It's simply a matter of character. His is poor.

And with that she packed trunk after trunk of elegant clothes, handmade in London or Paris, and a pale gray visiting suit, and a couple of black gowns for the balls she imagined I'd go to, and some pert little frocks for playing bridge at the club. She even had some lightweight jodhpurs made for me in Bond Street. As if any of this were relevant. She made her view of Neville plain, but never once did she say to me: Don't do it. Perhaps she didn't think she had the right to counsel me in the matter of love. It was an area where her intelligence had slipped; this is what she made you feel. So she was unable to say to me: This is a mistake, I forbid it, or even, For God's sake, Isabel, don't be such a damn fool. Of course, had she tried, I'd not have given her the time of day. I rolled around in her disapproval voluptuously, and I have to say it made me more determined to put my own questions about Neville aside. I certainly had a sense of Neville's character; his eyes have a sleepy, predatory look, and I should have known that night in Porthcawl—but what's the point? It's like walking backward to see if you can find what you knew perfectly well you'd dropped in the first place.

I was willing to go to India with him because I'd chosen marriage more than Neville, and more than either, I'd chosen Life. It was nothing to do with money or security; we had pots of that. It was pure escape, pure rebound—nothing more. I had to get out of Wales. And I had to forget the dead, whose bones were filtering through the rainy battlefields of France, and I had to get away from all those who'd come crawling back, dragging wounds and amputations behind them, their minds crazed by the memory of what they'd seen. My brother talked about it once, when he was drunk, but then he clammed up and never mentioned it again. The ones who came back are all like that. They can't get over being alive when everyone else is dead. Jack told me that an officer of the Queen's Regiment had set himself on fire and that soldiers got medals for valor when really they were throwing themselves at the guns. It was hard to believe, after all we'd once believed about the glory and honor of war. Jack spoke about Ed from Cardiff, who'd ended up wandering around no-man's-land, holding his blown off arm like a bouquet of roses. Once Jack saw a soldier digging a forward trench slice through a human face, and one night he stumbled over a corpse only to find that it was a boy he'd sat next to in school. I couldn't take it in. All I could think about was Gareth's scribbled words on a scrap of grubby paper: *My dearest love, the frontline trenches are ten miles away and we are marching to Arras, dead horses everywhere and men tossed in ditches, mangled and headless. No one bothers to collect the dead anymore. None of us have the foggiest idea what we're doing, we're civilians, amateurs. All the real soldiers are dead.*

OFTEN I FEEL as if I were in the same desperate rush that he was when he first went to France. Off he marched to war, boarding the troop train at Waterloo to have a grand adventure: Can't wait to get to the front to do my bit; am waiting for orders and desperate to go. I had the same feelings about India, going out in search of a grand adventure, an idea in my head. Mine was a vision of what lay at the end of the shipping lines, where the East began: a world wild and exotic beyond anything our little island could offer. Gareth left behind childhood and innocence and the first passion of our youth; I was leaving behind all my shattered hopes, the haunted, backward glances at places where the dear dead had once run up the blue hills and talked about how it would be tomorrow.

SUDDENNESS CAME ON the minute we reached India. It wasn't that way going out. The voyage out was a continuation of all I'd ever known, a slow glide through deep water, a casual changing of light as we moved eastward, until one morning everything was lit up like the huge diamond in Queen Victoria's India crown. We were heading into mystery and magic, into that gorgeousness I'd imagined since the days of flying about in my head, reading *The Arabian Nights*. On the boat, you see, we had so much time to get used to change, that's the thing, even going what's called the shortcut. Naturally, I was sick as a dog crossing the Bay of Biscay, felt my insides would fly out of my mouth any minute. I was so ill and green I thought I'd be happier if they just hurled me over the side and made an end of it. Whenever I lurched up on deck—only at night, of course, because one can't be vomiting in broad daylight—I saw the regulars hanging on to the railing, the same green faces puking over the side. We recognized one another, but turned away, each enclosed in a shameful cell of sickness, not saying a word.

The minute we got to the Mediterranean, I got my balance back. I began to feel the beauty of the sea again and my old kinship to it. I remembered the way we'd run down to the children's beach near Porthcawl early in the morning when no foot or paw had dented it. I'd wait for Jack to come down with Gareth, and we'd make sand castles, the three of us, I in my woolly bathing suit, which scratched so horribly between the legs, and the two of them running, kicking up sand. They buried me in the sand so that just my face was showing and then stuck a jam sandwich in my mouth to see if I could eat it without making the sand crack. In the old days, sailing to India meant dragging all the way around the Cape, instead of nipping across the Suez Canal and then down the Red Sea, past Mecca to Aden. The voyage out was so lovely. We had long, dreamy days with only the steady pulse of the ocean pulling us toward the Arabian Sea. At Port Said, little boys dove for pennies, and if you lowered a basket with money in it, they put in oranges, black grapes, bananas and pineapples, dates and little purple figs that were so much nicer than the dried ones we got at home. Once a chameleon came up in the basket, and it was so interesting to see such a peculiar Darwinian little chap; he was like something out of the Stone Age. The boat was oh, so glam, reclining on the water like a magnificent white hotel on a blue hill. It had a monumentalism about it. India has that, and I suppose the empire had that once too. Pater, using his Liberal Voice, insisted all that was over by the end of the century. The imperial ideal is dead, he'd say wearily, and the imperial race is weak and corrupt at its core. You certainly wouldn't know that on the *Viceroy of India* as it swanned across the ocean toward its glittering destination, ruling the waves, riding the crest of glory.

Naturally, Neville and I didn't have the money for first class, but it was the thing to do to travel POSH—port side going out, starboard coming home. That way one avoided the worst of the sun. For

Neville, sailing P & O was a new experience, just as it was for me. When he'd sailed to India, it was on those ghastly troopships that take months to reach Bombay. But it was odd how, at first, as we embarked, the whole thing seemed to rub him up the wrong way. He was snappish and seemed to want to get away from it all. There we were, civilians and military together, and even on the quayside he was upset and surly. He wouldn't speak and stood stiffly beside me while my head was whipping this way and that, looking at all the expensive luggage, the porters and passengers, some wearing their new topis just for a laugh, the women dressed up to the nines, as if they were at Ascot. A few beautifully dressed Indians were strolling on the deck: exquisite women in saris the colors of exotic birds, men wearing impeccable suits from Savile Row, with snow white turbans on their heads. They were a handsome people, intelligent and cultured, with lovely deep brown eyes. I couldn't stop staring. I'd not seen Asians before. Well, of course one doesn't, certainly not in Wales, though Mama told me that after the grim Mutiny business, in eighteen something or other, Queen Victoria always kept two Indian servants by her side whenever she went out in public, as a sign of solidarity, and of shame, for our acts of vengeance after the sepoy uprising. The Indians on the ship dipped their heads in a wonderful way, and I wanted to get close to them to see the exact color of their skin.

My eyes were out on sticks. Going down into the hold were vast mahogany cabinets and chests, pianos, dining room tables and chairs, rocking horses, oil paintings, carpets, saddles, a grandfather clock or two, crates of china and crystal, tea chests full of English silver, and even a spanking new Bentley. Must have been for the Viceroy, or a maharaja, but then I saw the little flag all aflutter on the front, so that settled it. Such extravagance, and all this for hoi polloi, the Raj of India, who were sailing off where destiny and duty drove them. But perhaps that's not fair, and maybe those days are over just as Pater says they are. Maybe going to India was their way of getting away from what had happened to England, leaving behind dead sons and lovers,

or blank eyes in melted faces that look out of windows, seeing nothing. Maybe they have their own soldier who jumps out of his skin if a
door slams or a firework goes off. I read in the paper about a doctor
who works with the shell-shocked; the marching dead, he calls them.
They quiver when the wind blows or start screaming when they pick
up a smell that reminds them of poison gas. We don't have shell-
shocked soldiers in India—or do we? Thousands of Indian soldiers
died on the western front. Why were they willing to go off to die for
something they couldn't have cared a fig about? All those regiments
blown to bits, all those faces turning to mold on the cold hillside.
Mother told me that in India, during the war, sacrifices were made,
contributions to the war effort, socks and sweaters knitted, that sort of
thing, but it couldn't have been the same as what happened to England, because for us it was right on the doorstep, far too close.

Sometimes, at home, when the wind was up, I seemed to get the
smell of the dead wafting over the washing line or the cries of men
dragging their boots down the lane. Even though I'd only heard about
it—breathed or whispered in drawing rooms, or read in the columns
of the dead in *The Times*—it was more real than the soup on the stove.
There was a pressure in the air, a certainty of doom that never left.
Even in Wales, protected from it, I remember how it felt to see the
regiments marching past the post office to go to war. I'd look at one
face and then another, thinking, You won't come back, and you
won't, but you might, and you will, on and on down the marching
line, ticking them off, trying to hazard a prayer, or barter with God,
to spare the one soldier that absolutely had to come back, because
without him life was unimaginable.

ON THE SHIP, for the first time really, I got to know the soldier I'd
married—not the one I'd wanted to marry but the one I did marry.
I'd never thought of Neville quite as a soldier until we were sailing to
India. Later I began to understand how significant a part this played in
his character, but in those first days, when he was not much more

than a stranger to me, I wasn't looking that hard. Neville can be charming even as he can be peculiar, and you never know quite what you'll be getting from day to day or even from moment to moment. He has a vulgarity that's offset by a kind of meticulous neatness, and I think he gets that from the army. I first spotted it in the way he dressed and took care of his clothing. On the boat he was always hanging up and polishing, sending clothes off for washing and pressing, buffing up his shoes and brushing his hair with a hard palm-down smoothing motion, like someone ironing. He carries a uniform well, and he's handsome in a Celtic way, long face and melancholy eyes, but he doesn't look quite as good in mufti. There's something impressive about khaki. Khaki, so I'm told, began in India when they mixed up some curry powder and turmeric to get a less visible, more jungly shade. God knows how splendid our soldiers must have looked in the days of scarlet and gold or in pure, brilliant white, but khaki is the color of conquest, no doubt about that.

I noticed that women stared at Neville as he strolled on deck; he stared back. But that's natural enough. I look at men, and why not? At least I wasn't one of those girls going out to India to try to nab a husband. Neville sneered at them, and I didn't quite understand why. I mean, they weren't riffraff, not by any means. They were elegant and young, wore slim skirts and high heels, little hats set off to one side on gleaming hair, their faces delicately rouged, wearing lipstick that deep plum shade fashionable in London last season. One woman wore a navy fedora with a brim that hid most of her face. She had the loveliest pale gray traveling costume with simple and expensive lines, and it held her body in a tight embrace. Those girls made up what's called the Fishing Fleet; those who sail back alone are called the Returned Empties—odd that they're thought of that way when they're the daughters of distinguished Anglo-Indian families. Have people forgotten that there's a shortage of men or that the officers are all dead?

As I was thinking this, almost as if he could divine my thoughts,

Neville came out with one of his truly ghastly remarks: Bunch of desperate bitches; fat lot of good their looks and lolly will do them with
all the eligible bachelors rotting in Flanders and Ypres, all those pam-
pered bodies feeding rats and worms.

Lucky for you, I snapped, that you could hide out in India and
not have to risk your precious life for England. He went red in the
face and his hands knotted, and I swear that if we'd not been surrounded by other people, he might actually have struck me. I thought
this but immediately shoved the thought aside. He'd never strike a
woman, but the language, to say *bitches* out loud like that, it was awful, and even worse when he grabbed my arm and yanked me down
the steps to our cabin. He slammed the door, stood in front of it, and
rapped out: I'm a soldier, Isabel, get that through your head. I've been
one since I was sixteen and ran away to join the Royal Artillery as a
trumpeter. My ancestors have all been soldiers, men with blood on
their hands, professional killers. We're not the landed gentry out for a
fox hunt on the plains of Belgium and France, to bag a few Huns, to
take a few potshots from the top of a hill. I've been fighting since I
was a boy, killed my first man when I was fourteen. I like it. I'm good
at it. I don't do it for England. I do it because it's the way I make my
living. I've been on more campaigns on the North-West Frontier,
fighting Pathans and savages day in and out, than that bunch of faggots
on the fields of Normandy will ever know. So don't you bloody well
question my courage or talk to me that way again.

I stared at him with my mouth ajar, and then I had one simple
desire: to take his head off with one sweep of my hand, even if it
broke all my fingers. My anger was so precipitous that it stunned me.
I almost looked around to see where it had come from. Neville
stormed off out of the cabin and spent the rest of the night knocking
it back at the bar. I wanted to keep my fury going. I needed to have
something out with him, even though I didn't know what it was. I
kept thinking: Why on earth did I ever have anything to do with this
lout? Why had I even thought of coming with him in the first place?

What madness had come over me? Much later that night I was sleepless and still furious. I wanted to go up on deck but was scared of the drunks who roll about out there all night until a steward escorts them to their cabins. It was only at dawn that I realized what my anger was really about, and then of course it was gone in a second. I crept deep into the covers and sobbed with grief for what had happened to Gareth and me—to have lost him that way, after I'd left him that way. It was more than I could bear, out there on the vast ocean heading east.

There was a strange kind of truce between Neville and me after that. It was as if we'd both become real for the first time. We'd had a good look at each other, and it wasn't attractive. And that remark of his about his family being in the army for three generations in India, and especially the bit about men with blood on their hands, it was ugly, and it stuck in my head. As the days passed, I came to realize just how much my husband was a soldier and how well it defined him. On deck we'd be strolling, sometimes up ahead of an officer, and quick as a wink he'd step aside, almost clicking his heels to let those "faggots" pass. Life on the boat was like that; the soldiers were always on duty, pandering to the officers night and day. And though he hated them, Neville was right there pandering too. The traveling empire was divided up according to prestige. The Indian Civil Service came at the top, with high-ranking army and government people thrown in; then the Indian police were off on their own, as were the planters, who drank like fishes. Then of course there were the despised types that were making a fortune in India out of tea, cotton, and the spice and gem trade. A couple of planters, who were said to be "retired from tea," were heading back to India because they couldn't take life in England. They told stories about fabulous estates and exquisite pleasure gardens up in the hills, in places like Assam and Darjeeling. The military were of course separated by rank, with the officers getting the best of everything: cool smoking and drawing rooms, a vast room where they played billiards and snooker, dining rooms and bars, roomy cabins, and the run of the decks. There were stewards hovering at their elbows with ashtrays and gin and tonics. They barely needed to raise a finger. It's like that here, of course, but here we all get that, not just the officers. Here everyone can afford a servant problem.

When I remarked on how the officers behaved on board, Neville snorted. There they lounge, he said, fretting about what exactly should be worn in the Punjab Club. Will it be white jackets and black trousers, or the other way around? It was the same on the troopships. Our boys got barely enough room to turn round. Battalions were herded onto the troop deck or under the boat deck, conditions no sepoy of mine would be subjected to, flooding latrines and vomit everywhere, terrible food. No officer came to check on the men, to see if they were being fed, or if the latrines worked, or if we had water. Worse than the front. I buttoned my lip and strolled on. But as we got farther and farther from England and closer to India, which of course was home to him, Neville got sweeter. His bitterness vanished once we were out in the middle of the ocean, with no land in sight for days on end. When an occasional ship came along, we'd all rush to the side and wave like mad. I saw sharks way down in the indigo blue, and flying fish broke the smooth, flat water. We kept on sailing, and every day it got hotter. People gave ominous little warnings: Oh, this is nothing—they'd laugh grimly—try the Hot Weather in Delhi or Bombay. Or: Wait till you get a taste of it just before the monsoon. Then you'll know what India's all about. Every day on the ship it got hotter and hotter. It was so bad in the cabins at night that the stewards came to take our bedding up on deck. It was such a laugh, all of us girls in our nighties, clutching pillows for modesty's sake, and men in pajamas, traipsing up to the upper deck to get air. We lay there chummily together, looking up and counting the stars, and we sort of camped up there, feeling the soft, cool sea air restore us to sanity and sleep. A woman was reading by moonlight, and so I nipped down and got my Kipling and did the same. One man stayed up all night, resting his back against the railings as he slugged down an entire bottle of gin, and by dawn he looked exactly the same as he had at the beginning.

Neville liked to sleep on deck; he said it was like camping in the hills or on the frontier. It was the first time he'd spoken to me about his life in India, so I heard it romantically, under moonlight, with the soft rise of the ocean taking us closer. He told me about encounters with wild natives beyond the United Provinces—what they call the UP—north of Punjab and into Afghanistan, where savage tribes are constantly warring each other and where the warlords cut each other's throats in broad daylight. This part is out of England's dominion, and no one can tame or subdue the tribal hordes, try as they might. Neville told me about the close shaves he'd had but said that he was like his father, Major Webb, of the Fifth Royal Gurkha Rifles, who'd never got nicked by a blade or gun. It seemed to me, listening, that he loved and admired his native troops. He called them those bloody browns, or even bally wogs, in a feigned common soldier's accent, but he usually ended up saying that they were great soldiers, fine fighting men, the best, and the empire would be nothing without them. It's that to-and-fro tendency about Neville that's perplexing, but now I've been here a bit, I've come to see that it's one of the things about the English generally in India. It's as if some kind of natural fondness between the English and the Indian has to be constantly repudiated. You notice it particularly when you first get here, and then you begin to notice it less.

Up on the deck with the stars swimming the sky Neville was on top of me all the time. It was odd because he'd been rather proper and restrained in that month that we first got to know each other in Wales, before we married. I remember a time when we came upon a couple round the back of the pub and he was incensed by what they were up to. I excused it by saying that the war mentality was still around, as indeed it was. I used to think that the war was actually in me, as it had been in Gareth, only in me it wasn't visible. I was impatient about everything then, agitated and tense, and, as I look back on it, my body was like that too, wanting to get over what it remembered, desperate to forget. It seemed sex could do it. But we had no sex in Wales, Neville and I, and we were married the day before we sailed. The strange thing is that the minute we were on the ship, he couldn't get enough. I couldn't move but that he'd grab and maul me, shoving his hands down my front and up my skirt. He was like a starving person, and three or four times a day were nothing to him. Thinking like this is both invigorating and terrifying at the same time, especially here, where everything's at least twenty years behind the times, and not a word is ever mentioned about what goes on between men and women in the privacy of their bedrooms. Sometimes I think that even the word *body* is too much for the English. It's worse here because you simply can't get away from bodies. The human form is rammed in your face at all times. Brown bodies, eating, crouching, spitting, mating, stinking, sleeping, rotting, and dying, in the streets and drains and in the brown shroud of the river. They're always under the feet, under the eye, in buffalo carts, tongas, and rickshaws, in shadow and sunlight, in the jungle or the Ganges, in our bedrooms and kitchens, in our dreams and nightmares. It's as if these bodily sights have sent the English scuttling into fortified cantonments where one can pretend that nothing carnal goes on, or at least not among the English.

I should be fair and say that Neville started off tenderly enough with me. After all, he thought me a virgin. He was slow and considerate, perhaps even nervous at first, and he had a sense of me, of my body. And he most certainly knew what he was doing. I was curious about that, and I wanted to ask, but how could I without seeming to be in the know myself? We moved gently and rhythmically, rocking with the waves into our conjugal life, and though it was a relief to feel intense pleasure again, it was also a grief. I wasn't always sure that I could hide that from him, and sometimes I think he knew I was sad, and then he was particularly gentle and he would hold me as we lay together afterward. And though I've come to see that there's something about him that's always on duty, he wasn't that way when it came to love. He'd experienced carnality in a different way, that's all I can say, or maybe I'm just saying that he wasn't English about it.

Once I asked him if he talked about sexual matters with other soldiers. I could talk quite freely with him then; it was only later that he put a curfew on all that. He spoke to me about things I was terribly interested in: about the way men talk about women—how soldiers talk. I think I was still wondering if Gareth had talked about me to the men in the trenches, on those long, lonely nights with only the sounds of the shells dropping, or a shot aimed at a head that like a swimmer's had come up into the moonlight to breathe. When Gareth wrote those words, he made it so real. And now I see that when you write, it becomes less dark. Neville answered my questions easily enough. In the officers' mess, there's no talk of women, he said lazily, lying on his back on the narrow berth, with the little porthole to one side and the sheets fallen down on the floor. There's no swearing of any kind either; that'd be bad form. Among the NCOs, wives are never discussed in that way, of course, but we might talk of certain things, now and then, when we've had a keg or two and got carried away. In the barracks and mess, the talk is naturally foul. Men discuss women in the brothels—women called black velvet, or ramjanis, or rum johnies. Some men get hooked up with Eurasian women, who are desperate to have sex with white men. There's talk of that kind, but never about *our* women. And you have to understand that there's so little opportunity to meet or even see women in India. There are the wives, missionaries, and nuns, of course, and the fresh meat that comes out on the boat, but they'll be picked off quickly by officers, because our caste system's no easier, and it's impossible to find a middle-class girl in India.

So that's why he came to Wales, to find a middle-class girl, marry her, and bring her back to India. Mother would be appalled to think of us as middle class, but surely her upperclassness has been watered down by Pater's lack of it. On the other hand, they both rather tried to elevate the Indian bit of the Pater's past—all that talk of the plantations in Assam and how Grandfather had made his money in tea. But they left out the bit about no public school and about the scandal, followed by the hurried departure from India to cover up something I've never been able to get to the bottom of. There was a huge oil painting on the wall of a child who drowned in India. That's when they cleared out, buried the dead boy and took Pater to England. He was seven when he left, but still, he was born here, and that comforts me, makes me think I have a link with India—not quite a stranger.

On the boat going over, as the days grew hotter, the lovemaking changed. Sometimes I'd walk into the cabin after taking a stroll on deck and he'd be lying on the narrow berth and would push me down and enter me with a force that would leave me swollen and raw. I began to beg off, or I'd spend hours in the lounge, reading, so as not to be alone with him. On the deck, on those hot, hot nights, when you'd think he'd be more restrained because of the proximity of others, he was less. In fact, the idea that the other passengers might know made him even more determined to get sounds out of me, which at one time wasn't hard to do, but as his ways got rougher, I got quieter. And then I cut off from him. There was something odd about it, peculiar; it was as disturbing as his remark about men with blood on their hands. On deck, when the stewards brought our bedding up, the men slept on one side and the women on the other. Only we two were off on our own, which was frowned on, but he didn't care. What people think—civilians, I mean—never bothers him. What the army thinks is another matter entirely. When I look back, our honeymoon makes me feel peculiar. I used to admire Neville's body; it's a bit like a sculpture, each muscle and curve defined and hard-edged. Men's bodies amaze me because they're so unlike mine, which lolls and dips and curves this way and that and, to be honest, is just plain full—not brimming like Mother's, but full all the same. Fat is not a word we use, Mother and I. There was a time when that word might have applied, and Mother would say it was the Italian tendency. She said that in my case it would pass, because I had enough Welsh blood to thin me down. The longer I'm in India, the narrower I get, which is not as pleasing as I'd imagined because it emphasizes my tallness, as well as the heaviness of my breasts. But to Neville: His hair was longer then, so it was more curly, dark brown and soft. He was a little like Gareth when you looked at his face sideways. Now of course the army's got him, and you can see each hair and follicle the way you can see each muscle on his chest and abdomen.

Once I asked him where he'd learned so much about women's bodies. He said it was because of what you saw on the temple walls, and watching the dancing girls, and how sex was not shameful in India, just part of religion, part of life. He talked about the things he'd seen up on the frontier, where the natives were insatiable for women's bodies, though despising women at the same time and using them as an excuse to kill each other. He said the maharajas were the worst and had harems full of young girls and used them all, a different one every night. I said I didn't quite see how hearing about women would make him such an expert. Oh, he said, I got to know my way around by reading the *Kama Sutra*. And he toppled me backward onto the sheets and started up again. Neville is insatiable in exactly the way he says the Pathans are. I began to wonder if it might be like opium for him, something he just couldn't get enough of or do without. Then I thought that perhaps it was to do with having no women for so long, there being so few in India, but then that made me think about the brothels, but it was harder to ask him about this. I suppose I was really trying to understand something about the kind of man he was, and I was beginning to see him not so much as a man but as a soldier, a person altered by war. And that was eerie, to have another version of what I'd left behind. Gareth was destroyed by the experience of war, first his mind and then his body, and Neville was brutalized simply by being a soldier, a man with blood on his hands, liking to kill.

I learned nothing from Neville about what went on with Englishmen and native women in India, but I'd already got some veiled information from the Pater. Pretending to be instructive about life in India, he'd told me about the bibis and the way Englishmen, in the past, had not only one mistress but sometimes several. When India was first colonized, Englishmen had even married Indian women. Intermingling was encouraged then, to settle the men—make them stay and all that—and it still goes on, though more clandestinely now. It sounded as if at one time the bibi was almost official, the approved alternative to an Indian wife. She had her own house in the garden with her servants and her children. And all this was quite congenial until a wife came out from England, and then no more bibi; no more coffee-colored issue. The Pater said that Indian women were wonderful and knew entirely how to please. He gave me a clue, in the most delicate way, of course, that perhaps this was part of the grandfather scandal and the reason his parents had left India, but as usual I didn't get the whole scoop. He implied that he was talking about domesticity and submission rather than erotic matters, but now I think he was trying to warn me. The English wife put her foot down, he said, and that changed the whole bang shoot for everyone and made relations between English and Indian a very different matter. I was to hear that tone about the Englishwoman, the memsahib, a great deal when I got to India. It's a tone of disapproval and annoyance, implying that Englishwomen in India are a nuisance and spoil the fun for the men. On my first day on station I heard one of Neville's pals say: You got hooked up, Webb? What rotten luck. Your life's done for now, old man. Too bad.

WHEN I LEFT HOME, Mother gave me a cutting from her favorite lilac tree, the only one that survived the worst winter in living memory. It was in the middle of the war, when things on the front couldn't have been worse. The snow kept coming down until it was above the knee, and the cold had a ferocity that made us think, Is it like this for them in France, are they dying of cold and exposure as well as the horror? It was when I first started wondering about survival. Why had that particular tree made it through the winter? And then, when it bloomed again, it did so in such a spectacular way that it made mother cry. Look, she said, it's blooming for all the dead ones that can't. And she walked quickly away with her head down. Whom was she crying for? I'll never know. Our boy, Jack, was safely back; sent home with a head injury after the Battle of Loos. But she was crying for someone. It was a time when something was loose in the house; it made us full of tension—something more than the war, something to do with Mother. The Pater kept his distance and was struggling too, but with him it's another kind of retreat, very unlike Mother's. There are secrets about Mother, one knows that, but she won't let you near them, so I don't try to winkle anything out of her. She's so open and direct in many ways—says it's the Italian in her—but she can also be impossible to understand. I felt lonely with her so wrapped up in herself. So all that winter I just read on, deep into Pound and Yeats, and swallowing *Sons and Lovers* and *Dubliners* in one go, trying to find life in the pages, our own life being too full of dread to stay in it for long.

When I told Mother I was going to India, she went straight out to the garden to cut and pot the lilac. I said it couldn't possibly survive the heat. Of course it will, she said, it will just have a different extreme to bear with, but it can manage that, having learned how. And anyway, you'll be in upper India, the Punjab, not Calcutta or Bombay. It will settle if you take care of it. It may have worse winters to contend with if you go as far north as Jalalabad or Peshawar, but at least it has that memory in its bones already. She was tucking the little twig into a small wooden box with some stones, earth, and a dollop of manure from the stables, all of which she pressed down firmly. It will be perfectly fine, she said, you'll see.

There were no flowers in the gardens when I left, not even a snowdrop, but whenever I think of Mother's garden, I see it awash with lilac, lavender, and wisteria, and I see her elegant, staked perennials beautifully massed in long beds—blue and white and pink. She tends them herself, adding more varieties each year, always making sure that the flowers in each bed are the same color. Sometimes she'll allow a white lily or peony with an edge of pink, or a blue hydrangea with a fleck of white, but she tolerates no real digressions. When you wake at dawn and look out across the gardens, those tranquil pools of blue, silvery white, or rose have a gorgeous stillness that's almost un-earthly. I'd stand at my window and look at my mother's garden and try to work her out, but I never could. Perhaps I'll always just admire and adore her, but never really know her at all. Up on the rise, the rose garden with its soft-headed beauties was a lake of pale pink, yellow, and white. Never a red rose. Vulgar creature, common as muck, she'd snap, putting on a lowbred English accent. She hates anything garish or crude; the marigolds here, their harsh orange and yellow and the pong that comes off them would drive her to distraction, but she'd love the lilies, orchids and frangipani and the small wildflowers that pop up when the rains come.

I see my mother walking among her flowers, wearing her floppy straw hat, her basket piled high with roses as she walks slowly down the long path that leads up past the croquet green and the tall poplars that remind her of Tuscany. I see her as she stoops to free a tangle of vine or snaps off a dead head, and I watch her climb the stone steps that lead to the kitchens, where Lucy will arrange the roses in vases and place them all over the house. Mother will put a little bunch close to my pillow so I can smell them as I dream. And she'll have one on her side of the bed too, next to the picture of her own mother, who died when Mama was eleven. I need sometimes to remember how beautiful it all was. Our gray stone house surrounded by tall trees nestling in the valley, which opened up into deep meadows. The bridge over the stream is clear, full of mottled trout flickering in and out of watercress and reeds. Beyond the gardens, the green swell of the orchard dips down to the river running along the valley floor. I'd hear the familiar sounds of the coal mine, and the church clock striking the hour, but even that is sad now: *Stands the Church clock at ten to three? And is there honey still for tea?*

There's a railway line near here, but when I hear the snorting, clattering Indian trains, I seem to see the track that looped around the long rows of colliers' houses on the hillside, with the view of the ash-pits and the blue mountains behind them. The miners' boots came clomping on the cobbles as they trooped home, their faces black as sepoys', their voices musical, and yet so close to the chichi rhythm I hear in the voices of half-and-half Indians here. I thought I knew about poverty, having seen it in the valley, but it's nothing compared to the destitution and squalor I see here. I find it quite heartbreaking, and I want to run away when little mothers scramble after me: Memsahib, my child, please one anna or she will die. Memsahib, this is the child of an English officer, see how fair, see the blue eyes, help us to live, memsahib, do not walk away. The minute I step beyond our lines and into the countryside beyond it's appalling. I can't get used to it and I won't. But I feel so helpless with my ridiculous little bag of coins, and I want to smack them when they call after me: Memsahib, you are an angel of God, you have given this child one more day of life . . .

Mother used to make me come with her when she visited the miners' wives when they were sick, or to give them food and clothing when the mine wall collapsed, or that ghastly time when the shaft gave way and all the miners were crushed or buried alive under the rock. She went every single day, and she made me go with her: You're coming whether you like it or not. Your grandfather bought this mine and got all three pits back to work when there was real poverty in this valley, so don't imagine that you're not going to do your bit. She was a different person when she was sitting with the sick, and it made me think about going to university and about taking up medicine as a career. Sometimes I'd have to go down to the cottages late at night to bring her home, and she'd be sitting there in the darkness, cradling the back of a neck, holding a cloth to lips that were spitting up lung blood. She'd be talking softly, not minding the coughing, the fevers, the pneumonia, the slow deaths. Even the little I picked up watching her is of use, in little ways, here. And I'm sort of beginning to see that little ways shouldn't be despised. When she was a little girl, living in Florence, her own mother had visited the sick and poor, even though her family was very grand and certainly didn't need to do more than send out donations. Mother continued the tradition, and she wanted me to do the same, but it's very different here—because ugly and poor as the hovels were at home, and with all the sickness and dying that went on, you could get away from it, because beyond the mines and ashpits stretched long pastures and meadows, hedges and hills, and the green watered valleys. The miners would sing coming up out of the earth in the evening and turn into the Miners' Arms to wash the dust out of their throats. They'd stroll home to a supper of stew and mashed potatoes, and a warm fire when times were good. I see all this, I keep it close to me, but it's also getting mixed up with India. Here the extremity of need can't be contained; the country can't feed its people. Here people just die with a promiscuity that appalls, and sometimes, on the tide of the river, you see what looks like a log bobbing along, but it's a dead body, or part of one.

When I'm most happy looking back, I see Ellen and me racing the horses up the hill, our hair pouring down our backs. And I could just howl for the freedom of our youth, our happiness, then, before the war came down on us, so that before you knew it, all that you'd ever known and loved was gone. Just like that, in a moment. Our lovely world had collided with a brutality that wouldn't go away. It left us broken, unable to go back to where we were, or who we'd been before the war, because with all the young men lost and gone, the young girls vanished too. Overnight we were women—widows or mourners, mothers of orphans, sisters and daughters of the dead, our darlings lost on foreign soil and our own childhoods sucked down into the trenches, never to come back up again.

TWO

Such joy to sit on the front veranda with the sun splattered on the red polished floor and read *Howards End*, where everyone behaves with such gentility, and the passion is measured and orderly, while mine's like a volcano. Neville's off on active duty on the North-West Frontier, what they call being "on the grim." Another Afghan War, he says, that's impossible to win because the terrain is impassable, and the enemy is girded with such ferocious religiosity they're unbeatable: seventeen thousand English soldiers slaughtered up on the frontier in Queen Vic's time. When the army infiltrates the villages, the villagers poison the food and medicine and cut the arms and legs off anyone suspected of giving us information. All this has been going on since the Crusades, when we certainly did our full share in the atrocity department. But our Tommies can't take on an enemy like this; poor devils, they're just out for a spell and don't even know how to fight. Raw as carrots, Neville says, lads out from Manchester or Durham who don't know who Allah is until his faithful come screaming down

the hillsides to cut their infidel throats as happily as our boys butter
their bread. They live on a pinch of rice a day, waiting it out in icy
caves for a moment when things become auspicious. Then suddenly
there's a bloodcurdling shriek that rips open the dawn, and there they
are, thousands and thousands of them, devoted to death, earning a
place in heaven each time they mutilate an English face or run a
sword from gullet to groin. Their troubles are ancient as mountains
and will continue till the world ends. Every time we go in, we're certain we'll win, because we of course have the modern army—and
every time we lose, one way or another.

I hate myself for getting involved. It was the way we were waiting
for news about the Somme or Gallipoli, glued to the wireless, scouring the papers. I thought I'd put that behind me, though this is different, more of a mopping-up operation, since the Afghan War is
supposedly over. I'm using it as a distraction from the things closer at
hand, which are ghastly, small human things that break a heart as
cleanly as a dispatch will curdle a sunny morning. So here I am in
Ferozepore, with a strange husband, and the most horrible scene
when we first arrived, and then another so tragic I can't bear to think
about it. We're into another month and moving closer to the Hot
Weather, and I'm trying to separate out what I imagined India to be
from what it really is. When I was little, I thought of India as a face
with a pointed chin, lying flat on a blue, windless ocean, which coiled
around a land teeming with adventure and beauty. I'd spend hours
staring at those tiny names on the atlas, memorizing the musical
sounds of the places strewn along the rim of the Indian Ocean: Zan-
zibar, Dar es Salaam, Comoros, Mombasa, Mogadishu, Lamu, Bombay, Mangalore, those dreamy faraway ports bringing slaves, gold,
ivory, and mangrove from Africa and dates, carpets, and whale oil
from Arabia. I saw the sailors following ancient trade routes on long
dhows with white sails, sailing in and out of port on the monsoon
winds. So when I sailed away from England, I'd already imagined India, I'd dreamed it; it was in my mind, just waiting to come to life.

It was dazzling from afar. From the ship, Bombay seemed to be made up of shimmering white palaces, ancient stone fortresses and temples, and mosques with gold and sapphire domes. Beyond the city, the mountains loomed five thousand feet, and the grand buildings on the shore were radiant across the smooth blue ocean. As we got closer, I could see that the Victorian splendor was fading fast, and in fact, it was all rather tatty and down-at-heel. But that didn't matter a bit. I'd seen what I'd seen, an illusion, perhaps, but one that could last a lifetime, and I understood why we came here, why we were entranced by its voluptuous grandeur. Once we were at the quayside, the whole squawk of life started up: vendors yelling, porters babbling and shoving one another aside to take our luggage and whirl it onto carts or rickshaws. The docks were like a bazaar on fire; the frenzy, the rushing crowds—it felt like a disaster in progress. And then things slowed. The Bentley was lifted from the hold by a crane; it hung high in the sky like a glittering toy. Everyone gasped, looked up, and pointed. Luggage was placed in lines, crocodile skin and calf leather, hatboxes and gleaming saddles, chalk marks on the right-hand side, porters with white gloves jumping to attention. Dignitaries rolled up in carriages to meet the toffs off the boat; much bowing and scraping and bands playing. Uniforms and pale pink soldiers. Garlands round the neck, salaams and salutations. Horse-drawn tongas, rickshaws, bullock carts, and grand carriages lined with scarlet satin and gold tassels, and then the line of motorcars, which seemed rather dull in comparison. The opulence made you feel you were off to a ball. The wind and the heat suggested you'd entered a trance, and there was an actual snake swaying to the music, dancing to the tune. I was bowled over by the smell of spice and incense overlaid with a dark, musky, earthy smell of human sweat, garlic, and animal dung. So excited I was. And my husband wasn't even looking around him. Closed off like a pea in a pod. He took my arm and moved me right along: For God's sake, stop gawking, and let's get out of this stinking hole and to the railway station.

I knew instantly that India was the place for me. I actually felt as if I'd been born here, that my first gulp of air must have been Indian, and my first mirror the smile in my ayah's brown eyes. I don't know why I felt this. I kept questioning it, not wanting it to be phony. Was it ancestral memory? Or love at first sight? I've been told since that it might have something to do with the fact that the first missionaries here came from Wales. They were called the twilight people because of that touch of the supernatural we have. Of course there are other twilight people here, the Eurasians—the half-and-halfs, the in-betweens, and mixtures of this and that who are so varied in tone and color that you're endlessly startled by a pair of green eyes in a nut brown face or a complexion as pale as a rose within a rope of shiny black hair. They talk just as the miners in the Rhondda Valley do, same rhythm with the drop at the end of the sentence. The memsahibs hate that singsong sound so much that they make their children learn Hindi right away so they don't pick it up. I keep remembering what the Pater said: Learn the language, Isabel; if you don't, you'll miss the whole thing.

In Bombay I was being roasted alive. I had images of insects frying as they flew, turning to ash as they fell, and of things going up in smoke without anyone really noticing—a mango or apricot exploding into peel, pith, and pips in midair and vanishing into the haze. All these little deaths created by combustion. Then the flies, millions of them, and at first they're as unbearable as the sun. They crawl into children's eyes, and between babies' lips, and cover wounds with a black, creeping scab. The Indians don't even bother to shoo them away. They don't sweat either. I'm wringing wet all the time. We passed through the grand marbled Gates of India on the waterfront and headed for the railway station to begin the long journey to Delhi and then all the way north by Frontier Mail—days of travel ahead of us. Getting to the terminus, the people, the sheer magnitude of their number on the city streets was frightening; so many of them and so few of us, and we're supposed to be in charge here. Garish orange garlands are flung around your neck as the tonga takes you through the rushing hordes. The music of a brass band collides with shrill, wailing Indian music, and the din makes you feel a bit touched in the head. I couldn't get air, and it was at that moment so hideously unlike the cool distance of the hills and valleys of home that I had second thoughts and wondered if I, let alone the poor lilac, would ever be able to survive here.

But thank God, before too long we were at the train station and climbing aboard the tropical train, a steaming, grunting gray brute long as a river. Once in our carriage, I tried to hide my fluster. I was stinking like a polecat, wet as a rag, and desperate for some chilled Évian. Neville of course was cool as a cucumber in his crisp khaki drill. He doesn't sweat or stink; he doesn't fluster. Lord, what a strange concoction of a man. He had under his arm a cane with a round silver knob that I'd never seen before, and he seemed to march rather than walk the minute we arrived on Indian soil. The train was astonishing, and soon I was transfixed all over again. Platforms here are like hotels. Locals sleep on them day or night, and if in doubt as to what to do, sleep's the thing. Heads covered, feet sticking out, they look like corpses wrapped in white muslin. The minute a train pulls in, they're up, frantic with activity and noise, grabbing their bundles and babies and heading for the crowded second- and third-class carriages. And when the train actually takes off, they hang off the windows, or lie on the roofs of carriages, or balance on tiny footboards by their toes. A furious stationmaster yanks at the naked feet from below, yelling and hitting, and people fall like flies. The station vendors make an incredible racket, so many different languages banging into one another, all so damn *loud*. Everyone has something to sell: chapati and sweetmeats, tea, hot and sweet, and water—some for Hindus and some for Muslims—cigarettes and betel nut. All of this is accomplished with a great deal of spitting. Beggars, with tiny, broken legs, hang on to the carriage windows as the train pulls out. People simply flick them off or pull down the windows hard on their fingers. The upper-class carriages are like fortresses, impossible to storm, hard even to see into because the venetian blinds are drawn right down to the bottom and double-latched. The stationmaster waits for the Collector or some other top dog to give permission for the train to depart, and off we go with a snort of steam and that nice clunkety-clunk sound of wheels as behind us a mass of humanity runs and slows and then finally vanishes into the distance as Neville snaps: Close the damn window, for God's sake, what's the matter with you?

Our carriage had polished mahogany squares like a library, with gauze and green shades to keep out the light, and a great block of ice in a tub in the middle of the compartment to cool us off; ceiling fan didn't work, so it melted fast. You wait for the next station, when a new block is carried in, and this goes on the whole journey, with awful swampy hours when the ice is a warm puddle in the tub. Whenever I thought I was going to die of heat, I rested my naked feet against the block until my feet were ringing. Neville barely noticed. He wasn't interested much in anything until he wanted a drink. He had his own supply and propped it up against the ice. His face was turned away from the window and the rushing world outside that had me all agog. If I suggested cards, he shook his head or went back to reading the *Civil and Military Gazette*. He rolled slim cigarettes in a smart silver box bought on leave, of which he's most proud. But talk he would not. Often, then, I just wanted to be his pal, nothing more, and to sit and talk the way we had on the ship very late at night. There was a lot about Neville and his soldiering side that interested me, but once we got to India, and he out of mufti, he seemed to be trying to be someone he wasn't. He was always going on about "my" regiment—Fifth Royal Gurkha Rifles—and showing me the button and shoulder badges and mess kit, huffing and buffing, even though his bearer would do it again the minute we got on station. I wanted to know more about him, not because I was in love with him, I'd never been that, but because he was unlike anyone I'd ever known before. He'd been born and bred in India and had gone to a military school in Sanawar, near Simla. He hated it, but wouldn't say why. It was as if, on that train ride, he were moving into a space where the army had claimed him, and he were just waiting to be free of me. It was as if he were already on station, longing to give orders and plan the next trip up to the frontier. He'd leave our compartment and wander down to the carriages reserved for the other military chaps going back after furlough. When he returned, he was all of a pose, trying to acquire qualities and be a certain kind of man that I imagine he thinks he's *supposed* to be in India: confident, masterful, and in command. A pukka sahib. He was attempting to construct an identity through being a soldier in the British Army with all that that means in India. I knew full well that he'd have been a very different man in Aldershot. In India he's a soldier in relationship to dark-skinned soldiers, and that defines him. It gives him enormous prestige and power, but he can't use his power because his own race has passed judgment on him. He's of an inferior caste. Perhaps he knew that when he went, at seven, to that military asylum for the children of British soldiers, up in the hills of Sanawar?

I did manage to force a little conversation out of him at dinner. He's better at night, loosens up a bit, and stops cracking his fingers so much. On the train, if you fancy dinner, you wait for a stop, get down from your carriage, lock up, and take off down the track to the European dining car, where a splendid fellow, robed in radiant white with a scarlet middle, flings open the carriage door and hands you up. You linger in the sumptuous splendor of the dining car—food and wine worthy of the Ritz—and stay there until the next stop. This can be hours and hours away, and all this is leisurely and lovely, a kind of getting used to that was perfect for me. So I was relaxed and I was feeling for Neville, seeing his irritation when some of the officers heading up to Quetta snubbed him. He was distant and preoccupied, but I wanted him to tell me about the life we were going to have, how it would be. He'd told me about the pigsticking at Meerut, which sounded absolutely gross, and the tiger hunting, and all of that, but really what I wanted to know was how life would *be*. He warned that I would not be permitted to do much. I wonder, he said, if you're up to army life? Ferozepore's a first-class station, and there's a decent club, and a tennis court or two, and a freshwater pool close to a spring. But the women aren't like you; they play tennis and bridge and gossip a lot and are very concerned about doing the right thing. None of them have even imagined going to university, so you'd be well advised to leave Edinburgh out of the conversation. Whenever I offered something in answer to his questions, he'd interrupt me: No, it's not like that. You can't do what you like; there's a lot of protocol, and everything's laid down with a trowel. I don't think you understand. It's very easy to be made to feel pretty miserable and unwanted. It can happen in a minute. If one of the wives takes against you, you'll be out in the cold in no time. Have to mind your *p*'s and *q*'s. No, Isabel, no on all counts; that is just plain bunk. This is not England, and certainly not Wales; you'll be on a military station, pretty much confined to it. You will not be gadding about to different parts of the country, not by train, or any other means. Where did you get such an idea? India, in case you don't know it, is an extremely dangerous place. Yes, of course, but what I do is distinctly different from what you do. If I get transferred, you will of course accompany me—unless it's up in the tribal regions. Otherwise you'll not go anywhere without me. No, of course not even with other people. There's no traveling about India. India is a place of work, and that's all it is. You'll go up to the hills, of course, and summer there with the other women, but no, you will not go further than Simla. The Himalayas are not to be climbed. One looks; one does not climb.

By then I was hooting with laughter. He glared at me, crossing his legs neatly not to spoil the nice crease: I'll be gone a great deal, up on the border. Probably the minute we get back they'll put me on active service. You'll be on your own. I'm sorry about that, but it can't be helped. Regiment's gone sometimes as much as ten months of the year. In a situation like that you won't want enemies. I know you like your own company, made that pretty clear on the voyage, if I may say so, but you can't be carrying on the way you did at home. This is India. I told him he was a stuffy old fool and poured myself more wine. Later on he stopped being such an arse and even became a little romantic, which is unusual for him. He brushed my hair and plaited it—rather well, I thought, all the way down my back, like a girl's. I didn't want to tell him that at the first opportunity I intended to cut it off at the neck.

GOING UP into the provinces by Frontier Mail is so utterly unlike an English train journey as to be unimaginable. It's like crossing the world and watching it change every hour. You watch as India passes by: rivers vast as seas, dotted with steamers, dhows, and boats packed to the gills with humankind, the stern perilously close to sinking. Women beat clothes on the riverbanks as buffaloes stir up the currents and meander through the paddy fields. You see scuffed white tracks with tiny people trailing back to hovels set into hillsides, groves of oranges and mangoes, fields of mustard and indigo. Beyond the green fields I imagined dark jungles stuffed with tigers, bears, gorillas, and serpents. Empty, treeless plains stretch on for days. Elephants stroll along, holding one another by trunk and tail, camels step down dusty tracks, and gazelles graze serenely at the edges of forests. And there you are, staring out of the window for days on end. There's nothing else to do. You're curious and excited, and the train is nipping along nicely, but you can't keep your eyes open for long because the glare blinds you. And you sleep and sleep, and not even Neville's persuaded to be amorous. When you wake out of this stupor, it's as if the sky's grown a few thousand acres; the horizon's beyond the stretching of an eye, and there's nothing behind or in front of you but India—wide open, spectacular, and beyond reckoning.

And yet, for all of its vastness, there was something familiar about it too, something about it that made me love it. I could almost imagine I was high on a hill, looking down at a long, low valley in Wales;

there's the same immensity. Everything is beautiful. The dark birds swirl and dive. The sky is silver, and the clouds pull the moon through it. But then you fall asleep, and when your eyes open, someone has conjured up a landscape so bleached and bare that there's only an occasional bush, or the scarlet splash of a mohur tree, or a banyan, and coming closer to it, you see tendrils growing down from the branches, making a writhing mess of roots and old men squatting. In another second you're passing a field of yellow marigolds, or you're racing against acres of linseed, and on and on it goes, very beautiful, very ancient, with the snowcapped mountains forever watching, and the miles of green sugarcane waving in the blue.

By the end of the journey I was exhausted, and I was stricken by a kind of silence that had reached in through the window to mock the smallness of all I knew. Out there a vast continent was going on its way, not giving a damn whether we lived or died. I was an alien, an untouchable, in a place incomprehensible to an Englishwoman. What on earth was I doing in India? What had possessed me to come? The smoke from village fires goes up in a straight line here, none of that curling nicely as it does from a chimney at home. And when you see gray smoke smudging the sky near the great rivers, you know that bodies are burning in the ghat. The white cows plodding through the pale gold dust are sacred, and I in my pink scrubbedness am polluted. But it's really too exhausting to think: too much sensation, too much beauty. Night comes down, BAM, and in minutes the temperature drops thirty degrees. The window turns black as a boot, and there's nothing to see. Back to sleep, until a new riot of morning wakes you, and the inevitable tea is brought in at the first station stop of the day—usually at four in the morning. And you drink it with the greatest relief.

WE WERE GOING to one of the fourteen provinces of the Raj, each one subdivided into districts that make up the vast up-country stations of India—the mofussil—with its shades of Kipling and the images he's left in our minds. Lower India is, I hear, rather rank and inferior in comparison, a place where people make money instead of doing their duty. We were off to our cantonment—you say it cantoooonment— the military bit where Neville's regiment is stationed. We arrived at Lahore in the middle of the night. Trains roll in at two or three in the morning here, and nobody knows why. It could be because time is different here; it seems immense, having little to do with us and our makeshift calendars and clocks. At Lahore we waited for hours before our driver and tonga turned up. Outside the railway station, caravans from Bokhara were arriving in the dawnlight, off-loading bags, bundles, and rolled carpets. Camels knelt at the wells; people set up little fires, taking a second to make their breakfast, before settling down to lie about under the trees, talking and eating as if they had all the time in the world. Neville hustled me inside. He was impatient, striding up and down, looking at the clock. When the driver finally arrived, bowing and scraping, we took off, hoping to be in Ferozepore for breakfast.

Just as we were nearing Ferozepore, there was a man lying on the side of the road, almost phosphorescent in that last hour of darkness, when the light is soft and blue. Neville got off the tonga and poked at him, perhaps to see if he was dead, and the man reared up and looked as though he'd cut our throats. Something about his face, the stark hatred in it, frightened me. I don't know why it was so shocking, but it had something to do with my idea that we're loved here, that Indians are happy to have us, and respect and admire us, white man's burden and all that. It was shocking to see that naked hatred. I kept seeing it burst out of his black eyes the way, later, I kept hearing the screams. But the morning breeze was ushering us in, passing over the earth and shaking the trees so that the birds woke up in a rush. That coolness would be gone in fifteen minutes, but now it was lovely, like ice pressed up for an instant against the neck. The trees were full of doves and parakeets, pink camellias, jasmine and trailing bougainvillea, small

animals were scurrying about in the pale grass, and all of it was delicious because of the breeze.

We'd crossed the river that separates Ferozepore from the civil and
military lines and drove down the back roads and on toward the cantonment. In a tonga, you're facing backward, looking at what you're
leaving behind; it's rather nice. We passed villages and small shrines
along the road and then came to a well-established plot of England. In
the civil lines, where the administrative people live, Neville pointed
out the club. That's where the ICS types all meet for a drink and
gather for swimming and tennis and tea dances and so on. We have
our own club, of course, but it's not the same. I didn't care about all
that rigmarole, not the way he did, but looking back, I had no idea of
what it meant, to *me,* never mind him.

That first morning in Ferozepore was too strange to be entirely
real, what with the piercing sunshine and the noise in the treetops
coming from scrawny black-faced monkeys flying through the air or
dangling from a branch by one finger. Elephants were making their
way back to their stables after a dip in the lake, swaying from side to
side in the shadow of astonishingly tall trees. Blue blossoms fell like
rain through pale leaves with emerald underlays, a deep shade overlit
by intense sunlight, and then suddenly there'd be a red canna lily, like
a splash of blood. The scent of jasmine wafted into the tamarind and
frangipani. The military barracks have neat bungalows laid out in
lines; everything's in lines, and everything's clean, whitewashed and
red-ochered. It looks as if someone sat down with a ruler and then
did the simplest of grids: roads and wider avenues; parade grounds and
a maidan to play polo and have gymkhanas; barracks and big and small
bungalows, all neat as can be. There's a brisk, simple kind of orderli-
ness. The flat-roofed bungalows have gardens in the front and back,
and spacious red-painted verandas shaded by ferns and bougainvillea,
and everywhere there are rows and rows of chrysanthemums in pots,
because of the transfers. On our way in, I'd seen some much older

bungalows facing the northeast, with wide verandas and tall flowering trees on either side and elegant little orchards of apricot and peach, with pear trees espaliered against red-brick walls. It had an Edwardian look about it and reminded me of Cardiff. It was all familiar and friendly, and in these surroundings of course I felt perfectly at home.

Neville suddenly turned rather peculiar. Sitting beside me in the tonga, he seemed uneasy and on edge. We'd arrived at the barracks, and instantly I sensed an atmosphere. It was just a short while after the early parade. A few of the soldiers' wives were standing at the entrance to the married quarters, huddled together, talking in an agitated way. Soldiers were gathered silently in another huddle, watching, their eyes directed across the way to another bungalow with an open door. It was as if everyone were waiting for something to happen. Only the sweepers kept on stirring up the dust, and a few native soldiers wearing breeches and puttees stood in neat formation on one side of the white church, as if waiting for orders. The other bungalow doors were shut, and there was a sense that something had happened. Neville was pale, waiting and watching too, and when I nudged him, he didn't notice. His face was hooded. His eyes were pinned to that open door. And then, from behind the open door, a woman began screaming blue murder. Everyone froze. The screaming went on until there was a shot. Then another. And then a horrible silence.

Neville threw himself out of the tonga. And so violently that the horse reared up and the driver began to whimper. The compound came to life, and everyone began to move, either back into his own quarters or farther out into the open. Soldiers talked intently to one another. Neville ran across to the open door, where a tall, dignified man in a blue turban came slowly out, preventing entry. Neville shoved him hard, but the man wouldn't budge. Beneath the blue turban was a pale and beautiful face. It wore no expression, and the man's stillness was eerie. Neville strode back across the compound and began to talk to one of the soldiers. Then the scene froze again. Someone had given orders that no one move or leave the scene, so we all stayed there in the sweltering heat, waiting. After about twenty minutes, a man, who I later learned was the CO, strode across the compound, buttoning up his jacket as he came. Neville immediately left the soldiers and began to walk briskly back to the open door. When the CO arrived at the door, the tall man stood aside, bowing briefly. The CO strode into the dark interior of the little bungalow, and Neville followed him. The man in the blue turban was walking away from the married quarters, but though he was walking fast, there seemed to be no emotion attached to his movements. The arm of his white tunic looked as though it had been dipped into scarlet paint. And for a fleeting second, deep in some subterranean strata of my mind, I seemed to see a woman fall and his arm reach out to catch her. As he vanished behind the gathering crowd of soldiers, it was as if he'd never been there, never even existed—so much so that for a moment I thought it was all an illusion.

The compound was emptier now, with only a few soldiers and even fewer women. Some glanced across at me as people look at strangers, but their real attention was focused on the door that had been open and was now closed. I got out of the tonga, feeling annoyed and awkward, not knowing what to do with myself. Suddenly a woman started to whimper and then to sob; she began running toward the door, but a soldier grabbed her arm and pulled her back. I was oppressed by the tension in the little compound, with its hard, dry surface and clumps of stony-faced people, and I stayed fairly close to the tonga and to our things, waiting for Neville to come out of the door again. I was standing like this, by myself, when an older woman, with some authority, approached me, introducing herself as Colonel Pendleton's wife and apologizing for what she called this ghastly introduction to Indian life. She put out a long, strong-boned hand: You must be Sergeant Webb's wife. She insisted that I come to her house for tea, until matters were cleared up. We were expecting you, she said, but the trains do get so badly held up here, and I know the line's out at Ferozepore, but now that you're here, we'll get everything sorted out. She was nice enough, but I wasn't budging. Neville had gone in that door, and I wanted to know what was happening inside it.

I'll just stay here for a bit, I said, and make sure everything's all right.

It would be better, really, if we just let the men handle this.

Do you know what's going on?

She flinched a little. I don't get involved in the soldiers' lives, she said, but I do have a responsibility to their wives, particularly when they're first out and don't know the drill. She was looking at me, her body turning aside, away from the closed door.

What were those shots?

Just an incident. She smiled. In India there are always incidents of one kind and another. I couldn't understand why she was so uncurious, and then I realized that she was simply playing a role: being the wife of the highest regimental officer on station. She was looking me up and down in a particular way. Up to that point I had thought I was wearing a rather elegant cream traveling suit, but now I wasn't sure.

You don't have your topi on, she said briskly. Come along, you have to get out of the sun. I looked across the compound and saw a man carrying a doctor's bag, walking toward the bungalow. We both stopped for a moment to look at him.

That's Dr. Singh, she said. He's the doctor on call at the hospital at the moment. She looked across at him. Awkward for him, she said quietly. I looked at her. Well, she said, clearly there's been a shooting. She retracted her chin. Mrs. Davies could well be injured, perhaps even dead. Her husband's just got back from active duty in Burma; he's been gone a long while. She stared at the doctor, who was about to enter the door of the bungalow. I noticed that he wasn't hurrying, that he was wearing a very elegant suit, and that his hair was more brown than black.

How do you know that it was Mrs. Davies who was shot? I was watching Mrs. Pendleton, who was still watching Dr. Singh.

Well, she said, almost as if I'd startled her, she's not settled well here. She's been troublesome, indiscreet. Women, she said, when they first come out to India, often don't do well here. It's not just the climate and the natives; it's the problem of their husbands' being on active duty so much of the time. They're alone, you see, for many months. This can cause problems. Mrs. Davies is one of those women who don't manage well on their own. That won't do in India.

What sorts of problems?

Well, she said with a laugh, you could certainly join the cavalry, the way you charge at it. She turned me around smartly by my arm. Let's get you settled, she said. No good waiting for Sergeant Webb; he'll be gone a long while. And then it seemed to me that she looked at me with pity, as if she knew something about him that I didn't.

Please, don't worry, I said. I'll go back to the tonga and put on my topi, and I'll just wait here for Neville.

I'll come with you, she said, and the tonga can take us back to my bungalow, which is along there to the right, close to the officers' mess. Come along now; let's get out of this beastly sun as fast as possible. For some reason, I followed her like a lamb.

Her bungalow was rather dignified, with white pillars, wide verandas, and yellow roses trailing up the walls. It was set back and looked cool and elegant in the rising heat. There was a garden with a child's swing in one of the trees to the left of the house, and I spotted a little pagoda near a pool with weeping willows shading the water. Once inside, I was in a genteel English country house, and it was comforting.

We're not really settled in yet, she said, pushing aside a pile of magazines so I could sit on a button-back Edwardian chair. The bungalows are so much nicer in Lahore. So much of one's furniture gets destroyed on the voyage over. I lost all my Limoges. I do hope you sent on some of your things, but don't be surprised if they turn up smashed to pieces. Of course you'll probably just rent your furniture. I don't do that myself, as the colonel and I have a standard to set, but our lives are so transient that sometimes one must rent, and occasionally you can pick out a jolly nice piece of furniture. Of course, she said, stripping off white gloves, it's considered rather smart to have your own furniture. But only the business people and planters stay in one place year after year, and so their houses are far more lavish, full of nice English pieces and so on. She now seemed a little distracted and kept patting her hair, which was gray, short, and permed.

She rang the bell, and the bearer appeared with a silver tray covered in white damask, loaded with little sandwiches, tarts and biscuits, and even some fruitcake. It was more like afternoon tea than elevenses. I was starving and didn't mind showing it. Mrs. Pendleton began firing off questions to her bearer, who was in turn laying out the tea things. He hadn't looked at me once.

I see that you speak Hindi, I said.

Enough to get by. You'll pick up the bits and pieces that you'll need, she said reassuringly.

I thought I'd learn the language.

Oh, there's no need to do that!

Well, one can only get a very cursory knowledge if one doesn't speak the language properly, don't you think?

I think we've arranged a servant for you who speaks English, a good fellow from Calcutta, Christian, agreeable, and clean, although his English is a little eccentric. Only men learn the language here, she said, elevating a sharp chin. Matter of fact, they have to pass exams in Urdu. But Indian life only really affects the men. She frowned, stopping as a servant in white padded in with an envelope, which she laid to one side. You'll find things very different here, she said, and it's best, I've found, to take the advice of old hands. We do things a certain way, and we have to set the right tone. It's expected of us. I used to be put off by all that bowing to the ground, but it's an Indian custom, d'you see? Indians don't respect anyone who doesn't do what's considered the right thing. It offends them. They're defined by whom they serve, and we rule by prestige here; they understand that. For them, as well as us, it's all about prestige, protocol, and hierarchy. One visit to a maharaja's palace makes that perfectly clear. We have much in common, but much also that separates us. D'you see?

She gave me an earful, told me everything I should know to survive in British India, like respecting caste and religion, and when to wear gloves, and how to curtsy and walk backward when royalty was around, and how to talk to servants, and how not to. Too much bullying here by women, you know, courtesy is best with natives. They are very courteous people, and that's certainly not something they've learned from us. By the time she stopped to take a sip of tea, I knew exactly how the collier wives must have felt after one of Mother's visits to the cottages in the valley. Mrs. P. also said some decent things about Neville: Good soldier. Diligent. Excellent horseman. You can never tell how a soldier will turn out even if he comes with certain disadvantages. All her talk was about placement and the hegemony of rank and status. What I really understood was how a soldier's prestige fell upon his wife, even as his rank was defined by his battalion, as well as by the prestige of his regiment. Clarissa Pendleton, with her paper-thin teacup, knew exactly where she stood in society, and she made it equally plain where I stood in the demarcation lines of the station.

She wasn't entirely clear what to make of me. For my part, I'd decided that she wasn't a bad old bat, and she'd come round to me too. I buttered her up by complimenting her silver, or recognizing a nice piece of Dresden, or commenting kindly on a chaise, which was in fact a truly ghastly piece of melodrama from the last century. Of course she was checking my pedigree; she found out what the Pater did and was delighted to hear that Mother was a horsewoman. I suppose, in her way of talking, she'd have said we were In Mines, as people always had to be placed in some category. I decided to move the conversation another way. I wonder, I began, if I might ask a question. I hope it wouldn't be impertinent, or indiscreet, to ask you what was going on this morning at the barracks—really, I mean? I smiled innocently. Is it too awful to ask?

She gave me a shredding look. The woman's dead, she said. Her voice became droll: Of course there'll be an official inquiry, or there might be, but it could be hushed up. Less likely these days, except it is an army matter. We don't like a soldier dishonored, particularly by this kind of thing. We like it even less if the wife was wrapped up somehow with the Bengali.

The Bengali?

Did you notice a handsome Bengali leave the Davies' bungalow this morning? I nodded, relieved to have his existence confirmed, since my impression of him had been so strange. She reached over and opened a silver cigarette box with a crest on it and took one. I took one too. There was a time before, you see, when . . . well, never mind the details . . . but Polly was injured in a way that didn't quite add up at the time. She inhaled deeply. India is not a place for women. Women are hated here. They burn them on pyres, blame them for all the feuds and acts of vengeance, and mutilate them for any act resembling impurity or infidelity. And as white women in India, we're considered a bloody nuisance and given no role to play bar decoration, which destroys character and brain. Must be the point of it, I suppose. India, I'm afraid, has not been touched by the emancipation movement, and may never be. In fact, to get by here, you have to become pretty odious.

May I ask another question?

Oh, by all means.

What did you mean about it being awkward for Dr. Singh?

Ah, you noticed him. Well, to be precise, I was wondering if matters would be complicated by his being involved in this incident—he's not army—and if this goes to trial, his presence would be difficult for all sorts of reasons.

What sorts of reasons?

She looked at me, hard, and seemed to make a decision. This is your first morning here, she said thoughtfully, and I'm going to be frank because I can see that for the present anyway, you are unusually direct. This would be a virtue, in my mind, anywhere but here. But we'll waive that and speak freely. Dr. Singh is an exceptional man, cultured, sophisticated, and brilliant. He can on occasion be utterly charming too, but on the whole he's rather distant and self-absorbed, and he tends not to remember people's names, or even people, which of course rather causes offense. Also, there are questions as to his pedigree, and that makes him rather complicated. She looked as if she were going to stop there, but I made it clear that I wanted her to go on. Let me explain: In India we like to know everything about everyone in our circle, and Dr. Singh, for many reasons, is almost in our circle—almost one of us. What we know is that he was born in London and educated at Eton. An Oxford man. Qualified in medicine at St. Thomas's in London, all of which I have to say he rather tossed over the side when he came back to India. I say back, but in fact, he has not spent much time here, and when he is here, he won't play the game, isn't even interested in the game, by which I mean our rules and protocol, the glue that keeps the whole imperial structure from falling to pieces. The colonel admires him greatly—excellent chess player, I gather. And you see, he's the one person that the colonel would call in to handle an incident like this, but that's the problem. Dr. Singh's position in society is—well, it's awkward, as I said, and this incident is bound to turn into a mess. We're all on thin ice here since that terrible business at Amritsar in April. The army and police are very much on edge. Dyer's not going to get away with it, of course; only a monomaniac would have considered such an action. Firing from horseback into unarmed people is not considered fair play these days. It's precisely that kind of thing that could bring the Raj to its knees. She looked at me. I rather hope it does. But of course that's easy for me to say, since our days here are numbered, the colonel's and mine.

Am I correct in assuming that the awkwardness you're referring to comes from Dr. Singh being an Indian?

She rescued a crumbly edge of jam tart from the corner of her mouth. That, she said, is a very interesting question. In some ways it's the only question to ask about him, but at the same time it's impossible to answer. Dr. Singh is a Hindu, reputedly a descendant of the maharaja Gulab Singh, an astonishingly brutal chap who was responsible for merging the Kashmir Valley and Jammu into a princely state. Matter of fact, we sold him Kashmir, after taking it from the Sikhs of Punjab. Don't ask me when—I'm hopeless with dates . . . However, like everything else about Dr. Singh, this is speculation and rumor. Some say he's an opium warlord, part of the Rajput dynasty; some swear that he's made a fortune from the trade that moves up and down the Silk Route to China. The only thing that people agree on is that his father is a scoundrel of the first rank. It's all bunk, in my opinion. Dr. Singh makes up outrageous stories to confuse people even more, and we don't like to be confused, because above all we like to put people in boxes, and we don't like them to get out. D'you see? She poured us both more tea. The important thing to know about Dr. Singh is that he is in no way confused about himself. He considers himself an Englishman, or rather an Indian-Englishman, or if you look at it the way the colonel does, he considers himself a Black Englishman. This, to my husband's mind, makes him an impossibilist, there being no such thing.

He *was* born in London.

Eaton Square. But what's your point?

Well, only that my grandfather was born here and spent most of his life in Assam. Mightn't we think he'd have a similar claim?

She gave a laugh a horse would be proud of. My dear girl, what an idea! Interesting, of course, when one reverses it, though of course one wouldn't. Did, by any chance, your grandfather consider himself an Indian?

He was very fond of India.

But did he, being country born, consider himself an Indian as well as an Englishman? In the way Dr. Singh sees himself as both?

I don't know.

I do.

I suggest, she said patiently, that you meet Dr. Singh and then you can tell me what you think. Personally, I think it's rather splendid to cancel out the racial divide in that way, outrageous to some, sublime to others, but it definitely has something of the aristocratic aspect. Dr. Singh has the sky blue eyes of his mother's side, the Kashmiri side—descendants of Alexander the Great, and all that. But of course we are drawn to him primarily because he has been of infinite help to us. There was the matter of an uprising near here not too long ago. Ask Sergeant Webb to tell you about it. It was a bloody and stupid business, religious, but with a touch of terrorism, usual thing, but it could have been much worse. Dr. Singh's intervention helped us out of a very bad scrape. She put down her cup and looked at me. Don't imagine I'm suggesting that Dr. Singh is with us and against his own people. That is not the case. He insists only that he is of both worlds. I am both Indian and English, he said once to me. And then he laughed and tossed off a couple of lines of Kipling, to the effect of having two separate sides to his head.

As she'd been talking, I'd been guzzling her words with the same intensity as the tea. I was utterly fascinated. This subject hadn't touched my mind before. Class I'd thought about, often, particularly in relation to Pater and his past, and now of course because of Neville's lack thereof. But color hadn't entered my consciousness, so to me there was nothing obvious about it, not the way it seemed to be for the colonel and his wife. How could I not have known about this? Had I been too young and self-obsessed to care about the far-flung empire? Had I been dozing when Mrs. Firth was droning on from *Our Empire Story*? Or had the color of our human possessions somehow not been part of the discussion? I wanted to do what the Pater suggests when I'm considering serious matters: Just let the wind blow through your mind, Isabel, empty it, and then begin to think hard not only about what is interesting you but *why*. What interested me was this: Had Mrs. P., somewhere in her words, actually suggested that there were shades of whiteness, with English being somehow the most lambent? And above all, if Dr. Singh might be permitted to be Indian and English, could Dr. Singh then be permitted to be black and English? Or did the blackness cancel out the first permission?

She was looking a little nervous, as if she might have gone too far, and she put out her cigarette and turned to me in that emphatic way certain Englishwomen have. Well, she said, the colonel and I are off to Peshawar soon. There are rumors of his getting a K at some point. Nice feather in the cap after our long years of service. Of course we won't stop long in Peshawar; orders are to try to stabilize things for the time being. Peshawar guards the eastern exit of the Khyber Pass and protects the Punjab, important station right now. I said I'd taken a look at the map. Good, she said, keep informed. And as for you, Isabel, she said kindly, now that we've been so blunt, perhaps you could tell me what brought you out to India in the first place? What I mean is, she said thoughtfully, one might have thought you could have snapped up someone, you know, in the Indian Civil Service, what we call the heaven-born, the top drawer. These things have significance here, and they give a woman a certain protection, particularly if her mind's good and she's not entirely conventional—attributes that can put one at risk. Believe me, not every Englishman who comes to India is worth his salt, far from it. It's an opportunity for some, nothing more. But the people who make it to the Indian Civil Service—well, for a start they've survived Rugby or Eton, before coming down from Oxford or Cambridge with first-class honors, and then they will have had to score very high in the Service exams. I have found that the people at the very top, the ones who run India, are on the whole incorruptible. She brushed the palms of her hands together. That's essential when all you really rule by is prestige.

Quite.

And then she stood, and so did I. She rang for the bearer and ordered that my tonga be brought to the front so I could be taken to my bungalow on the other side of the cantonment. We shook hands, and she looked me right in the eye, but as I was driven off in the boiling heat, I felt oppressed and uneasy. She knew something, and if I didn't find out what it was, I could find myself an object of pity and derision in this little English tribe, where caste was everything and breaking ranks was punishable by death.

Three

On either side of the door of a tiny bungalow stood my two servants, dressed in white, one turbaned, the other bareheaded.
When I walked up the narrow path, they salaamed. I did the same,
liking the formality immensely. Introductions were made, and I noticed that the cook was called simply by his function, Bobajee. Joseph
used his name, and his English, to welcome me. Immediately the
bobajee nipped out of sight, and I was left with Joseph. Inside
the house there was not a breath of fresh air, and as I moved to fling
the windows open, Joseph was instantly at my side, hands flapping,
distress visible: Oh, no, memsahib, please allow me to avail rooms of
air. At that moment I understood a fundamental aspect of my new
life. I was no longer permitted to lift a finger on my own behalf, neither to open a door nor to pick up a hankie from the floor. I was rendered useless. Joseph escorted me around the house, moving quickly
in anticipation of my needs. I put up with him, but once he'd taken
me through the two rooms leading off the veranda, to the two bed-

rooms behind, I asked to be left alone. I sat on the single bed with my suitcases at my feet, and the small cardboard box with the lilac cutting—well established after its time under a sunny porthole on the *Viceroy*—and felt distinctly irritable. The memsahib will take tea? Joseph murmured from the door. The memsahib will *not* take tea, thank you, but I will call if I need you. He retreated to the other side of the door: Memsahib will be resting. Certainly. The day is hot. The journey arduous. Rest is good.

I looked at the bed and thought a nap might help, but of course I couldn't sleep. The unfamiliar birdsong and the sharp light coming through naked windows gave me a headache, and there seemed so much to do, and yet how was I to do anything, and how was anything done in this place? And everything was, well, really rather ugly. The floors were plain concrete, and there were a couple of ratty cane chairs with their feet sitting in saucers filled with water in which ants were already drowning. There was a rickety chest of drawers, and that was it. The ceiling was made of hanging muslin cloth. I knew snakes and bats lived up there, and no doubt there would also be lizards and spiders big as toads waiting to flop down on a sleeping person. Everything was spotless, that much I'll say. But oh, what a far cry from our beautiful house in the Rhondda Valley, with my bedroom tucked into the eaves, where I lived like a swallow in a spun nest, gazing down on the gardens with their cargo of roses.

When I unpacked, I felt better, but I was careful when opening a drawer, having read Maud Diver's terrifying little offering, *The Englishwoman in India,* with all its looming warnings about nasty, germy things, deadly illnesses, and man-eating beasts, not to mention how India developed the emotional, pleasure-loving sides of an Anglo-Indian girl's nature, while obliterating her higher aims and sterner disciplines. There it was again, that perplexing phrase, *Anglo-Indian,* but another version of it, this being a book written for Us. I decided I did need a cup of tea after all. I headed for the kitchen, but there was no kitchen. I went in search of one through a covered gangway, with neat flower beds, a few trees, and a compound wall that closed it off from its neighbors. At the other end was a room, or more accurately a space, with an Indian type of oven and a couple of pots and pans, black and battered, draining on a scoured wooden counter. As I was looking around, a great shriek went up in the servants' quarters, and in a second a disheveled and very flustered bobajee entered. Joseph rushed in after him: Memsahib, please, it is not accustomed to enter. On no condition. The cook, he is distressed. It is his domain; only he works here, only he cooks. A babble of Hindi followed between them. Well, I'd had enough of this, I can tell you. I told Joseph to please impart to the cook that I respected his kitchen and his knowledge, but it was my kitchen too, and I intended to use it from time to time, to make tea, or a batch of scones, or whatever. I would not come to inspect, because I could see that everything was spotlessly clean, but I would not be barred from my own kitchen, such as it was. That shut them up, but I could tell that Joseph was trying not to look at me with—what? Pity? Amusement? Patience? Bobajee then meekly showed me how to make a pot of tea using a saucepan as a kettle. No strainer and only one teacup, and I, who had been mocking the blather that Mrs. P. had been rattling off about her nice English things, now felt firmly put in my place. I drank my tea sitting on my hard mattress and longed for England. There were no sheets, and nothing even resembling a towel. I suddenly, urgently, needed my mother, and I bawled for a good ten minutes, but it soon occurred to me that since she wouldn't be coming, I'd just have to be her. So I snapped to attention and yelled at the top of my lungs for Joseph, and he appeared, neat as a pin, ready for action. I gave him a list of basic necessities and told him to find someone at the barracks, some quartermaster person, to get them for me. Pronto. His face was aglow with usefulness: All will be as the memsahib wishes. He slid the list into the folds of his clothing. No money is needed. Chit is all. I will be back double time. He put out his hand: At the bazaar, rupees needed for memsahib's dinner. I gave him a handful. Fowl or fish? Fowl, I muttered. He bowed and went off to find a rickshaw, with orders to take a tonga on the way home, bringing essentials for the house, things that my miserable husband hadn't even thought of. Surely he might have applied himself a little by sending a wire to the supplies wallah, or a request to the new wives' committee, or whatever is done in the army? But no, I arrive to a stripped, kitchenless house, with a couple of territorial strangers who'd be better placed in a trade union in the Welsh valley.

Joseph, before he left on his errands, was kind enough to draw me a deep and deliciously cool hip bath. Since he brought the water in brimming kerosene cans that weighed down his arms, I didn't assert any claim to share duties in this department. I was out of my tight, sticky clothes and in the tub in a jiffy. All the while I kept my eye glued to the hole in the floor, which Joseph had explained in simple terms: Water goes out, snake comes in. I couldn't stand the strain of waiting for a scaly, tongue-flicking little face to appear out of that hole, so I nipped out of the tub and stuffed my knickers into it. I decided that it would be possible for me to dry myself simply by standing by the open window for a minute or two, and this was accomplished with quick success. I looked through my things to find my favorite pink dress, which in its threadbare state should have been retired to dusters long ago, but I loved it too much to leave home without it. The minute I had it over my head, barely before I'd done up the row of pearly buttons down the front, there was a knock on the door. It threw me into something of a panic, but since Joseph was away on house business, I was obliged to get to the door and answer it myself.

HIS EYES ARE NOT BLUE. They're pale green, with an edge of gray, and they're deep enough to drown in. His face is not as beautiful as the Bengali's, but it has a strong shape, a good nose, and an interesting mouth, serene and edgy at the same time. Eyebrows black, hair brown and longish, not thick and wedged, but slightly curly instead. The earlier-glimpsed suit was made of pale cream linen with a slash of silk to water it down. Mother would have approved of the way he carried it, but she'd have been less pleased by his mocking smile. He was looking at my hair, which, tousled and sopping, was quietly drenching my frock, and then his eyes dropped, as mine did, to my nipples, which were perfectly outlined by the flimsy cloth. And lo and behold, within seconds, the wetness had smoothed and tucked the pink fabric around my breasts so neatly that they sat before us like two peaches on a plate. I yanked at the cloth, and felt the seam give, and watched as a button broke free and bounced to the floor, and nothing was helping until I leaned forward and began to wring out the ends of my hair. Even so, it was too late, and he and I both watched as the wetness quickly expanded the radius of gummed cloth, which, when reaching my navel, sucked in its breath, exposing the full glory of my hips and belly. I gave up and folded my arms.

Forgive me, he smiled, lifting a hand apologetically, not a good time. He took a step backward, and instantly I found myself out on the front step, blinking in the glare and protesting: No, no, really, it's not a problem. Come in, do. It's just that I've barely got here, and there are no towels and . . . well, everything is all over the place, including me. I closed the door, with him inside it.

I was actually looking for Sergeant Webb, he said, standing with full bodily comfort in his exquisite cream suit while I cringed in my wet rags. He looked amused, which rattled me. I noticed then that he was quite old, perhaps as much as thirty, and that gave him an edge I didn't care for either. He held out his hand and opened it: Your button, he said. He put it in his pocket and strolled into the room, looking back at me. I couldn't find Sergeant Webb at the barracks, he said, and of course I wouldn't have disturbed you, except that the matter is quite urgent. He turned to face me: Naturally, I can come back later.

He'll be back any minute, I said, lying through my teeth.

I'm Dr. Singh, by the way, he said, smiling through deeply fringed eyes. His English was straight out of Oxford; it had no inflections, but it had a rhythm that wasn't precisely British, though I couldn't have told you why not.

I know, I said quickly. I saw you up at the barracks after the shots went off. He gave me a quick look. You were there?

Just got off the train as a matter of fact.

Must have been a shock for you. He was staring intently at my face. I blushed and walked with him out of the hall and into the first room, which was empty, of course, and I was so embarrassed I wanted to creep into the corner and disappear. I'm sorry, I mumbled, as you can see . . . there's not much here, and I can't even offer you tea as there's only one cup, and if I risk the kitchen again, there's a very good chance that the bobajee will shoot me. He laughed in a wonderful way, as if this were all foolishness and could be resolved in a moment. He went out to a blue American car, which I hadn't even noticed, and brought in a small crimson rug and two bottles of Évian. He flung the rug down on the floor and sat in a fluid way, putting out his hand to help me down. I was standing there rather lost for action, but I took his hand and sat, trying to fold my legs into the damp dress. I don't drink tea, he said, or only the sweet, spicy kind, which you probably loathe. He pulled the top off one of the bottles and handed it to me and then looked at me very directly and said, with quite astonishing sincerity: Tell me how you're managing India?

It took me a full moment to reply, and when I did, I was talking too fast: I don't really know how I'm managing India. As a matter of fact, I rather think India is managing me. I spent some hours with Mrs. Pendleton and came away in rather a muddle.

Ah. Clarissa. His manner was cool and suave, but I wasn't going to be intimidated by this kind of maturity.

I liked her, I said defiantly, assuming from his manner that he did not, but I thought she was rather cagey about what had happened at the barracks, called it the Incident, and I don't think I was getting the whole picture somehow.

Do you really want to know what happened? His hand smoothed

the rug, which was exotic and rather beautiful, with strands of gold and violet merged with the scarlet.

Well, yes, why wouldn't I? Mrs. Pendleton said the woman had been murdered, but I'm not sure how she could know that since she'd not been into the bungalow at that point.

Well, things like this are seldom simple, and the relationships get very involved, often in ways people are not inclined to acknowledge. His face was remote now, and his mouth rather solemn.

I think Neville—that's my husband . . .

I know Sergeant Webb, he said, his tone neutral, his eyes laid flat on mine.

I wanted to keep on talking because he'd gone quiet, but then, for no reason I could fathom, I couldn't think of a thing to say.

After a moment he asked: Are you sure I'm not holding you up?

Me? No. There's not a stick of furniture in the house, and I've not a thing to do. He reached out a hand and said: Sorry, we forgot to shake hands. I'm Sam.

Sam?

Samresh.

Isabel, I said, taking my hand back. He repeated my name, as if getting the hang of it. He seemed to have all the time in the world. About the barracks, he said, what appears to have happened was that Mrs. Davies had been standing in the bedroom when her husband came in and shot her between the eyes. He was watching to see how I'd react. I couldn't seem to feel anything. There was buzzing in my ears and dizziness in my head. My bearings had come loose, and my sensations were adrift. I stared at him, and he at me. His attention had the same breathless quality as mine. I couldn't take my eyes off him, and I had a peculiar feeling that we were both afraid. We kept staring until I seemed to feel an invisible nudge, as if Mother were right beside me, telling me to pull myself together.

Was the Bengali involved? I asked, as if there had been no lapse.

Her lover, you mean? No, I don't think so. Once, the murder

would have been pinned on him, but that's too risky with the Congress Party breathing down everyone's necks. We have had, he added gravely, a few incidents of our own recently.

You're talking about Amritsar, I imagine?

He nodded but was now looking a little beyond me.

You're not saying there's a connection?

No. Just that everyone's jumpy. His face, for a second, held no emotion, just like the Bengali's as he'd walked from the bungalow where the woman lay dead. And then he smiled and seemed to move the whole thing to one side, out of the way; his intense gaze was back, and he focused it entirely on me.

What will happen? I finally whispered, and as I heard my words, they sounded far away.

Very little, I suspect. It will be an army matter.

It was as if something terribly important had happened between us, but the consequences were as yet far beyond our comprehension. The way he'd said: her lover, and then immediately canceled it out, was a double image, like a shadow within a shadow. Heat and desire had come up in me at the word. It was immediate and startling, making me shiver, as if he'd touched my thigh. I was so scattered that I could only whisper: I can't help thinking that everyone here knows something that I don't.

Only the servants know everything, he said. The husband shot himself after he'd shot her; they're both dead. It's done. He turned away from me, and his face in profile was melancholic, dark. I began to feel that submerged feeling again, a sinking under water or beneath a great weight, and having no capacity to rise up out of it. I leaned back and closed my eyes, trying to empty my mind.

What do you want? he whispered, so close to me that I thought his voice was mine.

HE WAS GONE and I was adrift. A lorry was noisily braking on the road outside, and through the window I could see a private leap out of the door of the cab and begin off-loading some truly hideous items of household equipment. Where his blue car had been was a stack of cheap furniture. I watched the private without moving, feeling my dress turn to paper. Here was my furniture: a charpoy bed, two hardback chairs and a table of no distinction, two plantation chairs for the veranda, a tea chest of china and glass, another of linen, and another with *Household Items* written on top. I folded my arms across my breasts and shuddered. The items entering the door were all army issue and used. I looked around me in a daze. All I possessed was contained within three suitcases. All I remembered of my quiet life in Wales lay shattered on the floor. I went to my bed and collapsed at the enormity of what can occur in the hour between two and three in the afternoon. When I returned to the front room, I saw that the red rug was still there, a bouquet of roses.

I WAS IN SUCH DISREPAIR that I'd no choice but to be practical. I called for Joseph the minute he got back. When he stood before me, the logistics of our relationship became clear: If I sat, he had to stand; if I walked, he had to be some paces behind me. He gave me the details of my new life: He'd shop at the bazaar for me each day, or else I would be cheated. He'd make up accounts and present them for my inspection. He'd liaise with the cook, who would present daily menus for my approval. Cooking would always be done by the cook, unless by prior arrangement. Joseph would engage a gardener, a sweeper, and a maid of some sort for my personal care. The problem seemed to be that certain tasks went with certain people, and there was no crossing of lines. The sweeper could sweep inside but not out and would be a person of very low caste, who couldn't touch anything but the broom. The mali was an untouchable, and I'd need to remember not to touch his gardening things and should even avoid stepping in his shadow, and so on and so forth. What a weird and unmanageable way to live, I said wearily. No, memsahib—Joseph smiled—I am assuring you, it is simple matter, stick to the rules and no bother. Sahib is sahib. Untouchable is untouchable. Hindu is Hindu. Brahmin is Brahmin. Muslim is Muslim. This is simple, na?

I managed to beat Joseph down to just the mali and sweeper and said we'd think about a maid later. The dhobi would come to collect and deliver laundry every day. There was a tailor, and traders who'd come to call. Flowers would appear every morning, and vases and shears would be laid out for me. I was permitted to arrange flowers but not to pick them. Anything I desired could be made available. Every wish I had could be fulfilled.

I LAY ON MY BED and in the wink of an eye fell into a most brazen dream from which I woke gasping. I jumped back into the tub to cool off and lay there a long time. I then retrieved my knickers from the snake hole and stuffed it up with wrapping paper from the emptied tea chest. It had now become a pretty good writing table, with pen and ink and paper lined up on it, and a journal that the Pater had given to me to jot down my impressions. Joseph brought in a note from Neville announcing that he wouldn't be home for dinner. No endearment. No hope you're managing all right in your new and squalid quarters. No can I be of help, or is there anything I can do for you? No flaming nothing. I felt less guilty.

I DINED ALONE. And of course I changed for dinner. One changes for dinner even if dining in the jungle, but mostly I changed because I wanted to wear something long and silky, and I wanted to see myself as beautiful. Had there been a mirror, I'd have liked to gaze at myself as the green eyes had gazed at me such a short time before. Joseph came in to announce that dinner was served. I followed him with the easy grace of a memsahib, scanning the table for smears and the glasses for dust. The ghastly table was now covered with a white tablecloth and made elegant by a mock-silver sugar bowl full of rather lovely pink roses. I'd no idea where they'd come from, and asking him proved fruitless. I'd decided, anyway, during my reverie in the bath, to be less insistent on answers. So I waited, as was expected of me, for Joseph to wait on me. First, he arrived with sardines on toast. No chance, I thought, of going native here. I scoffed them down to the last tiny, throat-snagging bone. The rest of the meal was entirely Indian. Joseph brought in little bowls and dishes, explaining everything to me as he doled and spooned: Fowl is scrawny, underbreasted, but curried is superior. Memsahib, first night on station, be persuaded try a little vegetable curry, with fresh herbs and spices? Bobajee has made effort to overcome bad start with screaming. A little of the tamarind chutney, very good, I assure you, and the sweet mango you will definitely be enjoying. Take, try, all very delectable. He served me fragrant rice and uncovered a bowl of golden chicken with some interesting squiggly green things on top. Perhaps a small amount, memsahib? It is spicy, but no harm done. I took a pale pancake with nicely blackened edges and a spoonful of some dark kind of pulse. Joseph hovered, but I dispatched him back to the kitchen, where I presumed his own dinner was waiting. I was starving and now wanted to get the taste of sardines out of my mouth as fast as I could.

When I stormed the kitchen, the two of them were sitting on the back step, eating happily away. I couldn't speak, and they stared at me in that appalled-looking way they both have. My face was scarlet; my hand was clutching my scalded mouth. The chicken curry, which had been utterly delicious for that second before the green firecracker went off, was now down my front. I'd already gulped down the contents of the water jug, and these perfect imbeciles didn't seem to realize that I must have water or die. Memsahib—Joseph was shuffling around me—Memsahib, water will provide scant improvement. He tore off a flap of pancake and passed it to me on a plate: Memsahib, take the chapati, chapati is best. He then turned furiously on Bobajee and began hurling abuse at the man, who rushed off and came back with an enamel dish. Joseph snatched it from him: Memsahib, take yogurt, I beseech you. Do not be fainthearted. Chili is all, I assure you. He escorted me back to the other room and immediately made a pitch for another item on his shopping list: Memsahib, with hot curry, and in this bloody awful climate, icebox most essential. Allow me to purchase tomorrow. I nodded fiendishly, imagining the solace of a lump of ice in the mouth at this moment. I assured him I was perfectly fine. Memsahib, take a little rice, and perhaps the vegetable curry? I shook my head, and he looked disappointed that I wouldn't deliberately throw hot coals down my throat again. In a moment he came back with a tall glass of sweet lassi, and bowed low: Condolences, memsahib, from the cook. I sent Joseph back to his dinner and, with my tongue, made delicate investigations to see if the roof of my mouth was still there. Meanwhile, in the kitchen outhouse, a fierce row was raging between the two executive branches of my household. Joseph was yelling at the cook, in English, for my benefit: What is this lunacy? Inflaming the memsahib. She will be indisposed by flux. First night and disaster on our hands. This was followed by a string of virulent Hindi, which I longed to understand, but couldn't. Bobajee was silent. As well he might be.

Before long, Joseph was back to let me know that the cook was unaware that I'd just arrived from over the black water. He'd presumed that since the sahib liked his curry very hot, I would too. It's not a serious matter, Joseph, I said, still sucking in air; it's just a matter of getting used to it. I'll try again tomorrow, but I'd appreciate it if you held back on those little green things. Assuredly, memsahib, try again tomorrow. A sublime attitude, memsahib. I applaud it. I beg forgiveness. This I should have foreseen. Better safe than sorry. And then we had a little chat, he and I, during which he told me that he'd been educated in a mission school and had found Jesus and Christianity, but, being Hindu, had merged the two religions for his greater pleasure: Two is better than one, na? He then told me about his previous employer, Lady Enid Watson: Wife of burra sahib, many, many years in India, lady of distinction, severe in duties, ruling with iron rod, counting grains of rice, riding her horse, inspecting gardens. Oh, she sounds *very* interesting, I said blithely. To which he replied with a sweet, soft voice: Memsabib, she was incorrigible.

I now understood what Mrs. Pendleton had meant by his eccentric English. I thought it distinctly subversive. Joseph and I would manage very well. He was, he'd told me, more than forty. I knew that was quite an age in India. He had things to teach me, and the language came first. Even so, later that night, I said nothing to him about planting my lilac. I knew that the mali would arrive tomorrow, and I wanted to get in first and plant my little tree before being banned from gardening. The garden was small, but well tended, with bougainvillea trailing up the kitchen wall and lots of scarlet geraniums in pots. It was cool outside; the moon was full, and it lit my way. I thought I should start the lilac off in a pot and found a biggish one with an ugly chrysanthemum in it, which I yanked out and stuffed behind a sweet-smelling jasmine. I planted the white lilac, watering it in well with the mali's watering can. As from tomorrow, this watering can would be untouchable for me, even as I was untouchable for the mali.

NEVILLE ARRIVED a few hours later, just as I was falling asleep. A formidable, bearded, turbaned person was at his side: his Pathan bearer. I'd heard about him and had once thought he'd be part of our little household. I stared at the man, whose ferocious face seemed carved out of the high hills, and whose jaw lunged like a precipice below the ravine of his mouth. Neville announced that the Pathan would be returning to his quarters at the barracks. The two of them spoke in the vernacular and ignored me. The Pathan helped Neville out of his uniform and all but undressed him. There was something so intimate about the connection, Neville holding out his arms to have his shirt removed, like a child, resting his hand on the bearer's shoulder to step out of his trousers, and sitting to have his shoes taken off his feet. I watched in amazement. It was as if they were alone, enacting some ritualized form of service. It seemed a little revolting to me. Neville walked naked past the Pathan and into the bathroom, where he shouted for water. I'd been told that this man had accompanied him on all his campaigns and took care of every detail of his daily life— when he was on active duty and also in the barracks. The Pathan filled the hip bath, and when the bath was drawn, vanished.

Meanwhile, Neville was in a foul mood, displeased by everything I'd tried in some way to make pleasant about the house. I need to speak to Haskins, he snapped; this is not up to par. The bed is filthy, and the furniture is flimsy.

How interesting it was, but before Neville got back, I was more than ready for a scrap, mad as a snake about his complete disregard for me. But the moment he strolled in with his servant, something shifted. I saw the advantage of his crudeness, and I absolved myself of all responsibility for him. The ugliness of his manner exonerated those blissful moments as I'd stood, and then sat, in my glistening frock, and given my heart away to a stranger. Of course part of me knew that the best thing would be to pick up my heels and run. Love is no more than a reflection of our own excessive love of it. But now, of course, I was well on the way to persuading myself that Neville's purpose had been fulfilled. He'd brought me to India as he'd needed to, even as I'd needed to come. It was obvious that once here, we had no further use of each other. He'd reclaimed his old world, his true love, the army, and I was free to be whoever I wanted to be. And suddenly I was all milk and roses, because I wanted him gone. I did consider, for a moment, speaking the truth and saying: Marriage got us both out of a jam, so let's leave now before things get ugly. Instead, I heard myself ask: What happened at the barracks this morning? What were those shots, and what did you have to do with it?

He was sitting on the bed, and I on the charpoy.

One of the corporals shot his wife, he said, holding his ankles, his head dipped forward.

Why?

She was a slut. Messed around with a lot of soldiers, and God knows what else. When Davies got back from Burma, the CO had words with him.

But why were you so agitated about it?

He was my responsibility. He was young, not very bright. I should have handled things better.

So you knew what was going on?

He nodded.

Did you have an affair with her too?

He didn't reply or look at me, but his face was pale, and in a way he looked crushed. He said, still without looking at me: I was told when I left on furlough to get myself a wife, almost ordered to, if you want to know. I said nothing. After a long silence he looked up and said: I appreciate the way you're taking this. He seemed to slip into that vacant place inside him, but I recognized his flatness as a kind of grief. I reached over to touch his hand for a moment. I thought that he was grieving for the woman who'd been shot between the eyes, and for a moment I even had the effrontery to feel slighted, wondering if he'd loved her.

I have to leave the day after tomorrow, he said, to go up to the border. Another dispute with horses, and some land issues with the warlords. He was clicking his fingers, and the sound was driving me mad. In the Hindu Kush, he said dully, the Afghan War's still straggling on, pockets of fighting, and I might get sent there if I'm lucky. He looked directly at me: This business could go badly for me; the army has strict rules about moral conduct, and the colonel won't tolerate anyone letting the regiment down. Ah. I smiled; he was grieving for himself, not for her. I remembered how he'd told me once that he dreaded above all losing the respect of his regiment or being thrown out and shunted off to something ghastly, like the Army Service or Signal Corps. He was very gloomy that night. Neither of us could sleep, and we lay in the dark, in our separate beds with our separate thoughts. He knew I wasn't asleep, and under cover of darkness he began to talk in a way that he'd done once or twice on the boat. Listening to him, I knew that he and I wouldn't speak this way again.

He talked about his father, calling him the major, with a mixture of awe and admiration heavily laced with hatred. In all my time with soldiers, he said, he was the most ruthless. I barely saw him, of course, because he was always off campaigning, up the line, killing Pathans. But I heard the stories. Nothing better than an Afridi warrior coming at you with a sword a yard long, he'd say. No better or braver fighter, but what you don't want is to be left on the field, because they'll carve you up and take their time about it, lingering over the amputations, cutting slowly and deeply through the flesh and muscle of an arm. Neville would talk and then stop for a while. He loved violence, he said. He thought it clean. Effective. I don't see it that way. It leaves a bloody mess.

Instantly I had an image of a face blown away by a bullet between the eyes. His voice slowed: When I was a child and I saw him, it was as if he was always on a horse, high above me. The officers were gods, better men than we could ever be, always gentlemen, always in action—on the frontier or off in Burma or the Sudan. He knew his duty, and he did it. Once he let me climb up onto his horse because I wanted to be high up like him, sitting on top of a horse like a cavalry officer. He said, If you want to ride, come out pigsticking with me, why don't you? I'll show you great sport, a real man's sport. He had me sit up front on his mount, and he sat behind me with his long spear. It was the only time in my life I felt like a god, or the child of one, but when the boar charged out of the tall grass, I was terrified. His rage when he heard me blubbing was too much for him. He tossed me off the horse. I lay there on the ground, watching the boar make straight for me, its head down, curved tusks ready to gore me. I heard the major roar. Get up and run for it, you fool, get up. I felt the wind when his horse swerved to face the boar. I can still hear it, the thunder of the horse's feet, the way the breath steamed out of his nostrils. He stuck a spear in the boar, smack in the shoulder, but he did it at the last moment, taking his time about it, just as the Pathans do.

I could hear the glass clinking on the cement floor, and I knew he'd been drinking for hours. I listened as he continued to talk, almost to himself, on and on; once or twice I asked him a question, but he just went on regardless. His voice wasn't remotely slurred, but it sounded like a voice in a cave. I haven't seen him for years, he said. Didn't come up to scratch, you see; he'd known it from the start. I spent my childhood with servants, in an ugly barracks bungalow with a blasted tree in the garden and white, blinding dust all around. All day and every day there were parades; a call went up: On parade, on parade. The barracks jumped to life, and out they all trooped, never seemed to stop. I didn't leave the cantonment until I went to military school, and I used to wonder which was the worst, the school, or the major, or life in that filthy bungalow with the servants, so small and dark, smelling of oil and Indian food. When the major came back for a day or two, I could barely contain my excitement, but then the fear would set in. I was sometimes taken to see him riding in a ceremonial march, up ahead of a column miles long, with five hundred men behind him, all marching, nobody falling out, all perfectly in step. I only watched one of them—the one at the head, on his fine Persian horse, a soldier, and nothing else.

And your mother? I asked. He laughed. The major buried three wives, he said. Pictures of them were lined up on the mahogany chest of drawers where his medals were laid out. When I was very young, I asked him which one of them was my mother. I liked the look of the middle one because she was smiling. I wanted to know which one was mine. Before walking out of the room, without even turning, he said: You choose.

BY COCKCROW the sympathy I'd felt listening to him talk in the dark was gone. I told myself that his philandering had drawn attention to him, and now he needed me as a screen. From our bungalow I heard the sunup reveille and the crack of the morning gun. The crows all leaped to attention. And there he was, pacing up and down the cramped room, before leaving for the barracks square. He came back later with the Pathan, who drew him a cold bath, shaved him in it, and dried him when he came out. He had breakfast out in the open, served on the veranda. It seemed as if the Pathan had brought the whole camp along with him: egg-wallah and dudh-wallah, with their brown speckled eggs and enamel dishes of milk and butter, and fat hunks of bread, which Neville ate without saying a word. He didn't put his uniform back on. He told me he'd been given a day to put his household in order before heading north. There was something a bit scary about him when he was out of his khaki drill. He sat on the veranda in one of the cane chairs, yelling at Joseph to get a bloody move on with his whiskey and soda. And then he'd demand slices of buttered toast spread thickly with anchovy paste, and then more whiskey and soda, and then it was char and toast. His cane, with its round silver top, was tucked neatly under his left arm; it was as if he were always on the lookout for someone to hit. He was miserable as sin, bored out of his mind by being cooped up in the house, perhaps even remembering his childhood days of incarceration. He had a small piece of newspaper stuck to his cheek, where his bearer had made a small nick with a razor. He seemed to think it my fault. Everything seemed to irritate him. It was hard work to get him to talk about anything. My questions about how I was supposed to proceed in his absence infuriated him. It was to be an indefinite tour of duty, with short furloughs once in a while. How on earth am I to spend my time? I asked. I'm not used to being waited on hand and foot, and I can't be bone idle. I'll go bonkers with nothing to do all day.

Just do what army wives are supposed to do, he snapped; you'll get the hang of it. He provided me with the details of his pay. I was appalled by the amount and felt the deepest mortification at the idea of dragging myself each week to some pay station for a handful of shillings. Thank God, Mother had organized money to be deposited in the Imperial Bank of India for me. I didn't mention this to Neville because she'd advised against. At the end of our first day of married life we were reduced to silence, and it was the greatest relief when he went off to his mess that night. He came back drunk as a skunk, just like the night before. Drinking was part of army protocol, and essential to a regiment who were, according to Neville, hard drinkers to a man, from the colonel downward. In spite of it, he was up the next morning before six, impeccably turned out and ready for action. When he left, I pretended to be asleep. Later, from my bed, I could hear the army marching out, band playing and, no doubt, flags flying and rifles gleaming in the morning sun. The officers shouted out their commands in their loud, proper voices, and the boots went clickety-click on the hard dark road, while I, for a moment, was transported back in time, to the day when the Welsh regiments went marching off to war, taking Gareth, taking our future, and burying it deep in the trenches of France. But now, remembering what was gone, I was a little less sad, because something in me had come back from the dead.

Four

I wondered if I should just vanish. I wanted to get a good horse, a Kabuli or, even better, a Gulf Arab, and just disappear into the immensity of the country. My life was wide open, or so it seemed to me, unencumbered by Neville or by the army, and I wanted to try it out for the first time. I had a new, fearless kind of enthusiasm: to push out into deep water, to take things as far as I could, and not mind the consequences. Then I remembered how, when we'd said goodbye, my father had looked me squarely in the eye and said: Now, Isabel, my love, beware of your reckless heart. You're going off to a small community in a vast country, where the English are an endangered species. They've drawn in their ranks and won't tolerate change or difference, just won't put up with it, so don't stir things up. I seemed to see ahead, darkly, but I didn't want to. I remembered the shots, the Bengali and his beauty, the dead soldier and his wife. I wanted Mama and the Pater to be wrong. I wanted Mrs. Pendleton to be part of history, nothing to do with a new world that had been birthed by the war.

I sat in front of my beautiful breakfast, listless. Joseph had brought me sliced pawpaw and scrambled eggs. The mossies had attacked my net all night, breaching the fortifications. I was scratching myself like a monkey. Dreary it all seemed. In broad daylight, my enthusiasm of the night before turned out to be just plain lunacy. I was trapped in darkest India, in an army cantonment, with a husband who'd just headed off to the hills. The quartermaster came to do an inventory of army property; the major's wife dropped by for a chat; the padre came creeping by with requests for Sunday participation. Army wives came to call and had their cups of tea and looked me over. They were yellow and worn out, though none of them was older than twenty-five. The only one I liked, Bridget, had some spunk and a sense of humor, though Mama would have considered her common, with her brash blond hair and red, shiny mouth. I knew she'd be good fun, and she told me how I could get my hands on a pony. One of the junior officers' wives was looking for someone to share the exercising and costs of her horse. I felt better when I knew I'd be able to go off riding.

Joseph and I had our first tiff. I wanted to go to the bazaar, and he said I was obliged to go to the army-approved bazaar, a drab little place compared to the sprawling extravaganza where the Indians shopped. Joseph was firm: Memsahib, Indian bazaar full of thieves and incorrigibles. Definitely not advisable. Perfectly satisfactory for me to go for memsahib. Sorry, Joseph, I said, you're not going without me. You can come with me, so I won't be cheated, but we're going together, end of story. He was standing in front of me, hands cupped tidily in front of him, as I sat in one of the cane chairs on the veranda. He held his ground. I tried to argue with him. No reply. In the end I took the imperial line: Get me a rickshaw and let's go.

I put on my smart traveling suit to go to the bank, took out a lot of money, and we headed down to the bazaar. We ran our hands up and down great swatches of muslin, damask, cotton, and silk, pulling and tugging to get the feel of it. We smelled incense wafting from dark corners, sweat from unwashed bodies, and garlic from yesterday's curries. Babies screamed, and vendors kept up a constant stream of invective and seduction. We had to be shown everything, even the bales from the rear. There was Manchester cloth and the homespun kind. The vendor was trying to get me to buy British, but I really liked the soft open weave of the local and went ahead and bought yards of white muslin, in spite of protestations. We took it instantly to the curtain-wallah further up in the bazaar; he was whirring away on an old Singer under a shady tree, spectacles on the end of a long nose. He knew the exact length and width of the windows of the cantonment bungalows. Chota, chota, Joseph kept insisting, closing in his hands to convey the smallness of mine. Both he and Joseph were frankly disappointed in my taste: Why buy Indian cloth when it was possible to order lovely English linens and have them sent out? Perhaps the memsahib should reconsider? Joseph said he was just trying to swindle me. I told them that the plain white would be just lovely. We moved from stall to stall and were offered sticky sweets wrapped in silver after each sale. Joseph walked beside me as I stocked up on thick brocades, silky sheets, and Kashmiri satin. I was dreaming of lush cushions and a bedspread that gleamed in the moonlight. I bought a length of sari silk, with a gold edge, for the fun of it, and one of those short cutoff blouses that go underneath. Joseph turned his back while I was making this purchase, but he encouraged me to buy a few pairs of chapplis, so I wouldn't die stepping on scorpions and spiders.

We whirled off to another part of town, to a vast warehouse, which echoed like the interior of a sunken ship. It was stuffed with Victorian furniture, frozen in time. The furniture-wallah sold me a mirror, a gorgeously carved, ornate oval, with not a blotch on its shimmering surface. I later decided that it must be from the time of the Mutiny massacre because on the back the name Meerut had been almost obliterated by a dark stain. English blood, no doubt. We ordered it sent, along with a small round tea table, a delicately carved writing desk, and a matching chair. I threw in, for good measure, a couple of armchairs covered in squished velvet, a blue oriental rug for near my bed, and a pair of china paraffin lamps. We went home in two rickshaws, packed to the gills, hoping no one would catch us as we sidled in with our treasures from the out-of-bounds bazaar. Exceedingly fine day, said Joseph. Memsahib has a delight in life. Very commendable.

In a day or two—such is the speed and efficiency here—I had my white muslin curtains billowing in the breeze. The furniture was in place, and there was a plump little footrest, a red and gold floor cushion, a deep blue silk quilt flung over my bed, and an aquamarine dressing gown of shot silk, which stirred quietly as the punkah fan moved the stale air. When Bridget came for a drink, she blew out her breath and said: Blimey, you've turned the place into a harem. She was jealous, of course, but she settled in easily, lying on my bed. She likes to drink and smoke. She says she's a bad girl with no one to be bad with: Too damn risky. If you do it more than once, you get caught. It's the damn servants; news gets round the station in a minute. Bridget turned out to be the only one I could have a real talk to about the Davies Incident. The other women I met avoided the subject, except to mutter: Bad business or very bad business. If anyone mentioned the wife, it was: That Woman, or That Damn Davies Woman. Bridget said that Polly Davies *was* knocking off the Bengali, quite a dish in his way, but how *could* she do it with a nigger? I'd thought that word only referred to Africans. Don't be daft, she snapped. Black is black; there's no in between. She delicately positioned her cigarette in the ivory holder and told me that though sleeping with natives went on in India all the time, it was completely against the rules—especially the white woman/black man way round. The woman carries the can, she said, but the darky'll get bumped off one dark night or have his goolies chopped off and thrown to the pidogs. According to Bridget, Mrs. Davies had been lonely, and the soldiers took advantage of her. Her husband knocked her around, and she'd had a miscarriage or two. You know, Bridget said, she was just plain miserable here, poor cow, and I don't blame her. I hate it too,

being confined to barracks all the bleeding time. Can't go anywhere—no fun, no dancing, no money, and fuck all to do. When the
men are here, they're too drunk to be any use, or certainly Frank is.
She raised her glass in my direction: No matter who you marry, luv,
after a year you'll want to put him out with the rubbish. But who'll
take a husband off a girl's hands when she's sick of him? She poured
herself a pink gin and promised me that things were going to be much
more lively in the hills, where we'd take up lots of evening dresses, go
out dancing every night, and might even see the Viceroy at one of the
garden parties.

Of course I could have taken Bridget's information as a warning,
but I didn't choose to. I was happy in India, and I didn't want to think
further than that. I was falling in love with my first home. It was a
world away from my room in the rafters at home, with its white walls
and rose and honeysuckle curtains, and Mother's elegant Italian
pieces. This little bungalow was all mine. Joseph was a marvel; he
could hang or fix anything and even invented a way to make the
flimsy wall hold the mirror. He had a way of using his toes to pick up
the tiniest object off the floor—a safety pin, a piece of string, a scrap
of paper. Go on, I said, challenging him. Try a grain of rice. He was
shocked: Wasting food is sinful, memsahib. What foot has touched,
mouth cannot. When he wasn't around, I practiced with the easy
things, like a napkin or pencil, and I intended to get as good as he is.
Once he cottoned on that I was willing to learn from him, we had a
conversation about his teaching me the language. Memsahib, he said,
standing with his hands folded together, Urdu of no value. No one
will be understanding a word. Punjabi I will teach. He told me he
knew some Latin, a little Persian, some Sanskrit, Hindi, Kashmiri, and
Punjabi, but he didn't make me feel a fool for having only Italian and
French myself. He told me most Indian languages were a mix: Learning one, memsahib learns many. Excellent method. Economical and
speedy. We decided to devote the morning hours to my learning of
the vernacular, speaking nothing else. He wanted me to correct what

he called his impoverished English, but I was reluctant to because I love the way he sort of kicks the English language in the pants, making it verbless and to the point. He also uses his own brand of English to have a go at us when it might appear that he doesn't know what he's saying.

I was moaning to him about the maid he'd hired, a tiny girl with hands the size of a leaf: I can't stand it that Gita's so petrified of me, Joseph, what's the matter with her? He sighed at my stupidity: Accustomed as she is for memsahibs to bellow and shout, and for sahibs to kick up the backside, when she sees memsahib come, most certainly she will hide. Well, tell her to stop right away. I can't bear that kind of submissiveness. He smiled in an interesting way and murmured: Memsahib will get her way—as is customary. I gave him a sharp look, and he quickly ducked his head. Don't think you're pulling the wool over my eyes, Joseph, I said.

Memsahib?

You know what I'm talking about.

WORD GOT ROUND that I was a sucker for pretty things, and all the vendors and tailors in the province came knocking at my door. The derzi came and squatted on my veranda with his traveling sewing machine, wanting to mend, to alter, to fit new collars and cuffs. He told me if I showed him a picture from a magazine, he could make me anything I desired: Any kind, memsahib, simple for playing bridge, formal for Simla, silk or satin, large or small, any gown handmade in three days. Then the merchants from Srinagar arrived, sitting under the tree until the locals had gone. They turned my veranda into a bazaar, bringing in piles of gorgeous hand-stitched shawls, quilts, embroidered sheets and pillowcases, and underwear too beautiful to wear. A silk-wallah was showing, against the backdrop of a Persian rug, a pair of silky knickers, or an exquisite bra, or a long petticoat with match-thin straps. And as he kept putting out his wares, he'd murmur seductively: All handmade, I assure you. Please to touch, come closer, memsahib, feel the quality, touch the beauty, no obligation to buy, look only, no need to buy. I was transfixed by a beautiful nightgown of cream crepe de chine with a plunging neckline, delicately bordered with pale pink roses made from silk thread gathered up into knots. My pile was growing by the second, and all the while he crooned: Please to touch, look only, no obligation to buy. . . and all the while I was loading up my chair with every delectable item I simply had to have.

Joseph kept beating down the vendors' prices, and sometimes things got so rowdy that I thought we'd end up with the two of them having a punch-up. I'd learned the magic words: Kitna pice? (how much?) and would happily have passed over the amount, because everything was dirt cheap, but immediately we were given a price Joseph would throw up his hands and hiss with horror: This is an outrage. Memsahib, allow me to remove the thief. The two of them would be at each other's throats till I made Joseph stop. He'd end up hurling a furious final snarl: Malum? Which I think means something like: Understood? Did you get it? Now pipe down and bugger off. Joseph has to have the final word, and once a sale has gone his way, butter won't melt in his mouth. He was different with me by now, more himself, and had stopped all the bowing and scraping and smiling like an imbecile. He also likes to get his own back. A moment ago he came in, furious, after delivering a note to Bridget. I'd asked him to take it over to the club, which is a little way off. He'd refused my offer of a rickshaw, on the grounds that memsahib is excessively free and loose with money. He came back an hour later, hot and bothered, his face puckered up with distaste: Memsahib, what is it I am seeing at the English club? What is this running around with no clothes on? I looked up with interest. He went on, unable to conceal his disgust: Memsahibs in white underpants, hitting white balls. This is revolting, na? Fifteen love. Thirty love. What is this abundance of love? And clapping. And shooting: Good shot, oh, well done, jolly good shot. My explanation was of no earthly use to him; he whammed it aside with a snort: Naked is naked; legs uncovered deplorable and shameful.

We had another problem when I rose early one morning to ride my new half horse, shared with a pretty blond thing from the officers' part of town. A couple of words out of her mouth were enough to place her in deepest Gloucestershire: Such a pity we have no hounds here. Don't you miss the hunting? Ever so, I said, but chin up, there's lots of shikar [hunting and shooting] to make up for it. She left in a hurry with a: Do let's take Pearl [the horse] up to the hills; the riding there is so divine. Afterward I could hear Joseph quietly imitating her accent: Do let's take Pearl up to the hills. The riding there is *so* divine. But as I came out for a cup of char before heading off for my ride, his mouth dropped to his chin. He took a long, silent look at me: Memsahib, what is this I am viewing? Joseph, I said sweetly, shoving my helmet down hard on my head, you are not my mother, and this is simply what a woman wears to ride a horse. These—I yanked at the sides—are called jodhpurs, and women wear them all over the world. He folded his arms: I am not understanding this word *jud purrs*? All over the world women are wearing such things? Memsahib is definitely pulling my leg. Last madam rode one side of horse in full skirt. Memsahib is wearing trousers like a sahib and telling me this is world-class apparel? Yes, I am, now please stop dithering and ask the syce to bring my horse round to the front. He sniffed: Memsahib will do as she pleases, but I remain out of eyeshot.

I rode off and left him to take his irritation out on Bobajee, who had orders to make me, on my return, a breakfast of mangoes and pawpaw, followed by scrambled eggs and soft chapatis. The bread is lousy here because the yeast is ages old by the time it gets to us. Bacon and ham is of course off the menu, except when Bobajee has his day off and Joseph cooks. He uses a different pan, and will do much scouring and boraxing afterward, so there's no trace of the evil pork fat that we both adore. I took off at a demure walk, but once in the open avenue and under the trees, trotting past the English church, with its graveyard filled with the English dead, and beyond the maidan, suddenly I'd left England and the army behind, and I was happy as Larry.

Out here the trees fall back, the bungalows disappear behind a hill, and there are just the flat, open fields and the spread of a village with its Hindu temple and fat white Brahman bulls. Thin women move down the narrow, dirty streets, trailing emaciated children and carrying babies on sharp hips. Yapping dogs and mutilated beggars take up positions on the street, and without even showing itself, the sun pinkens the sky. Fruit and vegetable vendors set up stalls for the day. A woman in a green sari piles up cowpats to boil rice in a tin once filled with condensed milk. I begin to canter and then to gallop past the paddy fields, past the glowing mustard and bean fields—all fresh and fragrant in the cool morning. Dew glazes the earth, and it's as though everything's breathing a sigh of relief. Partridge and pea-cock move through the tall grass, only their pretty heads and necks visible. In half an hour I'm at the river. On the stone steps a few bathers step into the slack water, and fishermen sit out in their boats with their poles. The river has a dark, sulfurous smell. The lily-trotters walk on little islands of mud; downstream, people are shitting directly into the water, while upstream, women scrub clothes on the rocks and rinse their pots. A small, ruined fortlike building, draped in vines and cascades of purple flowers, makes a jagged clothesline, and a man lies asleep behind a shard of wall, his head hidden in his arms.

Riding back was entirely different because I was on fire. My limbs were floppy, and I was shaking badly. Even though it was still early, the heat was booming down, and shadows fell darkly between the hovels and the trees. The plain had become a wasteland, treeless and ugly. Each child, man, or woman I passed seemed intent on just mov-ing trancelike through the heat, each one struggling for life under a vicious sun. It was hard to see, and the inside of my head had an echo. The heat seemed to press me lower into my saddle with hard, thud-ding blows. My bones were rattling. I felt minute under the weight of the sky. I didn't understand why the birds didn't just drop. How could they fly when the air was dense enough to shovel? When I got home, I slid off the horse and fell flat on the ground, dead to the world.

IT'S NOT INFLUENZA, a voice snapped.

Who said it was? I croaked. And who the hell are you anyway? He gave a light laugh. Joseph was lurking in shadow, saying nothing. It was night, or maybe it wasn't. The English voice was chiding Joseph, who was being obsequious, which annoyed me even more. I wanted everyone to clear off and leave me alone. I wanted to sleep. The obnoxious English voice kept asking its questions, and it exhausted me. A hand picked up my little box of quinine and looked at it. I've been taking it, I snapped, two grains a day. It was perhaps the end of the day, or the beginning, who knows? Twilight of some sort. Joseph stopped talking, and I was left with the voice, which was chockablock full of breeding, intelligence, and authority, asking its questions, sometimes in English, sometimes in Hindi, but not shutting up. Then I fell down a well, and the walls were clammy. I was giddy and shaky, light-headed and panicky, hanging on to the walls by my fingernails. My hearing and sight were blurred. Small creatures were running up and down the walls; the ceiling was billowing, it had turned dark red. A hand came under my waist and raised me, then propped me up against the pillow. I was sopping wet, and the wet seemed solid, as if I'd vomited. Another hand brought a tumbler of iced lime juice to my lips; the rim pressed against my tongue, and I tried to swallow, but the liquid spilled down my front. I was furious because I was wearing the cream crepe de chine with the tiny pink roses made of knotted silk thread. It had risen above my knees, and my legs were free. I wanted to kick them in the air. I wanted to laugh or cry, and I didn't know which.

After a bit my head cleared, and I could think again. Someone laid me down flat, in a firm way. I heard the voice say: Malaria, and then, from the structure of the sentences, what sounded like instructions. I heard Joseph say: Yes, sahib, but which bazaar? And then: That is far, sahib, many miles. The voice rapped out orders: Take a rickshaw. Make it wait. It will take time to get the prescription. Show him my card. Bring me another basin of water and a clean towel. Now get along. The way he spoke irritated me; it was rude, and Joseph sounded afraid, but there was nothing I could do. I seemed to swoon, and it was rather lovely, except that my brain was scrambled. I began to croon softly: Mah . . . lar . . . ia. Mal . . . air . . . ia. Mal . . . lairi . . . a Mah . . . lai . . . reeeaa. Even in this strange disordered state, some small scrap of my brain was alert, and the thought passed through me: If it's malaria, I'll end up yellow. I laughed. And then, for a brief second, I was asleep.

When I woke up, everything pierced me. My quilt shuttered one of the white windows; the other was a square of moonlight. I felt air around me. Someone had lifted the end of my nightgown and was rolling it up like a bandage, working very slowly and carefully until the silk reached the top of my thighs. Two hands at the small of my back lifted me for a moment, and then the nightgown was rolled again. The hands were strong and steady, practiced, moving slowly, almost tenderly. I had no will of my own, no curiosity, nothing. I was floating on the embers of a fever, my mind locked, my body asleep. The hands continued to roll the silk up over my belly and over my waist, uncovering my breasts. An arm slipped to the back of my neck and raised my head; my dangling, matted hair, reeking of sweat and sourness, fell away and spread over the pillow. Gathered silk moved like water across my face, up and over my head, and then it was gone, and I was naked. The sweat on my body was cooling, and I lay silently, as if in a rain forest. I was weak and yielding, an invalid, or a newborn infant. My feet were rubbed with something wet and scratchy. I laughed. I could hear the cloth splash into a basin to be rinsed and wrung, and then my legs were bathed, starting at the calves, front and back, and then hands parted my legs, moving the cloth along the inside of my thighs. I shuddered, and my hands clutched the sheet for a moment. My skin was taut and filled with tension, and at times I felt I was on the rack, stretched to breaking point. The cloth was rinsed and wrung, and then it began to circle my breasts, moving from the edges to the center, and then I was tipped on one side, so that my back and flank were exposed. The cloth sponged and cooled me all over till my spine was tingling. Not one word was spoken, not by me, not by him. I gazed up at the ceiling where the curtain fan of the punkah moved back and forth rhythmically, back and forth, wafting its soft breeze over my body. The cloth dipped one last time and came back to my throat and face; my hair was pushed back so that it was gummed to the top of my head. The coldness was exhilarating. I was in suspension, an insect, eyes roaming but not moving, waiting. Then a hand, warm and gentle, rested lightly on my brow, my cheek, and the side of my throat. I began to weep, and I couldn't stop, and seeing his hand come to rest for a moment, I leaned over and kissed it. I heard a sharp intake of breath. I kissed his hand again, and now there was silence, except for the tears streaming from my eyes. I was crying because he'd taken me in all my rage and fever and filth and had washed and cared for me with more tenderness than any man had ever shown me. I lifted my arms and folded them across my eyes. He pushed my arms out of the way and kissed my eyes. Holding my wrists against the pillow, he leaned over again and softly kissed my mouth. I went out like a candle.

When I heard him walk to the door, the chills started up again. I felt absurdly vulnerable. I heard the click of the lock and then the whisper of his naked feet as they returned to my bed. I pulled myself up and leaned against the pillows, and when he sat on the edge of the bed, I raised my arms and put them around his neck, and I hung on to him like a child in a shipwreck. When at last I let go, he moved back, looked at me, and smiled with his beautiful Indian eyes. He was wearing a soft, loose white cotton tunic with a high neck. He looked quite unlike the man wearing the cream silk suit who'd walked across the compound after the shots went off. And he wasn't the same man as the one who'd sat on my floor and handed me water from an Évian bottle. I wanted to see his body, but when I reached for the buttons down the front of his robe, his right hand reached my left and held it still. I was clear in my head now, and my body was entirely mine again. I was more than willing to give it away.

I wouldn't dream of taking advantage of a delirious woman, he said. How would I know if you loved me?

TWO DAYS LATER I was well enough to offer him tea.

I like the new digs, he said. It looks very different from the first time I was here.

He glanced over where his rug adorned my wall, and I said: I thought of returning the rug—as an excuse to see you—but decided to keep it instead.

It's all yours, he said, and sat opposite me in the chair and stared. Joseph brought tea and poured it in his laborious way, and the doctor and I sat for a while, making small talk about the weather. I poured some of the tea that he likes, the stuff with hot milk and spices, and passed him the cup, which he took and held in such a way that I couldn't let go of it. He smiled at me over the steam and said, exactly as if he were talking about the cricket score: I'm dying to kiss you. He continued to sip his tea, as I did mine.

Are you entirely better? You look rather radiant this afternoon.

Well, I don't know about entirely. I slept until three and feel weak as a lily. You were very kind to me the other night, I said, feeling shy. He dipped his head slightly and smiled: It was an honor. He leaned forward in the round chair and let his hands fall between his knees. He was wearing white flannel trousers and a blue shirt, and he smelled of hospital. The first thing he'd done when he'd come into the house was to wash his hands with carbolic soap.

Do you always wash your women? I asked, reaching for a cigarette, which he lit for me, brushing his fingers against mine.

It was the first time.

There was a table between us. He rose abruptly and pushed it out of the way, then looked intently at me and frowned. Don't move, he said, there's something on your forehead. He moved toward me, in slow motion, and then very softly and slowly kissed me on the mouth.

For God's sake, I whispered, someone will see you.

He returned to his chair across the way. I'm going to send Joseph on another long expedition, he said. I can't stand much more of this.

Put it out of mind.

He stood up, went to the door, and yelled for Joseph: I need a bowl of water. And, please get the towels from my car for the memsahib. He turned to me: I brought you some towels, made in Madras. It was rather difficult drying you the other night with that rag.

Army issue, I said defensively. Somehow, whenever you come here, I seem to be in a compromised situation, either dripping wet and naked or lunatic and naked. I should warn you that right now I'm sensible and mentally alert.

Glad to hear it.

He took the towels from Joseph and turned to me with a firm directive nod: It's time for your medication. Joseph, he said, would you be so kind as to bring in some boiled water? He picked up a battered doctor's bag and headed for my bedroom, opened the door, and ushered me in. I stood with my back to the door, and watched in amusement as he dug into his bag and brought out some needles and phials, which he laid out on the table. When Joseph knocked on the door, Sam was the one to tell him to come in. He took the jug of boiling water: Thank you, Joseph, that will be all. Joseph took a moment or two to be dismissed; he looked at me reproachfully.

What the hell are you doing? I asked. Being so bossy? I was under the impression that this was my house. He took my hand and led me over to my bed and sat me down: I've asked Joseph to go to the hospital to pick up a package, which is waiting at the desk. It will take him at least two hours to get it.

Joseph is not a fool.

Nor am I. Now, listen, this is the situation: Joseph's cousin from Delhi, who is at present staying at a village a few miles from here, is in dire need of ointments for his rheumatism. Joseph is going to collect these even as we speak.

When did this all take place?

Before I came in to see you. And I should add, it was Joseph who asked me. It was not my scheming idea.

I looked at him: Two hours?

One hundred and twenty minutes. If he's decent, he might give us longer.

Half the street will have seen you come in.

The hell with them, he said, moving his arm around the small of my back in such a way that I almost lost my balance. He looked me right in the eye. I've been careful and discreet all my life, he said, and I'm tired of it. He kissed me again, with his eyes closed, and when he moved back, he opened his eyes and smiled: Time to be bold.

I knew that this was altogether too bold, and far too sudden. I undid the top buttons of his shirt. My fingers shook. He undid the cuffs because I was incapable. He was patient as I fumbled with the rest of the buttons, and his smile was a little mocking, the way his smile always is, but it had in it something quite new that I couldn't fathom. When the buttons were undone, he lifted my hand and kissed it on the palm, then quickly drew off the gold band, and tossed it into the bowl on the floor. He stood up, and I pulled his shirt over his head, and when I first saw him, and again when the fluid darkness of his body moved over mine, it was as if my fever were back. I pulled him against me and kissed him. But he moved away and back again. His hands began a different exploration of my body, lingering excruciatingly over the places where the towel had once been, making me want to scream. He brushed his palm across my nipples. I remember these, he said; they startle easily, but I'd no idea they'd be so pink.

Five

We had less than an hour left, and during the first hour it had become clear to me that during the malaria crisis, I'd been far more delirious than I'd realized. That night now seemed like a screen punctured with holes in which snatches of conversation and hazy actions seemed to have taken place almost as if they'd happened to someone else.

How did you know I was sick? I asked him. It was as if you appeared out of nowhere. And why did you take so long to come back?

My love, this is India, not Belgravia. Did you think I'd hop on a bus the next day? I was waiting for an excuse. I suspect you'd have liked me to have done something rash and foolish. He smiled: As a matter of fact, I thought about it. And it scared me to realize that I was thinking about it. That time, when you were wringing wet, it was as if a monsoon came through and knocked me over. I drove away, and then I circled back, but when I reached the end of your street, I saw your furniture being unloaded, and I talked myself out of it. It didn't seem fair. I didn't want to foul things up for you the minute you arrived. And it was too dangerous—for you, particularly. And so it was a perfect move on your part to get sick. As soon as I heard that, I came. He narrowed his eyes and gave a small, confused shrug: It's not like me at all. I'm usually rather cautious.

I'm not very good at cautious, myself.

It's what I like about you. It's what brought you to India. I've spent my life avoiding anything that resembled passion. You told me last night about the boy you lost in the war, and I realized that I've never felt anything quite like that, not with such intensity. I've kept out of it, lived in my head.

Well, you're heading into trouble with me.

I know that.

You say it so calmly.

It's done.

Tell me what exactly happened last night? I fell off my horse and then somehow landed up in bed. I seem to remember being delirious and violently sick and being given an injection. I thought quinine was the thing with malaria.

It is, but you can take quinine and still get malaria. Malaria's ubiquitous here.

Will I go yellow?

We'll see if we can turn you brown.

What am I going to have to take? What's all that stuff you took out of your bag?

Arsenic.

Arsenic?

It's a perfectly sound treatment for malaria. He gave a louche smile: But we'll be careful with the dose . . . nasty way to die.

Tell me about last night. You sent Joseph off into the wilds to find an Indian quack. And I vaguely remember him coming back. I remember that you wouldn't let me undress you, but I don't remember you leaving. I do remember you telling me something about your prep school in England. The other peculiar thing is I seem to remember you reading me *Little Black Sambo*, or was I completely out of my mind?

Yes, you were, rather. And I didn't read you *Little Black Sambo*, but I did tell you that it was a name I was once called. And since you've forgotten, and for the record, I told you that I left India for England when I was six—like Kipling and every other English kid . . . any of this coming back to you?

Sort of.

You insisted that I tell you about my childhood, and I gave you an edited version.

Why?

He shrugged: Well, I don't think about it. It was an uneventful childhood, really, just the five-star Indian kind.

When he spoke in this way, it made him impenetrable, and it made me impatient. Can we start at the beginning? I asked him. We might not get two hours again. Were you really born in London?

Nine Eaton Square, as a matter of fact. We returned to Kashmir when I was two, and my mother took me back four years later, to go to prep school.

Would it, I asked, be possible to move off the record a bit?

He laughed: If you insist. What d'you want to know?

I'm just trying to understand. Mrs. Pendleton made you seem so mysterious and complicated.

All right, he said, like someone grasping a nettle, we'll go back to the prep school, because how can an English story be told without including the prep school? His distance and coolness were a barrier, and I struggled not to knock it down. As I told you last night, before you dozed off, I began my English life being called Little Black Sambo. He hesitated. I don't want you to get the impression that I dislike the English. It would actually be a lot easier if I did. As to the name, in English schools, as you know, we begin by chopping off the last bit of a name, and adding an *o* or a *y* or an *er*. It's a form of castration. The point is to infantilize a boy and make him someone smaller, someone faintly ridiculous. But if you're black—and I learned a long time ago that an Indian is black—the naming goes much further. The name needs to be humiliating. They call it putting you in your place. Even the teachers joined in. If we were reading about India or looking at a map, the master would say: Let's ask Little Black Sambo, our friend from the colonies, let's see if he has anything to say.

When Sam saw me wince, he said, in a perfectly English way: All in good fun, nothing to get worked up about. Then he went down a bolt hole for a moment and didn't say a word. I tried to help him out. When I think about *Little Black Sambo*, I said, the book, I mean, I remember the Indian boy being rather clever. Didn't he outwit the tigers, so that they turned into ghee and were made into pancakes?

I suppose so. He was clever, quick on his feet. If you see the tiger as a symbol of empire, the story's really quite subversive. The tigers take everything off the black kid and put it on their own backs. And that little black boy losing his identity one bit at a time, as he gives up one piece of clothing after another to the tiger, was me exactly. England was stripping me of everything I'd been in India and letting me know what I could and couldn't be. I was too young to understand all the subtle shades of it, of course. All I knew was that the name humiliated me. Crying was of course simply not done, so in a few months I stopped blubbing, and once you stop, it's hard to remember how to feel anything strongly enough to let yourself do it again.

He was staring up at the ceiling, where the fan blew the slight breeze back and forth, back and forth. He'd moved into a private place, and I left him there until he was ready to go on. I knew, he said, that I had to be several steps ahead, much cleverer than the rest of them. So I skipped a form, I think as a way of getting out of there sooner, but of course it only made me smaller and more abusable to them.

When I tried to ask him about the abusable bit, he became philosophical and dry: Everyone gets institutionalized cruelty and perversity in an English school. It's handed down from one generation to the next. Eton was no different. My father wanted me to go there after the prep school, and he put my name down the minute I'd cleared the womb.

Did you ever tell him, I interrupted, that you were having a difficult time?

He laughed. I was too English for that. Besides, by the time I got to Eton, every boy was being toughened up for conquest or war, and I became part of that way of thinking, even though the conquest would inevitably be against my own kind. The public schoolboy, whether he's in the Sudan or India, carries his public school on his back. He gave a dark laugh: He does not snivel or whinge; he's an Englishman wherever he goes. I wasn't spared that particular brainwashing; it took hold, but of course, for me, the Indian side of me complicated the whole thing. I was divided, but most of me wanted to be one of the conquerors. Obviously, he said dryly, that was not something I was going to pull off at Eton. Humiliation is a devilish thing, and the English are very good at it. The nicknames, the jokes and cutting remarks—they're all part of the system. It's the way they are to one another, and they don't see that there's a difference if it's done to a foreigner. But for them, foreigners don't count. They're phobic about anyone who isn't English. Only the little red island lies beyond contempt, and for that matter, only a very small section of it. When the empire is gone, he said lazily, the contempt will still be there.

He sat up, laughed, ran his hands through his tangled hair: I should stop talking about this, makes me want to put my clothes back on.

I rested my cheek against his back and could feel the tension. My brother, Jack, I said, went to Marlborough, but he never really talked about it. Sam turned his face so that I could barely see his mouth. Boys don't tell, he said. The silence was back, but I was getting used to it. The whole system stinks, he said, in his mild way. I was a dark boy surrounded by white ones who had subdued my country and would do the same to me. They considered it impertinent of me to be sleeping in the same dorm or to be close to their flicking towels in the cold bathrooms at dawn. At first I hated India for giving me a visibility that made boys brutal to me, but later on I came to see that to be black among the English actually made me invisible. It happened in India as well as England. I was invisible wherever I went because wherever I went was colonized.

The peculiar thing, I said, drawing him back into the pillows because he seemed to have moved away from me, the really bizarre thing is that you're so damn English. I feel completely at home with you. He moved right back into my arms in a second. The stupid thing, he said, is that for a while I actually believed that I *was* English—part of the empire, part of them. England, you see, was the only world I knew, the only language I spoke fluently. I was in every way one of them, more and more as each year passed. I could never go home to India in the holidays, of course, so I stayed in London with my aunt, or sometimes at school, so as each year passed, India faded, and England became the place I grew attached to. People, he said, always told me how much the English love India, that it's their jewel, their favorite colony and all that. And the English certainly do love India. It's the Indians they can't stand.

Has there ever been an English person who loved you?

He sat up. What an interesting question. He smiled: I can't think of anyone, but I'll keep trying.

May I be the first?

By all means.

IT WAS EASIER AFTER THAT. He became tender and relaxed, and he didn't mind telling me about the rest of his time at Eton. He spoke in a different way, less defensively; his voice was less clipped: By the time I got to Eton, I was tougher, and I'd developed my own form of mockery. I think there was a minute amount of affection in the cruelty of the naming at Eton. I was called Niggly. A plummy voice would call out: I say, you, Niggly, what d'you think you're doing in the library when you're barely out of the tree? The name would be thrown at me, like a javelin, as I walked down a corridor or was going out onto a field, but I'd got physically tougher by then. It was the best I could do, until I determined to break them with my brains. I remember the exact day, December eleventh, when I decided I wasn't going to play the game anymore, not be the black to their white. By then what they imposed on me was determined solely by coloration. I wasn't willing to accept that. There were two Indian boys at Eton, but I avoided them like the plague. I didn't want to be lumped together with them because we matched. Nor did I want anyone telling me how to be an Indian; it took me years to learn how to be one.

Turning his face sharply toward me, he said: What do you make of all this? You're not saying much.

I'm trying to decide whether you're angry, or hurt, because for some reason, you don't sound bitter.

I was always more hurt than angry, but it would have been fatal to show it. Self-hatred doesn't appeal to me.

Did it change when you went to university?

The big difference was that by the time I got to Oxford, I was ruthless. And I needed to be. At Balliol the competition was vicious, and the scholarship boys, who were partitioned off in their own kind of hell, were some of the toughest academic adversaries I'd ever met. At Oxford I was baptized again. I remember that day perfectly too. I'd been talking about a composer—Berlioz, I think, pontificating about the *Grande Messe des Morts*. And by the way—he smiled—I'm actually much better on detail than you give me credit for—just for the record. Anyway, there I was spouting a lot of undergraduate rot, and I heard someone laugh. His name was Duncan Lambert-Smythe. Hark at the darky, he said. Quite the Black Englishman, isn't he?

There were howls of laughter and knee slapping all round. It was a perfect name for me. It could be used with the elegance of a fencing strike and was delivered in a droll, almost friendly way. At that moment I understood that I was a serious problem for them, not just because of my accent and the way I dressed, or the way I conducted myself, but because I'd created a version of Englishness that was superior to theirs. Brutality had forced on me a humanity they lacked.

He dropped the cool suavity, and although he was talking calmly enough, the emotion was up. He kept trying to control it, and it was interesting to watch the two sides of him fighting it out. When, he said, I'd shot to the top of my form, my problems intensified. The hostilities were endless, and I knew that once again I'd have to get out of there as fast as I could. So I pushed them to let me complete my degree in two years. At first they thought me outrageously arrogant and dismissed me with a curled lip and a laugh. But as I kept on devising ingenious ways of getting through the syllabus in a couple of years, they decided to take me on or at least to allow me to take the syllabus on.

Soon after that, bets were being placed on me, and money changed hands. The masters were in on the race. Lambert-Smythe set himself up as a bookie. The odds kept shifting. The speculation mounted. It started with a shilling or two, then went up to ten, but soon rose to pound notes, and then fivers and up. Most of them thought I hadn't a hope in hell. One or two thought I might conceivably pull it off. Lambert-Smythe was one of these. I could hear them debating and arguing in the common rooms, in the bathrooms, and while running on the track. It caused quite a stir. I never questioned whether I could pull it off; I just knew I had to. I was already a year younger than I should have been, but I was ready for a marathon. I was in top form. And I shoved my certainty in their faces. I could out-English them in coolness and bluff, and it drove them mad. There was scorn and amusement, that gazing out of the window at the spires and saying: Well, let's see if Singh can pull it off. Why not? No harm in trying, what? Let's see if the Indian can make it.

I had to take them on in this particular way because for the English an intellectual is equal to a war hero. By then the name had been divested of its mockery, the tone was different; there was a breath of respect in the way it was uttered. I thought of it as my coat of arms. I learned to love it. And as the last year was coming to an end, the excitement was exhilarating. Lambert-Smythe sat in his study, drinking brandy and toasting bread in front of the gas fire, discussing the bets, and speculating on my chances of success. He seemed to be taking an absolutely fair-minded approach to the race, but he was upping the odds and listing them on the bulletin board every afternoon. The masters told him to lay off, but he kept on going. It was being called the Indian Derby, and, he said drolly, I was grateful for the restraint because other alternatives were possible. I was finding the going harder the closer I got to the finish. The masters were piling it on. I was working day and night, though pretending to knock my papers off in a couple of hours. Duncan spurred me on. He came in with barley water every few hours, and at night brought me strong coffee and intoxicants. And in the end he was as much invested in the outcome as I was. He used to wake me up at night, to make me swat for an exam, or he'd get me out of fencing or rowing so I had more time to study.

In the end, he said quietly, I managed to come down from Balliol with a formal first, and when I went in for my interview, the examiners stood up and clapped. There was not a trace of sour grapes. I was carried on pure white shoulders across the quad; the masters joined in with the applause and thrown caps. After that, I even managed to salvage a couple of friendships. Duncan Lambert-Smythe was one of them. He was a queer—openly, flamboyantly—and a great oarsman, as well as a brilliant Greek and Latin scholar, the best classicist of his election. He'd been kind enough to do some of the legwork for the papers I'd been turning out every week. When I asked him why he was helping me, he'd smile and say: Just for the pleasure of seeing you take them on, old man, just for the fun of watching you knock them down. We had a common outsider status that we encouraged in each other. There was mutual respect and affection. But, by the end of my time there, in spite of my straight alphas, I was considered reckless, if not downright self-destructive. It was as if my feat had struck a little terror into them. One wonders what will become of you, Singh, a don said, looking at me sideways. What will you achieve, one wonders, with your great brilliance, your furious arrogance, and your little Achilles' heel?

JOSEPH GOT BACK in just over two hours. Sam had left. I was a bit nervous that Joseph might be on to us. I asked him if he'd got the medicine for his cousin. Most definitely, he said. Now he will be on the mend. Grateful we are for Dr. Sahib's generosity. I was looking closely at him, but there wasn't a trace of irony in his face; for the moment he seemed uncorrupted by us. Bridget came to see me the next day and seemed particularly fidgety. She spotted in a second that my ring was off. I told her it had become loose. Never thought I'd see you getting scrawny, she said. She was pinning up my hair, which I still hadn't got round to cutting. She stuck the last pin into the chignon and said: What's going on with you and the sexy doc then?

What are you talking about?

You can tell me, you know. She winked at me. I won't say a word.

Tell you what?

About you and him. Think I'm blind, or what? He's here all the bleeding time.

That's bunk. He only came yesterday, to give me an injection.

Oh, yeah? How long does it take to stick in a hypodermic?

Bridget . . .

No need to convince me, luv. I'm all for a girl having a bit of fun, but it seems to me you should know better after that business up at the barracks . . . anyway, none of my business and all . . .

We were having sundowners on the front veranda, and Bobajee had made some delicious cheese straws. Bridget, I said, pouring us both a stiff gin, your mind's running away with you. Dr. Singh and I talk. We have some things in common. He happens to have gone to school with my brother.

And where might that have been?

Marlborough.

She gave me a funny look, both disappointed and sad.

Isabel, your doc went to Eton, not Marlborough. I've been doing a bit of checking up on the prince of darkness.

My fluster got the better of me. Why on earth would you do that?

Call it protecting a friend. Know what I mean?

I lit a second cigarette from the first.

Look, I'm not going to spill the beans, she said. I'm not an eejit, but you know what it's like round here. Even when he leaves his fancy car behind and comes in a rickshaw, you can see the faces at the window. You're lucky that next door's gone off to the hills, can't take the heat now the kiddie's got some kind of fever, and Maureen—you know, the redhead—she's going first thing tomorrow, and the others will soon be on their way. She put her hand on my arm in a complicit way. Now, don't look so worried, luv, she said, I've been keeping an eye on things. I told them the doc had been sent by the CO's missus. That shut their traps in a minute.

Well, I appreciate that, Bridget, really I do, but you don't need to cover up for me. Dr. Singh and I are friends. You can't say that isn't permitted. After all, he's chummy with Colonel Pendleton—they play chess all the time—so there's no need for all this cloak-and-dagger stuff.

She made sure that she was looking directly at me when she asked her next question: You know of course—being that you're such friends and all—that he's married with a kid?

I drove my half-smoked cigarette into the ashtray and mashed it to pulp. Of course I know, I said, looking her straight in the eye. They marry awfully young, don't they?

She was quiet, blowing smoke into the distance, where the pale hills were doused with shadow.

You don't scare easily, she said, I'll say that much for you.

FOR DAYS ON END there was no sign of him. I was in torment and then in a rage. Joseph told me he was at Kasur every day and that the influenza had spread to a second village. A nurse came to give me injections, but now the idea of letting someone inject arsenic into my arm felt bizarre and even dangerous. I thought he might write a letter, but the dak-wallah came and went and no word from him. Once I got a letter from Neville, which I kept meaning to respond to, but didn't. Bridget didn't say another word to me about Sam. Instead, she started on about Gandhi. Well, she said, that's another way of being a nigger all right, wearing nothing but the loincloth when he's asked out to tea. Sort of shoving it in our mugs, like, as if the skinny little bugger's saying he's proud to be what he is, and take a good gander at me in all my darky splendor. That takes the biscuit all right. But it's right peculiar to hear a voice like that coming out of a face that color? Know what I mean? Confusing. Darkies should talk like darkies. Otherwise it's hard to tell the difference, in it?

Quite.

THE HOT WEATHER was with us and gathering force. It was tiring just to think, and I was trying my best not to. Most of the army wives had gone up to the hills, but Bridget was waiting for me. She said the hills would make me better in a flash and get rid of the trace of yellow in my complexion. I couldn't leave. I couldn't decide what to do about Sam either. Not a word from him. More days dragged by. Now I wanted Bridget to leave, and did everything I could to get rid of her. I knew that eventually, she'd take off, with the last of the wives who were still on station. And sure enough, the minute she got prickly heat she was packing. I've seen people tear themselves to pieces, she said with a shudder. Rip their skin off and have to be tied up. I'm off with or without you, luv, and that's the end of it. She snooped around in my cupboard and drawers and fished out a few things she liked: Mind if I take this nice paisley scarf of yours? Nippy up there. And you don't need this little jacket, now do you? Ta ever so. Oh, and I like these shoes, but my feet are smaller. Not to worry. The hat will do nicely. See you when you get to Simla then.

I'd been getting pressure from Joseph too: Memsahib, why beating about the bush? To the hills we must go. Allow for me to arrange dooly. He was talking about an antiquated thing, a kind of covered chair, on a stretcher made of bamboo, where you lie back in complete seclusion and are carried by two porters at each end. Joseph, I said, I am not an invalid. I'm just not quite ready to leave, but I will most certainly tell you when I am. Health will deteriorate, he said ominously, most definitely. When he saw that I was staying put, he had me sleep in the garden. He'd make me a bed out there on the lawn and hang the mosquito net from the peepul tree. I'd have a small table, a book, a pen and writing paper, a paraffin light, water in a thermos flask, and my sandals on a chair. The net was weighted down with stones to keep the snakes and scorpions from sidling in to join me. It was romantic out there, under the starlight and the huge moon. Sometimes I read; mostly I just thought and dreamed. The dream was that Sam would suddenly appear in the moonlight and say: Here I am. He'd be wearing a soft white muslin tunic, one that he loved as much as I loved my old pink frock. He was a person who'd somehow just materialized out of nowhere, and I thought he could do it again. So I'd wait for him, listening to the servants as they settled down to sleep on the roof, comforted by the sounds of the night birds and the cicadas in the trees, the far call of a jackal, and the silence when the day fell under the spell of the night. But he didn't come. Night after night I waited, and he didn't come. My doubts mounted. The wife and child put on flesh, until I could draw a picture of them.

And then one night, when I was about to give up on him, he came. It was late. It was hot as hell. He looked exhausted but wouldn't admit it. He was standing in the front room, and his eyes had lost all their mockery. I couldn't, he said wearily, stay away another minute. I had to see you. I miss you so terribly. He looked at me: Is it safe? How many people are still around?

Just the soldiers who aren't up at the frontier, but they're all in their messes, drinking themselves silly. That's why, I said briskly, I decided to let you in. He frowned: Is everything all right?

Why wouldn't it be? I wanted to be excited to see him, but now that he'd arrived I was angry.

I could hear him scrubbing his hands in the next room. I never did tell you . . . he called out, but then stopped mid-sentence when he saw that I was standing at the door, watching him. He looked at me: What is it?

There are quite a few things, actually, that you haven't told me.

He came in drying his hands. Such as?

I took a deep breath: Well, about your wife. And child. For a start.

I went and sat on the end of my bed, and he took up a position in one of the chairs, facing me. Ah, he said, I'd rather presumed you'd have worked that one out.

Was I to presume that your names had been put down at birth? That's how it's done, isn't it?

He sat forward and let his hands fall between his knees. Something like that.

Well, will you tell me about it?

How much do you want to know?

I realized then that the less I knew, the easier it'd be. I want to know everything, I said.

Are you sure?

Positive.

Your decision then.

Absolutely.

Well, he said, I avoided marriage for as long as I could, which wasn't hard because I was in London, and I didn't come back very often. We had the betrothal, and afterwards, I left again, for years. She was very young, of course, and it had all been arranged ages before. A suitable match, caste-wise, wealth-wise, all that. He gave me a sarcastic smile, but this time I wasn't quite sure whom he was mocking.

Can I have a name?

I'd rather not.

Why?

Once you know a name, a person becomes too real.

This, I have to tell you, Sam, is agony.

It's separate, my love, you have to see it that way.

It's still agony.

He moved his chair right up to my knees. No, stay back, I said, just tell me what I need to know. Don't touch me right now.

So he told me. He was trying to be kind, sticking to the facts: auspicious dates, how the wedding worked, all the days and nights of celebrations—all that sort of thing. I cut him off midstream. And I wasn't very nice.

I just want to know the obvious thing, I said sharply.

All right, he said softly. I don't love her.

I didn't believe him, entirely.

It's not as if I'm spending my time there instead of here. I'm very seldom at home, or rather, at the house where my wife lives in Anantnag. It may be hard for you to understand, but many arranged marriages work, functionally, and often at a deeper level. It wasn't that way for me. In most families the wives all troop into the parental home and create a huge family unit bolstered by religious rites and customs. Men have a rather separate existence. This has enabled me to live my own life. No one questions me about anything. He grimaced. Except you. I'm an only son, and my wife has remained very close to her own family. I keep away because there's nothing to draw me home. My wife is entirely traditional; she lives within strict purity codes of health and cleanliness. This kind of thing infuriates me, as do all the endless crises of pollution—nonstop washings and purifications with holy water from the Ganges. Hindu rituals are too numerous and intrusive to be borne, at least for me. I find purdah ridiculous, always have. He stopped and looked at me, a bit awkwardly. It's hard for me to know what you know about Hindu customs. I don't follow them anymore, and couldn't anyway after I got to England because I had to eat what was put in front of me. And—he smiled—it was often beef. So when I returned to India, I was given even more leeway than the average Indian male. I went through a cleansing ceremony when I got off the boat and then returned to my own existence. He was silent again. I didn't say a word.

The minute we were married, he said, my wife turned into a matron. It happened overnight. She's bound hand and foot by her rituals, obligations, and fears. She's at her prayers as soon as the sun rises. She's a placid woman, and, he said dryly, that has been useful too. We reached a reasonable understanding many years ago. This is not so unusual. The life of women here is diabolical, he added grimly, and then went quiet—for ages, it seemed.

You should have told me, I said.

You're right. And I would have if you hadn't been married yourself. He got up and paced around. No, I take that back. I didn't tell you because saying it would have made it too true, and I didn't want that. I was waiting for the right time, and that's always fatal. It got harder each time I saw you. It's entirely my fault. I'm really sorry. Did someone tell you, or did you just work it out?

Both.

He didn't ask me who told me. He seems always not to want to give or to get more information than he needs. He looked unhappy.

It was my fault as much as yours, I said. I didn't ask.

You shouldn't have had to ask.

I didn't because I knew. I just didn't want to know. I suppose I rather wish the clock could be turned back, that we might have met before those other lives had happened to us.

I don't believe that. This is right. Five years, or even two years ago, it wouldn't have worked.

And your son? I asked him quietly. Where is he? And how old is he?

He's eight, and he's at a small prep school in Wiltshire.

How could you? After what you went through?

I understand why you say that, he said quietly, but I convinced myself that the advantages of an English education outweigh the disadvantages. In any case, the schools, the English schools here, are no different. Sammy is very bright . . .

I wish you'd hadn't told me his name, I said, because now I want to go and get him. His face dissolved. The conversation was causing damage. I stopped immediately.

SO, THAT'S WHAT I WAS LEFT WITH. She, or Her. I was grateful not to know her name, because now she was real enough, from even the little he'd said, to have taken up a whole room in my brain. As soon as I'd let her in, I wanted her out, because it was my mind she inhabited, not his. She actually lived miles away and right now was summering in the Mussoorie hills, where she had a house, which seemed to be filled with female relatives. Sam had a number of houses that she never went to, one some miles out of Ferozepore and one in Simla. He wanted me to go to Simla immediately. As soon as he could get away, we were going to see each other there. I'm not going to be able to see you here again, he said, you've been malingering, but there's absolutely no reason for me to come anymore. It's too suspicious. I'll come up to Simla as soon as Ansari can take over. You should have gone to the hill station ages ago. He looked at me sharply: Your complexion is getting quite dark. He said it, I thought, with slight disapproval. It's my mother's Italian blood, I said. I can take the heat.

You're going to have to, he said, with that heartbreaking smile.

Six

The heat, under a banyan tree, is more than 110 degrees in the late afternoon. The air's as dense as concrete. The cuckoos sing all day long, and the wretched brain-fever birds scream their heads off, getting louder and louder. At night, in the garden, I often hear jackals in the distance, and later, the comforting sound of the night watchman, whistling, making his rounds. I lie there on the long, lonely nights, drenched in sweat, remembering that he barely sweats, however wildly or desperately he makes love to me. I don't hate the hot weather, I just find it trying, but I won't allow myself the indulgence of constantly complaining about it. Perhaps I'm like the soldiers, not letting it in. I don't know. But perhaps something in me just doesn't find it as unbearable as the others do. In the evenings, the bheesty, a sweet-faced man, comes around with his sodden goatskin bag, and he walks around the bungalow, sprinkling water on the ground. As soon as the water hits the dust, there's a delicious smell—as good as the smell of cut grass.

I get up very early and go riding for over an hour. Sometimes, when it gets so hot that I can't stand it, I'll sit in a tubful of cold water or lie wrapped in a wet towel. Sometimes, walking around, I'll lift the ends of my skirt and fan myself that way. I'm beginning to see the hot weather as a challenge, something I need to overcome if I'm to stay in India, because I'm going to stay in India. In this kind of weather I think I'm getting to know the real India, not the cantonment type of India. But the heat also raises the temperature of my body: My passion runs high, the sexual tension is unbearable, and the longing drives me crazy. Some days I think of wearing my sari and of taking off to the field hospital where Sam's working, or even to his house. I spend hours in front of the Meerut mirror, painting kohl onto my eyelids and daubing crushed rose petal paste onto my cheeks. I do it on those stinking hot afternoons when I'm bored out of my mind. I tell myself that I'm wearing the sari because it's cooler, and it is—much. The short silk blouse is lovely; the sari is shot with gold, and it's like being bathed in cool water. It makes me walk differently. I'm conscious of my skin against the silk, and the way the air gets to my upper body in the gap between sari and blouse. I bought some junky rings from the bazaar and put rings on every finger and toe. I rub sandalwood paste over carefully plucked, arched eyebrows. My skin is nut brown. I scrape my hair back into a rolled knot. It's cooler than if I cut it. I thought of oiling my hair the way the women do here, but it's too disgusting. I wear scarlet lipstick on my mouth and put a vermilion dot in the center of my forehead. I think a diamond in my nose would be rather fetching, but would probably be going too far.

I'd rather thought I'd feel demure and mysterious, the way I imagined women in saris felt. But instead, I felt wild and free, giddy and on heat, released from my white skin, my Englishness, and the requirement to live within the bloody awful conventions of womanhood. I was sexually on edge, and on the prowl, always hoping that Sam might turn up. I wanted him to see me Indianized, because a woman wearing a sari is beautiful. Most of all I wanted to know what he'd say, but he didn't come.

A COUPLE OF SOLDIERS have cracked up from the heat. Joseph passed this on to me, and my ears pricked up, because I wondered if that would bring Sam back to the station. It didn't, but I knew that that was because no one from the army would have called him in. The army has no word for a mental breakdown; they ignore it, like the heat. It's considered a breakdown of discipline, a weakness—a poor show. The soldier gets a court-martial and is stuck for months in detention, where he might put a bullet through his brain. I knew about all this, of course, from long ago, from another life, a different incarnation—from Gareth's crackup in the trenches. I suppose one might call the soldier's affliction here heat shock instead of shell shock—just another form of cracking up. I don't see the soldiers; they're stuck in their barracks, day after day. I seem to see them lying on their bunks, staring up at the punkah, bored crazy. I hear the morning sounds from the barracks, and I know that their routines go on, undiminished, throughout the hot weather. For the common soldier, there's no summer relief. I didn't give my husband, who was sweating it out on the frontier, a second thought.

Soon I was seeing no one but the servants, who were getting increasingly grumpy. And when Joseph, for the umpteenth time, said: Memsahib, it is time to go to the hills, I gave in, and told him we could leave at the end of the week. I will help you pack, mem, he said, hoping, I know, that once he'd packed me up, I might clear out sooner. For heaven's sake, Joseph, I can do my own packing. I'm not a complete imbecile. He shook his head. Mem. Nothing to do with imbecile. It is my job to pack—some things for me to pack; for Gita to pack others. It is not for you to lift finger. Hard for you to remember this.

Well, all right, Joseph, if you really think we need to start this now, get me the tapestry bag and the caramel leather thing with the strap around the middle. And my good saddle and all the tackle. He looked brightly at me: Mem, we will take dooly, and gharry for luggage? No, we will not take a gharry. Please arrange a tonga, with two strong ponies, and an ekka, which if I remember correctly, is smaller than a gharry. I like to travel light. His face was a picture: As the memsahib wishes. No need to be clarifying. I too am not an imbecile.

I wish now that I'd left when he told me to. Everything had been conspiring to draw me up to the hills, but I wouldn't go. If I'd only left then, when Joseph had asked me to, perhaps it wouldn't have happened at all. The heat got unbearable. Everyone got more unpleasant. I was still waiting for Sam, on the off chance, and he still hadn't turned up, though he'd sent a note round with promises that he would be in Simla in a few weeks. I was impatient and cross, thinking he could do better. I was still planning to go and see him, but I knew it was too risky. So I paced up and down instead, unable to read, write or sleep; even eating seemed a waste of energy. Bobajee's curries and delicious banana fritters were barely tasted, and I lived on sweet lassis and small slithers of coconut cake, with endless cups of masala tea, which I'd taken to drinking. And then, on Wednesday, two days before we were to leave for Simla, I had an unexpected visitor.

It was quite early in the morning, and the heat was a little less oppressive. Joseph came in with a peculiar expression on his face. Memsahib, he said, bowing slightly, there is a woman here, and she will not go away. Who is she? He shook his head miserably: I do not know, mem, I cannot say. I was curious: You don't know her, or you don't want to tell me who she is? Please be clear, Joseph. He was upset: Mem, I do not know this woman. For some reason, even though Joseph is scrupulously honest, I was certain he was lying. I suddenly had a chill. Well, is she one of the memsahibs, or is she a native woman? He didn't answer my question, and I said: Send her in, Joseph, I will see her. He shuffled his feet: Mem, possibly I try again to make her go. Bullock cart still outside. I got up: Don't be ridiculous, Joseph, just tell her to come in. As he was turning to go, my instinct got the better of me, and I said to him: Joseph, if you think there's anything I should know, please tell me now. He hesitated a long while. Mem, he said, this is a woman who existed before memsahib came. She has met her fate.

When I walked into the room, a girl, almost a woman, was standing there, light streaming behind her. In her long robe she looked like a saint. She was so beautiful that she took my breath away. I stared at her. And she stared back, out of eyes that looked almost black. Her cream sari swirled up and over her shoulders and throat, covering her lower face and leaving naked only the deep velvet of her eyes, her small nose and finely etched pink mouth. She didn't smile, and there was something about her stillness that made me nervous. My heart was racing like a freight train. I was thinking: This is her, this is she, this is the end of everything. I pulled myself together: Won't you sit down? I gestured to a chair, suddenly grateful for my punkah-cooled room with its morning light and beautiful, exotic furnishings. They became her, as she did them. I thought for a hysterical moment that I'd arranged the room just for her and that this would be her house now, because my life was over. She moved toward the chair, and for a moment almost stumbled. When I moved to help her, her eyes conveyed such torment that I suddenly had a sense of her sorrow, and I was wracked by my part in it. She immediately righted herself and sat down. The scarlet brocade of my new cushion lit up her golden skin, and she shifted slightly in her silk so that it arranged itself around her until she was cocooned in cream. I could see nothing of her body, except that she was slight, like a young tree. Her eyes burned so much that I wondered if she was feverish. And then she spoke. Her English was perfect. Oh, wonderful, I thought, something else he forgot to mention: His wife went to Oxford too.

I am the daughter of Fahad Naseem, she said. She spoke slowly, and very formally: I have come to speak to you about a matter which has caused great concern to my family, and to me. I regret that it is necessary to tell you these things. Although you are not directly involved in what has happened to us, you are by implication. My father, she said, raising her chin, is a highly respected merchant, of excellent caste, known in the community for his good breeding and honesty. We are Muslim, and we abide by the teachings of Allah. Even so, my father has educated each of his children to high standards, including his daughters, of which he has two. He has also departed from some of the most sacred duties of our religion, particularly with regard to me. I am the older. I am seventeen. Unlike my sister, I was not obliged to live in seclusion, and because of the liberties given to me, I was granted, for a year, to take employment as a tutor to one of the officers' children, two little girls. The officer's wife did not want her children to disturb their English accents with the local dialect, and so, every day between nine and eleven, I would teach them how to read. I liked this work. It gave me freedom I had not known. It gave me a sense of another life, a different fate from the one laid down for me. I was grateful to my father for permitting this, but he allowed it only because he hoped that once I had tried the life of the Feringhi, I would see its waste and foolishness and would be willing to marry. She tilted her head slowly. You will understand that seventeen is late for a girl not to be married. My parents were concerned, but it was my wish, and I insisted upon staying as I was. I had hopes of going to England, or perhaps to America, to make a life for myself there. These thoughts I kept to myself, of course, for my father had other hopes. It was my father's wish that I would marry his business partner, and as a result, the business would be secured. But such is the clash that education creates for us, because like an oyster, once the mind is open, it cannot be easily shut. She looked down, and I saw her mouth tremble.

Joseph chose this moment to come in with a tray of tea, which he set out, at an infuriatingly slow pace, on the table, and proceeded to pour two cups of tea with the speed of a tortoise. Finally, he bowed and left us alone. But her mood had shifted.

I believe—she began again—that I should move to the point, but it is very painful to do so. For a while, there was no sound but the creak of the fan curtain being moved back and forth, back and forth by the punkah-wallah. I thought of him, lying on his back on the veranda with a cord attached to his big toe, moving it to stir the air in the room, for no other reason but that my life could be made a little more pleasant because of it. I was distracting myself from thinking about the girl who sat opposite me because during the course of her careful speech—after the first astonishing relief—I'd begun to feel a mounting dread about what she might say next. I'd no idea who she was or why she'd come, but what was very clear, in spite of her valiant attempts to hide it, was the extent of her distress. I moved a little forward in my seat: Please tell me whatever it is you came to tell me. I should have shut up. Somehow, by speaking at all, I'd distressed her more. I apologized. Quickly she said: I have thought often of you, Mrs. Webb, and I had not imagined you to be a kind lady. So it is harder for me to tell you the things that I must. Another long pause. I knew your husband, she said, as if the words were knotted around her throat. I didn't want her to say another word. I didn't need her to say another word.

I see, I said quietly.

You do not see, she said bitterly, because by knowing your husband, I have polluted myself. I have been defiled by an Englishman, and as such there is nothing for me but death. I stared at her in horror. My father warned me, she said breathlessly, he even warned Sergeant Webb, but still he pursued me, and still I succumbed. I was vain, and I was flattered. I knew how grave the risks were, but I was pulled by my senses until I lost myself. Even then, knowing this, my father showed me mercy. Her cheeks were flushed now, and she was so agitated that I thought she must be ill or on the verge of a nervous collapse. My father ordered me never to see Sergeant Webb again, or I would have to face dire consequences. I agreed. And in return for his mercy, I agreed to the betrothal that he had always craved. Arrangements were made for the wedding, in the customary way.

Sergeant Webb was away on duty and remained so for many months. In these months I resigned myself. But as fate would have it, very close to the time of the marriage, Sergeant Webb returned. It was just before he was to go on leave. He waited for me outside the officer's house and then followed me home. He did not care that he would be seen. He did not care that for this I could lose my life. I did not speak to him, not one word, but this meeting sealed my destiny. At least, she said softly, for this life.

All this while I'd not known what to say to her, but now I did, and I spoke urgently and with passion. I don't know quite why you have chosen to tell me this, I said, but I'm glad you did. I'm terribly sad that this has happened to you, and so carelessly, without thought for you, your family, or your future. You say that for you the price is very high. I don't know what you mean by this, but is it really as high as you say? You're educated and clever and beautiful; you can get away. Perhaps I can help you. It is dreadful to marry a man one doesn't love.

It is too late, she said, dully, beginning to rise. It was only then, when she was getting to her feet, that I realized that throughout our entire conversation she'd moved no part of her body—not once. I wondered if perhaps she was afraid of falling, or if, in her stillness, she'd been holding herself together all this while. But now she was looking at me with pity, and with disgust. How can you help me? she breathed. You English, for you, money is all you can give. I am talking about the loss of honor. I have polluted myself with an Englishman. I must take the consequences of that with my life. For him, for you, there are no consequences; there is only the taking. For me, there was love that was deep as hate. It is done. Watching her, I kept trying to understand, but I kept failing. And then she said: I came here to dishonor you, as I have been dishonored. That is why I came. In my coming, you too have lost honor. I have come also to show you the price I have paid for your husband's little fling with a native. The long, swathed shape of her body stirred, and I saw a glimpse of gold as for a moment her elbow cut out of the cloth. She moved toward me and thrust out of the cream silk of her sari two golden arms. Her hands were cut off. The livid, severed ends were sealed with long black stitches.

SHE LEFT IN A BULLOCK CART, veiled and curtained, as she'd come. I sat on, as motionless as she'd been a moment ago. I felt that she was still in the room or that I had taken on her presence, that we were one. It seemed preposterous to think that, but slowly it dawned on me that I was trying in some way to keep her with me, to stop her choosing her fate, or being chosen by her fate, whichever it was. Presently, Joseph came in and stood to one side of me, saying nothing. We stayed there together for a while, until he went to pick up the tray, and then he walked to the door. When he'd gone, the shock lifted, and I began to sob, and I couldn't stop. All morning long I waited, looking at her chair, until, at noon, I got up and went to sit on the veranda. Joseph came out and stood very close to my chair. I didn't look at him, but I said: I know, Joseph. You don't have to tell me. I know what has happened. He stood awhile longer, and then, very gently, he reached over and rested his hand on my shoulder and patted it, once, twice, before he walked back in.

THE NEXT DAY I woke before dawn and began frantically shoving things into a heavy velvet bag bought from the silk-wallah. I was surrounded by heaps of clothes on the floor when Joseph came in with my tea. Resting back on my heels, as I'd seen the mali do, I could see the way he was looking at me, but he said nothing. Joseph, I said, we must go as soon as you can arrange things. He nodded. I continued to pack. Joseph, I said, I need you to get this letter to Dr. Sahib as soon as possible. Can your cousin take it, as before? I gave him the envelope. It must get there today. Here, give him this. He shook his head: Money not necessary, memsahib. Later I'd see that I hadn't even looked at what I was putting in that bag; I was doing it automatically, one thing after the other. All I was fully aware of then was that I had to get away, and I had to tell Sam where he could find me. Bridget had given me two addresses in Simla. I'd looked at a map of the hill station and decided on one that looked a little farther from the center of the town. I was worried that once I'd left the bungalow, it would be hard for Sam to find me.

When everything was packed and ready to go, I was glad I'd chosen the road over the train, even though I knew it would be a hellish journey. I needed the hell. I needed things to slow down. I wanted to find a new way of seeing. I wanted to learn how to empty my mind, because that way I might forget the motionless girl in her cream sari, and her black eyes, which were still staring me down. I was anxious and jumpy, and I noticed that when I sat or walked, my arms were crossed across my breasts, with my hands tucked under my arms.

We set off in the softest light and took a shortcut through back roads that led past sugarcane fields and mango groves. Cattle were moving through sluggish streams, and dark forms crouched in the fields, looking up as our small entourage passed by. I was in the tonga, my things on the spare seats, with the syce at the reins. Joseph sat in the ekka, surrounded by all our provisions, luggage, blankets, and water bottles. We drove in silence. People were walking to the lands, carrying food in bundles. Children sat in the dirt, chewing on sugarcane; skinny dogs lay in the shade. Later we came to where the hovels and huts of the untouchables were spread out in a rough circle; they stared as we passed, crouching in a wasteland of debris and filth. The river stank like a dead fish. The earth was bone dry and empty. Their poverty and their misery disgusted me. My compassion had frozen over. We moved on at a clip, putting them behind us. Soon the land opened up, and on a rise the great flare of the plain was visible. On and on it went, absolutely flat, and way beyond it stretched a horizon of pale mountains, a blue wall shimmering in the haze. The sun wasn't quite up, and we moved quickly along, throwing up dust.

When we reached the Grand Trunk Road, we moved up the

steep incline and landed on a wide, well-made surface. All human and animal life was traveling on it, going north, to towns and cities, or to the hills beyond. People glanced up as we joined them. Their look wasn't hospitable, but neither was it hostile; it was merely indifferent. We were passing, they too were passing; it had no significance in the life of things. We were joining a flood of people who were moving slowly and steadily through the morning. People of all castes used the road, but certain people kept to one side of the road, moving along quickly, not speaking, while others kept well apart. They knew who was, and who was not, polluted. The road was divided into four lanes, and the syce moved swiftly into the middle of the road, the only part that was flat and paved. We joined the fast-moving traffic. The outside lanes were choked with country carts, loaded with crated chickens and geese, and sacks of vegetables and rice; children were tucked in between the sacks, a baby lay curled up with a pregnant woman wearing a pink sari. There was a rough lane for heavy bullock carts carrying rice, salt, grain and timber, hides, cotton bales, and clay pots. And everywhere there were people, walking slowly and steadily, men in front, women and children behind. Babies slouched on hips, and women gossiped and laughed, the rims of their saris stirring up the dust. They looked as if they could go on walking for a hundred years. Occasionally we'd come to a solid stretch of British and Indian troops, marching in cork helmets and dusty drill. They were going up to the hills and were merry about it. Long wooden carts filled with provisions and lines of horses, elephants, and camels, with heavy bags drooping from their saddles, followed the marching soldiers. They waved and moved out of our way and regrouped when we'd passed.

Most of the road was shaded by trees, with camps, shrines, and police stations along the way. A Punjabi in bright yellow trousers was watching the passing crowd, smoking a pipe. He gave us a quick, sly look and then lazily puffed on his pipe, on the lookout for bandits and troublemakers. Some of the resting places looked disheveled and dirty, with trampled fires and beggars waiting for their next benefactor. Others were clean and shady, with stalls selling food, tobacco, and piles of firewood. As we passed, I'd catch a glimpse of a water trough, or a well, or a fast-moving stream, and there'd be people gathered there, in groups, with spaces between, as if they were always aware of the danger of contamination. In the more secluded places, you'd hear the high voices of the purdah women behind shuttered litters with embroidered canopies and tasseled curtains. Once I watched, hypnotized, as a pale, ringed hand emerged from the curtain for a moment and then vanished into concealment again.

The road went straight on, heaving with traffic sometimes and empty at others. It was level and without turns, but now and then the hard surface would raise itself a bit, and then all India was spread out below, with the soft blue of the lower hills leading to the far Himalayas. Often you felt that those mountains didn't exist because the plains were endless, and at these times it was as if we were traveling under a scorching sea, waiting for some evidence of coolness, height, and air. We were heading for Ludhiana, where we'd stop for the night. Joseph was kind, making sure that we stopped often so I could rest, setting down a quilt under the trees, and bringing me water to wash my face. We barely exchanged a word. I couldn't seem to feel. All I could do was look around me, as if immersing myself in all this, trying to understand all this, would somehow save me. Across the way other travelers were resting, cooking, or eating, and sleeping, always sleeping. Sometimes a collection of walkers—perhaps an entire village—would leave the embankment to take a narrow path across the plains. Tall men walked beside creaking cotton and grain wagons; whips looped the air; tongues lashed at anyone who got in their way. You sensed their impatience and exhaustion, but they didn't show it. The sun was filtering through the lower branches of the trees; the day had reached and then passed boiling point, and now the sky was merely simmering. And all the while, up ahead, the veiled majesty of the Himalayas was hidden behind cloud and snow. Now and then a sudden jagged slope would slice through the clouds and then vanish again.

We found an inn just before Ludhiana. It was an ugly, flat-roofed building set back from the road. The innkeeper, a sour and sozzled Scot, was surprised that I'd set out without an army or police escort, and he seemed to think I must be a tart because of it. I didn't like the look of him and took a room at the back of the inn, close to where Joseph and the groom were unloading the horses and setting up camp for the night. I envied them the stars and the cool night air. In my ugly little room I could hear them talking, making a fire, laying down blankets under the trees, and getting their supper together. As the air cooled, doves and parakeets came to roost in the branches outside my window. A little later the bats swooped through the night sky, and a little after that I was fast asleep.

WE WERE still crossing the plains the next day, but by now there was a slight easing of heat. Each time we reached a stream or waterfall, Joseph would bring me a bucket of water. As we got closer, the water got colder, and it was delicious to put my hands down into it, and splash it all over my face. Approaching the lower hills, we could see deodar forests in the distance, and as we climbed higher, the wind was sharp and invigorating. By the side of the road, boulders, rocks, and gravel lay piled up in heaps, as if the hills had risen up and emptied their laps. The next European hotel was a short way off the road and well signposted. We turned a corner onto a dirt road and moved up to a little hill. Perched on the slope was a beautifully proportioned Victorian manse, with a stand of oak trees behind it. The minute my tonga clattered up the gravel to the front door, a woman came out on the wide veranda and rushed down the steps toward me: Are you all right? She was peering at me, determined that I was a calamity from the road. I said I was perfectly well and asked her if she had a room for the night. She stared at me: Surely you're not traveling alone? I lifted the diaphanous net that swirled around my wide-brimmed hat and put out a hand. I gestured in Joseph's direction and said I'd been well attended. Well, *you're* new to India, she said, with a touch of horror, turning me into the cool of the hallway. Come in, and let's make you comfortable. She led me into a drawing room full of pale, sun-bleached sofas and round mahogany tables. On the piano top was a tall arrangement of deep blue delphiniums in a copper vase. There were prints of exotic birds on the walls and heavy, blue silk draperies at windows that were as tall as doors; you could step out of them onto the veranda.

Some of my deadness began to lift. The familiarity of the hotel, and of the woman, was restorative. For the entire journey on that roasting road, I'd watched the world move, and it hadn't touched me; none of the beauty, or wonder, or the squalor or poverty could penetrate the wall. Everything I looked at was alien, strange, beyond my comprehension. Now I was reentering a world I knew, and something began to shift.

This house, my hostess said, offering me a chair by the window, used to be part of a small parish; now, as you see, only the house remains. The church was burned down twenty years ago; there was an insurrection at the time. We bought it from the clergyman when my husband retired. At that time the Grand Trunk was the only thoroughfare going right up from south to north. India changed utterly when the traffic moved away from the rivers and onto the roads, and of course it changed utterly again with the railways. Years ago, she said, settling her ample frame in a button-down chair opposite me, when we bought this house, we thought a pleasant, small English hotel would be just the thing for people coming up to the hill stations for the summer retreat. The whole government comes up, you know, with the Viceroy and all his officers—in fact, the whole bang shoot: the Commander in Chief as well as the Delhi and Punjab secretariats, not to mention all the officers and the wives and children from the plains. The road was knee-deep in sahibs in those days, and we put them up for the night and entertained them before they set off on the last bit of the journey to Simla or Mussoorie. It was all great fun. Of course now—she trailed a hand through her hair—it's very different. But we still keep the place open, and guests do still turn up—she smiled—like you, though it is late in the season, I must say, to be heading up. She spotted the empty finger: You came over with the fishing fleet? I laughed: No, I came over with my husband; we're stationed at Ferozepore, but he's been on active duty from the minute we arrived. It was her turn to laugh. Ah, she said, I know all about that. We're army too, though my husband is of course retired. She looked around her. We like it here, very much, and didn't want to go Home, so it works well enough. The odd visitor is a nice thing, and sometimes army chaps will turn up, and my husband likes that. But—she landed her palms down hard on her lap—enough of all this chatter. You must be exhausted. Let me show you to your room, and then why not come down and have a glass of sherry with us?

I followed her up the stairs to a room overlooking a croquet lawn and a square swimming pool, surrounded by weeping willows. In the middle of the room was a four-poster bed, heavily draped, and there was a mahogany dresser, complete with Victorian lace and silver knickknacks. An overstuffed chair and a large wardrobe pretty much filled up any walking space there might have been. The mantelpiece was covered with army regalia, but there was a grate made up with wood, and I was glad of that, since it was cold. She left me for a few minutes and returned with a vase filled with scarlet geraniums and several thick white towels. And, oh, joy, there was a bathroom, with pipes to the tub. I was in heaven. I thought I could just about manage a sherry and a conversation for the sheer bliss of such comfort. Settle in, she said. I'll send someone up to make a fire and bring you an extra blanket.

And as it turned out, sipping sherry and nibbling on canapés were the best things that could have happened. We were on the veranda, sitting on tall-backed cane chairs draped with soft tiger skins. The mists came down from the hills and hovered at the end of the lawn, and in the distance the vast expanse of the Himalayas towered above the trees, cut off at the snow line. As night descended with its usual severity, the mountains disappeared entirely. I was having my sherry and giving them a version of my life—in order to explain the waywardness of my travel arrangements. They were all ears. But when Lily Saunders heard where I was staying in Simla, she was utterly opposed: Oh, Albert Street won't do at all, not after you've been ill. One thing if you want to be gadding about all over town, rushing off to luncheons and dinners every night, and being part of the social set. But from what I gather, you want to recuperate and have a quiet time of it. She sipped her sherry. Of course, she said with a sniff, Albert Street is very far from the elegant part of town. It's the busiest, and the noisiest area, with rickshaws dashing to and fro all night, and the Lancers getting up to their high jinks. I hear that there are some quite awful people nowadays who just come up to view the proceedings. They're not invited anywhere, but just their presence, gawking, as the Viceroy goes out to the theater—that kind of thing—is rather frightful. There are also a couple of rather unsavory hotels at the end of Albert Street, and it's a bit too close to the bazaar. Not the spot for you at all.

I remember, as a young child, she said wistfully, coming up to Simla from Bikaner. In those days there were only a few houses, and certainly no Albert Street, and it was all a great deal nicer than it is now. Simla is not what it was; riffraff is creeping in, and there's no stopping that kind of thing. And of course, as the major will tell you, being a married woman does not shield you from the sudden little romantic exploits and trysts that will spring up. I can't tell you how enormously romantic the place can be. When I was a girl, we used to ride out at moonlight and swim in the lake, taking a picnic of cold fowl and champagne, and stay out under the stars all night. That sort of thing was all right when it was just officers. Now, I hear, some of the liaisons are not as harmless as they once were. So, she said, turning her beaming brown eyes on me, I have a much better plan for you. You can stay in our cottage; it's off the beaten track, of course, but that just might suit. It's quiet, and secluded, and perfect for someone who doesn't want to be disturbed. The first houses were built on the base hills, d'you see, with the newer ones rising up the hill, all jumbled together, and looking, now, well, really rather ghastly. But ours is old, and though it's just a plain summerhouse, it will be perfectly adequate for you, and there's a lovely lake not too far off to go boating.

Oh, but I *couldn't*, I protested feebly. It's *much* too kind of you. I wouldn't dream of putting you to so much trouble.

Nonsense, said Major Saunders, coming abruptly to life after his second whiskey and soda. It's my son's house—we don't use it anymore—and he's on leave until December. The cottage is empty and a temptation for merrymakers. George will be glad of the rent; he's always penniless when he gets back from England. My wife will give you instructions in the morning, and you'll find the key behind the door in the potting shed.

Oh, I murmured, this is just so kind. I can't tell you how grateful I am. May I give you a check in the morning—for rent and whatever else is necessary?

My dear girl, don't bother your pretty head about all that. We'll settle it all in the morning. How about a spot of supper?

I'd played my malaria card to good effect, and Lily had already decided that after two sherries I should go straight to my room, soak in a deep bath, and then get into my night things. I'll have your supper sent up to your room, she said, ringing the bell for the bearer. You look absolutely whacked, poor thing, and one wonders how you made the trip at all. You're clearly quite convalescent. And rather thin. Fancy that, dear, she said, turning to her husband, alone on the Grand Trunk Road. Quite takes me back to my childhood, when we all trooped up in doolies, with all our toys and pets in litters with us. It was such fun for a child, going up to the hills, stopping for picnics along the way. Everything was immaculate then. Whatever is said about the English, we certainly know how to build roads. Learned it from the Romans. You can't *imagine* the traffic the Grand Trunk has seen over the years: elephants and camels, regiment after regiment of soldiers, convoys of unbroken ponies, cannons, a gold carriage once for Lord Curzon, a circus from China, and, not so many years ago, a consignment of diamonds hidden in the linings of a hundred dinner jackets that were being sent up to Srinagar to pay for an assassination.

Seven

That night was the last time I dreamed about the Muslim girl. In the morning I took a long walk by the lake and didn't look behind me to see if she was following. The last link connecting me to Neville had snapped. If its purpose had been to warn me, then I was warned. If my fate was sealed, then so be it. I was now very close to Simla, and I wanted to be there. I was determined to be with Sam. Joseph and I were going to take the Grand Trunk Road to Balka and then go on to Simla—he on foot, I on a pony. There was of course a perfectly charming miniature train, which offered one of the loveliest rail journeys in the world: up through the Kasauli hills, crossing Summer Hill and into a tunnel that takes one into Simla's glorious Victorian station. But I wanted to ride. I needed to ride. I was looking for a different kind of immersion into the life of the country. Riding was the thing to do, according to Lily Saunders, though her husband thought I was bonkers.

It was cloudy when we set out, and the air was cold. Leaving the

Grand Trunk, we turned immediately onto a narrow road that began rising in increments, slowly at first and then dramatically. As I rode steadily up the track to the mountains, my heart seemed to open up. I could almost have been in a remote part of the Welsh mountains, where icy winds roar down granite outcrops, lash the stone cottages, and blow dead leaves into the alleyways. I found myself restored by the familiar and the dear, and it was as if I'd let go of a breath I'd been holding in from the time I left the bungalow in Ferozepore. I breathed out hard, and then again and again, and inside me something lifted. As I continued to ride, a sense of relaxation, almost of nakedness, filled me. The cool, spiced air was heady, and the water in the streams carried flakes of melting snow. I stopped on a rise to look back to where other ponies were making their way up, and I could see Indian and British soldiers marching in single file, their topis like cones, their uniforms black where sweat poured off them. There were a few Europeans traveling in dandies, followed by porters laden with luggage. One was pushing a bicycle, and another carried a huge tin drum on his head, complete with regimental colors. I could just make out Joseph, who was walking steadily. I recognized him by the scarlet turban he'd promised to wear, so I could see him from afar. I waved my arm back and forth like mad till he looked up and saw me. He lifted his hand straight up in the air in salutation. Tears came to my eyes as I remembered his kindness on the road and the way he'd stood silently beside me when he'd come to tell me of the Muslim girl's death. He'd put his hand on my shoulder like a comrade, a true friend, and now there he was, slogging up the hillside to accompany me on the next stage of my journey.

I broke out into a sweat as the going got tougher. The pony knew the path, which was just as well since I hadn't a clue, and once up in the hills, it was nothing like Wales. The surges of the hills made for hard riding; the undergrowth was often like a jungle as it reached out over the trail. Joseph had instructed me never to depart from the path: Shortcutting, mem, will end in China or Tibet. Stick to path, or God will lose you. The path was narrow as it backed into crowded hills and then spread out again into open places. Goat pastures crouched at the foot of terraces dotted with mud and wood huts. The cattle were very small. The people were small too; they looked Mongolian, with narrow eyes, high cheekbones, and thin smiles, and they smelled. It was wonderful to watch them walk or climb, because they're astonishingly quick and agile, sprinting along the hill paths that lead in and out of the woods and valleys, light as deer. The best times are when the road takes you into a dark wood and shade drips over you like rain. You hear the sounds of running water and the wind moving between the oak and walnut trees. The birdsong is deafening, but more musical— doves, barbets, and cuckoos rather than parrots and brain-fever birds. These woods feel sacred and mysterious and sometimes a little eerie. Coming out of the dark, you see birches and pine trees bucking in the wind, and heavy white rhododendrons big as trees, with custard yellow butterflies fluttering in and out of the brittle leaves. The air seems to crackle, and it really fills a body with energy. It's also hellishly tiring, to clamber up rock-strewn passes and steep paths littered with shale and fallen rocks. Going down is the awful bit because your calf muscles lock, and stiffness sets in instantly. Quite often I'd dismount and walk, to move the stiffness to a new place. I wanted to keep going till I dropped, to have my body be absolutely spent, because it was reminiscent of sexual love, and what I wanted above all else—what drove me up those perishing hills—was Sam. We stopped often on the way, and sometimes I'd wait for the rider just behind me—there were six of us going up together—and we'd drink water together and share raisins or hard biscuits and have a quick chat. We kept asking the same questions: How long do you think it is now? How far to go? To which the answer invariably was: Haven't a clue, but I do hope it's soon. And on we'd go, determined to get there ahead of the others.

In the hills my mind just plain shut up. I was just there, present and alive, among the ferns and waterfalls, watching the rabbits scurry into holes and the clouds make shadows on the hillsides. At a precipice I'd stop and look down a sheer drop to a dark green crown of pines below; it was breathtaking to be so high, so vulnerable, like a twig the wind could blow away. When you toss a rock over the side of a crag, no sound comes back to you, no echo, and below stretch infinite abysses and silence. In the immensity it's as if you'd almost ceased to be. The wind in the pines and the sounds of the doves seem oddly human, or perhaps it's just that you feel at one with them and become a pine or a dove yourself. Somewhere up there our hill path joined a broad, open road, which had branched off from the Grand Trunk Road at Umballa. I was relieved to see it since it would lead us in greater comfort to Simla.

As we got higher, I felt a touch of euphoria, and I told myself that I was freezing the malaria out of my blood, burning fear out of my body, becoming hard and strong for whatever lay ahead. I had a sense that we were going up to the top of the world. More people were moving north now. At the wayside stops there was a buildup of human traffic: herdsmen and woodcutters, stonemasons, troops, Hindus, Muslims, Sikhs, and Persians, all walking, all very merry. And you had a sense that mingled in was a different crowd, more like musicians and singers, accountants and moneylenders, lawyers and hairdressers, whores and strippers. As we came closer to Simla and the land flattened out in places, we passed elephants half lost in blue-blooming grass and others cavorting in the river. The inevitable horses, camels, and bullock carts kept on coming. Occasionally there was a white face in a Ford or a glittering maharaja in a Cadillac; once a caravan of young princes in white Jaguars went roaring by, honking their horns. Government officers clicked by on sleek black stallions, and there was a whole regiment on the move, with flags waving and bugles playing. All this brought bustle and excitement to the road, but for most of the time it was just people walking, stopping to pray, eat and drink, to take ritual baths in the rivers, and to sleep close together for safety and warmth. We stopped sometimes to look back at the low, flat bowl of the distant plains before the view was lost to sight again, always this shutting off of a view followed by an opening up of another. The great mountains beckoned, the snows of the Himalayas and the famous towering peak of Jakko moved in and out of cloud shadow, like a woman behind a veil. Far, far above, in the high Himalayas, were twenty-foot snows and mountains with glaciers wide as the sea, untouchable as stars.

And then, finally, there it was, up ahead: the city of Simla. From the distance, with night coming on at a gallop, it was breathtaking. Lights were going on all over so that it looked as though pearls had been tossed at the slopes of the mountains. The main road led into lower Simla, where rickshaws rushed between shops and alleyways and out beyond the bazaar into a courtyard with rows of stables. The racket was almost unbearable after the silence of the hills. I was talking to a few of my traveling companions, an officer and two corporals. By this time we'd become quite chummy, as one inevitably does at the end of a journey when everyone is going his own way. I was offered advice, and caution, and drinks and dinner, but I was anxious to get away. I wanted to make a plan. I needed to find a way of existing in this city slapped carelessly against the hills. It was impossible not to keep looking up; the eye was drawn to the hills and then to the mountains beyond the hills, on and on without horizon. The houses were an odd mixture: Swiss cottages, Victorian villas, bungalows, and boxes. But what was astonishing—up there at about eight thousand feet above sea level—was how these dwellings were perched, like seabirds huddled on cliffs, on narrow terraces with sheer precipices below them. The sides of the mountain were littered with houses, line upon line of them, reaching up into the peaks, cluttered at the bottom, more sparse the higher you went. I wondered how on earth you got up there. I also wondered if the English had turned this pleasure palace into some kind of garrison. There was a sense of claustrophobia, of a closed and defended community hiding out in the hills, with their balls and garden parties, tennis and theater, and full evening dress every night, a last fling of the empire, hanging on to glory even as it was passing away.

One of the grooms from Balka came to relieve me of my pony. He told me where I could find a horse for my time in Simla, an indispensable choice of transport in a carless city. I hailed a rickshaw and gave instructions to the driver. I avoid rickshaws if at all possible; you can't help but be aware that the man pulling the vehicle has somehow taken on the role of a horse. There am I, sitting in a chair, and there he is, running between poles. He has no problem with this arrangement and keeps calling out from time to time: Hold on, memsahib, sharp bend coming, but fear not, Allah is with us. It was very clear that nothing but a rickshaw, a pony, or a bicycle would be of any earthly use in Simla. I was rushed away at breakneck speed, up and down, in and out of lanes, and then suddenly I'd look down and see that we were dangling over an appalling precipice with a drop of a hundred feet below us. Gradually the narrow paths opened into slightly wider pathways. After ten minutes or so we reached a part of the city that was somewhat flat, with wider ledges. We'd arrived at a row of small cottages tucked into the side of the hill. The rickshaw driver stopped abruptly, and I stepped out. My cottage was directly in front of me, hedges on either side, with a little garden full of pansies, sweet peas, wisteria, and honeysuckle. Behind it, shimmering in snow, loomed the vast fortification of the Himalayas, peaked and crenellated, ghostly under the moon.

WHAT I NEEDED, and this was going to be quite something to achieve in an imperial city with the season in full swing, was complete anonymity. Simla was crawling with government officials, dignitaries, administrators, and half the civil service—not to mention the army. White skin would be an automatic invitation to inclusion, and I wanted none of that. I'd come to find Sam and to be with him, and

I'd be happy to hurl the rest of the world over the cliff. But how to find him, and if I did, how to see him? I couldn't sleep, and as a result, I had a most peculiar night. First there were the aches and pains of the long, hard ride; this was followed by dizziness—mountain sickness, I presumed, and something like the nausea of the Bay of Biscay stretch on the voyage out. I gave up on sleep, unpacked my bag, and settled in. There was a single paraffin lamp, which was just about enough light to manage on. The cottage was Spartan but adequate. I found bedding and towels but couldn't work out how to get water. All I could make out was a well and some kind of pulley contraption. Fortunately, there was some bottled water. I washed and got into bed and curled up with all the blankets I could find. Lying there, I tried to track my thoughts and saw that for some reason they kept returning to Sam's wife. I imagined he was with her. Up to this point, or, more distinctly, up to the point of the incident with the Muslim girl, she hadn't caused me any loss of sleep. Once we'd spoken about her, she'd gone back into shadow. Now she was in clear relief again.

I'd got a book out of the club library, called *The Hindoo Tradition*, and had read the whole thing through. It had helped me understand Sam's life a little. Having read it, I felt both impressed and removed. But up to this first night in Simla I'd not felt an iota of guilt about his wife. Now I was filled with it. More than that, I was fearful of the consequences: for her, for me, for Sam. How much suffering would there be? And would anyone be spared? I didn't particularly like this shift. It was inconvenient, an impediment and a nuisance. But there it was: guilt, green, slimy, and adhesive, tangled in my brain. I was no longer invincible. I was just an immoral girl on the loose, desperate for love. And here was the wife taking shape and form, almost pressing her face to the windowpane. I found myself trying to see her more clearly, as if I hoped I could return to the rather cynical way I'd thought of her before. Now she was a lot more than an idea in my head. She was a woman, veiled and purdahed, but real and alive. A woman who'd been given in betrothal to Sam when she was twelve years old and who led a life in which I supposed she considered Sam her lord. That was frightening enough in itself, that a woman could think of a man that way, or see herself as a vessel for sons, and a keeper of clean utensils. I had to distance her, not allow her to get right in the middle of us. I couldn't give her legitimacy. I began to think of her as a girl who'd once married the man who was now my lover. There was a comfortable distance in the "once," as if that were all over and done with, and now another reality existed. Half of my head was trying to take her on and vanquish her, and the other was wrestling with whatever power she might have that I didn't. And then, without warning, I began seriously to doubt Sam. Perhaps she'd actually reclaimed him—through a sudden illness, a death in the family, the son's return from England—some wretched wifely pull that could make me secondary—or even irrelevant. I was so agitated that I went to the bookshelf in the corner of the front room, my lamp spilling light over the wooden floorboards. I'd glanced at the books on my way in, and I took myself back to the second shelf, where the Kipling was. And there, in a poem called "The Two-Sided Man," I recognized not only the Black Englishman but also myself. The longer I stayed in a country that was not mine, but was owned by people who were mine, I was split right down the middle, just as he was, fighting two sides of my head:

> *Something I owe to the soil that grew—*
> *More to the life that fed—*
> *But most to Allah who gave me two*
> *Separate sides to my head.*
>
> . . .
>
> *I would go without shirts or shoes,*
> *Friends, tobacco or bread*
> *Sooner than for an instant lose*
> *Either side of my head.*

Neither the poem nor my thoughts of that night in any way resolved a damn thing. The more I attached myself to India, the more complicated the questions: Who was I in India? Could I be myself and do as I'd do elsewhere? Or did being in British India determine who I was and how I was to behave, as it must for Indians? Did that include the wife? Or was she untouched by the Raj, living as she did, not baring her face to the world because her religion, and not the British, refused her this? The way she lived irritated me. I wanted to think of her as a foolish sister one would like to be shot of or perhaps as an older wife who'd lost her edge, her grip on the sheet, on the strings of his heart. But in spite of that, I couldn't avoid the bitter knowledge that she'd been the one to know him before he had facial hair; she'd accepted him as her husband before she'd put on breasts. She'd had no say in the choice of him, of course, nor felt the blow to the heart that I'd experienced watching him walk across the white, blank compound the day the woman was murdered. But her claim was as solid as the accord that linked the generations and defined the bridal transaction. It was set in the alliance of caste, the purity of bloodlines. Beside her, I had no claim. I was a woman of no account, a Feringhi, an untouchable.

Suddenly, in desperation, I wanted to be her, and to have what she had—merely to make myself more accessible to him. I saw her, veiled and sheltered in domestic seclusion, walking through perfumed rooms, performing ancient rituals, kneeling at her shrine, making morning prayers and sacrifices to the gods. Occasionally she would glance through a narrow, latticed window at the far hills in the distance or look beyond her balcony to the gold and blue domes of the temples. Did her narrow view permit a glimpse beyond the lovely hanging gardens to the thick, churned water where buffaloes rolled beside camel thorn trees and where untouchables crouched in the dirt to wash their filthy rags? When she lingered in the cool of Mussourie, would she be surrounded by whispering women who painted their hands with henna, oiled and coiled their hair, and spent long days lolling on satin cushions, adorning themselves to express an inner purity? A purity of which I had no inkling, and no chance, since I'd already polluted myself beyond redemption, as he had by touching me—and is that why he'd washed me?

I felt better thinking of her inspecting her pantry and linen cupboards, to see if a napkin or a cup of rice had been pilfered, or screeching at the cook, or slapping the servants for not obeying the proper cleansing rites when boiling the pots. I imagined her flinging dal puree at a wall because an impure hand had smudged the bowl. But I simply could not imagine an intelligent person spending hours planning a meal for a husband who'd take off into the next room to chomp his dinner down with his own sex, while she waited with the women in the kitchen for the scraps. It was too much for me. I tossed and turned all night, not knowing what to do, but in the morning all became clear.

When I woke, I took a good look at my face and my arms. They were brown and toughened from the ride and would do nicely. No English rose. No Italian olive either. I was dark brown. And as I knew by now, brown is black; anything not white is black. I opened the medicine cabinet and found a large jar of Brilliantine. Smearing the gunk into my hair, I brushed and brushed until the whole length was black and glossy. I parted my hair down the middle and pulled it back into a tight bun. I lined my brown eyes with kohl. And added a light touch of Vaseline to my skin where the sun had bestowed on it a strong trace of the Italian tar brush of my maternal ancestors. I carefully lined up a round red dot on my forehead. I poured on the sari, tucked it into my knickers, and wrapped it loosely around my shoulders and face. I was now fully prepared to take on the city of Simla.

I kept telling myself that I was an Indian, a Hindu, to make it sink in, to make it stick. But the wild thing was that the minute I'd put on that sari, I was no longer who I'd been. I was at liberty. I was ablaze with possibility. And I was fearless. I'd observed how white people looked at Indians, and the simple fact was that they didn't. No white person, even if I set myself on fire, would give me a second glance. I wanted to go out there and see if I could pass. I wanted to know what would happen, and most of all, I wanted to know how I'd feel.

On the corner a young boy was squatting on his haunches in the dirt with the patience of a wise man, and when I asked him to find me a jhampani, he instantly became an entrepreneur. I could see him urging a commission from the rickshaw-wallah, who told him to get lost and followed this up with a kick in the pants. I quickly slipped him a few annas and got into the rickshaw. But now I was nervous. I didn't want to be around my chosen race, because they'd sniff me out in a second. So I kept my head down and showed the rickshaw driver the address on a piece of paper. I'd also taken the precaution of writing a letter to give to the owner of the flat on Albert Road, to ask for any letters that might have been sent to a Mrs. Webb, and I didn't want to attempt that in the vernacular. I hoped I'd get back a letter from Sam.

We jogged away from the pretty gardens of the small English enclave and moved on up, through houses with back verandas overlooking the rooftops of the houses below. From a distance you had the sensation that you could jump from one roof to the next, like a child playing hopscotch. From below, everything looked diminutive, and there was that sensation again of being high above the world, in an atmosphere that shuts the brain down, cools the blood, and sets the soul free. My spate of bad conscience had vanished. I was burning with excitement and desire. We made our way to the Mall and on to where the European shops were located. Here I had to get out and walk since only certain vehicles can use the Mall. As I walked, I saw windows dressed with silk frocks, evening coats and scarves, wideawake hats and gentlemen's flannels, tweed jackets, white linen trousers, and dinner jackets. There were silk umbrellas and fabulous hats, with yards of tulle to keep the sun off the blanched complexions of the memsahibs. The Angrezi were well installed in Simla, and they had taken full right-of-way. The glamorous shops and the lofty road were cooled by trees and graced by establishments reminiscent of Bond

Street or the Burlington Arcade. Smoking shops sold Turkish, Russian, and American cigarettes. Well-stocked shelves offered French wines and spirits; one had an entire window of champagne bottles stacked in a high pyramid. A store lined with crimson silk walls displayed a collection of Tibetan masks, and another was stacked with rubies, diamonds, and emeralds, the stones all big as your thumb. One window, with a dark green awning, seemed to be filled to the brim with pale pink pearls but when I looked again, I saw a black sequined rope sidling among the pearls and then the golden eye of a glistening mamba, its wicked tongue flicking between pink pearls.

I longed to see more but didn't dare. I could hear snatches of conversation as I passed close to the strolling dames: What fun it was, quite splendid the view from the shrine, but I do so loathe those vile monkeys. Did you hear that Mabel was not invited to the fancy dress party? I know, isn't it shocking? She spent the whole night bawling in the ladies' of the Grand Victorian. Can you imagine? God knows what will happen if she's not asked to the garden party. Serves her jolly well right, I'd say; some men are simply off limit, even here. How many on your dance program tonight, Lydia? Oh, bad luck, but it'll fill up, no doubt. Let's lunch at the little Chinese place. I adore their noodles. And then we can be back in time for tea at the Auchinlecks'. Oh, look, what a divine dress! Perhaps Mother can be persuaded to splurge on that one for the Viceroy's dinner on Friday. Not going? Oh, dear me, whyever not?

Beyond the Mall I took another rickshaw since I hadn't the first idea where I was going, and knowing that, the jhampani took the long way round, past the Town Hall and the Administrative Buildings and on to the less flamboyant part of town, where I had originally intended to stay. I blessed Lily Saunders for her intervention, but I couldn't make up my mind where I felt less comfortable, here, where the hotels, Edwardian shops, and buildings were somewhat down-at-heel, or up above, with the cool social crowd milling among the chic shops. Women, I noticed, were strongly in the majority. And the men were pink, flaxen-haired, and none too handsome. I knew, though, from Bridget, whom I kept expecting to see on some corner, that officers came up for their hols, and that's where the fun and glamour were to be had. The rickshaw brought me rather roughly down to earth. The jhampani pointed to a house which, by the look of it, appeared to be divided into flats. I paid less well than I would have had I been white and let him go. I nearly made the mistake of walking up to the front door but remembered in time and scuttled round the back, where an old servant sat on the step, smoking. I nearly lost my nerve. But then I thought: What can he possibly do, turn on me and say: Memsahib, you are not black?

I hid in my veil, ducked my head, and put my hands together in greeting. He did the same. I walked up slowly and wondered if I was afraid of being found out or afraid because I'd become a servant approaching the house of a sahib. I asked the man if his memsahib was at home, and when he nodded, I asked if he'd take the letter to her. I spoke formally, as Joseph had taught me. In a moment or two a woman in a floral cotton frock came to the back door and shouted for me. Of course this bit was easy because she barked at me in my own tongue: Why had the letter been sent here in the first place? I looked vacant. The old man translated. I shrugged, as if I hadn't a clue, but then she didn't expect me to. She handed me a white square envelope, and I took it, bowing my head. Don't lose it, she ordered, it's from the General Hospital at Lahore. I ducked my head again and headed for the road like someone who'd won the Derby.

My darling, come immediately, right now, right this second. It's easiest to ride, and you, being so efficient, will find a horse easily. I'm giving you instructions for the way through the woods. When you get here, go round to the gate at the front; the key will be under the large red stone on the right hand side. Hurry! I can't wait another minute. Forgive me if this sounds like a batch of orders—I know your sensitivity to all that—but words just can't convey my utter, utter desperation and longing for you. Your Sam.

When I got home, who should be sitting on the doorstep but Joseph. I wanted to hug him—but of course . . . so I dipped my head, and he dipped his. And I fooled him for just a fraction of a second. Then his mouth shot open, and we were back to appalled again: Mem, out of your mind, na? He hustled me into the house as if I were naked: What has been going on in my absence? Very good sentence, I said, unlocking the door, perfect, in fact.

Sentence construction not of interest, memsahib. About clothing I am asking. He collapsed onto the step, his head in his hands. I sat down next to him. And how lovely not to have him immediately jump up. I patted his arm. Come along, Joseph, I murmured; it's not as bad as all that. I needed to go into Simla to see the sights, and there are a great many grand people in Simla. I didn't want to be bothered with them. So the sari was perfect. He looked at me and pointed to my wrist: Mem, sari and watch not going together. I clapped my hand over my elegant little gold watch as if to vaporize it. He looked at me as a mother looks at a stupid child. All right, Joseph, I said. *All right*. I will go in and change, if you would do me the honor of working out how that bloody silly well over there produces water out of that bloody pump.

As memsahib wishes.

Memsahib also wishes a good horse. Double quick.

Where to find a horse?

I can tell you precisely, but you will need a rickshaw, and do not tell me that you'll walk, because that's out of the question.

Too much walking, he said, softly, looking at his feet, which were broken and bleeding.

Oh, God, Joseph, why didn't you tell me you needed some boots?

Mem, accustomed I am to walking, but path dangerous going and painful.

You stay put. I'll get the horse.

He looked at me. Memsahib, I have anticipated. Syce is bringing horse and also luggage. Let us enter house. Not loiter on doorstep like coolies.

I LEFT BY THE FRONT DOOR, another woman entirely. I was dressed in a long blue skirt and riding boots. I looked ridiculous, of course, but for some reason—not hard to locate—my jodhpurs and helmet hadn't come up with the other things. Joseph couldn't explain the matter. I rode sidesaddle through the streets and got back to where we'd entered Simla the night before. Looking at Sam's map and instructions, I took the road east up through a little copse of fir trees and followed it for a couple of miles. Not a soul to be seen. Here and there the icy green of mountain water. Sharp blue of sky. Air touched by mercury. Mountains lost in deep cloud. By now I was riding with my skirt yanked up around my waist and my legs bare to the sun. I cantered for a mile or so and then stopped, because suddenly, on the level road, I felt I was approaching a precipice, and though the feeling was located in my mind, it was also a bodily sensation. I had to think. I got down and paced a bit. This was the last time I could make a choice. The minute I saw Sam I'd be done for. The future beckoned, and I could sense its darkness, its potential tragedy. I considered that for a moment and took myself to the worst calamity. But the fact remained that I just didn't give a toss. I was too far in. I got back up. I rode the horse, and I found myself following a lovely path, clear and sunny, with the smell of jasmine and honeysuckle in the air. Sometimes the foliage of the trees would meet above my head, and between the green I saw the cleavage of the sky. The mourning doves calling to one another were heartbreaking; the cuckoos flung out their alerts, but on I rode until I reached an imposing stone house, set back among trees, with a vast expanse of cropped lawn surrounding it. It was closed off with a high ironwork fence, with nasty spikes on top. I rode round to the front, as directed, and now saw a long road that led up to the gate. The road was wide enough for cars and was in good condition. The front entrance was intimidating, and I was glad I'd come through the woods. I dismounted, found the key under the stone, opened the gate, and led my pony in. There was not a servant to be seen.

The minute I turned the curve in the driveway and saw the house fully for the first time, I fell in love, all over again. I knew a house so much like this that they could be mother and daughter, the most beautiful house in England and Wales. I was looking at a replica of Wilton House, near Salisbury. I stood there, gaping at the pale stone frontage, the stately Italian corner pavilions, and the distinctive Venetian window. The sun lit up the house and crossed the low line of its turrets before cascading down its flat frontage. Everything about it was restrained and elegant and utterly gorgeous. Over the great sweep of lawn and beyond the formal gardens, a small Palladian bridge crossed the river to a forest, and beyond the green rose the soft blue of the mountains. I wanted to cry. I knew the original so well. It was built somewhere around the thirteenth century as an abbey and had then passed into the hands of the earls of Pembroke. Mama had a whole shelf of books about it. I walked the horse slowly up the gravel pathway to the entrance porch. And then I felt utterly disoriented, and I wondered if this was the right house, whether I was on the right road, or even in the right country. I tethered the horse to a stone urn and turned to face the flight of stone steps. As I was trying to decide whether to bang on the heavy door or flee back into the woods, it opened. And there he stood, smiling, wearing pale cream flannels and a white shirt, a country gent standing at the door of his manor house.

Neither of us said a word. We were both in the grip of some strange paralysis. He stood looking at me, and I at him. Finally he said: I can't seem to move.

I'll come to you then.

But when we were facing each other, for a moment we still didn't know what to do. Then he grabbed me, and I crashed into him, my face at his neck, my lips on his skin. We both hung on for dear life, and we stayed that way for what seemed a very long while, till his arm threaded around my waist and led me into the hall. Inside, it was plain and simple. Nothing like the baroque extravaganza of Wilton, but the shape of the rooms was the same, and there was something pleasing about the geometrical design. Its regularity helped to contain the wild sprawl of my emotions. I followed him through, not saying a word. We went into a drawing room with cream walls edged in gold and long saffron drapes, held back, so that sunshine flooded the floor. He sat me down in a gilt armchair, upholstered in cardinal red silk—very much à la Wilton—and I was so excited that I had to tell him: This *is* a copy of Wilton, isn't it? A miniature? It was an absurd thing to say when all I wanted to do was to ask him where the hell he'd been all this time.

This one, he said, is only a hundred years old. He'd taken up position on the floor, and we stared at each other again, shy as strangers. I couldn't take my eyes off him. The white shirt was rolled up to his elbows, and his arms were brown and gleaming, lightly covered in dark hair. The gold watch was too large for his wrist, and I noticed for the first time a narrow white scar above his elbow. He looked very serious until he smiled and then said in that insouciant voice: This was my mother's house. I used to come here in the summer, before I was sent off to school. He looked around him. It's very different now. One of the Pembrokes had it built as a whim, thought a touch of Tudor splendor would be just the thing in India. The man turned out to be a homicidal maniac and ended up being cloistered here for several years. When my mother bought it, she got rid of a lot of the marble busts, gold paint, and hoo-ha and turned it into a family house. I only use the front. He went on, telling me about the house, which was very interesting, of course, but entirely beside the point. I couldn't decide what was the matter with him, blathering on like a tour guide when he'd not seen me for what seemed like a lifetime. It dawned on me that he was nervous. Perhaps, like me, he'd had his moment of doubt on the road and didn't have the same certainty about going on.

What worried me more was that he didn't look the same; he was pale, and thinner, and there were dark hollows beneath his eyes. I blurted out: Have you been ill?

Do I look it?

As a matter of fact, yes. And why do you always have to be so oblique?

Am I? Didn't know that either. He looked down and seemed to be considering the matter. He was sitting in that marvelous Indian way, one leg stretched out, the other draped over, a timeless, languid pose, beautiful in its ease. I wondered if he was aware of his grace or any of his bodily gestures that I found so appealing. He looked at me: The thing is, yes, I have been a bit ill, as a matter of fact. He raked his hand through his hair. I got a touch of the influenza, almost impossible not to, though my immunity is pretty high. This strain was particularly vicious. He frowned, and the double lines above his eyes were deep. There's always, he said, something mysterious about influenza, the way it suddenly materializes out of nowhere. The Latin word for it suggests that it comes from hidden influences—astral or occult—it's a bizarre kind of affliction—

Sam, please get to the point, and tell me exactly how sick you've been.

He laughed: Such impatience. I've noticed this tendency in you before. Let me at least give you a few details so you'll know what kept me away from you all this time. He was deliberately trying to drive me crazy as he rabbited on about influenza being a febrile zymotic disorder, highly contagious, with symptoms and sequelae including rapid prostration and severe catarrh of the respiratory mucous membrane . . . and blah, blah, blah for several more minutes when it was all I could do to keep my hands off him.

Sam, I said patiently, could you spare me the details this time? I was worried to death about you.

He moved until his bare foot was touching my shod one. And as he was pulling off my boots, he kept on talking about the killer flu—

on and on about contagion and contamination and the precise nature of this epidemic, and what worked and what didn't, and the difference between Western and traditional treatments, and so on and so forth until I said: Sam, I'm going to hit you unless you stop.

Sorry, he said, grimacing, I always talk too much when I'm scared.

There's nothing to be scared about.

It's just that I'm so happy to see you. And I don't know quite how to behave or what to say. The fact is I'm utterly crazy about you, even though you're appallingly blunt, not to mention terribly rude, and given to violent outbreaks rather similar to influenza. He smiled: What were you thinking? That I'd forgotten you? That I was never coming back?

No, actually I was wondering if you'd been unfaithful to me.

He looked shocked. With whom?

Your wife.

He laughed out loud. Then he looked down and seemed to be studying the floor for quite some time. Ah, he said, it would seem that I've not been able to put your mind to rest on that matter. You're going to have to learn to trust me, as we'll have many separations, you and I, and it seems that you doubt me already. I must say I think it's rather unfair since I've given you no grounds. He'd leaned forward and ran his hands under my skirt. I grabbed his hands to keep them where they were and said: For a man always going on about the uselessness of words, you've been very tedious today. I slipped off the chair and onto the floor and held him around the neck and kissed him like mad, and his hands whooshed up under my skirt and circled my waist, and I was aware for a split second of wide golden planks and a rug of red and cream which I was tipped back onto in no uncertain terms. He glared down at me. I have not made love to my wife in years. Nor will I, from this day forward, world without end, Amen.

Eight

He was wearing yellow pajamas and soft leather slippers turned up at the toes. I wasn't wearing anything, and it surprised me that it should be so easy. It was dark outside, and the stars were beginning to make an appearance. He'd given me two things: a braided gold bracelet from Russia and a padded quilt from Kashmir, crimson with tiny black stitching. I loved them because they were completely what they should have been: the first shoots of a life that we might have together one day. I kept thinking, Perhaps Neville is dead in the mountains. Perhaps some Pathan killed him swiftly in the night, and I'll never have to see or speak to him again. I also thought: Perhaps his wife will have a mysterious and painless illness and pass away quietly. I shivered and drew the quilt over me and smoothed its silky skin. I saw the tiny stitching making circles all over, like ripples on water, and at the outer edges, shadows turned the crimson to black.

Sam lit the hurricane lamp and blew out the match. Its chimney was just beginning to grow sooty, and he rubbed his finger on the inside of the glass like a woman checking for dust. I stared at him. There was something about his expression that was remote, almost uninvolved, until suddenly, like a propeller, his face turned to me. What, he asked in an agitated way, are we going to do about that damn horse?

I thought you put it in the stable at the back.

You said you wanted to go back tonight.

I don't want to, but Joseph will worry.

You two are quite the pals.

I gave him a look.

He sent one back: Perhaps you just like black men.

The silence between us was tangible as a creature stalking the room. I stuck it out. I've made you angry, he said. The remoteness was back.

You certainly have.

His hands were held in front of him as he sat forward on the bed. He has lean hands with small wrists, and they shook a little. I'm sorry, he said, that was a pretty vile thing to say. He was rubbing the side of his face, and I wanted to kiss his hand, but I was furious. I wasn't censoring my words, he said, the way I usually do. I must be more nervous than I thought. Forgive me. I'm so sorry. It was an appalling thing to say.

I suppose I should be grateful that you said it out loud. How often have you thought that?

Well, actually, I never have, but I'm just becoming aware of how dependent I am on you, and I don't like the feeling. Unused to it. He turned to look at me, his face ajar: Must you go? It's sort of put me on edge—your going so soon. Is there any way you could stay? There are so many things we should talk about, so much I've thought about since I last saw you.

Seeing him that way, with his mockery gone, turned me around.

It was as if the Gulf Stream had moved through, warming the air between us, greening the atmosphere. Are you worried about what we've got into? I said, taking his hand and tucking it under my thigh.

I suppose so. This whole affair could blow up so badly. You're much more vulnerable than I am, and I can't stand the idea of that. You've moved so far beyond the pale. I can't bear to think of people turning on you or making you suffer. We can't hide this for long. You know that, don't you?

In the long run I wouldn't want to.

We've both had some time to look at what we've got into. You had your breakdown with the malaria, and now I've had mine. I think what I can't stand is not knowing the future, not having any control over anything.

What's the worst that could happen—to you, I mean?

He gave me his list: I'd be an outcast from my family and community. I'd have to give up my practice, probably, and certainly the research I'm doing at the asylum at Ranchi, which is funded by an English philanthropist. I could lose the job at the hospital in Lahore. But on the bright side, I could continue to be a doctor—abroad, if we couldn't take the heat, or in another part of India, if the heat was manageable, though we'd be much poorer. What about you?

I'd be thrown out too, but I don't think I'd go home. I'd stick it out here, if you would, but I couldn't stay in India without doing something. I took both of his hands and looked at him: What I really don't want is for you to think that you've put me at risk or will ruin my life, that it's your fault in some way. Don't imagine I'll be a stone around your neck, or that you'll have to set me up in some house in the middle of nowhere and watch me go round the bend. That's what happens, isn't it, in situations like this? The man somehow manages the ostracization, and the woman gets stuck in the attic or hurls herself in front of a train. I'm not doing either of those. I can take care of myself, whatever happens. I wouldn't have got into this if I didn't know that.

Spoken like the best of your breed, he said, moving across the physical divide and joining me among the pillows. But we wouldn't be able to marry, he said quietly. It's only fair to make that plain.

I would have liked to marry you, I said softly, but it would be all right just to live together. It would be more than enough. If I didn't have money of my own, we wouldn't be having this conversation. I can't imagine myself being dependent, or idle or useless here. If I stay, I must do something constructive. If we have a life together, it must be on equal terms.

He laughed at me: My view of the future is a little more romantic than yours. I see us living on a houseboat, or in a house, perhaps in Kashmir. I suppose I could do my research on my own, but it wouldn't get published. I'd just be a doctor and do the best I could with the limited resources we have here. That would be all right. My father would visit us, but probably not for a year or two. My son would be furious with me for at least ten years. My mother would be unhappy, but she'd understand, without saying that she did. I would certainly go to Wales and see your family and the house where you grew up. And for the record, I wouldn't mind a child or two.

I was so stunned by the last remark that I couldn't say a word. And it was as if he were shocked too, because in a moment he became all busyness and purpose. Well, he said, I need to see to the horse. You're going to stay. I'll drive into town and get a note to Joseph. Say you're off to the theater, or something. He looked up. Can Joseph read?

Joseph, I said coldly, can speak five languages.

I can see, he said, that you haven't entirely forgiven my vulgarity of a moment ago.

I'm putting it down to the cruelties of the past.

Generous of you. I should be back in an hour at the latest. Do you need anything?

I need to kiss you.

AFTER HE LEFT, I lost my nerve. I suddenly felt exposed in the huge house, not knowing what to do if anyone should come. He'd said that no one comes here. The house is kept up in the summer, but it's closed all winter. It has something of a ghost life. The servants, he said, come before I do, but not while I'm here. My old ayah is in charge of everything, and she's scrupulous, particularly about my privacy. He'd got up and stood looking down at me: Thanks for saying you'll stay, but you know, if you'd gone, I'd have come right after you. Remember that. I put my hands on either side of his face and kissed his mouth. He still looked wretched, and I couldn't bear that: Don't let's be melancholic. I love you so. Just hurry back and make me that kichree you promised. I'm starving.

I LIKED HIS FANTASY of the future, and I wanted to believe it, but something in my bones told me it would be otherwise. When I heard him drive off, I suddenly thought that he was going forever, and I rushed to the door. He'd already gone. I strolled around the house, lighting lamps. I seemed to see his mother in the rooms, talking or reading to a small boy. I even had a sense of the maniac earl locked up in an attic. The Singhs had certainly swept away all the pomp and glory. No more crusty old paintings of Jupiter caressing Juno, or Salome dancing with a head on a plate; no stags in the mountains, or family portraits of people on horseback. There were no marble hounds chasing foxes, and no collections of Sèvres porcelain. The Brussels tapestries and Aubusson carpets were gone, as were the heavy paneling and marble friezes. There wasn't a single Grecian statue exposing a breast, nor were there staterooms or ballrooms, or staircases decorated with murals. But there was a perfectly delightful boudoir, pale gray and old rose, with sweet round sofas and velvet chairs, and a chest of drawers with a collection of irresistible saris, neatly folded into squares. I chose a gold one and took it with me when I strolled into a sumptuous library, every wall lined with scuffed leather-bound books that had all been read. The fireplace was huge, and there were scarlet Persian rugs, and carved teak tables, and an old leather chair next to the fireplace. The vaulted cloister corridor was exactly like the original, but without the busts on pedestals. In the front hall, Shakespeare lounged against a pillar of books, his hand propping up his chin, his legs crossed. The house was refined in its Englishness, made glorious by its dash of Italian, and the combination of balance and order made it utterly peaceful. It was a house a person could live wonderfully in, but it seemed no one did.

There had once been a magnificent formal garden, which Sam had turned into an eclectic kind of sprawl, with a circular pool surrounded by banks of roses, and a glade of rhododendrons. The rhodies were not your common garden variety; they were pure white shot with an edge of pink, like a peony—a special breed from China. He'd also created a whole jungle of lilies—every variety and color, from pure white to a strong purple that could pass for black. I had to be careful not to ask too many questions, or he'd give me an entire history. It wasn't an English garden, because although there were oaks and yews set into the lawns, the walls of the house were cluttered with peach-colored bougainvillea and white jasmine, and there were gardenia bushes with soft blooms, and jacaranda, frangipani, and pomegranate trees all mixed in together. A lilac tree gave my heart a turn. Everything was fragrant and flourishing, and it all had a slightly wild, uncultivated look about it, and for some reason, I thought that perhaps this was the kind of garden a bibi might have liked. I saw pale-skinned, dark-eyed children running across the lawn on stick horses made of sugarcane. I saw a woman strolling among the rosebushes with a basket like my mother's, and I didn't know if what I was seeing was myself in another life or whether the figures on the lawn had once lived here.

I sat on the edge of the circular pool, my feet dangling in the water. I looked down. It was as if the water with its sprinkling of water lilies were mesmerizing me. I let myself fall into the deep water. I dropped like a rock, and so deep was the pool that I kept falling. The water was freezing. My skirt rushed up over my head, and I was like an animal trapped in a bag or a kitten drowning in a sack. The cloth got tangled around my head and neck, and it bunged up my eyes and mouth. For some reason, I remained calm. I stopped fighting the water and let myself go. I kept sinking, but I had the strongest sensation that I'd be all right. I was still going down, and I was drowning, when suddenly the pool was filled with light. I touched the rocky bottom, and I shoved off, hard. The upward thrust began to unravel the cloth until my face was open to the water again. At the top, I gasped like a fish, lungs tight and bursting, my body solid as ice, my hands blue. I scrambled out, teeth chattering, ran back into the house through the French doors that led into Sam's quarters, and fled to the bathroom and sat on the floor in a puddle, too shocked to move. Even wrapped in thick Madras cotton towels, I couldn't stop shaking. When I collected myself, I decided that some dark god of the underworld had yanked me free.

I lay back in the tub. It was made of thick porcelain, and it was long enough for me to lie down in. It was Victorian without question, and very elegant. There was actual *plumbing*, so you could turn a tap and hot water would come gushing out. And there was an actual lavatory, which flushed—peculiarly, I have to say, with some spluttering—but it did flush. Sam told me that Lord Curzon, when Viceroy, was very keen on inventions and always had the newest thing. Sam's mother had once treated him for snakebite fever, and he'd had these ultramodern conveniences shipped over from London as a present for her. There was a basin, which was particularly lovely, with hand-painted pansies spilling down the sides. I lay in the bath and let my body thaw. I dreamed of him, with the sheer bliss of knowing that he'd be back in thirty minutes. We had a whole night ahead of us. A whole night.

WE'D MOVED from our earlier position in the drawing room to his bed and hadn't moved from there all afternoon. He'd said: You're too extravagant in your emotions to be English. There's also something about your face, your eyes especially, that doesn't seem Anglo-Saxon.

Could there have been, in the far past, some liaison with the other side? He was laughing, of course, but the remark stuck with me. He'd also wheedled a pretty full and detailed sexual history out of me and had been singularly reticent about his own. He was more willing to talk about celibacy, a state that had never even entered my consciousness. He'd said he'd been celibate sometimes for a few years, and when I asked him why, he said it was to clear his head. I didn't understand that because for me it's sex that clears the head. He seemed to be talking about some kind of retreat or a surrender of the senses after a period of decadence. He told me about the decadence but rather skimmed the sexual side of things. And I thought later that was wise, because those are the things that get snared in the heart and cause a heap of trouble later on. The wild time of his life came after Oxford, when he'd gone to Europe on his version of the grand tour. I wanted, he said, to drift around in blue silk pajamas all day and to consume five-course dinners at midnight. I'd worked so bloody hard, and I just wanted to let go. I began wandering the streets, looking for God knows what. Had an intense interest in the unusual and the bizarre, and became one of those people—there were plenty of us at the time—who were desperate for sensation. I seemed to attract some odd and interesting types. And of course my wealth took me into that fashionable, feckless world of the fabulously rich. They had mansions in Salamis, Nice, or Palermo and exquisite garrets in Paris, where they hung around with dangerous émigrés from South America or Constantinople. We spent the summer season at balls and picnics in the hills or going to the opera and the Russian Ballet. We were constantly touring and château hopping. I spent hours talking about Picasso and Cocteau with doped-up artists, slept till two every day, drank from three onwards, not remembering the faces of the women from the night before. The war was coming, and because of that, life was on edge and tragic, as if we knew that Europe was about to be turned into a graveyard.

But, he said with an ironic laugh, in all the decadence and waste,

I still had the public school manner. I was an exercise in British un-
derstatement—and a complete sham. I tried smoking opium; it seemed
a natural thing to do, culturally in line and all that. I told myself I was
conducting research, and that I could be disciplined about it and live
within the delicate rituals. Opium smoking was all the rage; it was
considered intellectual and civilized, and for a while I was pain-free,
floating through the days and nights without a care in the world. But
one night, on a beach in Monte Carlo, I saw how close I'd got to tip-
ping over the edge. I hurled the stuff into the sea and stopped—but in
such a precipitous way that my brain went into shock. I was a mess for
a while. When I'd recovered, I decided it was time to go back to England. I took up my medical training and immersed myself in work.
But a strange thing happened, because as the years sped by, I began to
long for India for the first time. My friends thought I was crazy. War
was imminent by then, and everyone was gung ho, desperate to sign
up. I wasn't prepared to die for England, though I was still being English in my own way. Like all of us, I'd been prepared for what was
about to happen. Our whole education had trained us for service in
war or in the British Empire. I knew that going to India was still part
of the game, but I didn't care. It was where I wanted to be. So at the
end of 1915 I took ship for India, and the minute I got here, I threw
myself headlong into work. And, he said quietly, while I toiled day
and night in poorly equipped hospitals and down-at-heel village clin-
ics, most of my friends were ending up in the dead and missing
columns of the London *Times*.

I WONDERED if I might be another stage of decadence for him. And
whether I'd become the English to his Black. When I asked him if I
was a way for him to complete himself, he said: Aren't I the same for
you? He thought I was losing my nerve. I wasn't, but I was beginning
to wonder if we'd get out of this alive. His life was entirely bound up
in the way he was perceived, by his hospital, his clinic, his patients,
and, above all, though he would have hated to admit this, the British.

They'd granted him a rare inclusion, but his immunity was maintained by delicate boundaries, as much as by his exemplary record—both in his doctoring and in the vital British matter of character. I had less to lose, or so I imagined, having not made a life for myself here. But I wanted that life, and I was determined to get it. I wanted to work and to be able to stay without being an outcast. Sam had made it clear that the Englishwoman's record in India was paltry or nonexistent, arising out of a complete lack of role. Her own conventions and prejudices made her useless, and this was confounded by the fact that her children were sent away at an early age and shipped across the sea, often not returning for years; that also I was not going to put up with.

I lay in the tub, looking out of the long windows at the garden, mulling over what he'd said. The French doors were wide open, and I could hear the doves in the lime trees, and when the wind blew, it brought in the scent of gardenia. I missed him so badly that I went back to the things he'd said in the space opened up by bodily love. You keep asking me, he said, to take off my mask, but I'm not sure I want to. I thought once that sex would be enough. It couldn't be misunderstood; there was no subtext, no innuendo. All my life there's been a silent language going on in the heads of people around me. They're saying one thing and thinking another, and so am I. There are facades within facades, mirages everywhere, and as a result, I watch myself, and I'm scrupulous about what I give away. I'm not used to a woman like you. At first, I thought you were just naive, didn't know India, hadn't really encountered anything much about the racial divide. You were like a goose egg in a jungle. You're not naive, but you are astonishingly unconventional. You look at things differently, and that puts you at tremendous risk here. I don't think you realize how much, or if you even care.

SOMETIMES WE FELL ASLEEP for a while, his arm beneath my head. He could enter sleep easily, through a crack in any window or door, and be completely out for ten minutes or two hours, waking easily, completely rested. We're all half asleep here, he'd say, lying on the floor with his head on a pillow or stirring out of deep contentment in the hammock under the trees. Sometimes we lay in silence for a long while until one of us would ask: What are you thinking about? As time drifted by, we'd slip in and out of a silence that bound us more tightly together, seduced by sex and sleep, unable to resist either, until I came to see sleep as the Hindus do, as the first slumber of eternity. He got up once and brought me a painting of his parents the day they'd married: very formal and elegant, entirely traditional. We were lying in what had once been his mother's room. He said it had been rather Indianized in her day, with low chairs and carved tables, Persian pieces from her home in Kashmir. The room couldn't have been plainer now. Cream walls, white drapes, apricot-colored mahogany floors, a bed, small and low to the ground, a long table covered with medical books and journals, and well-read magazines and newspapers. An ashtray or two in need of emptying. *Sons and Lovers*, and a battered copy of *The Upanishad*s in Sanskrit. A pair of glasses with slim metal frames. I put them on, and the distance blurred out of recognition while the printed word rushed into focus. A rosy, translucent Buddha sat on a black stand. There were two Picassos, both nudes, and a large wall clock from St. Petersburg. On the far wall hung a collection of erotic sketches, which had belonged to his father and which his mother had stuffed in the attic.

My mother, he'd said, is very conventional, very formal. She's remote, and quite religious, although she isn't one of those pious women. When she left me in England, she came back here and trained to be a doctor, and she's never stopped working, though she's often been ill and is rather frail now. Her philosophy of work came from the background of her caste, and I always loved that about her. It was sincere—not that throwing of food on the ground for untouchables and dogs, or the obligatory alms and offerings, but hard, daily work among people who are suffering. She taught me how to think and how to float above thought. She taught me the pleasure of doing absolutely nothing for hours on end. I also learned from her that the flesh knows more than the intellect and that what our blood feels is true. She had me reading the paper at four. She spoke to me in Hindi, English, and Persian until it became effortless to move among the three. Any discipline I have, he said, came from her. She rammed it into my head. Samresh, she said, you must try harder, not for my sake but for yours.

He showed me a box full of letters she'd written to him when he'd first been sent away to school. Not a single letter had been opened. When I stared at him, he said simply: I couldn't do it. The loss would have been too vivid. I kept an image of her in my head throughout my school days and always sort of hoped she'd come back and take me away, but of course, once she was back in India, it was five years before I saw her again. When she left me the first time, she gave me an amulet and said: Do not look out of the window to see me leave, because I will not be there. You must go on now without me. I touched his cheek and said: That's not something you'll be hearing from me. He smiled. You have a way, he said, of repairing things.

She was, he went on, always Indian, unpartitioned, whole, but my father was a hybrid—brilliant, tender, unstable, and capable of great violence. There was passion between them, but it was explosive, and it frightened me when I was small. For many years my mother despised my father's life. They had arguments that went on all night, and sometimes she wouldn't speak to him for days; she'd retreat into a silence that sometimes included me as well. He looked at me and smiled: I think that's the bit of me that you find hard to take. She could be cold, and when she retreated like that, I was stranded, and of course I learned how to do the same. I was very aware of the differences between them, and nothing made it clearer than the fact that they occupied different parts of the house. We have our own partition here, my father would say sarcastically. What the British did to Bengal in 1905, my wife imposes on me.

There was a sadness about Sam when he talked about his mother, but it was absent when he told me about his father. I loved his quarters, he said. He had this large, leather-topped desk, with a line of clocks announcing the time in all the different parts of the world. He always sat on the floor, or he'd lie flat out on a sofa, his bare feet balancing on one arm. He'd be smoking a Cuban cigar and arguing with his cronies about politics; it could go on all night. He'd constantly switch from Kashmiri to English, and it was as if the two languages were at war with each other. I adored him, he said. My mother did too, but she wouldn't admit it. She couldn't live with him, or without him, and later the hospital became another kind of partition for her. She had to separate herself from what she called his criminal ways. I heard her accuse him once of being as unscrupulous as the British. He said that everything he knew about corruption and double-dealing had been learned from them. He was larger than life, exuding power and bonhomie, and there was nothing better than being in a room where he was having a meeting with his cronies: dark men sitting together drinking tea, smoking, cracking jokes, and making it seem as if the world were entirely under their control. Apart from the business side of his life—textiles and the arms trade—he had a great fondness for explosives. You are better at making money than a Pakistani, my mother would snarl. And there was the espionage too, with terrorism thrown in. The British didn't mind the ethnic stuff, in fact, stirred it up and profited by it, but terrorism was another matter. It was bad for business. My father felt the same way. He spent money in an extraordinary way: jewels, racehorses, railways, warlords, palaces, and princes. He thought he could buy anything or anyone, and he pretty much could.

Sam got up suddenly and walked to the cupboard and pulled out a peculiar looking prosthesis made of porcelain. See this, he said. This is my father's leg. One of many. I kept this one because he used to stomp about in it and say: Look, one white and one black leg. What does that make me, eh? When he was angry, he'd accuse the British of blowing off his leg, and when he was morose, he'd accuse himself: My own train, my own dynamite, and my own bloody leg—they all turned on me the same day.

Wait, wait, I said, jumping off the bed and taking the leg from him. Start at the beginning. This is fascinating, I said, peering at the workings of the leg. Look at all the little screws and the way it bends; it weighs a ton and must be ages old. Tell me how he lost his leg, and don't leave anything out. So he sat at his father's desk and put his feet up, and I sat in a chair by the window and listened. My grandfather, he said, my father's father, was involved in the delicate process of passing over lavish payments to the warlords who controlled the passes between Kabul and British India. It was vital to keep the doors from northern Afghanistan shut, to stop the Russians from sneaking down into India; that's been a British preoccupation for centuries. It was a lucrative but bloody business, and he was up to his neck in it. Anyway, somewhere along the line, it seems that he'd been used to keep British hands clean by setting up an assassination. He pulled off a barbaric little incident a few miles outside Kandahar, and some uncooperative fellow lost his head one dark night. This incident had unpleasant repercussions for my father. The British government expected him to go on doing their dirty work for them and arranged for another assassination that almost cost him his neck. He was offended by them and outraged by their arrogance. He was a Rajput, a ruler in his own right, and the British were trying to get him involved in an uprising against the Russians by passing blood money to some Afghan tribes. He was having none of it. The British then made a deal with the Afghans, but it ended badly, and it somehow looked as though my old man had been involved in a brutal incident where many innocent people had lost their lives. He immediately broke his connection with the British.

The problem was, Sam said, smoking, the old man was as ruthless as they were. In fact, he was so like them that he couldn't help seeing the English as brothers, and he wanted to join the firm as an equal partner. He shared the English passion for exploration and expedition, and he walked the same line between exploration and intelligence gathering that the British had mastered from the old days. They would be secretly mapping the courses of Indian rivers, while appearing to be delivering a gold coach to a maharaja; that kind of thing was right up his alley. He did it all the time, using business as a foil for espionage and sending out expeditions that were in fact military operations. But unfortunately he slipped up. He made a deal with the Russians to keep the British out of a major part of the arms trade, and the British found out about it. While huge supplies of explosives were being taken up north as part of the tunnel construction in the hills, my father, who always traveled in his own private train, stopped for a moment just outside a tunnel to take lunch by a stream. The minute he got back on board, the train blew up. The explosion blinded him in one eye, and he lost his right leg. He'd probably have hemorrhaged to death but for the expertise of my mother. You're too evil to die yet, she whispered to him; you're not permitted to go until you've earned some merit in this life.

Perhaps he listened to her, he said thoughtfully, or perhaps he lost his nerve, but either way, after this episode, disillusionment set in. He had his conversion to the Swadeshi movement and got very involved in the boycotting and burning of British goods. It was about the time that he took off to South Africa to meet Gandhi, and his life changed radically after that. So you see, he said with that lovely smile that somehow managed to reconcile the East with the West, there's a family history of radical change as well as all the terrorism and skulduggery, so don't despair of me yet.

COMPARED WITH ALL THIS, I was a milk pudding. The simplicity of my own identity—Welsh, part of England, part of Great Britain, and part of the empire—it all fitted together as tidily as the Union Jack. No hacked-off pieces, no migrations created by rupture and war, no subjugations or humiliations, no religious exterminations, no genocide, no conflicts or choices—I had a single, stable national and personal identity. We have no such luxury, Sam said. My father folded under his conflicts, moving first into the British camp and then out of it as he became increasingly involved in the home rule movement. And I suspect, he said, swinging his legs down off the table, that's what he's up to right now. Whenever he goes quiet, he's hiding out somewhere, planning some kind of unpleasant incident to shake up things for the Brits.

Nine

When he came back from town, I was standing by the window of the drawing room that overlooks the fountains and rose gardens. And I was wearing the gold sari. A peacock had just disappeared into an arbor of wisteria; a line of ducks flew over the Palladian bridge. The green, green grass rolled down to the copse of fir trees; beyond them the mountains barricaded the sky. I'd chosen to wait for him in the drawing room. It's the only room a visitor would be ushered into; the other rooms are too personal and, without servants, usually in a state of disorder. When I heard him come down the corridor and stop at the door, I hesitated a moment, and then I turned around. He stared at me, hard, for a full minute. I didn't move. I looked down, and then I looked him straight in the eye and began to walk the length of the room toward him.

Not bad, he said, with an approving laugh. In fact, rather impressive. You could almost pass.

Why almost?

You walk like a horsewoman. And your demeanor lacks humility. He laughed: You're going to need a little practice.

Don't imagine I'll start eating in the kitchen.

So we began. After I'd showed him my skill at picking safety pins and paper clips off the floor with my toes, we got into the serious stuff. Back and forth I'd stroll with a heavy book on my head as he surveyed me from the armchair: Keep your head up and your eyes down. Move your hips more seductively and walk *slowly*. You're still striding. That's much better. Think of yourself as a girl walking in a religious procession. That's it. It was all very amusing, a kind of play, but it was also more than that, and it always landed us back in bed, till the sari was scorched and the caste mark was no more than a pink blur. The next day we began in earnest. We drove to the bazaar in the car, and if I spoke English, he ignored me: You have to be more fluent. Forget the Punjabi; just concentrate on basic Hindi. At least you're not talking British Hindi, which is only good for giving orders. Joseph has done a pretty good job.

The one thing I'd been practicing to say to him was harder than learning Hindi. My precise words were: I'm going to train as a doctor.

Fine, he said, but you're going to have to do so in your English incarnation.

I was startled. I thought you'd tell me I was being ridiculous. That it couldn't be done.

Why would I?

Why wouldn't you?

There are women doctors in India, he said, and you seem to forget that my mother is one of them. Some trained here, though the majority did medical studies in England or France. It's not impossible.

You think I could pull it off?

Of course.

Would I have to go back to England?

He shook his head. Delhi will be fine. Lots of our doctors earn a medical degree quickly; there's no time for the seven-year stretch, not in India or not for many Indian doctors. Those who'll be going out to the villages do what's called a modified degree. They learn what they need to know to treat the population, takes two years or so; it sounds patronizing, but in fact, it makes sense. You might be able to convince them to let you do it that way. Either way you'd get an excellent training.

Delhi's a long way from you.

I'll be in Bihar Province, and that's a long way from everywhere.

You're going back to Ranchi? When?

I work at the asylum from July until December and spend the rest of my time in Lahore. I have independent relationships with both hospitals and a private practice in Ranchi as well.

Could I come and see you in Ranchi?

Of course. And I you in Delhi, but the distances are vast, and the trains are slow. Also, you'll have a lot to do. There's only so much I can do to help you, and I have no affiliation with the hospital in Delhi, though I know it's as progressive as a British institution can be. My mother might be able to pull a few strings, but that might be tricky too. Even though she's broken out of her own restraints and conventions, she wouldn't approve of our connection.

You mean I'd never be able to meet her?

I think anything can be done, he said quietly. It's just a matter of will. If you want to train, I'll dig out some of my books for you. I have a beautiful copy of *Gray's Anatomy*, and I'll see what else I can find. We kept on talking about it as we drove through the back roads to the Indian market. In the outlying villages, people were praying in the river and taking their ritual baths; gray eagles rose up into the sky and a man in a small fishing boat hauled in his net. There was a strong smell of sewage and decayed fruit; it lay splattered on the dark earth under the fig trees, and the crows picked at the mush. We were driving in silence. It was the late afternoon, and the heat coming off the river was somnolent and smelly. I was seeing India differently now.

Once I'd said what I wanted to do, out loud like that, I knew I'd have
to find a way of navigating the country on its own terms. And at that
moment, watching the people squatting under the trees or walking on
the dusty road, I couldn't imagine where they were going, what the
insides of their huts looked like, and how each day would be for that
woman over there in the white sari or for the man fixing his bicycle
on the dirt road. And suddenly, I was terrified of being in the market
dressed in a sari. I had an image of people laughing at me, turning on
me, being exposed as a Feringhi and hated for it. I wanted to tell him
this but couldn't.

We'd stopped under the trees with all the rickshaws and empty
bullock carts. The bazaar spread out like a stain, and its boundaries
were unclear. It was the end of the day, and rotting fruit and vegetables were piled up in dusty heaps, beggars were shuffling through the
waste, one was walking through a mess of fish entrails on the stumps
he used as legs. Children were stuffing squished black bananas and
split oranges into their mouths. A man came out and began lashing at
them with a stick. The hubbub and babble of voices were overwhelming; streams of people walked by; animals were being loaded;
water carriers screeched; the sweetmeat sellers were aggressive and
loud. The children hanging off their mothers' hips looked starving,
and the flies were getting unbearably close to their eyes. The beggars,
in their willful mutilations, were grotesque.

Sam reached over in front of me and opened the door. I got out
and forced myself to walk toward the bazaar. Immediately the stench
made me gag. I stood perfectly still, my hand to my mouth, trying to
stop myself vomiting. I saw a dead dog lying in its filth and the severed head of a goat in the drain. A beggar came up and clutched at my
sari, and when I tried to get away from him, he followed me, be-
seeching, clawing at my skirt. His eyes were milky, and his mouth was
covered in sores. I turned and ran back to the car, and to Sam, who
was walking toward me. He stopped: What's the matter?

I can't do it.

Can't do what?

Go in there. I gestured wildly with my hand: Into all that, all those Indians, all that noise and filth and stench.

Can't do it at all or just this?

I began to sob: I don't know. I just can't do it.

He stood sideways and looked at me, his arms loose at his side, his expression wary. We've taken an action, he said quietly, the consequences of which are beyond our control. His voice hardened: Are you in or out?

I'm supposed to decide *here*?

And now. Get out of the car and walk in among all those filthy, stinking blacks, or I can drive you back to Simla.

I was shaking. I didn't like the tone, his expression, and I certainly didn't like the ultimatum, and I said to him tightly: At this moment I can't think of anything nicer than being driven to Simla to an elegant cocktail bar which serves champagne and smoked salmon sandwiches. But then I looked at him and saw the concentration of misery in his eyes. He was trying to disguise a sense of outrage, and of hurt, and a piece of steel entered my spine and lodged there.

Give me a moment, I said.

Take as long as you like, he snapped, moving back to the car. He leaned against it, his back facing me, and lit a cigarette. I got into the car on the other side. A woman with a small child walked up to him and salaamed, and with infinite economy of gesture, he returned the greeting. They spoke for a moment, and her way of looking at him was strange: It was a look either of supplication or of gratitude, and I didn't know which. I'd only seen that expression on the face of Indians who were speaking to Us, and I wondered, numbly, whether it was because she knew he was a doctor or because she knew he was rich. The problem was that I had no idea. He came around to my door and opened it and reached in his hand to help me out. I took it. He leaned back against the car. Isabel, he said softly, this must for you be the way it was for me walking down the corridor at my prep school and waiting for a senior boy to yell out something revolting. And to tell you the truth, what you felt just then, I often feel. I moved closer to him, needing a cigarette, which of course I couldn't have.

Stay close to me, he said. It'll be all right, I promise.

I shook my head. I need to go by myself, I said. You get the vegetables. I'll get the fruit. I'll meet you back at the car.

I took a deep breath. Ahead of me was a densely packed flood of busy, impatient, hurrying humanity, all trying to get the best fruit and the best prices in the shortest time possible. They were utterly at home in these exchanges and knew entirely how to get what they wanted. I took another deep breath and pushed myself through, and in a moment I couldn't see Sam at all. Something in me went calm. It was a little like the moment in the pool when I thought I was drowning. I made my body compact, and I negotiated my way through the crowd, moving into the shoving stream. No one gave me the time of day; they laughed and bickered and talked to one another, and it was impossible to get anywhere near the front, where the pyramids of mangoes, bananas, pineapples, and coconuts lay waiting for me. I thought of my father, who always said: Just get a move on, Isabel, grasp the nettle. And I thought of Joseph's reprimanding voice: Mem, what is this shilly-shallying? Move forward, or be trampled to death.

I began to imitate the women around me. I pushed and yanked, lifted and sniffed, turned over and scrutinized, grabbing what I needed, discarding what I didn't. I passed my money across a sea of other hands and took my fruit and shoved it into my calico bag. I used the minimum of language to get what I needed, and then I moved back out, away from the heavy trading. It was there, where I felt less crushed and intimidated, that I could fit more easily into the swarm of strangers. I felt the fear go, and I was suddenly at peace. Some harness fell off me, and for the first time in my life, I saw myself as neither one thing nor another, but simply as part of the common herd. It was astonishing. And liberating. It made me happy. After that, I simply did what women the world over do best: I shopped.

IN THE CAR DRIVING HOME, Sam and I began a serious conversation about the future. We put everything on the table. He didn't seem to care about the risks. There comes a point, he said, when you get beyond worrying about what might happen and just try to make a plan for when it does. It got dark on the road, and he stopped talking; he needed to concentrate. Animals and people would suddenly appear in the headlights, materializing out of nowhere. He turned to me in that sudden way he has. How, he asked, are we going to get rid of your husband?

I've left him.

Officially, I mean.

I'd rather hoped that I'd never have to set eyes on him again.

Could be more difficult than you think. He may not let you leave, and you're here because of him. You're an army wife. You can't disappear, and he might well come after you. When he'd parked the car, he sat in silence for a moment and then asked me: How far are you prepared to go?

In what way?

In any way. What's the limit of your commitment?

There's no limit.

So—he smiled—if he became a problem, we could have him bumped off?

WE WERE IN THE GARDEN ROOM, having tea. All around us, circling the gardens and the fountains, the lawn stretched as far as the eye could see. It was at this time of day that the mountains came to visit us, becoming intimate and close, while the vast snowy peaks in the distance were like mirages. Did you know, he said lazily, taking down my hair, that Alexander the Great thought that if he reached the Khyber Pass, he'd see to the end of the world? He came here with all his poets and engineers, scientists and surveyors, to measure each step from Greece to the end of the world. We called him Sikander, and he was considered a great god. Think of it, his soldiers following him for eight years, epic marching in a brutal landscape, the two greatest civilizations clashing, India going under his wave. But in the end the resistance stunned him. He couldn't get further than Delhi. He'd flown too close to the sun, and for the first time his army refused to go any further. Many of them stayed, of course, settling in Afghanistan and Kashmir, adding some gold to our dark. It's a good combination, Greek and Indian. I probably have some in me, along with all the rest.

But your eyes are green, not blue.

Let's be grateful yours are brown.

My eyes were enmeshed in the garden. How is it, I asked, that I've never caught sight of a mali in all the days I've been here? There must be scores of them, undergardeners and weeders by the dozen.

They weed by moonlight.

I hear the night watchman doing his rounds at midnight, so I know at least he exists. They all whistle like birds; it was the same at my bungalow.

I don't like to think of you there, of you ever being there again.

I sat up from my position on the floor. Where should I go then?

Well, perhaps we should take a trip to Kashmir and see if you'd like it there. There isn't the same jagged divide, the same squalor and poverty, the things that make you so squeamish. He tossed me an ironic but tender smile. It's a wealthy state and very beautiful. And Kashmir's not occupied territory, so it feels as it must have in the days of the Mughal Empire. The lakes are frozen solid in winter, and everything stops, and then when the thaw comes, the shikaras return, and the ferrymen, carting goats and vegetables back and forth, passing the English houseboats, and the raja's palaces on the shore. It's not the real India, of course, but it's an illusion that seems to remain, whatever occupation's going on around it.

IT WAS THE END of another lazy day, and we were in the garden room. It's an odd room, with its vaulted ceiling and panoramic frescoes of the Alps, though why one should want such a view with the Himalayas right outside the window was beyond me. I'd picked a huge bunch of roses, yellow and pink, with sprays of dark blue flowers threaded in, and they sat on a high, carved table. There were narrow chaises with curved arms, but we tended to sit on the rug, books spread around us, tea cold, and drift off to sleep because it was too far to the bed. Sometimes Sam would play Beethoven or Bach on the phonograph, and other times he'd dance with me, playing American records with strange music that I loved but didn't quite understand— moony sad tunes, with lots of saxophone and trumpet, strings and horns all jiggled up with a tinkling kind of piano. Nigger jazz, he called it. There was a touch of sullenness in the air, and sometimes, in the early morning or at night, there was dampness in the wind. It reminded me of being by the sea at Porthcawl, when the summer was coming to an end and the flowers had lost their splendor. Here they were still in full bloom, and every day I went out with a basket and brought it back loaded. Some kinds I knew, and some I didn't, but I arranged them together in tall vases. I felt close to Mother and home while I did it, and on each side of our bed I put little bunches of flowers, just as she'd have done. That world seemed so far away now that I wondered for a moment if I'd ever lived in it. I'd gone so far beyond thinking back, or trying to see myself as others might see me, that I couldn't imagine what Mother might say if I told her I'd fallen deeply in love with an Indian. I lived in the moment, knowing that before long Sam would have to go back. Before long the monsoon winds would blow and the whole imperial structure at Simla would vanish into thin air. The Viceroy's court would return to Delhi for the rest of the year, and our little raft of love would be gone with the wind.

WE FELL ASLEEP in a state of disarray. I remember waking to the far-off sound of the grandfather clock in the hallway. Once I thought I heard something but immediately fell asleep again. When next I woke, Sam was curled into my shoulder, and the room had a pearly gloom to it. The sun was down, and the air coming in from the flagged terrace was cool. A sound from the garden startled me. I carefully separated myself out from Sam and listened. Footsteps were coming from the outside, clicking along the stone of the terrace, turning the corner, coming closer. When I looked up, I saw a soldier standing just outside the French windows. For a terrifying moment I thought it was Neville, but the man was too tall. He was looking at me with a strange, impassive half smile, impossible to decipher. He was in full drill, his topi on his head, his arms stiffly by his side. He didn't walk into the room but just stayed where he was, silently watching us, staring down at me with no expression on his face. I pulled the quilt closer to me and for a moment thought of covering Sam with it, but it was too late for that.

I was wearing Sam's salwar kameez, and the cloth was all crumpled up. I pulled the top down, and shook Sam, hard. He sat up. The officer stayed where he was for a moment, but when he saw that we were awake, he removed the topi and tucked it under his arm. Without coming into the room, and from the French doors, he said: All the doors, sir, were locked, and I took the liberty of coming round to the garden. As we both clambered to our feet, he continued to watch us. He spoke stiffly: Please excuse the intrusion. I'm Major Turner. Colonel Pendleton gave me instructions to contact you at all costs. He made a small bow in my direction, and in that moment, I saw the first trace of emotion: It was part shock, part disgust. Slowly Sam reached his hand over and took mine. Allow me, he said, to introduce you to my friend, Miss Herbert, who's just come from Cairo. The major bowed slightly and looked away. Sam took a cigarette from the box on the table and offered the box to me and then to the officer. I took one, but the officer did not. Won't you sit down, Sam said, pointing to a chair, and would you care for a drink? Major Turner didn't sit down, but he put his topi on the table for a moment, to get some papers out of his pocket. There's been a very unfortunate incident, he said, outside Pindi. A train, carrying Hindu women and children was set on fire in the early morning of the twenty-fifth. All those trying to escape were cut to pieces.

Sam flinched. How many deaths?

Over two hundred—mostly women and children—with hundreds of serious injuries.

Who was responsible? Sam asked.

Muslim militants have claimed responsibility.

Sam sat down, as did I, and the major followed suit. I'd be grateful for the details, Sam said.

Well, as far as we can tell, the train came to a halt just outside Pindi station, close to a Muslim slum, where there have been a few other incidents lately. The train was hijacked. Some sort of religious incident erupted, and stones crashed through the windows. Soon afterwards several carriages at the front went up in flames, and anyone trying to escape was forced back into the train and burned alive. Police investigators say gallons of petrol were poured in through the windows. There was no possibility of rescuing anyone in the first ten carriages. By nightfall a Hindu mob retaliated, committing acts of unspeakable savagery. Hard to see which side is more barbaric.

Unfortunately, Sam said coldly, all sides resort to the same tactics at moments like this. You will, I'm sure, not have forgotten the British barbarity at Amritsar?

Quite so, said the major, looking down. I should tell you, he said quickly, that this incident has been further complicated. A small regiment of the British Army, for reasons not yet ascertained, became involved with the hostilities. There seems to have been a question as to which side the British Army was on. Several British soldiers were beheaded. There's some fear that this could develop into an insurrection. He stopped for a moment. The details are in the communication. I have orders to accompany you to Rawalpindi at your earliest convenience. I have transportation outside.

For a moment Sam sat very still, with the cigarette smoke coiling up between his fingers. Perhaps I should see the communication, he said. He read it silently and then put it aside. His face was grave. He asked a few more questions and got more figures, which revealed that in the final count, Muslims had overwhelmingly been the victims of the violence. The police's part in the affair, as well as the army's, appeared very murky. Sam folded the communication and handed it back. Perhaps you could give us some time, he said. The major got swiftly to his feet and moved to the door. He disappeared into the darkness.

The two of us walked calmly out of the garden room but collapsed the minute we got back to the bedroom. Sam was stiff and silent, and I felt dizzy with dread. We looked at each other. I was shaking. We were both white. He sat down abruptly, his head in his hands. Shocked and afraid, I crouched down in front of him and held on to his knees. Do you think he believed that I'm a visitor from Cairo?

Not a chance, he said tersely. He'll try to locate who you are among the officers' wives, and when he can't, there are other ways of finding out who you are. I sat next to him on the bed. It all depends on Pendleton, he said. He could hush it up, but he won't do that unless there's an advantage in it for him and for the army. He's a decent man, and he likes me, but he'd sacrifice me in a shot if I wasn't willing to cooperate. He smiled bitterly and said: My old man has something to do with all this. It's why Pendleton wants to see me. There's a lot you don't know about my father's political activities, and there's a lot I don't want to know about them, but he's involved; it's his neck of the woods.

Suddenly he turned to me, and he seemed rather calm. He lit two cigarettes and handed one to me. Did Turner say anything to you—before I woke up?

Not a word. He barely reacted. You'd think he was on parade. It was only later that I caught a flicker of something in his eyes. Mockery, distaste, something like that. But he was very careful with you, I thought.

He's just following orders. I don't know anything about him, but I don't think he'd take the risk of blabbing about this, but the British communicate so obliquely. A remark would be enough.

Do you have to go? I suddenly had a powerful sense of unease, of some mystery unfolding.

I don't want to go, he said, finally. But I think the worst thing to do right now would be not to go. What do you think?

I agree.

He looked at me seriously: Do you want me to stay? Because if you do, I will.

Was I at this moment hoping for a grand gesture, a surrender to the moment, to the personal over the public? Did I want him to nip back to the major and say: Sorry, old chap, I'm staying put? I certainly did.

You should go, I said.

What about you? What will you do once I've gone?

Suddenly I was calm too. The future was the present. It was done. I'll go back to Simla, I said. I don't think I can go back to Ferozepore now. I don't know what I'll do exactly. I need to think. Will you be all right? I asked nervously.

I'll be fine. But we might as well accept that our cover is blown. He took my hand. I don't think it will affect you immediately. The

British, he said dryly, don't tend to actually stone adulterers, but their methods are equally deadly. I'm not worried about my personal situation. I'm compromised, but not politically and professionally. The awful thing is that what happened at Pindi will turn into something even more tragic than the burning of the train. There'll be rioting. The British will try to suppress Congress, Gandhi will get involved, and he'll probably end up in jail. Nehru will have his say. There'll be more deaths. He got up and began pacing around. I really don't know what Pendleton wants from me. He's asking for my counsel, and no more, but he knows that my father has a lot of control in Jammu and Peshawar, and, he said sarcastically, he thinks I'm more amenable than the old man.

But you're a doctor, I said. You're not involved in all this political stuff, or are you?

There's no separation between the two, he said. I've been walking a fine line, but I'm going to have to make a decision one way or the other. He got up and began throwing some clothes into a bag but then suddenly stopped, and sat down on the bed. You, he said softly, need to stay calm and not worry about me. I'll have some time to see what kind of man the major is on the journey. I'll find a way, if I can, of shutting him up. If not, it will be all right. He sat with his right thigh close to my left, just as it was when we made love. I'm not going to leave you, he said, tucking a strand of my hair behind my ear, or have you locked in an attic. Nor will I abandon you to the rage of your husband. You're the love of my life. I'll come back and get you, and we'll sort out what to do next. Just stay in Simla. That way I'll be able to find you. You can leave messages here for me if you like. He reached over to a table and grabbed an envelope. Let me write down some addresses for you. You can reach me at any of these places, he said, picking up a pen and writing quickly. Did those people give you a box number I could write to in Simla?

I wrote it down for him, and he stuffed the scrap of paper in his leather bag.

Don't go tonight, or if you leave, let me know where you are. I'll write when I get to Pindi, and I promise I won't be long.

I had a terrible foreboding, but it wasn't about me. Before he walked out of the door, he kissed me very slowly, and then, with his lovely mocking smile, he said: I suggest you reacquaint yourself with *Othello*.

PART TWO

Ten

We were in Simla, Joseph and I. He was bringing up a bucket of water from the well, and I was looking down into the darkness. There was a smell of iron, which reminded me of the mineral waters in Bath and Tunbridge Wells. We'd been scrapping. Joseph wanted us to get out of Simla immediately: Mem, for you there is the habit of going beyond not auspicious to brink of downright dangerous. I waved him off: I'm waiting, Joseph. He paused and put his foot down on the rope to steady it. For what is mem waiting? I wanted to come clean with him about Sam, but I couldn't, so I mumbled: I'm waiting for someone, Joseph. Without looking at me, he muttered: Someone is not coming, mem. How do you *know*? I wailed. His mouth gave its side shuffle, and precisely because I find his prescience so irritating, I said: I should have told you about this a long time ago, Joseph, but I want you to know that the person I am waiting for is Dr. Singh. His hands moved one over the other until he'd hauled the bucket over the rim of the well. He set it down on the ground, brimming, then turned to look at me, dark eyes shining with anger and pain: Does memsahib think that I do not know what it is to love a woman?

WE LEFT the minute the telegram came: *Isabel: Meet me in Jammu on Friday 20th. Take the night train from Simla via Pathankot. It arrives at midnight. Please be on that train. Things here terrible beyond words. S.*

When I saw him from the window of the train, he was taut and lean, stripped down and dark. I wondered if he was in some way decolonizing himself because now he blended in with the mob on the platform. I'd never seen that before—not when he walked across the barrack grounds after the shots went off, or when he wore a salwar kameez or ate with his fingers off a banana leaf. He was Indian now. When I got down from the train and when he came toward me, his eyes smiled quickly, with relief and a sudden blurt of love. But then the lights went down, and shadows pushed his eyes back into his sockets. His skin was gray, not gold, and something about the silty color was horrible. He was scanning my face, and then, while I hesitated, knowing I shouldn't kiss him but wanting to, knowing I shouldn't touch him, even though I wanted to hurl myself at him, I was left standing there, not knowing what to do. I hoped he'd at least take my hand and tuck it under his elbow the way he used to, but he raised his hands and barely folded them together and bowed his head slightly. I did the same. His fingernails were black, and his hands were bruised and torn.

We walked quickly along the platform, not speaking. He helped me into a car, an older, less flamboyant one than the blue, and I even wondered for a moment if it would actually manage the long drive to Srinagar. He drove expertly through the press of rickshaws, bullock carts, cows, and taxis. The sky had cleared, and the mountains towered against a deeper darkness. I'd seen the blue mountains from the train, and a glimpse of Ladakh covered in snow, but then the clouds came down, and I didn't see the peaks again. He told me only that we were going to a houseboat, off the tourist track, at the northern end of Dal Lake. He wondered if I would want to sleep. Had the train journey been terrible? Had I been bothered? Where had I changed into my sari? Ludicrous questions, and then not a word more. Even the way he drove was circuitous, avoiding the main road but then driving so fast on hairpin bends that my heart banged up against my ribs. I asked him if he was trying to kill us both; he looked startled and slowed down immediately.

It was still dark when we reached Srinagar. We sped down alleyways and skirted the boulevards and the grand Victorian hotels illuminated by moonlight. I saw flashes of water or a lit window, caught a snatch of music or quick, stunning glimpses of the mountains, radiant at their peaks, but it was like a dream. The images in my head were of fire, not ice, screams, not symphonies. As dawn rushed in, I could make out the Jhelum River, with its spangled bridges, the fishing boats, the nets of water lilies made visible by first light. As we passed through Dal Gate, the city was coming to life, the bazaar filling with porters and vendors constructing stalls out of wooden crates and draped fabrics. Tiny shops were piled high with copper pots and silverware; rows of carpet weavers and shawl sellers chatted together, drinking coffee among embroidered silks, parasols, and red tasseled cushions. Old women smoked hookahs, and a few boys played cricket in an alleyway. Animals strolled about, and the drains were heavy from the rains.

We took a shikara at Dal Gate. Everything in me slowed as the boat made its dreamy way through old Srinagar, past the mosques and the grand lakeside houses, their balconies smothered in roses. Sam said very little. Occasionally he'd point something out in that clipped way he sometimes has: That's Turko-Afghan. Those bridges are five hundred years old. That mosque, the one with the minaret, inside there's a sacred hair of the Prophet Muhammad. Or he'd turn and say: That's Hari Parbat Fort; the wall around the hill was built in the sixteenth century by Emperor Akbar. I'll take you to see it one day. I was grateful for the future tense, because when he's this way, there's no telling if there'll even be a one day. Sometimes he was almost formal: By the way, do you ski? Normally, I'd have whopped him with a snooty remark of my own, not only because of course I know how to ski but also because it infuriates me when he makes his cultural forays into the antiquity and grandeur of India's past. I'd done my reading on the train, thank you, and I'd managed to wade through the history sufficiently to sort out the Buddhists and Hindus, the Sikhs and Sufis, not to mention the Mauryas, the Aryans, and the Guptas and the Mughals. I didn't need his instruction at this particular moment, but I didn't say a word because of the tension between us. It grew with every mile, and it was far from sexual, hard to pinpoint, impossible to break, as we drifted down toward the lake, winding past apiaries, floating gardens and lotus beds, tiny hotels half hidden by tall reeds, and houseboats that could accommodate a queen's retinue. And not a word from his lordship all the while. I seriously began to wonder if he'd decided to bring me to this place of unparalleled beauty just so he could tell me the whole thing was off.

I tried to forget him. *The Rainbow comes and goes, / And lovely is the Rose . . . / But yet I know, where'er I go, / That there hath passed away a glory from the earth.* The sun drew out the walnut and almond trees. Small, dark-skinned people were at work in wide saffron fields; children climbed trees in the orchards; bullock carts, piled high with vegetables, lumbered up the hills. I stopped looking in his direction and gave up trying to read his thoughts. Vineyards and rice paddies nestled between sycamore and cedar trees. Heavy pine forests flanked the lower slopes of the mountains. I was locked in the moment, enraptured, free: *There is only now.* Pir Panjal rose abruptly from the valley, and the Great Himalayas rose up in the north, snow-covered and a little frightening. My senses were fully awake: summer gardens built on graceful terraces, the scent of jasmine and roses wafting across the water, giant chinar trees studding the hills like cloves in an onion. The breezes were cool and tolerant, as the people of Kashmir are said to be. Even the heat was comfortable. But for all of it, my lover remained so silent and so sad that I couldn't find him. Now and then he'd reach across and hold my hand or touch my cheek, but words were useless, speech too treacherous. My heart began slowly to sink into the fathomless deeps of desertion, abandonment, and loss.

HE'D STILL NOT TOUCHED THE SUBJECT of what had happened after he'd left me to go to Rawalpindi. And I was so willing an accomplice in the silence that I left him in his aloofness and dreamed instead of making love to him in the spice gardens. Would the saffron make his skin golden again, would the cinnamon melt his heart? If we swam among the lotus blossoms, would our limbs tangle and our bodies join again, would his right thigh cover my left? Would he talk to me when we made love the way he always did, or would the silence keep going until we both fell off the end of it?

He'd rented a small houseboat, tucked back into the reeds and bulrushes, with old cedars and willows on the shore behind it. The only approach was by water. There was endless shade, as in Simla, and it was so different from the plains: high, dark-topped trees, tea green shadows with bright birds wheeling through patches of light. In the middle of the lake a man sat perched on the tip of his wooden boat, saying his prayers; a pregnant woman, her knees spread, poled her way through the water, with a cargo of lotus leaves at her back, and a red scarf covering her head. Ducks flew over the quiet waters, and a crane shot up from the bank, looking, from the distance, like a rolled umbrella. It was fertile and lush, brimming over with everything human and good; you could feel it in the breeze and the sunshine, and the smiles on people's faces.

When he said he'd been staying at the houseboat for two days and had spoken to no one, I asked him if I was an intrusion. He was startled: Of course not. Why would you say that? I glared at him: You should know. How can you be a doctor and not have a sense of how your coldness affects people? He said: I'm not that way with my patients. I can't be. I thought you understood me. I looked at him in astonishment: Sam, I know *nothing*, not a thing. How can I understand when you haven't told me a word of what's happened to you since the major came and dragged you off to Pindi? Now, I can of course read newspapers, and I know what happened there. But that's all I know.

By the time we drew up to the side of the boat, his face was ashen. He helped me up onto the deck and threw up my rolled bag and almost, for a moment, lost his balance. I watched him with fear, not understanding him, not knowing if I'd said terrible things that couldn't be unsaid. The deck jutted out into the water, and the roof and shutters were latticed so the sun spilled through in checkered patterns. Most of the roof had become tangled up with wild roses, ivy, and honeysuckle so that you only caught glimpses of the wood. I went straight inside. It looked as if he'd lived there all his life. His battered doctor's bag was stuffed to the gills, and some of his papers and instruments were scattered on the floor. It broke my heart. In Ferozepore and Simla I'd come into a room, and his bag would seem to have arrived before him, sitting obediently just inside the door, while he went to scrub his hands. When I wasn't with him, I thought of myself as his bag, or the watch on his wrist, or his slippers as they walked him to his bed.

The sitting room was spare. Two plantation chairs on either side of a stove, an armchair with a cushion, a table cluttered with newspapers, a stack of Gold Leaf cigarette packs. The kitchen was a slip of a room, barely big enough for one, which would suit him as he liked to cook alone. Next to a Primus stove with two rings was a pile of peppers, chilies, onions, and aubergines. A bottle of brandy, half empty, or half full. A scalpel next to the garlic. A bowl of plums. A small bag of tea. A bag of rice. Another of Turkish pistachios. Rimbaud facedown in the wilting coriander. It took me less than a minute to take all this in, and then I waited for him to come in from the deck. But he didn't.

He was smoking in a corner of the deck, so much in shadow that he'd almost disappeared. For a moment I wanted to shake him, but I took control of myself. I went up and crouched in front of him, my hands on his knees: What on earth's the matter? I can't go on like this with you. He leaned forward and grabbed me so hard I thought my bones would crack. His body shook as if it'd been taken over by wind or the tail of a hurricane. He wasn't crying. I waited a long time, holding him until his body went quiet. He drew back into the chair, and for a moment I could have sworn that his eyes were no longer green. His eyelashes were like black scythes all in a row, his mouth a dark line. His voice shook: In my first years back in India, when I was working with the poor, sawing off a leg, holding a melted face in my hands, stitching women half hacked to death by demons, or children cut into pieces . . . it was like being in the Dark Ages . . . and I didn't know how to take it. Since then I've thought nothing would shock or pierce me to the heart again. And then you. And then this. He drifted and was silent a long time and then, almost inaudibly, said: Nalini is dead.

I was so shocked that for a moment I couldn't find anyone to join the name.

Your wife? I stammered. Do you mean your wife? He moved his head from side to side, which means yes. His hand half covered his mouth: They'd been laid out together, he said, those from the train and those from the rioting. The bodies were all piled up together . . .

Don't talk about it, I said . . . not now . . . I wanted it left the way it was in my mind. I'd read the reports in the paper. I wanted to go on seeing it that way. I couldn't get any closer to it at that moment because if I did, I'd be no good to him. He'd given me her name, and soon I might see her face, or the details of her death, and I'd be plunged into a pit of guilt and terror of my own. I had to see if I could bring him back because he was still with the dead. I knelt and took his hands; he was cold and shivering, in shock, exhausted, and I wanted to tend to him, save him, reconstruct him—do for him what he'd done for me in my bed in Ferozepore when the malaria had scorched and filthied me and he'd washed me clean. How could I do this when I was part of the blame? How could I ask him to speak and then silence him?

The bedroom was set back among the trees, and the only piece of furniture was a camelback wooden frame bed close to the floor, with white pillows and a blue Kashmiri quilt. I wrapped him in the quilt and curled up beside him. I wouldn't get into the quilt with him unless he asked me, but when he reached for me, I took off my clothes and lay next to him. And then I took off his and curled myself around him. There was nothing erotic about it. I was like a doctor, trying to bring warmth to a body in a state of extremity. He was still freezing, and in the darkness of the room his skin looked white and vulnerable. I felt that no one had physically loved him, or caressed or held him, or soothed him, and I knew from before, as if from another life, that death has to couple with life, with sex, immediately, so the darkness is lifted and life can continue.

He enters love with a gasp, like a swimmer diving into deep water, and then it's as if he swims underwater into the deep reaches of a cave without seeming to breathe at all. This is where I recover him— in his breathing when we're making love. I know him intimately from his breath, which says: Listen and you'll know who I am. When he surfaces, he lets his breath go like someone who's held it a very long time, and his whole body shudders. His breathing has a rhythm I can follow, as it comes and goes until it's sharp and hard. I move so closely with him that I feel his breath on my skin, and sometimes in it I hear a word, an endearment, an astonishment. With my hands at his back, I wait for the deeper sound of his breath after we've loved each other to exhaustion. And then he sleeps like a child in the hollow of my shoulder.

Eleven

It took months to fit the pieces together about the train burning at Pindi. I'd heard and read the British version, but of course it didn't bother with the names of the Indian dead. It was being called the Chili Field Incident, and there was a presumption that it had been a Muslim uprising against Hindus, followed by a horrific retaliation in the classic mode: eye for an eye, life for a life. A long article in *The Times* had appeared, and I remembered some snippets of it—something about a man in a black turban riding a bicycle beside the train as it slowed to take the last bend before Rawalpindi. Behind him was an open field, and beyond that the trees; in the paddy terraces, men worked knee-deep in green earth and sunlight. Close to the track was a chili field on which women crouched, sorting through a swarm of crimson pods spread thickly on the ground to dry. The train had just passed the chili field when the man on the bicycle threw himself on the tracks, causing the train to come to a shrieking halt.

It was our first night on the houseboat. Sam suddenly woke from a nightmare, his head in his hands, shaking all over. I tried to get him to tell me what he'd dreamed, but he couldn't. It took him a long time to tell me what he'd been told by his aunt, who was one of only two survivors. He spoke in a dazed, flat voice as if he were relating facts about someone else's life; it was clinical and precise, miles from feeling. It seemed that his wife's family—in all, fifteen women and ten children—had left the hill station at Mussourie to travel to Rawalpindi for a family wedding. There was a week for everyone to get to the wedding before the festivities started, and other family members were to join the train along the way. The wedding party had waited for a few hours at Lahore to board the train. When the first announcement came, they got up from the floor, rolled their mats, and made a bee-line to their gate. They'd reserved plenty of carriages, from R14 to R20, so that the servants could take the kids off their hands while they speculated on how much the wedding would cost. It was to be a grand affair. Sam's first cousin, who came from the hills around Um-balla, was marrying a girl from Rawalpindi.

As the train took the last bend before entering Rawalpindi, it jerked and screeched to a halt. A smell of scorched iron and steam filled the morning air as the rocking continued all the way down the line. The noise and vibrations brought sleepy passengers to the windows to find out what was going on. They watched as a stream of men came around the side of the paddy fields and were joined by others, moving around to the channels that ran in front of the paddy, walking toward the track that ran parallel to the railway line. Others came down the side of the chili field, but these were not workers because these men were carrying stakes, scythes and long knives, and tin cans that sloshed as they walked. At the moment when panic broke out in the carriage, the men let out bloodcurdling screams and ran full tilt at the train, where the people at the windows of the train began the stampede to the doors.

Rocks came crashing through the windows of the first carriages. In compartment R20 screaming mothers ran to R14 and R15, where children were crowded together on seats, and two babies were nestled together on blankets on the floor. It was 6:34 A.M. Nalini was the first to run out of the women's compartment. She sped down the corridor, picked up one of the smaller children, and slung her onto her hip, grabbing another by the arm. Auntie and her daughter snatched up two small boys, hoisted one on each hip, and followed. In the corridors rumors were circulating that a demonstration against the British was about to begin; a darker speculation said this was a Muslim mob from the village across the way and that Jafri, a terrorist who was behind a massacre some months before, was leading the mob outside. Some British bigwigs were in the front of the train, and some members of the Hindu Council, who were traveling up for a conference. There was also a small contingent of soldiers. Just as Nalini got to the door with the children, stones crashed through it. She ducked and ran quickly down toward the next door. Sticks wrapped in muslin and doused with petrol came flying through windows on both sides of the train, setting the floors on fire. A flaming rag soared into compartment R14, and landed on the seats. They caught fire in a second. One of the women tried to save a basket of orchids and white lilies. A child started screaming because the wings of the peacocks had caught fire. A rocket of fire landed on the luggage shelf, and baskets of mangoes, figs, and pomegranates pelted the cowering women before they ran out into the corridor, screaming, pulling their shifts around their bodies, snatching up shawls and silk coats to cover their skin. The carriage was rocking; windows shattered and blew in, spraying fragments of glass into the women's faces. The doors were jammed shut from the outside, and anyone who made it to the ground was cut to pieces or doused with petrol and burned alive. Auntie's last glimpse of Nalini was of her running, a child on each hip, away from a sheet of fire. Some of the passengers managed to get off the train, Auntie and her daughter and the two boys among them. They ran out across the fields, carrying children and babies, trying to get to the trees. Halfway across the field most of them fell flat on their faces, arms up, backs riddled with bullets, as close to the train, soldiers kept their fire coming.

Afterward it was impossible to say why those particular carriages had been targeted, or whether it was the British or the Hindus who were under attack that morning. There was also the question as to whether the British had had a hand in it because of the benefit received from Hindu-Muslim conflict, but the papers didn't dwell on this. Others sighed and said that the tragic history of the Hindus and Muslims had been present since the thirteenth century and would no doubt continue till the twenty-first. There was confusion about who had attacked whom, and where the mob had come from, and at whom the soldiers thought they were shooting in the field where forty women and children lay dead. Over two hundred bodies were collected and brought to a warehouse close to the railway station, piled so closely and burned so piteously that it was often impossible to say who was who, and of what caste or creed. And because British policemen had loaded the bodies and laid them out in the warehouse, head to toe, a Muslim hand touching a Hindu ankle, it was only later that outraged families came to separate, remove and cleanse, and bring back to order and decency what had been desecrated by the hideous ignorance of the Feringhi.

In the Muslim village close to the train line, the avenging of the dead began. A Hindu mob gathered in the late morning, and by the afternoon more than five hundred men had assembled, armed with stones, homemade bombs, and knives. They surrounded and tore into the village, burning shops and houses to the ground. As women and children ran out of their burning houses, they were skewered on swords; girls were raped, doused with petrol, and set on fire. Eight Muslim boys were beheaded. Four British soldiers were beheaded. Then the looting and pillaging began. And by the time the police arrived, having waited for reinforcements that never came, there was only dense smoke, the smell of burned human flesh and animal fur, and the stench of melted rubber and chicken feathers. Every piece of what had once been home had been burned and trampled into the ground. Three hundred people were dead, and every doctor and nurse in the vicinity was brought to Rawalpindi to set up hospitals in the fields.

Much later, in the twilight, the police came across a man, presumed to be the leader of the Muslim mob, who was standing like a scarecrow in the chili field across the way from the scorched village. When they got closer, they saw that his hair had been set on fire, and his feet nailed to the ground with carpenter's nails. He'd been standing that way overnight, and as the police approached him, he suddenly toppled backward onto the crushed chilies as his feet gave way beneath him.

The next day a small man wearing a dhoti and steel-rimmed glasses sat close to the chili field with his knees up, staring at the gutted train. He stayed there all day, speaking to no one, waving people away with a flip of his wrist. In the evening, when people gathered under the trees to hear him speak, he said two things: It is time for the British to leave India. It is also time for us to remove untouchability from our hearts and minds.

Twelve

We woke with the first premonition of monsoon; the mountains were wrapped in mist, and the trees swept by night rain. I wanted the rain to carry us over the land and out to sea. I'd barely slept all night, drenched in sweat, almost feverish with fear. Water was the only safe and clean element; I wanted to immerse myself in a lunar world, drown in waves, and be washed up on a tranquil shore. I needed to be forgiven, but who could forgive me? I watched Sam a long time as he slept. It was cold in the bedroom, and I put on one of his shirts; it was creased and worn, rather as he now seemed to be. I sat cross-legged on the bed for a while and then got up and made a fire in a small Victorian fireplace; it was drawing nicely, making a soft crackle. When he's asleep, he's unfathomable to me; it's as if the book were closed, the painting covered. It made me aware of how well I thought I knew him, before we were separated at Simla, before his wife died. I had no inkling of who he was now.

His hand was out of the sheet, small-boned and long-fingered.

His fingers were blackened around the edges, the nails torn, as if he'd been digging in the earth or in ash. When I asked him what had happened to his hands, he answered another way. It was the first time, he said, in a field hospital, that I'd seen Muslims and Hindus working together like that. My mother came and brought half the nurses from the purdah hospital. It was so appalling that it was beyond religion, everyone was untouchable, and no one was. In the end, I suppose, we were just Indians.

When he'd first woken, I could tell that he'd forgotten what had happened and didn't even know where he was, because he reached out to me with simple pleasure. Then he fell back into confusion and sadness. I got him a cup of tea and sat close to him as he pulled himself up to drink it. I leaned over and kissed his face. Guilt was attaching itself to us like a parasite, and I wanted to yank it off. Do you think we've done something terrible?

Like what?

Killed your wife by half wanting it. I did half want it, sometimes, out of sheer longing for you. And now I feel so utterly sorry.

He pulled back into the pillows. That's magical thinking, he said.

But did you ever wish it?

I had in mind a painless death.

You didn't say.

Nor did you. But if thinking does have any power, our thoughts chose the wrong target.

We'd reached that place, and it happened quickly, where it was too painful to talk. It kept on raining. He slept for twenty-eight hours nonstop. When he woke again, his energy had returned, and he could keep it for short bursts. Sometimes he talked about what had happened at Pindi, but only about the injuries, the rioting—the politics. He didn't talk about his wife again, or the future, and something about his stillness and withdrawal made me stop asking questions. He was fractured, and only time would put him together. Often when he'd start to tell me something, his voice would crack and he'd say:

I'm sorry, I'm sorry. He said it in such an English way that it was heart-wrenching. Once he looked out at the water and said: I'm falling apart.

Sometimes we had to eat, and he'd go off into the tiny kitchen and make vegetable korma, or brinjal and potatoes, and we'd eat sitting on the bed, leaning over the sides for bottles of water or beer. Soon, since we never left the houseboat, we were down to rice and curds. He'd mix them together and chuck in a handful of spices and the last of the coriander to cheer it up. Every morning he'd go down to the lake and walk down into the water for a few minutes and swim a few yards, his arms gleaming in the sunshine, only the blackness of his head cutting through the clear water. He went in not to bathe, but just to be in it, part of its flow, walking out into the deep water until he was submerged and then floating on his back. I couldn't go in. The water was perishing cold, it was just melted mountain ice, and my skin wasn't used to the extremes. I'd wait for him on the bank with a towel, and he'd yell: Come in, it's not that bad, really. Well, actually it is, but nothing's better than getting out of it. His voice would echo over the water, the lofty English vowels, the lovely inflections of education and ease emerging out of a face grown haggard for the price of the privilege.

He sat down on the bank with me, shivering. His hand was a block of ice. And then, by an act of will, he stopped shivering—just like that. He said: I've been thinking about what you said, about going to the medical school at Delhi. We desperately need medical women, and not just to attend women. I was never sure, when you talked about it before, whether you really meant it, so I didn't want to push it. But we're short of women doctors; very few came out during the war. You'd be a great doctor, he said, shivering just once and moving closer to me in my dry warmth. You have the heart for it. My mother says there are a number of women's hospitals run entirely by women, and Indian women have been training for years. He put an arm around me. It may not be as hard as you think. He added shyly:

In Pindi I spoke to my mother about you, and she said she'd be happy to help you with a clinical placement when the time comes.

We walked back together in the clouded sunlight and sat on the deck, drinking scalding coffee. He boiled buckets of water for me and washed my hair with lavender soap, and I sat in the sun to dry it. His nails were healing, but I now knew that the blackened skin around them was deeply burned, and parts of his nails had melted. I had a premonition that I was seeing the beginning of a complete physical change in him, a breakdown of his body as well as his mind. One night, as we were lying in bed, he reached under his pillow and brought out two long strands of small pale pink pearls. These, he said, belonged to my mother's mother. I'd like you to have them. He scooped up my hair with one hand, baring my neck, and wreathed them over my head; they trickled down my throat and between my breasts, and I shuddered for a moment. I looked at them, turned and touched them; they had exquisite clasps, rubies surrounded by diamonds, delicately set in white gold. I stared at him, and he said: You're right, they were hers, but she never wore them, which is why they're a little sick. If you wear them, they'll get better. I put my hand up to take them off, and his hand came down to keep them on: Don't think that way. I want you to have them. She had them as part of the marriage settlement, and the only reason I have them now is that I was going to take them to someone in Simla who mends sick pearls. I of course had never heard of sick pearls. Just leave them on for the night, he said. Do it for me. He was trying to move beyond, so I kept them on. They lay on my throat like velvet or fur, and I refused to let them be sinister or sad.

THE MORNING IT STOPPED RAINING we went out for a drive and ended up on a long, straight road of poplars. It's like being in France, he said, instantly cheerful. On one side was a small village hidden among trees, with an English graveyard above it. He glanced at it and said: Whatever they died of will have drained directly into the water supply of the village below. It's how so much European disease came to India. White bulls with painted horns drifted among the sycamores, and he began to tell me about how as a small boy he'd gone fishing and duck shooting on the lake, swimming in pools with maharajas' sons, playing with marbles made of turquoise and amber. There was a boy, he said, who got caught in the nets . . . and then suddenly he began sobbing, his right hand covering his face. He stopped the car and put his head down on the steering wheel and, without looking up, said: It's the exhaustion, please don't be concerned, it's just the exhaustion.

I couldn't reach for him because my mind was crouching in front of an image: Sam going to identify his wife and being able to know it was her only by the amulet around her neck, which he'd given her on their wedding day.

Do you ever think of the war? And all the people who died? I asked him, because I found myself thinking that way again. He looked at me tenderly: Yes, I do think of them. And of the boy you were supposed to marry. Although, he added softly, you do know, don't you, that the only man you were supposed to marry was me?

He could recover in an astonishing way by *doing* something and was utterly at home in action. Why don't I, he said, teach you how to drive? Here, get out and come round to my side. We swapped places, and he sat beside me as I jerked and stalled the car, until finally I got it going. I drove faster and faster, and he lay back and closed his eyes, but came to life if I took a mountain turn too fast or it seemed that we might end up in the paddy field like the raja we'd passed a minute before, sitting on his roof, waving his ringed hands at us. Sam waved back and said: There are centuries of excess in that face, keep driving. When I came to the forest and slowed down, he began to kiss me, little kisses on the sides of my face, my cheeks, the edges of my eyes and then on my mouth, hard, with his hands under my clothes, until we veered off the side of the road and the car shuddered to a stop. We got

out and ran into the forest, scrambling over the pine branches to find
a bed among the little trees coming up out of the peat.

ONCE WE'D GONE OUT into the world, it was easier to do it again.
Each day we took a little drive, and I got better at it. I like the way,
he said, that you've become less savage with the gears. Sometimes
we'd race way up into the mountains, through the passes and tunnels,
looking down at a world of such beauty that there were no words for
it. Death seems such a little thing when you're up here, he said, unty-
ing the ribbon that held up my hair. I'm even coming to believe that
when we die, it's like waking up from a dream. Then he told me that
he wasn't going back to the asylum at Ranchi and would conduct the
research on shell shock without the British philanthropist's money.
I'm tired of the strings, he said. And I don't want to be a racial mi-
grant like my father, dealing with English businessmen who make us
approach them by the back stairs.

On one of our drives in the valley, he told me he'd met Gandhi
with his father at Pindi. I was surprised. I thought your father was involved with terrorism and guns and making money, I said; he doesn't
seem a Gandhi type.

Oh—he smiled—Gandhi has no contempt for money, just feels
it's not for personal use.

What does your father think of him?

Oh, only that saints are usually foolish. He smiled. And he sees
himself as a homegrown Indian, whereas Gandhi's not. He also thinks
that Gandhi's views are against history. For him, machines and factories are the way ahead, not hand pounding of rice and spinning. But
we certainly need him to get rid of the British.

I had an image of them all there in Pindi, performing their rituals,
tending to their dead. I saw him working in the field hospital. I saw
his mother among the women with her band of nurses. And I felt
such a sense of uselessness, of having nothing to contribute, no duty

or skill to offer. Sam believed, as much as his mother, in the sanctity of work. And whenever he spoke about his family, it was such a blow to my stomach that I almost doubled up. They were people to whom I could never be legitimately connected. I could never stand with his mother as part of a gathering of women; never talk to his dad about Gandhi and the British. Perhaps never be more than part of a nation who'd taken too much, killed too many, and stayed too long. When he saw I was sad, he said gently: You shouldn't have asked.

I know, but sometimes I have to.

A few days before he was to leave, I asked him outright: Where are you going when we leave here?

To England.

Of course, I said. You must go right away.

Thirteen

When he'd gone and I was alone again, I went back to white. I didn't like it; I lost so much freedom and became visible again in a way that horrified me, but Joseph was pleased: This is good, mem. Gadding on trains as Indian woman frightfully hazardous. Time to settle down. He was in charge again, an accomplice as much as a friend, and he felt entitled to protect me once Sam was out of the way. In Lahore, waiting for the train, on the way back to Ferozepore, he wanted to know my plans for the future. I was nervous to tell him, but after strolling aimlessly around the station, waiting for our connection, we ventured into the quieter section, where the waiting room had just a few Eurasian women, and I took the plunge: The plan, Joseph, is for me to train as a doctor. I was sure he'd give me that look of incomprehension that he saves for moments like this, but as so often, I was wrong. This is not strange, mem, he said quietly. I saw the emotion in his face: Mem should know that once I had a wife and she was very ill. A doctor memsahib took care of my wife's disease when no one else could help her. He stopped. And, I said, what was the result? He looked at me: Mem, result is of no matter, for in the end my wife did die. Important only that there was a woman to take the pain from my wife. He put his hands together and lowered his head: Great honor to serve, mem.

WE TRAVELED TO FEROZEPORE, Joseph and I, in our separate parts of the train and for a short while took up our domestic positions in the military lines once more. Bobajee was reinstalled, as was Gita, but on a weekly basis. I was nervous as a hen, feeling too close to Neville's turf. There were a few letters from him, which I barely read, except to note that his tone was becoming somewhat threatening. I couldn't approach him, even on paper. If ever I allowed my mind to fix on him, I thought of the Muslim girl. Now, as I looked around me at the other bungalows, it seemed this part of my life was over. I was anxious to get to Delhi. Sam would be on the seas for a month or so and then in England for as long as it took to bring his son back to India. He thought that Sammy should leave England and be with his family now that his mother was dead. I'd said to him: Will I be able to meet him one day? And he looked at me and smiled: Of course. I believed him, as I did when he said he would do anything to help me. When he was that way, so kind and so encouraging, offering a sense of protection, without ever interfering with my liberty or choice, it was hard to conjure up the side of him that could go off wandering on the moon. I'd said to him, when I was going through one of my periods of rationalization and self-deceit: It's the sexual part that made it wrong, I suppose. If it wasn't for that, there would be no infidelity, not really, I mean. He looked up and smiled. For me, he said, my marriage was the infidelity.

WHEN I KNEW HIS SHIP HAD SAILED, I looked myself in the eye and decided that my life must take off on its own if it was to intercept profitably with his in the future. I was afraid of loving him too much and collapsing myself into his future, whatever that might be. I was afraid of being pained by him, and I was terrified of dependence. Mother had ingrained on me so strongly that I must at all times have money of my own, but she'd never suggested that I could actually earn it myself. And now I thought I could. India had not set me free. Nor had love. Perhaps work was the thing.

Bridget was my first and only visitor in the short time I spent at Ferozepore. She came on a damp, gloomy day. She was jaunty as ever, but India was wearing her down. Her blond hair looked brittle and brassy, fine lines were moving in around her eyes and mouth, and her dress was too tight. I saw her more clearly now, but still with affection: thin dark brows beneath platinum coils of hair; scarlet lipstick, too thickly applied; gestures graceless but provocative. There was something beautiful and slutty about her at the same time. So, she said, you've turned up at last. Thanks for ditching me like that. Ever get to Simla? She was shoving piles of papers out of her way and gave my velvet bag a covetous stare. She adopted a plummy accent: Lots of rumors going around about you, my de-ah. I thought I knew what you were up to, in fact, I was dead certain that you'd be all chummed up with the sexy doc, but then I heard he'd been in Pindi dealing with all those lopped heads. She sat down on a chair piled high with clothes. Got a ciggy? I gave her one. So what can you tell me about Major Turner? She took a deep drag and put up her chin to exhale it, holding me by the eyeballs.

The name jolted me badly. Bridget, I said, could you stop firing questions and talk to me properly? I haven't the faintest idea who Major Turner is. She pulled up the skirt of her summer dress, exposing her lovely legs. He's the one with the rod up his backside, stiff little prick, thin mustache, yellow eyes. Not your type, I'd have thought, but who knows? Once I'd have thought a darky would never get within an inch of you . . . All right, you can take that look off your face . . . Anyways, as to the major . . . he was asking questions about you, and that of course made people think something was up, his wife having died of typhoid a year back. He said he'd seen you in Simla, and since no one else had, they presumed the two of you had a fling and you'd run out on him. He seemed all bitter and tight-lipped, and that was enough for the sharks.

I don't know Major Turner, I lied, even as I saw him standing in the darkened room, looking down at us, and saying to Sam: Please excuse the intrusion. I'm Major Turner.

Well, Bridget said, it's clear from the look on your face that there was nothing going on with the two of you. So cough it up, what've you been up to all this time? Quite hurt my feelings and all, not hearing a word from you. She put the cigarette out. I've not said a word, you know, about you and the doc. Hope you know that. When, after a prescient pause, I still gave her nothing, she said: Well, not to worry. Best to say nothing, safest all round, I'd say. Things are right messy at the moment, so you could get into plenty of hot water, and we wouldn't want that.

We talked for three hours, and in all that time I managed not to say a word about Sam. It took every minute of that time to convince her that I could go to Delhi and make a go of it there. So, she said, this is the upshot of it all then? I'm thinking you're having it off with the doc when in fact, you've decided to dump your old man and go off and *be* a doc. She poured herself another pink gin, very heavy on the gin. I'd say you could do it. You've got the education, and the cheek, and the brains. I'm all for it. Education and hard cash's the only way out. Here or in England, it's the same; we're just an afterthought of a sex, not much different, think of it, to being black. Get yourself settled in Delhi, and I'll come down and see you, and you can introduce me to the white docs.

EVERY DAY WE SPENT in Ferozepore increased Joseph's anxiety. I am hoping that mem will not shilly-shally again, he said. Concerning me now is the matter of sahib. Soon regiment will return from the frontier. Any minute now, before monsoon, soldiers come back to base.

The plan is for us to leave very soon, Joseph.

He beamed: This is assuredly right action, mem. I commend you.

That is, if you wish to accompany me. It is of course up to you. You're not bound in any way.

He put his palms together. Bound I am, mem, hand and foot. Let us make a dash for it tomorrow.

WE LEFT FEROZEPORE on a wet monsoon day in early June, when the sky was about to release an ocean of water onto the plains. Down it came, a barrage of water, day and night, unceasing. After forty-eight hours of sheeted rain, roads turned into rivers, and cliffs waterfalls. The little bungalows in Ferozepore filled to the brim and burst their thin shells. I thought of my lovely curtains sailing out of the windows and the red armchair leaving on the tide; my embroidered pillows and the mirror from Meerut bobbing along with Bobajee's pots and pans. I thought of the one-line letter I'd left my husband being whisked to the top of a tree. The face of the Muslim girl came up for a moment as the veranda went under a wave. And through it all, the islands kept on floating, rising higher, catching the debris of the floodwater, so that a child clutched a top branch, a broken chair slept on the sand. The heavy curtains of rain gave an impression that the world was dissolving into whirlpools of garbage and sewage, river currents rushing up and entering jungles on a voyage to nowhere. A river burst its banks, jumped the gate, climbed the stairs, and came to rest on the bed in which a family lay sleeping in the early-morning sun. A swan gazed down from an attic window. Rats crowded on the chimney pots, and millipedes attached themselves to telegraph poles. When the streets had turned to water and the hills to mud, villages collapsed and then vanished. Small huts and wooden shelters fell flat on their faces, crops drowned, the paddy fields disappeared, babies died in their sleep, and old people huddled on the roofs of the infirmary like wet birds. Those who could run headed up to the hills and watched the torrents down below, bringing trees and every kind of vehicle, cart, and rickshaw tumbling down the slopes. They saw upturned human bellies, pearly as fishes, riding the tide, eyes wide with wonder, traveling gently to God. Lightning bolts shattered the windows of the hospital in Lahore as a flood clogged with trees, carts, bullocks, cows, goats, and camels went roaring across the plains, stampeding to the sea. The instruments of the Lahore Orchestra sailed majestically on, moving from stream to stream and finally joining the swollen ranks of the Indus, before sailing into the Arabian Sea. A vast mango tree broke free of the water, crashed into a bank, and lay quivering on the ground like a shipwrecked boat. Days later, drowned jungle birds in its branches came back to life, the golden snakes shook out their coils and sidled down its sodden trunk, and books caught in the foliage fell to earth and flipped their pages in the sunshine once more.

WE GOT TO DELHI, Joseph and I, leaving the floods behind us. Now nothing was left of that old life apart from the lilac tree that I would not leave behind. The army stayed up in the hills to wait for the waters to subside; the wives and children went back to the Himalayas to dry out. In Delhi I'd intended to stay at the Grand Oriental Hotel, but it was being modernized, so remembering Sam's suggestion, I booked into Claridges on Aurangzeb Road. I gave my name as Miss Herbert, and to my amazement, the manager said a suite had been booked for me, and paid for, he added, with a discreet smile. I was staying in the best suite, and it had been specially prepared for my stay. A little flabbergasted, I was led to the lift and whisked away to my suite of rooms on the top floor, with a magnificent view of the seven citadels of the medieval period, and a clear view of the Qubt area, girdled by the walls of Lal Kot. Sam had given me this since he couldn't show me the city himself, and it touched me very much. The Vishnu Temple, the Iron Pillar and the forts, the mosques and towers lay before me in all their splendor, and I had a bird's-eye view of the ancient calligraphy and lavishly carved marble, the domes and arches and the austere tombs with their buttressed walls. And from where I stood on my balcony looking out across the city, I saw also the wide boulevards that showed off the white buildings of the Raj, with their ornate Victorian carvings. I could compare the golden domes and towering ramparts of the ancient past to the temporary quarters of yet another invader, whose day, like the centuries of the Delhi sultanate, would pass in the blinking of an eye.

My rooms were most definitely not English. It seemed that the firm of architects who'd redesigned Claridges was happy to retain the Anglo-Saxon exterior, while making the interior exotic. Apparently, no offers had been forthcoming to take up this architectural and cultural challenge, until a certain maharaja, anonymous, stinking rich, and a staunch member of the Congress Party, had swooped to the rescue. He was known for his extraordinary wealth as much as for a tendency to bellow in the *Delhi Times* about the British: "Our illustrious masters, who first had the mendacity to use India to finance their industrial revolution, are now attempting to have India pick up the cheque for their blasted war costs." This gentleman, known as Raja V, a powerful magnate whose fortune had quadrupled during the war years with the huge textile demand, was now putting his genius into home consumption: "No point in hanging around; we must take the country back *before* the Raj is sent packing." He'd a clear sense of what the aristocratic and wealthy wanted. My rooms, though sumptuous, were cool and quiet, with elegant beds dressed in cream silk. The walls were papered with linen shot with a trace of gold leaf; three delicately sculptured columns separated the rooms from a balcony weighed down with bougainvillea and white hibiscus. The dhurrie rugs were deep blue. Wide windows brushed with a swath of crimson. Carved panels, Bengali in style, took up the central wall; a small niche housed a golden goddess. In the bathroom was a lotus-shaped pool with an arrangement of scarlet lilies in a black vase. Next to it, a telegram: *Isabel: Please find it in your heart to forgive my misery in our first days together, and believe that in spite of it, you have my wholehearted and eternal devotion. S.*

I lifted my head and saw a gorgeously decorated ceiling with blue and turquoise floral and geometrical patterns. I looked back at the scarlet lilies tipped with black and thought my heart would break with loneliness. In the mirror I caught sight of my face without its vermilion dot, and my hair sans Brilliantine, worn with a swept-up knot and tightly secured, and oh, how I missed my veil, the secrecy of it, its protection and quietness; its inclusion in a hidden world. Now look at me, white as a sail, all decked out in my buttoned lawn blouse and olive skirt, strangled at the waist, heavy on the thighs when what my body longed for was the silky embrace of my old sari. I was disorientated, an outsider again, and once separated from myself and Sam, I barely knew who I was.

THE FIRST TIME I stepped out of the hotel, Joseph hurried toward me and whispered frantically: Mem, I find myself in appalling circumstances.

Oh, dear, I said, are the rooms dirty?

No, no. His tongue clucked with impatience: Mem is not getting the picture. Quarters of sumptuosity, but it is I who am appalling—in rags and tatters. I looked him over: Seems to me, Joseph, you look perfectly all right.

He was almost hitting his head with exasperation: Mem, what I am saying is that in bearers' quarters are uniforms of unqualified finery—hard to see who is servant, who sahib. He waved his hands in despair. Low-caste servants not sleeping on bistra, but lolling in silk sheets, eating off plates. And here am I, ashamed of showing my face in the back quarters of honorable hotel, no credit to mem whatsoever.

What would you suggest, Joseph? I turned to face him. Tell me exactly what you need, I said, so that we can both continue in peace.

New clothes I am suggesting, he announced.

I agreed that this was probably something we should both invest in, but I was a little startled when he announced the sum. That much?

Mem, I cannot be looking like riffraff. If mem is to be saving lives and ending suffering, I cannot be letting the side down.

I KNEW THAT to take on the task of becoming a doctor would mean I'd have to go through it all again, just like university; I'd have to have higher ideals and work harder and longer than the men. Much of it would be a fight or putting up with vulgarity and stupidity. I knew how that worked, but I didn't know anything about how India worked. Did European doctors train in India? How many Indians trained at home and how many in Europe? How would it work with women? They'd obviously have separate classes and lectures, separate time in the labs and all that, so perhaps I'd be better off going to one of the women's hospitals and not putting up with the prejudice and annoyances of a mixed college. What I found in the library surprised and heartened me: Women of good caste had long been qualified to treat women and children in India. As long ago as 1872 the nawab of Rampur had provided a school so that medical women could treat Muhammadan women of all castes. Women were admitted to the medical college in Madras, and the Victoria Hospital had opened there with Indian money and the old queen's blessing. Rich Indians had established the Bombay Medical College to enable women to qualify as M.D.'s years ago. So, as it turned out, India had often been more enlightened than the illustrious universities at home, since Oxford and Cambridge *still* refused to grant women degrees with full privileges. I knew that I was in the right place after all. India would make me a doctor.

How to begin? After graduating from university, I'd done a few courses in London, but I was rusty, and I needed to find a tutor who could oil and hammer my brain until it ran smoothly with science and Latin and Greek the way it once had in the quiet classrooms of Scotland. Those strange days and nights when the *Lusitania* had gone down and the shocks and hauntings of war had begun to take hold of our imaginations, and the only thing to do was to keep on studying, keep on believing it would all come right in the end. Rumors about Gallipoli and the horrors of the trenches, the casualty lists so terribly long, and the way people began to talk of the dead in a particular way. A dead officer would have become intellectually brilliant and destined for great things, even if he was a complete dolt, while foot soldiers dying in their thousands were not given a second thought. And that notion so bald and vicious that you heard in every drawing room: Every man ought to be of use to his country, and if he can't, he's better off dead. And my old feelings returned as if it were yesterday, the pain and loss, the grief of Gareth's death: The War Office regrets to inform you . . . For it was as simple as this: He put his head up in the moonlight and caught a bullet in the brain.

When the Zeppelin raids were on, death could be shoved out of mind by cramming for the physics and chemistry exam. And even then it was: Doctoring for women? So unsexing, my dear. Must you? I have no objection to you becoming a nurse, if you must, but of course it's a different kind of woman who does that. And: Men are in short demand; this is not a time to tie yourself up for years of study. Only Mama stuck with me. She'd turn on her friends and remind them that Italy had never prevented women from going to university and had produced Maria Montessori, whose ideas had taken the country by storm just before the war began. This England, she would say, with that soft swipe of her right hand, is so unkind. If a girl is mathematically gifted or wants to be an engineer, well, she has to enter some obstacle race or travel to the University of Rome. What is so outrageous about a brilliant woman?

I SAT ON MY BED in my gorgeous hotel room and ordered chicken and chutney sandwiches on crustless brown bread and a jug of lime water. I scoffed the lot, reading through the curriculum for the first year of medical school. I already had chemistry and physics and I hoped wouldn't be reexamined. Anatomy was going to be the hardest.

I feared and dreaded it. I'd seen the drawings, so chaste and clean on the page, but how would it feel to be faced with a corpse? How see a dead body as material for study? Putting it out of mind, I stuffed my degree and certificates into my bag and took myself off for an appointment with the dean of the University of Delhi. And as I walked through the marble arch, I knew I was leaving my entire identity behind: married woman, army wife, visiting Englishwoman, and the lover of a Black Englishman. I was simply Miss Herbert again, with the aim of becoming a medical officer in India.

Fourteen

My dearest love, I miss you so terribly that it's as if my heart's been amputated. If your letter hadn't been waiting for me, I don't know how I'd have managed. The ship was bad enough—a couple of wretchedly bad storms with everyone in need of a doctor. The longing for you became overpowering in this room, which, for all its Victoriana, reminds me of Simla and you. Even the portrait on the wall, of a dark beauty reclining on pillows and a rug, on the grass in a garden, reading, wearing a black jacket and hat, is too like you to be borne. The club's all right, I suppose, comfortable enough, unchanged by even a chair, and Mayfair is of course as it has always been. It's as if these streets have known nothing of the tumult of love and sorrow that England has passed through. The echoes are all here: the stamp of boots at night, the names on school and university walls, *all the lost friends buried in far-off fields. England is utterly changed in the years since I left. I'm trying to understand what has happened here, what feels so missing, so bleak and lost, and I think it's to do with the peace as much as the war. England has made a grisly and revolting peace, which no amount of economic rattle can condone, and there's a sense of shame and bitterness left behind. One senses in the streets and pubs and eating houses an overriding depression, real and tangible—as visible as the black bands on people's sleeves. The horror of war is still here in every way—the stumped bodies of the survivors, the melted faces of those poor devils who barely survived the trench fires—you see them hiding in the darkness of bars. You sense the grief of the orphans, the widows, the poor—despair and hopelessness everywhere. And once out of the charmed quarters you collide with poverty and squalor, the dirt and grime of the workshops, people undertrodden and brutalized. The slums are no better than India's in that there's no sanitation and medical care and no real effort to address the needs of the underprivileged. And this an invincible people? Charitable, Christian, and kind?*

You must have known some of this before running off to India—on the rebound, I now see, from so many losses. It's a shock to be back. This is so different from the slump that hit England when the old queen died; there's no sense of a new ideal being forged in the lean winds blowing here, no excitement that the repression and rigidity can be replaced by reform and change, that the country can at last move out of the garden party and into the real world. I feel changed too; it's as if Oxford had gone down and those memories are lost, making my years of medicine and research just a dream, but I don't know how to go on any more than England does.

Your ideal is clear to me: You are becoming a doctor. That's a new beginning. You will achieve all that you dream of and more. I'm still part of the past. I hate what has happened to England as much as I hate what it has done to others. And yet I remain an Englishman. It's as immutable as my color, but I can't continue to live at this remove from the catastrophes of my own race. I can't observe or analyze it anymore. I have to change without feeling it a treachery. But then I wonder: Who am I? And what do I have to offer apart from a good pair of hands to tend the mangled bodies? You'll say this is enough; you'll also tell me to stop giving you the archi-tecture of what I'm feeling instead of the feeling. The truth is of course that the depression I pick up in the eyes and stooped postures of the English is my own.

As for Sammy, I shy from it here as I did when I first saw him. All my rehearsals of how I'd tell him were useless. I thought I could sit down and explain his mother's death in words that wouldn't sear him for the rest of his life—as if such words existed. I was speechless, as I am sometimes with you when I'm overwhelmed by the enormity of what I'm doing. And after an hour at his prep school, I wanted to beat someone up. I'd gone to see the headmaster—a moron with the name of Dyer—to tell him what had happened, so that they would take care of Sam in the days after my visit. But the minute I told him about the train burning, which he of course had read about, a particular English chill entered the room. My Oxford and his, a place we'd talked about a moment ago, no longer existed; he had ejected me from its hallowed halls. My Englishness was no longer valid. I'd become a color. This severance between us was so deep that it was as if a blade had moved right down it. And all because of the one word, Rawalpindi. Once it was uttered, his face changed, and I saw that gaze, that elevation of nostrils and that courteous revulsion that come right up to the surface in the English when they speak of the atrocities of others, meaning of course the four English heads on stakes, not the British soldiers dropping on one knee to fire directly into the backs of women and children in the chili field. "And you say that Sam's mother went down with the train?" He asked this in a tone that was more like: "And you say you have no kippers on the menu today?"

The old familiar rage began, and I wanted him to know how it would feel to be choked by my dark and savage hands. The level of my violence, and my total disregard for the consequences of it, shocked me so much that I left immediately. This kind of turbulence is new to me. I've lived so damn carefully, obliterating all passion, personal and political, and now I look at myself and part of me is exhilarated and the other half is terrified. But I

*do know it's because of you, who stormed my ramparts with your pink rag
of a dress and shook me till I had the decency to fall apart.*

Friday
*Had to stop. Too exhausted to think. Some days I sleep here as much
as I did on the houseboat, only here a man in a black waistcoat, rather
than an uncovered woman, brings my tea. He carries up a tray of smoked
salmon sandwiches and a dish of apple charlotte. I can't face the dining
room. There was a time when we used to come down from Oxford and use
these rooms and bar, staying up all night talking about literature and art.
I used to dine here with Duncan Lambert-Smythe. He was very fond of
darts and could thrash anyone, including the barman. They have a column
of the war dead on the wall here too, but I don't read the names.*

*I should tell you about Sam and the school in some detail so you can
understand enough to help me decide on what we should do. After the
headmaster, I went to see Sam's housemaster. He's a perfectly decent chap,
and he helped me quite a bit by just talking about Sam, saying how well
he does at school, how clever he is, and how kind. He said he'd take
Sammy under his wing. And all of this of course—all these conversations
with Sam's masters—was just a terrible holding off. I'm aware as never
before how much I do this, skirting round things, setting up evasions and
subterfuges, avoiding decisions—precisely in the way that you charge me
with. I kept waiting for the right moment to tell Sam. At first he was just
so happy to see me again that I couldn't bear to. He wanted to show me
around and have me look at his work and meet his friends, but finally, after we'd had tea in a room made available to us, I told him that I'd come
with very sad news and that it would be hard for him to hear what I had
to say. Then I said nothing for a full two minutes. He was crumbling a
piece of sponge cake in his fingers and didn't look up for a long time. "You
don't have to say it," he said, "if you don't want to." I said that I'd give
anything not to have to, but he was old enough to be told the truth. I then
told him a lie: I said a train had been derailed, and his mother had been
traveling on it to his uncle's wedding, with her aunts and some of his*

cousins, and that the train had gone off the tracks and a lot of people had died. I said she had died peacefully. His eyes whipped up to mine and then dropped. I saw that he was very frightened. They let me stay with him that night and all the next day. He asked me no questions, and most of the time just sat beside me, trying to be very gentle and kind, his face very still as if something had gone from it, some life, some energy. He didn't want to talk about it and only came to life when he talked about his schoolwork and the masters he liked. I'm not at all sure that he's able to comprehend the finality of death, and I suspect he'll keep alive a fantasy of his mother, in her absence, the way I did with mine.

When I was leaving, he asked me if I was going to take him back to India. "I like it here," he said. I said I'd come back on Sunday and take him out to lunch, and that I'd keep coming for a while, and we could talk about what he wanted to do. But he's so little. How can he know, at seven, where he wants to be? He stood by the door and watched me leave, and his face was just the way it had been the first time I'd left him there. It took me right back to the day my mother had told me not to look out of the window for her but just to go on without her. As we were saying goodbye, in the rotunda, I'd asked him what they called him at school, what name he'd been given. "They call me Singh," he said, "except sometimes when they call me Sammy." I can't tell you how much it comforted me to hear this. The school seems okay. It doesn't feel like Eton. The boys don't give the impression that they're expecting to enter the world and see it bow; they don't reek of privilege and class and money, not yet. England's changed in that there are more Indians here than there used to be, though whether that will help or hinder is another matter. Sammy fits in, and they like him. It's clear from the way boys and masters respond to him that he's part of the place. He seems so English already: his voice, his manners and his way of conducting himself, and that scruffy-haired, mussed look he has. He blends, he passes; his skin is rather creamy though his eyes are brown. He's also a hundred times more outgoing than I ever was, and much more friendly. So the difficult question is: Should I stay here so he need not be uprooted? And would you come? Could you go to medical school here—

would you want to? Can I ask this of you when for us to be here together would be monstrously difficult? We'd be getting away from some problems but encountering others just as unsolvable. If Sammy were to walk down Regent Street with you, people would think you were mother and son, but if I were with you, the dynamic would be utterly different. I can't pass, and I refuse to: I'm not going to give myself an Italian or a Jewish name and watch my back for the rest of my life. I belong in England and India, both, but I've only one skin. I'm beginning to think that if I join the Congress Party and commit myself to the movement, perhaps I'm merely trying to rid myself of one side of my head. But ridding India of the British is the right action; there's no question about that. I support that as an Englishman as much as I do as an Indian.

The other complicating fact is that you said to me, rather pointedly, I seem to remember, not to leave Sammy here, to bring him home, but I don't think he wants to come back. He has a sense of India that seems too alien for him. "I saw some pictures," he said, "and the natives looked so ugly." I told him that we were natives—natives to India, and he said: Oh, and then thought and said: "But I'm not like them, and neither are you." Something about the way he said it infuriated me, as if he were already beginning to despise his own people. But how could he not think that way when the only pictures he'd have been shown would be of creatures huddled in the dirt? He'd probably have said the same thing had he been in India. I wanted to yank him out and drag him up the gangplank and ship us both back to where we belong and stick him in one of the new schools before he's hopelessly warped and confused. But there's another dilemma. On the one hand, Gandhi's calling for boycotts of government schools while Tagore says that's absurd because there aren't enough national institutions. G's rejection of the West can only lead to a narrow, chauvinistic nationalism, rather than some kind of universalism that could unite the best of both civilizations—and what the hell does any of that matter when Sam simply doesn't want to go home? He's come to feel he's one of them, and how can I disabuse him of that fantasy because part of me wants him to achieve what I could not? And what is that? Simply stated, I think it's the right to have the ease and grace and sense of place that an Englishman of a certain class takes for granted, knowing that with it go certain responsibilities and duties toward others who have less. Isn't that the aristocratic ideal, the mystique that the English create around their possession of India—and surely there's a way of making it real?

I crumpled up the letter and stormed out of the hotel and walked the streets for hours on end, my mood veering drastically from fury to pain. When I came back, I rushed to the wastepaper basket, to see if I'd perhaps got it wrong. But of course the basket was empty, even as my satin sheet had been folded back, my shoes polished, and the floor licked clean of any speck of dust. I then upset the hotel staff by insisting I get the contents of my wastepaper basket back, which, miraculously was achieved. I stayed up all night. I was so torn. Did he think that I would up and throw everything to the winds, book passage and return to England? Did all that chaining to the railings achieve no advance in the balance between the sexes? What was Sam thinking of to set up his boy with the same expectations of ease and privilege, put him in a cadre of upper-crust twerps of the same level of breeding and money, only to come to the same conclusion that for all of it, he'll never get more than an elevation of nostrils and the revulsion that the English have for those who are not, and can never be, English?

It took me a night and a day to come round to some normality of response and to look at my own side of the matter. Sam was out of his bunker at last, which required me to do the same. I lay on my bed, sending rings of smoke up to the canopied ceiling. With whom had I fallen in love? What precisely had I been attracted to? What did I want? How much was I prepared to risk, or sacrifice, to be with him? And where did *I* want to be with him—here or there? And then, for the first time, really, I thought directly about his color. Would I still desire him if his skin were ebony—if he were one of the indigenous, dark-skinned Dravidians and not a tall, lighter Aryan? Would I still ravish him if his hair were patent leather black? His eyes black, not green? Would I still adore him if his mouth were dark; would I kiss him with the same abandon? What's the exact shade of rejection anyway, and when does otherness become revulsion? I love his shoulders and belly and cock because their color is not too different from mine, so perhaps it's a physical sympathy. But then there's the case of the beautiful Bengali, who walked across the compound after the shots were fired. With him, all of the above gets chucked straight out the window because his blackness took my breath away, his blackness was dissolved by beauty—*was* beauty. The Bengali had the mystery and grandeur of a god. He should have been decked in gold. The white and blue he wore were Grecian, and he was on a par with the Immortals. Does it come down to beauty then? Sam is not beautiful. I can't say I'd be crazy about him, besotted and obsessed with him if he were as black as a boot, but I can't say I wouldn't.

Delhi,
July 27, 1921

My dearest one,

Your letter made me furious for a while, but then it made me really think about what's ahead of us. You're saying that maybe we'd survive better in England and that uprooting Sammy from his prep school would do more harm than good. This is where I stand: I've thrown in my lot with India. Being with you here, and someday working with you here, is more than England could offer me. Starting a career in medicine has made that clear. I need to throw myself into more than just love and passion—I want to make my life useful as well—to be part of that English mystique you describe: an aristocratic ideal that can and does exist, in small ways, within the tyranny of imperialism.

Of course you're right: I did leave England on the rebound, from the loss of Gareth, and the war and all the emptiness it left behind, but above all, I was in flight from myself, not knowing how to create a life that was whole and good. What I feel now, about you and about having a life with you here, is far more than impulse, flight or fantasy, or the things that began when you asked me: What do you want? I'm a little afraid of what it will require of me to really love you—to have your mystery and exotica become the daily struggle to love and accept the whole bang shoot of another person. In the quandary of all this, I try to make our future tangible and real. After leaving Simla, I started to imagine a house that we could live in together. I didn't know where it would be, but I could imagine it fully. It came out of needing to be somewhere with you where we could be at home. A small house where we could pull the curtains, lock the door, light a fire, boil potatoes, and roast a chicken. Where we had time to talk and drink wine and laugh, and know that no one would come, no boots knock along the street or smash in the door. I wanted a time and place where there'd be no threat from Neville, no grief for Nalini, and, instead, down the corridor, a bedroom for a small boy with the same name as yours. I thought we might find this in the hills somewhere, and that we could stay a long time and not see anyone till we wanted. It's part of the sense I've always had that it must be possible to vanish into the immensity of India. At first, this seemed to be about hiding from the world. I imagined that ivy would tangle and cover the windows, darken the crack under the door, and shelter the two of us, so we could stay safe within, dressing and undressing, making love, sleeping, eating, reading, living together as the days piled up, one after the other, without calamity or change. You'd light the lamp and turn the wick up, and just to watch your hands would be enough. I'd read and learn and practice and begin to see myself not as a woman physician but as just a physician, part of a network of assistance and cure—the way you see yourself. We'd quarrel, and I'd watch you scuttle back like a crab that won't come out until the tide has changed. I have to admit that I like to quarrel and argue and shove rudely past your defenses and fear, and it isn't the end of the world, for God's sake. Why must an argument signal desertion? In the end, we manage to end up safely on the shore together.

For a short time there was another dream, and I tell it to you in case it might be a version of the one you're entertaining. I know it would be possible to live in England, in a quiet manor house, something small and anonymous—outside Oxford perhaps. You could work at the hospital for officers wounded in the war and help put their minds together, stop them screaming when the nurse drops a spoon or the fire engine roars by. I could continue my medical training, even if it meant going to the Continent to complete the process. I know that one day we'll go back—not in the sense of returning Home—but for visits and to see how it affects us to be there once I've become what I'm becoming, and you've become an Indian, uncolonized and free. I could imagine our house, our garden, your room, mine, our room, our children running across an English lawn, sturdy and tall, café au lait—perhaps more lait to be on the safe side. You'd rake up the leaves and burn them near a greenhouse filled with orchids and black lilies mixed in with the potato and onion seedlings sleeping in black earth, waiting for spring. I'd go out, drying my hands as the sparks flew up into the oak tree, and stand in front of you, taking you by the lapels of your good coat, tugging them together to keep your chest warm: Hurry up, I miss you. It's suppertime.

I had to move beyond that into a more difficult vision of the future, one that I can't see, one that I have to believe in by taking a wild leap into the void. I think that staying here will take us to the limits of our courage, but I want that as much as I want to work here in a way that will be productive. To put it simply, I'd like you to come back with Sammy, and I want to be part of the process that helps you become an Indian, the way you began. I want to love you here, without all the conflicts that create distance between us. I want to take root beside you, for us to grow down into the earth and make it permanent. India no longer belongs to England; to think it does is just to enter an English fantasy. And as for your dream of harmony, of integration, of combining the best of the West and the East, who knows if it could happen? The question is: Can we survive in India together, can we find sanctuary in its vastness and endless possibility? I don't see why not. After all, there are thousands of liaisons like ours going on all the time, darky-whites and half-and-halfs, twilight people leading full lives and getting away with it. The problem for you is that you've been too conspicuous in your Englishness. If anyone looks at me twice, it's because they wonder if I'm a Eurasian, or someone with a touch of white blood from the East India Company days, or the offspring of a white officer and a bibi. We care and worry too much about all this, and when we do, it becomes too powerful a force in our lives. We have to connect with others in ways that make all that irrelevant, and when we do that, the power of the Raj diminishes until it becomes nonexistent.

Come back to me, Sam; bring your boy home. If we do less than this, it's not because we fear the future or the consequences of what we've begun together; it will only be that we doubt our capacity for devotion. Get back over here as fast as you can. I send you abiding love,

Isabel

THE LETTERS went back and forth on the mailboats, and slowly we came to a decision that we two would stay in India and let Sammy, for the time being at least, remain in England where he wanted to be. It was more Sam's decision, of course, than mine, but I admired his generosity. He was saying that he'd let his son find his own England, and I knew that by so doing, Sam was in some way repairing his link with the mother country and at the same time turning himself over to India. He described himself as having been a self-hating Indian and trying to hide it by outdistancing the competition. Sammy wasn't that way. *He'll come back,* Sam wrote, *when he's pulled back to India, and he'll do better than I have. Already I see him overtaking me, because I doubt he'll be divided the way I was. I think I chose my isolation to avoid having it imposed upon me.*

As for me, I wanted Sammy with us, and with the children that we hoped to have, and I knew it wouldn't feel whole without him. I also had such a sense of the child's isolation, because of Sam's, but then, Sammy didn't seem to feel that way, though I kept thinking that surely he must. I also had a sense that the boy, small as he was, knew what was best for him, and England, for now at least, was where he wanted to be. He would make of it a different experience, and his blood, in the end, would pull him back the way the war had brought his father home. And so we left it there.

Fifteen

It was time for me to move out of the hotel, so I took up residence in a small, cozy place closer to the university. Joseph missed his fancy quarters, with a comfortable bed and a wardrobe full of interesting clothes, including a rather nice suit and a swanky pair of brown leather shoes. He sulked for days: Down-at-heel we are here, memsahib. Ashamed to put foot out of door. I assured him the digs were temporary, but personally, I rather liked living in the quiet cul-de-sac. It was more anonymous, and all that bowing and scraping at the hotel had become rather tiresome. Delaware Street was quiet and residential, close to an area of warehouses and a large shoe factory, and beyond that a sprawl of Anglo-Indian houses, close to the railway line. Several people thought me a darky-white and once, in a rougher part of the city, a soldier shouted an obscenity at me. Joseph threatened to cut out his tongue. Very Christian sentiments, I said. Joseph, I'm sorry that I can't keep you in the way you've become accustomed in Delhi. The fact is I'm broke. His feelings were hurt: Mem, misunderstanding as per usual. Concern is for mem in an area unsafe for walking. I smiled: Oh, I know that's a concern, Joseph, but what you're really saying is that you don't want me going native again.

My money had gone in fees and books and tutoring. I wrote to Mama and asked her if she could see her way clear to raid my part of the trust. It was discretionary, and the trustees might, for good reason, cough up some of the cash now. I also asked her to please book passage to come and see me, as I was lonely without her. Meanwhile, I was embarking on a medical training. On my first day I got to class early and sat at the back of the room. There were rows of desks on a platform, and on a dais, the professor shuffled her books together and untied a large rolled diagram, which she attached to a hook to the wall. The room was stinking hot, the air like soup. The door opened and closed as twinned women came silently in and sat down; from behind, they looked like sarcophagi in a row. Some wore saris, others long veils and jackets, a few wore loose pants; some were decked out in full chador and burka. Eyes behind bars. No skin. No scent. No smile. No breeze or touch of air. Did they even breathe, these gentle, modest maidens, heads sequestered in the secrecy of the veil?

Our professor has managed, with some difficulty, to hang up a diagram of a skeleton and, next to it, a full-length map of the human body, male naturally, but with very sketchy genitalia. Apparently, it's a special diagram for women students, with a fig leaf effect. Professor Thibault has some smaller scrolled diagrams, which I hope will reveal the female body. I watch my sisters draped in black, as they apply a corner of veil to a damp forehead in much the same way as they'd dry their cheeks after ablutions or tidy their children's mouths after lunch. A woman sits next to me. I can just see the outline of her face behind the burka. The room is quiet. The professor coughs and continues to stack her papers. The woman next to me makes a movement and then lifts her arms to remove the burka. Beneath it, her hair is peroxide blond, her eyebrows black as licorice, her mouth scarlet. She stands up and begins to strip. Off come the dark robes as she unwraps herself, rolling the shroud like a bandage and then tossing it to one side. Beneath the black, she's wearing European bazaar clothes, cheap but sexy: a tight skirt, low-neck black top, high-heeled shoes. The professor is staring, her mouth slightly agape. And following the professor's eyes, the women begin to stir, finally turning to look behind them at the woman sitting next to me. She stoops to yank her heavy bag up onto her desk, dragging textbooks from an interior littered with papers, lipsticks, packs of cigarettes, and a gold lighter.

My name's Gloria, she says to me, still scrabbling in the bag. I mumble my name, and she looks up and gives me a big smile. In the lower reaches of the lecture hall, a small commotion begins, like birds gathering in branches. Chairs scrape back; sandals shuffle; there's a whispering of cloth. One of the women flips back her veil, revealing a head sleek as a seal's, glossy and perfectly round. One by one veils fall as necks are bared, a plump cheek dimples into a smile, an elbow peeps through gauze, a golden throat emerges out of the dark, and a pink shoulder loses its strap. A woman with a fine, chiseled face lifts her arms, and her golden bangles jangle in the sunlight. The wind moves through loosened hair, caressing a chin, lifting small curls and wisps at the back of a neck. The women are breathing now. You can hear it. It's as if air had been pumped into their lungs. Hands appear, some decorated with henna, others with ringed fingers and delicately painted nails. Bare arms, white bodices, a half sleeve, a rosebud silk shift, which curls around a breast, nips a waist, slouches around a thigh. They're starting to giggle, some stand up and walk a little; one struts and wiggles her hips, another lifts up her skirts and shoves her bare legs out in front of her like a man. They're laughing into their palms, banging their lips softly with their hands, whispering to one another. A tall woman raises her arms on either side of her, and it feels like a blessing.

The professor, who, like me, is wearing a perfectly boring sundress, smiles at the women and says a few words of welcome. She has a French accent, but her English is excellent, as is Gloria's. Gloria's asking me all sorts of questions: How much money do I have, am I married, do I have children? Where am I living? Do I like her skirt, and should she shorten it? Would that be too tarty? Do I have nice clothes? Will I have coffee with her later? As she's chattering, she's leaning over the side of her chair, shoving the burka down into her bag, pushing her hair back out of her face. Then she straightens up and faces the front, her face expectant, the scarlet mouth voluptuous as a summer pudding. Slowly the room goes quiet; the professor begins her lecture. She turns to the diagram and points with a stick to the left-hand side of the diagram. The heart, she begins . . . She tells us that when we have studied all the parts of the body, dissection begins. The women begin to take notes as we look up and study the human body in all its beauty and wonder, in all its frailty and tenderness.

When the class was over, the women covered up and, two by two, walked out into the shuttered world. Gloria, still uncovered, took me off to a coffee shop on the corner. I was her disguise now, or perhaps being with me gave her immunity. The waiter didn't approve of us one bit. When the coffee came, Gloria tipped most of the sugar bowl into her cup and stirred it a long time. She had an odd way of sniffing and rubbing the end of her nose, and she looked out of the window a great deal, though with the rain coming down harder by the minute, it was impossible to see anything. After I'd answered all of her questions, most of which were downright rude, she pushed the coffee cup aside and looked at me. Let me tell you about me now, she said, gazing at me out of violet-black eyes. She gave me her life story, almost without taking breath, as if uttering these things might have some terrible consequence. Gloria's an assumed name, of course, she said breathlessly. No real names, no real places, just take it from me that I came from somewhere in the north, near Peshawar. My father was a bigwig, and I was a daughter of the intelligentsia. We went to London for a few years, when I was eleven, and I went to school in Baker Street, but then my father was ordered home, and it was back to Muslim for all of us, nothing but dear old Islam every minute of the day.

She reached into the leather bag and hauled out her cigarettes, and the gold lighter, which had fallen to the bottom. I was married in the usual way, she said, with a warped smile. I was the second wife, and the first was religious, and very lazy. I had to do all her dirty work. We all lived together in my husband's father's house. He was a pig. My husband too, a pig. I produced a child, who was added to the others in the house, making, I think, about seven or eight—but who really cares, they can be claimed by the family at any moment, for any transgression, so who cares? She drew on the cigarette and sighed. It was ghastly, she breathed out. The usual thing, up at five to make the bread and order the servants around, working all day in that useless way, doing nothing but cleaning, but not even real cleaning, because of course we had servants to do that. It was not work like an animal in the fields, not that working in a row, passing the bags along, which might be satisfactory in some way, but just spreading the cloth and serving food and obeying orders. And all the time, living with the beatings and kickings; and the endless hatred of women. Even being utterly as one should be, toeing the line, obeying the idiotic commandments—it made no difference. Women are to be beaten, burned, raped, killed. No one cares. No one sees. The windows are all bricked up, so there's no point in screaming. When the door opens, we retreat into the back rooms and hide. Once I had the temerity to actually listen to the men talking in the front of the house, and for my sin, they made me watch as they beat my daughter till she could no longer stand. If I smiled, someone hit me. If I lifted my veil or took my clothes off for a moment in the privacy of my room, I was told to cover myself, as if I was filth.

How old are you?

Twenty-eight. Look older, don't I?

No.

Liar.

Your English is exceptional.

It is I who am exceptional.

I didn't doubt it. When, after class, we talked, she would tell me a bit more of her story, and while she told it, she watched me like a hawk, needing my pity, my horrified face, needing me for something else, but I didn't know what. Of course, she said, it's perfectly nice to be an interpreter for the BBC Eastern Service, but the real money comes from entertaining. She'd already told me it was forbidden for women to work, and that anything she did to support herself could get her killed. I dance in music houses, she said. No one knows me here; no one could trace me back to the hills. I've been living like this, on the run, for nine years. The dancing brings in more money than anything else, and I like it. I feel alive when men are watching me. Her voice was defiant and yet plaintive, oddly compelling. I felt I knew how she'd talk to men. I had a sense of a smoke-filled room with men lounging on low couches, smoking, drinking, ogling her as she danced on a stage, singing love songs, maybe selling herself when the entertainment was over.

Another time, when she seemed very frightened, she wouldn't come to my house: No, not there. I'd stand out so close to the polo grounds. I have to keep to my own beat. Her own beat was at the far end of the city, huddled beyond the bazaar areas, in a vast, filthy sprawl she called the city of tents. At first she refused to take me there. But then, one day as we were walking to the main part of the university, she pulled me into a room and began to empty out her bag. I want you to come with me, she said. I think we can get away with it. She shook out what she called her rags and put on hijab. She'd brought the same getup for me. The burka she gave me was rather beautiful, soft silk, green-gray, a cap on the crown of the head, which remains in place when the veil is lifted, pleats at the back, flaring across the shoulders. The front is smooth, with pale pink embroidery around the grille, a honeycomb with a glint of eyes behind it. I was ready to go with her, curious in part about her life but also worried about her. She'd lost her job. She'd stopped coming to class every day, and when she did turn up, she looked thin and unkempt. I can't study, she said one day, her hands shaking. I want to stay in a dark room and never leave it. I can't stop thinking. The thoughts get stuck in my head like a song.

She gave me snippets of her life in London, how she'd wear a gray skirt and tie to school and then come home, put on the veil, and go to the mosque. She talked about going out to tea at the corner café and coming back to the prayers and rituals of her other life. Her father, when he was summoned back to India, told her to forget her English life, or the contradictions would be too much for her. But, she said softly, the contradictions were too much for him. One day, she said at the same breathless gallop, at two in the afternoon some men came to the door of our house. They made us all gather in the living room—music was playing; it was Chopin—and in front of us they stabbed my father to death, sixteen times in his chest and neck. And then, as they were leaving, one of them looked at me and, before walking out of the door, slashed me across my stomach with his knife. My mother put her hand to her mouth and took my sisters from the room, and then they ran away. I was left holding my sides together, but no one would take me to hospital because as a woman I could not be touched there. I dragged myself down the street and knocked on the doors, but no one would open them. Finally, a stranger, a Turk, found me lying on the street and took me to hospital, but none of the doctors would even look at me. Someone, finally, found a woman doctor and brought her to me, and she took care of me and stitched me up; the scars are thick and horrible, like dirty ropes. Would you like to see them? When I moved back, she sneered at me: I thought not.

I often went with Gloria after classes were over in the afternoon, just to sit in the park or to take tea or coffee with her. We wore European clothes, and she could pass if she wore a lot of makeup. The burka is a superior form of disguise; behind the grating, the view is perfect. But being on the street was dangerous. I began to appreciate her skill with the knife, but I wouldn't carry one. You're an idiot, she said. Just make sure you don't become a liability. One evening, after we'd had a glass too many, she said I could come with her to where she lived. She came to get me in one of those covered carts for women in purdah. We got in, and she snapped out directions to the driver, drawing the curtains around us. It took a long time to get out of the center of the city and to the underworld beyond. Inside the cart it was rather peaceful. Gloria fell asleep on my shoulder, and I sat there, listening to the commotion outside, trying to tell where we were by the sounds. Once I stuck my nose out to see what the holdup was about; a cart had overturned, and little boys were darting about among the vehicles, hawking newspapers and bunches of white tuberoses, narcissi, and lilies. It was getting dark, and then it was dark. Gloria slept on. I counted my rupees a few times, not sure how much this journey would cost. When the cart came to a stop, Gloria woke up; she looked disoriented for a minute and then returned to her edgy, vigilant self. She got out. I paid, and we began to walk, keeping our heads down. It's not far, she said, don't speak to anyone; don't stop.

We were in a bazaar, and then we passed close to a small temple; inside, men were chanting. The monotonous, droning sound of the priests made the air feel heavy. The moon was up, but the air was hot and sticky, and lightning ripped at the sky. We walked on, past lines of shopkeepers and traders, past drivers smoking at a corner. A few buffaloes swayed down the main street; plaintive music wafted through an open window. Children were crying, and women called out to one another over the rooftops. The houses were two- or three-storied, made of brick, the lower story usually a small shop, above which families, servants, relatives, and friends lived together. You could hear them laughing and shouting at one another as you walked by. Inside a shuttered shop, men's voices rose and fell and then began to argue. A policeman was propped up, asleep in a doorway. The walled city seemed to be fermenting. Vegetable, animal, and human— everything was rotting. Rats ran between piles of rubbish, and fetid breezes sent ripples of poison and sickness into the air. Outside the open square in front of the mosque men were sleeping on the white ground, huddled up, their faces covered. It was hard to be sure whether they were alive or dead. Pigeons and kites slept on the domes, and in the distance a sound went up: Allahu Akbar—God is Great—three times in a deep baritone, lovely as the sound of night surf hitting the shore. The low-caste women settled to sleep on the rooftops with the children; the high-class women lay down in their latticed zenanas, trapped in the stifling heat.

Someone shoved us from behind, yelling: Make room, make room. I turned to see a bunch of small boys, pushing and shoving, waving swords, making elaborate flourishes in the air. One was riding a hobbyhorse; one sucked a lollipop. I saw a dog's body spinning without a head; blood pooled in the gutter; the little boys shrieked with laughter. They're orphans, Gloria said. Warlords buy hundreds of them for the price of one British soldier's wages. They can be taught in a day how to behead, amputate, and cut people to pieces. They like it, she said, turning quickly down an alley. Her voice sped up as she dragged me along with her. I saw kids like that further south from here, she whispered. I caught them down in the basement of my house. It was at a time when no one was allowed to go out. We were waiting for reprisals. They were looking for Muslims to kill, and young boys were formed into killing gangs. They had clubs and machetes and knives. Sometimes soldiers with guns went with them; sometimes they went alone. They strolled into houses, made people come out, and killed them in the street. They were shouting and laughing, but you could see they were mad; their eyes were red and blind-looking, and blood was all over them. There were dead bodies everywhere, and the little boys jumped up and down on them as if they were mattresses. At night you would hear the shooting. I thought of walking out into the bullets because I didn't want to be cut again.

Just listening to her voice with its dead, dry tone was too much for me. When she told me what she'd been through, she had not a speck of emotion in her voice. Her stories stuck in my brain for days. I didn't know what I was doing with her. Some part of me was attracted to her fringe life. I told myself I was trying to find out how the other half lived, but really I was sneaking up on something dangerous and illicit. In the study hall I saw the women back away from her, and I began to do the same. I was ashamed of myself, but I did it. She lived on an outer ledge, moving through her disguises but always giving herself away. I could see her ending up barking mad.

I TURNED BACK TO MY STUDIES. I'd slipped behind in chemistry, and I used my coaching hours as an excuse to spend less time with Gloria. Her clothes weren't clean; she'd lost the earring in her nose, and her sniffing was constant. She no longer took the slightest pleasure in our classes or in the women; when she was with us, she fell asleep. She wouldn't go to the lab; in the dissection room she threw up. She lost her books, or sold them, and sometimes she sat on the floor and rocked. She was working in a rough part of town and swore that there was a man in the audience who came from her village. She was too terrified to go back, and when I gave her money, she took it. She was biting her nails and tearing the skin off the corners until they turned purple and black. Then, for a day or two, she seemed to recover herself. She came to the odd lecture, met me sometimes in the library or the lab, but before long she took off as if she'd just remembered that she'd left the fire unattended or a pot boiling on a stove. She wouldn't discuss anything or take any more help from me. When she talked, she kept turning the gold lighter in her hand, rotating it, rubbing her finger across the top. Then it was gone, but her hand was still clutching the absent lighter, rubbing her finger across its vanished gold. One day she came and sat beside me on a bench where I was smoking. She grabbed my hand. You just keep going, she said frantically, do your residency in one of the purdah hospitals in Delhi, finish your degree, and go into one of those maternity hospitals in the hills. Take care of the women and children. That's all I want. Promise me this. When she left, I saw that there were deep moon shapes where her nails had cut into my palms.

ONCE WE BEGAN THE DISSECTION of a human body, I needed all my strength to get through it. I'd studied *Gray's Anatomy* and read the dissection instructions carefully, learning the precise arrangement of arteries and veins, the alignment of muscle and ligament, the organs in their beds of tissue and bone, the heart guarded by the pericardium, the bones lovely in their perfection of utility and design. On our first day they brought in a corpse, a young woman whose body had been found on the street the night before. She was an untouchable. She lay in her bag, waiting to be cut and sawn to pieces, section by section, organ by organ, bone by bone. One or two of us had the temerity to ask Professor Fordham what it might be like to see a cadaver for the first time, and beyond that, to take a knife to it, skin it, and hack it to pieces. What if we vomited? Passed out? Fell to pieces at the sight of the inevitability of our frail human remains? Such ideas, he said, do not occur to a medical student. If you're squeamish, return to your embroidery. He looked around: Who wants to go first?

Her eyes were closed, but she had on her face an expression as if she'd been caught unawares: the echo of a smile, her mouth turned upward into a soft line. There was a dimple in her cheek, and her skin was ghostly pale. Her arteries had been cut to drain the blood, the severed ends sewn with thick string. Her pores were small and clear, and when you touched her embalmed skin, it felt like rubber. She had a pretty mole high on her cheek. Her nose was small and pert. Her hair had been carelessly shaved, so that tufts remained, and there were cuts in the skin close to her temple. Professor Fordham tossed a cloth over her face and exposed the rest of her. Heart's no good, he said, we'll get one from the men's lab. Male heart will be better anyway— larger, clearer, certainly more logical. I looked at her. She was thin and delicately made, but her breasts were round and full. I wondered who had kissed them, and whether a child had fed at her nipples.

There was bruising and contusion around her shoulders, as though someone had yanked her backward and knifed her from behind. Her brain was in a jar.

I tried to be manly about it. I told myself that it was essential to dissect a body in order to fully understand it and forced myself to look at her as if she were an object, a usable commodity. I read the instructions and tried to fulfill the task: *To skin a cadaver, take a scalpel and meticulously flay the epidermis, a small section at a time, without disturbing the capillaries and tiny veins close to the surface.* As the veins were cut, powdery blood emerged from the bruised skin. We were each given a piece of the woman, an arm or a leg. I was given her hand. I tried to work on it as if it were cloth or leather and concentrated on an inch, not looking beyond to the rest of her, repeating to myself the names—semilunar, scaphoid, metacarpus, phalanges—trying to dull the senses, to detach sight and smell, to bury feeling, but I felt myself tip, until suddenly I was no longer under the bright lights of the lab. I was in a lunar landscape, sleepwalking on a battlefield, knee-deep in a trench, looking down at my dead soldier, my hands buried in his flesh, my cuts and jabs the beaks of birds, the teeth and claws of rats, ripping my lover's hand, which once had known the sun and the breath of my mouth. My peeling back of skin let in wind and rain to fingers that had once written poetry, lingered over my body, played the piano, held a spoon, tossed a grenade, clutched the earth and died . . .

When, eight hours later, the hand is skinned, it's still a hand, though now it looks like meat and muscle, with slim bones showing through and severed vessels where the scalpel cut too deeply. The pads of fat have to be picked off by hand, and then we dig through the flesh to find arteries and veins, dissect tendons and muscles, and saw through rib and bone. Day after day, moving through acts of butchery to find the organs, we haul them out of their dark trenches, leaving the body gutted, cavernous, limbs scattered around a torso blown to bits. I drag myself out of the lab each night, too exhausted to think or feel, and sit shivering as Joseph fills the tub with scalding water, again and again, as I try to get clean. I scrub my flesh and hair to try to remove the smell of formaldehyde, which remains in the pores the way bits of tissue and bone cling to my arms, the way organ meat sticks, so that in the middle of the night I'll find a piece of liver or kidney adhered to my arm or caught in my hair. I'll wake screaming that the dead are crawling over me. Joseph runs in and holds my hand: Let me draw more water, mem. He's horrified that I touch the dead, the pollution of that. Unholy work, mem, he'll whisper, shuddering. And in the morning, I return to the mangled remains, to a severed head passed around for inspection, a carcass reduced to chopped joints and sawn ribs, bits and pieces of heart and brain tossed in a bucket, and bones bleached and lonely as those at the Somme.

THE MONSOON came late to Delhi. In the damp air, the cupboards creaked and the doors wouldn't open. Newspapers flopped like cloth; my textbooks stuck together or fell apart at the seams. Soft, creepy insects settled on the lamps or crawled over the windowsills. Pickles went bad; chutneys turned furry and green. Millipedes curled into the toes of my boots, and a scum grew on my sandals. The walls dripped. Clothes didn't dry; cuts and wounds wouldn't heal. Silk underwear turned moldy. Silver turned green, plates slipped out of your hands, and the sheets felt wet and slimy. The little garden at the back first sprouted weeds between the bricks, then moss took over; wooden window boxes collapsed with the weight of the rain. It kept on and on. No one was out on the streets, and the moon was blinded by cloud. I was so exasperated by it that I kicked the door open one night and yelled at the rain. Joseph, who spent his entire day drying every single thing I needed, wiping walls, killing caterpillars and snails, and trying to dry my papers by the fire, came out to see if I'd done any damage to the hinges. Mem, he said, monsoon is monsoon. It does what it does. Shouting of no earthly use.

The humidity was the worst; like a thick blanket, it hung over your body day and night. It was hard to sleep, and getting anywhere was impossible. Rivers were flooding, and bodies came whirling down, grotesque as the cadaver. Rain scoured the earth and tore into the shallow graves of the burial grounds. Seasonal sickness, they sighed in the hospital. Famine, Fever, and Cholera. Let's get you into the wards to take a look. Come on, Miss Herbert, give me a hand. Put on your masks. Where shall we start?

STILL, I was seeing him everywhere—side of a face, back of a tousled head, skin the color of coffee swirled with cream. I ran down the street, only to find it wasn't him. I saw a car like his and looked at the driver with longing, only to see it wasn't him. As I took lunch or tea at the hotel, a man would stroll up to the desk, and I'd have that sudden intake of air, and the pain that followed, because of course it wasn't him. All I had left to remember was the warm side of him against my thigh, his bare feet on mine. Without him, the mosquito net was a shroud twisting in the breeze, the memory of how he felt inside me lost in the dark. If life could be simple, if I could drink his essence from a coned leaf and feel the same intoxication that I felt watching him walk down the platform with his head up, and he waved and I ran—if I could. All I was left with was absence. And fear. Fear of the deep histories of hate; the chasms of culture, and the monsoon, a river out there behind the garden gate, black hens drenched, unable to fly, jackals creeping closer, snakes sailing in on the tide. Soon I'll sink into the sides of the river or float up to the moon.

Then, one afternoon, the rain stopped and didn't start again. I was in the garden in the early morning darkness, looking at the damage, seeing the swollen, battered lips of the gladiolus, watching water drain as doves, parrots, and orioles patrolled the blue sky. Mice darted through the falling leaves, the children were playing in the trees, when at my back, with utter certainty, I knew that someone was watching me.

Sixteen

I left Delaware Street immediately and got a flat on the first floor of a quaint and shuttered building called Queen's Mansions in the fort area. I'd decided that I didn't particularly like Delhi; it was crowded, noisy and chaotic, a world away from the open spaces of the northerly plains. I was restless, fidgety, working and reading, doing my papers, taking tests, finishing experiments, frantic with activity, exhausted by the stress and fatigue, the inhuman demands of becoming a doctor. And all the while, the traffic, beggars, pavement sleepers, and opium addicts were squalid and dismal, the noise unbearable. The city was extending itself, daily it seemed, as the villages were overtaken by a sprawl of slums and shantytowns, mud huts pushed against each other's backs, covered with tin and rags; streets running with sewage and rotting vegetation. But of course I was far from this. I'd put Gloria and my vagabond existence aside and dedicated myself to the acquisition of knowledge. Now I'd walk down the clean, wide boulevards, tree-lined and fountained, and stroll in the parks, or spend hours in the library, my mind ravished by the wonder of the body. Or I could drive in a taxi past lovely pink and red sandstone mansions with Sikh guards presenting arms, and imperial bungalows with deep verandas, neoclassical columns, and magnificent lawns. Outside the white mansions, supplicants lined up to see politicians, crouching on the street, smoking, waiting for hours. Delhi was thrumming with excitement and intensity, an ancient city rising out of a dusty plain, a place becoming impatient and agitated. But we, in our cool skins, were still holding the reins, and it seemed that all the talk of change would come to nothing. Occasionally a little scene would pass my study window: a string of shaven-headed men dressed in saffron muslin, the soft bang of a drum, a woman's low voice, chanting, a handmade sign leading the procession: *Nonviolence! Leave India in Peace!* Occasionally an uprising, put down with great force, the boot of the empire making its path plain.

I fell into a slump when we moved into Queen's Mansions. There was little trace of Sam left, only the crimson and black-stitched quilt and the pearls locked around my neck. I had the medical books I'd taken from Simla, and they sat among my textbooks and papers. Occasionally I'd open a page and see where he'd underlined a section or made notes. I studied his marginalia as if it held a message for me, but his notes were utterly clinical. Letters came, and I rationed them, reading a paragraph, and then, later, another, eking out an existence among his words, until the contents were licked clean. Wherever I went, his pages came with me, and the message that lingered was his ambivalence: *Why am I so tangled up with the pompous, ridiculous world of the past, with the strutting masters who have turned us all into slaves? Gandhi's not wrong; mentally we are still England's slaves. But are we likely to get rid of foreign rule by boycotts and peaceful marches? The very words* civil disobedience *stick in my craw because of their echoes of childish impotence . . .*

Without him, the bud was off the flower, every light dead in the windows, and food a waste—what use my body without his? What interest a good book when there was no one to discuss it with? Why wash and comb my hair, scrub the back of my neck, or brush my teeth when my mouth was starved of kisses and my teeth gnashed together all night in loneliness? I lay on the chaise with my hand over my eyes. Joseph came in with a tray of tea and set it beside me: Mem, no use lying about like fish out of water. Matters to attend to. And I would rise up like a bayonet: What *now*? Can't you see I'm exhausted?

I couldn't dent his dignity. If memsahib will permit, I will accompany to flea market, excellent places, all within budget; cheering up accommodations will do mem a power of good.

Queen's Mansions certainly had some problems beyond my ill humor; the servants' quarters were a disgrace.

This won't do, I said.

Fate has led me here, Joseph said, like a man about to take a bullet in the brain. He looked around him at the filthy walls, the greasy bed, the floor littered with the leavings of scorpions.

Fate has not led you here, I said firmly, closing the door.

He dipped his head: Humility is needed. Too much on the high horse.

Rubbish.

The solution was quite simple. The flat had two parts, a main section and a small part up a flight of stairs. Joseph could perfectly well use the second half. When I suggested this, he spluttered: Mem is wanting that I go to jail?

Please, let us be sensible, Joseph. You are altogether too dramatic. We're on the first floor of the building, and both parts of our lodgings are utterly self-contained, with separate entrances. The worst that could happen is that you'd have to move out, if someone objected, but why would they? Stranger accommodations must be going on all over India.

Memsahib is saying: What the heart doesn't see the eye doesn't grieve over?

Other way round.

He thought a little, then gave me a great smile. Mem, I accept offer with gratitude.

As of one mind, we began to discuss ways of making each section private and inviolate. I'd knock on the intersecting wall if I needed anything, three taps if I wanted him to come down. He'd knock twice and wait for an answer before coming into my quarters. It was a more private arrangement than before, when servants had always hovered around, knowing everything, able to walk into a room without even the ring of a bell. We decided a maid should be hired to attend to my personal affairs. But only when I am out of the house, at the university, I insisted. I don't want anyone underfoot.

Within a couple of days Joseph had turned our digs into an elegant and comfortable living space. We'd raced around the antique shops and flea markets and had bought a nice mix of Indian and English pieces: a teak table with matching chairs, pale dhurrie rugs and carved screens, a set of Crown Derby plates, linens from Belfast, some benches from Simla, a bevy of scarlet and gold tasseled cushions, and even a showy old chandelier that tinkled in the breeze. There was a big, old-fashioned bed, which had been in the flat when we arrived, and by the time all was done, the Irish linens were covered by the Kashmir quilt, Sam's red rug lay at the foot of the bed, and the lilac was installed in the garden. All was as it should be.

WE'D FINISHED OUR FIRST EXAMS and were chuffed with the results. Of the women students who'd gone up, all but Gloria had passed, and of the men—over 1,070—70 percent had passed. Five women were on the honors list, and one looked as if she would get the gold medal at the end of our studies. Our intellectual endowment had been tested, disproving the lingering prejudice that the admission of women would lead to the lowering of standards of medical proficiency. We were delirious and now had some weeks off, before moving into the long haul for the preliminary scientific exam. And Sam was coming home, his timing, as usual, impeccable. He'd sent two telegrams, one to say he'd got to Bombay and another saying he'd be in Delhi on either Wednesday or Thursday. My happiness was complete.

I began to prepare myself for him. I'd been having fittings for a suit. It was pearl gray, with a long skirt, tailored, ending at the back in a deep pleat with a tab secured by a black button. The jacket was short and cut to the exact curves of my body; the collar trimmed in turquoise, buttons the same color. And a gorgeous glossy black hat, tight in the crown, with a wide, dipping brim and a half veil that stopped just above the lips. The suit marked a dramatic shift in me. It was the first time I'd worn something to show off, rather than hide, my body. Nor was this the same body I'd worn for twenty-odd years, nor was it a body Sam would even recognize. It had been four months and 12 days since he'd left—136 days and nights. Once I'd have eaten my way through every one of them. This time I starved.

The night train arrived at midnight. It was a wild night, cold and blustery, and my taxi was late. By the time I got to the station, the wind was so strong that people listed sideways like sailboats, holding their hats, umbrellas inside out. The streets were slimy, and paper swirled and slapped up against doors and walls. I ran inside the train terminal, shaking off the rain, and looked around anxiously; the clock was past midnight. The station was less crowded than usual, and there was a hissing sound and the sudden shriek of a whistle. I didn't know the gate number, but I could see that a train had recently come in; steam was swirling softly up into the gloomy dome. The platforms were empty, and a few station guards hovered outside the locked gates. Farther down, a swarm of rowdy soldiers moved in and out of the restaurants and bars, their kit piled up by a gate.

I suddenly caught sight of him. My face turned into a smile, and I began to run in his direction, almost knocking into a couple of soldiers in my delirious haste. Sam was walking down an empty platform, completely ensconced in his own world. He hadn't seen me.

He was walking with himself, his face happy, his walk languid, his body utterly at ease. He was home; he was coming back to me. I couldn't move for joy. He did that thing he does, linking his arms behind him for a moment but, as if feeling too exposed, bringing them back to his sides again. His face was pale, and his curls had been cut, his hair brushed back from his forehead so his cheekbones stood out, making his face angular, Semitic. He was beautiful. His tweed suit, golden brown with a fleck of black, was very elegant, and I thought again of how he'd walked across the bare compound in his pale silk suit, my first day in Ferozepore. I came out of my trance and was moving quickly toward the gate, to wait for him there, when the two soldiers, deliberately, it seemed, walked directly in front of me. One knocked me sideways, and I lost my balance and fell, landing hard on my hands on the pitted tiles of the station floor. I pulled myself up, shocked and gasping, and surveyed my torn skirt. My heel had snapped; the contents of my handbag were strewn around me; my little confection of a hat crushed under a boot. There was glass embedded in the palm of my left hand.

When I lifted my head, I saw Sam running toward me. He stooped and picked me up in his arms. I staggered for a moment in my broken shoe, and before I could recover my balance, the two soldiers tore into Sam from behind, hitting him so hard that he reeled. He righted himself and looked at the two of them—pugilists, with faces like sides of beef—and he was quite marvelous in his composure and dignity. My heart rocked with love. He moved past them and closer to me. I'm a physician, he said tersely. Give me some room. One of the soldiers laughed, lunging at him. His voice slurred. No, he said, you're not a physician, now are you? You're nothing but a dirty coolie in fancy clothes, that's what you are. He grabbed Sam's lapel and said in a quiet and insinuating whisper: And don't you be putting your greasy mitts on her, coolie, or I'll knock your bleeding block off. Sam looked at the drunk with indifference, moving back, as if from a stench. But I completely lost my head, and I began shrieking: Do you know who you're talking to? How dare you, you little creep. This man, I said, is the personal physician of the Viceroy . . . The soldier stopped for a second, but jerked his head and sneered: Sure he is, love. And yours too, I don't wonder. For all his bluster, my comment had jolted him, and his face lost its cockiness. The two of them slunk away to join a posse of other soldiers who were gathering up their kit bags and heading for the gate.

Sam took my elbow, and I moved to retrieve my things. Leave them, he said. We made our way through the gawking onlookers, whose gaze, once on his face, had now dropped to my naked feet. They turned away and, by so doing, rendered us invisible. We walked on, not looking left or right. His body was a rod. Outside, the rain pelted down on us, and it seemed warm, cleansing. We walked through it and in a second were drenched. He had a car waiting, and we clambered into it. The minute we were in the back seat, he drew me up against him and kissed me all over my face and throat. Rain and tears were streaming down my face, and my hair had become serpent's coils. I began to shiver, and he held me hard as the car wove its way through the heavy station traffic and out toward the center of the city. It's all right, he kept saying, come on now, it's all right. But I was a broken pipe, sobbing and spilling. I just wanted to be myself again, I wailed, the person I once was . . . not an Indian woman, not an English one . . . I just wanted it to be like it was, when I didn't have to hide, or be in disguise. Just to meet you on our own terms, as ourselves.

It's going to be all right, he said. But I was bawling my head off . . . those soldiers, the way those people stared, the hatred in their faces, the disgust . . .

He held me tightly: They're ignorant, pay them no mind, just relax, simmer down.

I can't . . . because they can get us . . . and there's nowhere to *go*. Don't you see, I didn't know where to take you . . . I wanted to take you somewhere splendid and beautiful. And then I thought: We can't go to a hotel, or I can't go to a hotel with you, and I don't know where there are hotels you could go to, but there certainly are no bloody hotels we could go to together, and it's all so revolting and sad. And then I snapped: Why are you so damn calm in all this?

I have more experience of it.

We went home because in the end that's all a person can do. Once the door closed, I fell against it as if keeping back the hordes and stared at him in misery. He took my hand and drew me away, wrapping himself around me, kissing my neck, and then he led me to the big wing chair before he went into the kitchen and came back with the inevitable bowl of water. He went to his bag and took out a bottle of Dettol and sloshed it into the water and pulled out some cotton wool swabs. I was quiet a moment, and then I said: I'll have to be a Black Englishwoman for the rest of my life, won't I?

His lowered head was black as a bullet. It was all I could see because he was extracting with tweezers the pieces of glass that were stuck in my palm. He didn't look up. After placing each piece of glass on a square of lint, he wrapped a bandage neatly around my hand and smiled at me. Life is short, he said, why are you so agitated?

I'm afraid it's all going to go bad.

What did you think? He smiled with his old mockery. That we'd get away scot-free? That we could meet at the station like lovers? That I could pick you up from the floor and hold you in my arms and not have someone beat me up? He undid the top button of my jacket. May I? he asked, sliding a finger between the buttons, lifting each one, slowly, without actually opening the jacket more than a fraction. His hands slid through the parting and moved under silk, warm, accomplished, up and around my breasts. I was shivering uncontrollably. He got my black kimono from behind the door and, after taking off the jacket, and the silk camisole beneath it, wrapped me in it. I shook off my ruined skirt, and together we examined the damage. He swabbed the long gash down my calf, while I sniffed and whinged. He dressed it with a white bandage, a cigarette clamped in the side of his mouth.

JOSEPH WAS OF COURSE perfectly aware that Sam was with me, but he didn't say a word. I sent him messages in our wall-tapping code, but he stayed away. Finally, I decided to go and find him. Dr. Singh is staying with us, I said.

Indeed, he said, glancing above my head, as if looking for spiders' webs, or some such domestic problem. He muttered: Kindly permit me to go to the market, memsahib. There are things needed now that Dr. Sahib is here.

I smiled but in return got a turned back. Later, when he'd returned from the bazaar, he came in, bowed to Sam, and headed for the kitchen, where he stayed for quite some time. When he came back in, I noticed that he'd made us two different breakfasts. For me, there were scrambled eggs and bacon, with tea and toast, and for Sam, a paratha, a lime pickle, and a glass of lassi. His eggs looked as though they'd been stir-fried rather than scrambled, and there were easily as many onions as eggs. A heap of cumin, green chili, and coriander had been flung on top in a none too tidy manner. Sam said something to Joseph that I didn't understand.

What did you say? I asked the minute Joseph was out of earshot.

None of your business.

A moment later, in the same tone, he said: I went to see your mother while I was in England.

You *what*?

Well, actually, I went to see your parents, though it was your mother that I was primarily interested in.

Don't you think you might have asked me first?

It would have taken too long to get your answer. From time to time one has to take things into one's own hands.

And?

I found her charming, delightful, as was your father. I was interested in his Indian connection but of course didn't find out precisely why they up and left in such a hurry—family secrets and all that—but he did show me round the mine and took me to the pub, and he seemed very happy to be in the presence of an Indian again. Some of his Hindi came back, and he told me what he remembered of the tea plantation, and he wanted to know all about how Simla is these days. Of course—he smiled—your mother is so like you, or rather, you are so like her. She asked me to tea and then insisted I stay for supper and then positively pressed me into spending the night. He reached his hand across: I say, d'you mind if I have that last piece of toast? He looked at me: No good getting exasperated with me. I'm just trying to set the scene for you.

Well, start at the beginning then. Did you write, or call, or what?

He spread butter and marmalade thickly: Simply fetched up one Friday afternoon, hoping to find her alone. Fascinating woman, she knows a great deal of medicine, told me about her methods with TB and how much disease there is in the valley. She's very knowledgeable about the first stages of pneumonia, which so many physicians miss entirely since . . .

Sam . . .

Yes?

I really don't want to know every bloody word you said to my mother. I just want to know what she asked about you and me. I'm certain she was on to you in fifteen seconds.

Credit me with at least some ability to dissemble.

We are speaking of my mother.

Well, you know how it goes. We talked around everything without getting into anything. I'd told her that I'd met you in Simla and that we were friends. She was happy with that for a while, but soon her questions became a little more focused. Of course, being your mother, the next morning, after kippers and tea, she'd had enough of the chitchat and just came straight out with it: And what precisely, if

I may ask, is your real relationship to my daughter, Dr. Singh? Threw me a bit, actually, but fortunately I've become accustomed to this kind of thing from you. What I love about your mother is that she's so Italian, you know, the way she moves and talks, the carriage of her body, not a trace of stiffness. The accent is still there, but at the same time her English phrases are exactly and only English. I'm beginning to think that it's the language, and the way they use it, that make the English English. Anyway . . . since she'd asked the question, I was obliged to answer it, and I sort of lost my grip for a minute because what on earth could I say: Well, actually, Mrs. Herbert, I've been sleeping with your daughter for months, and I'm madly in love with her?

What did you say?

He poured some of my milk into his empty lassi glass and swirled it around for a while. It is, you know, he said softly, impossible for me to hide my devotion to you, and I decided, whether it was expedient or not, not to try to. He looked at me directly: I told her that we were going to make a life together, whatever that took. She looked me in the eye for a moment and then surveyed the handle of her cup for an interminable time. You know, she said, my husband and I know very little of the complexities of a cultural alliance of this kind. And of course we shouldn't forget that Isabel is married, should we? That, Sam said, really made me laugh, and she had the decency to let me. The interesting thing was that she wasn't hostile, not at all, and I was surprised by that. I wondered if she'd somehow been responsible for your peculiar lack of racism, or perhaps it's just a lack of familiarity with Indians, or black foreigners generally. I was foreign to her, no doubt about that, but much in the way a Russian or even a Greek might be. It wasn't a matter of color with her, and I can't tell you how unusual that is.

He had his hand open on the side of his face, and then he reached across and touched my cheek. I think she knew very quickly what was going on between us. Early on she'd told me that she appreciated my coming here, particularly when I had sad business to attend to, meaning Sammy. I like the candor that your visit implies, she said softly, and the seriousness of your intentions towards Isabel. I think, he said, she was able to react to it not as she should but as her own person dictated. But by the end I could see she was disturbed by the whole thing, mystified, and even afraid. You see, she said, I don't know where to begin with something of this kind. I've not been to India, I know nothing of the country, but of course I do know the English, all too well, and it's quite certain, Oxford or not, physician or not, what the English view of such a relationship would be.

I asked her what the Italian view might be.

Different, she said. The question in Italy might be: What kind of future would you have? How far would Isabel drop in society, not being married, being seen perhaps as a kept woman, even a—she hesitated—a puttana . . . ?

And there it was again, he said with a grin, your mother was looking at it simply from the point of view of conventional morality, not as a color problem. And when I mentioned this to her, she said: I cannot judge the color problem, knowing nothing about it, but is it possible for you to be openly together in India?

No, it is not.

I have of course been thinking about that, she said, trying to imagine how it would be for the two of you to enter a restaurant, or a church, together?

That would not be possible.

I see.

So a life of hiding? Of obscurity? She turned in her chair to face me directly. Would it be easier here? In England?

I'm afraid not.

This is very, very daunting. She turned her face to the window. One is allowed to get away with so little in life.

Mrs. Herbert, I really don't want to alarm you, but I didn't want to hide anything from you either. I'm not interested in hiding and obscurity, only in finding a way through. I should also tell you that Isabel doesn't know I'm here.

Would you have told me if I hadn't asked?

Of course. I'd like to speak to your husband about it too, but I wanted to tell you first.

I appreciate that. But I have another question to ask, the most important one: What of children?

AND THAT, Sam said, is pretty much where we stopped because the real question is: What of the color of the children, and who can answer that?

I was speechless. That he'd gone so far, laying out a future that he and I had barely dared put into words. But I was glad he had. It was as if we two, once separated from each other, had been able to look clearly into the future and had taken it on, each in our own way. We sneaked back to bed and lay sideways, and now that he'd said it out loud, to my mother and me, there was no question about it, no hesitation. We spent hours talking, and then he fell asleep, while I, in the twilight, lay thinking, planning, fretting. When he was fully asleep, I crept out. I wanted to get some air, and because we needed cigarettes, I took the half mile walk to the small cluster of shops around a miniature park, the kind of thing you might come across in Chelsea near the King's Road. It was misty out, and the air was heavy, but I walked fast and found a small shop selling sweets and cigarettes, smelling salts and the like, and I bought a few packs and began to walk home. It was only when I was halfway home that I knew I was being followed. I walked faster, feeling my skin become warm and prickly. There were plenty of people around, so I didn't feel threatened, and once I turned into a corner shop, to catch my breath and calm down. When I started walking again, the sensation of being stalked was even stronger. I knew I shouldn't go home and began walking in another direction to throw my pursuer off my track. I thought of Gloria and wondered if this was something to do with her. I was sweating like a pig, my heart thumping. I walked faster, knowing I should walk slowly. Then I was struck by the thought that whoever was following me must have been doing so since Delaware Street, and knew all about my life, knew about Queen's Mansions, my work at university, my habits, my travel route morning and night, Sam's arrival—everything. It was like finding a burglar in the corner of the room who'd been there all along. I went home a different route, unlocked the front door with clattering hands, and ran up the stairs, barreling past the lady who lives above us. The minute I got inside, I decided not to tell Sam. It was ludicrous not to, but I was for some reason prepared, willing even, to allow myself to believe paranoia had summoned the stalker. I didn't want to think about it, or make it real, so when I got home, I curled back into him and said nothing. I used all my willpower to think about what he'd said about the future, but hard as I tried, I couldn't get rid of a feeling of terror.

Seventeen

Mother came to India. She'd taken a detour to view the glories of Hyderabad. Oh, she purred, hands aflutter, I can't tell you how beautiful, a whole other civilization, so exquisitely made, and knee-deep in jewels. Did you know the nizams of Hyderabad wore ropes of pearls studded with diamonds around their necks and ate a paste of crushed pearls to make their skin creamy and pale? And that when the last nizam was given an egg-sized diamond, the poor fellow didn't know quite what to do with it, so he asked for six more, which he used as buttons for his best coat? She was perched on the edge of her bed at the Ritz, which was vast as a boat, and she patted a space on the cream satin for me to sit beside her. Digging through a leather bag, she kept fishing up presents for me. I went to see them manufacture raw pearls, she said, which are soaked in hydrogen peroxide and left to dry in the sun, until they acquire a lovely lustrous white. I bought you a bagful, she said, pouring them into my lap. Perhaps you can make a belt with them and thread in these exquisite little rubies;

really, one could eat them, they're as delectable as pomegranates. Her bed was piled high with presents from England: a Chanel suit made of crisp cream linen, with a black rim, rather like a funeral envelope, but très chic. And a cloche hat from Worth, a gorgeous pair of black Italian spiky-heeled shoes with bows, and a delicately carved ivory cigarette holder with emerald petals running along the length of it. Love has made you beautiful, she said, whirling a wool wrap around my shoulders. Of course, she said, kissing me on the cheek, you'll need to have the clothes adjusted. You must be at least two sizes smaller.

And all the time she couldn't stop telling me how wonderful Sam was, how much she and the Pater both liked and admired him, and how clear it was that he absolutely, absolutely *adores* you, Isabel. Could not stop telling us how *wonderful* you were. She said that the Pater had even asked him to take a run up to Assam and check if the tea plantation house was still there—the land sold years ago, of course, but there was still a small house on the edge of a jungle. Pater's younger brother had always thought he might take a shot at tea, but still hadn't got around to it, and now of course was too long in the tooth. Mother wanted to see as much as she could of Delhi. I took her around the city and showed her the sights, and we went together to the university and medical center, where she poked her head into the lab, recoiled at the smell of formaldehyde, but said the library was rather impressive, for India. She was asking a million questions and reading my textbooks like novels. I wish I'd had the nerve to become a doctor, she said. Such weakness of character not to have tried; Maria pulled it off long ago. Mother always spoke of Maria Montessori as if she were a friend: What eloquence, what brilliance, and do you know, she has a child tucked away somewhere—illegitimate, they say?

As Mother did her sightseeing, I was back in the lecture halls, hard at it, so I didn't have too much time to spend with her, but enough for us to take lunch together at the grand hotels. She liked to make a dramatic entrance, and an even more dramatic exit, leaving huge tips. Wherever we went it was, senora, senora, and rushing us to the best tables. She spoke her immaculate French to the maître d'hotel and was on amazing form. Mama, I said, you should really stop in India. You look divine, and you seem so at home. You could follow Maria's example and start another Casa dei Bambini right here in Delhi. Of course, I wasn't entirely serious about having my mother stay in India, but she was so alive, so kind, and so enthusiastic that I considered it. She was another woman, less on edge, less prone to the small incision, the tart comment, the downright slice below the knees that Pater, after years of painful endurance, now managed with detachment. I still hadn't learned how to do this myself; Mama could crush me in a second.

I found myself imagining how she must have been when she was my age. She'd always been a beauty, but why had she done nothing with her brain? Not easy to do, she sighed. The best I could do at the time was to learn how to treat the workers' ailments and bully your father into making the mine more profitable, which gets harder every day, of course, with the unions wanting their wages upped every five minutes. But I would have liked it, real medicine, what you're going to do with your life, here, where it's so sorely needed. But to do anything serious, I'd have had to go back to the Continent. And besides, I couldn't leave your father and pursue a life of my own—unimaginable. How you get away with it here is beyond belief, but you know, I do think you get a touch of the unconventionality from me.

We were sitting at a table by the window in the restaurant of the hotel, having coffee. I was desperate for a cigarette, but not a chance. We were talking about the old days, and how she'd come up to Edinburgh, spend a few days in a hotel close to the university, and do what we were doing now, just the two of us, without Pa and Jack. But she hadn't been this free then. She was asking me about the lilac she'd given me and was delighted that it was alive and flourishing, and I suddenly took it into my head to ask her about the time—it was when Jack was first back from the war—when she was so unhappy that even the survival of her lilac brought her to tears. She looked startled: I didn't think you even noticed. You had so much on your mind then, worrying about Jack and Gareth and brushing up on your maths and physics to get into university. Oh, I noticed, I said. She turned her face and gazed out beyond the blue columns and gold drapes to the miniature lake set with symmetrical precision into the Oriental garden. The sun was glaring off the water. Inside, the fans moved silently in the ceiling, and though it was barely two in the afternoon, it felt like four.

Well, Mother said finally, I suppose it wouldn't be too bad to tell you, in the circumstances, but I must ask you not to question me. I mean it, Isabel, not one question. And here she gave one of her famous glares: I'm not up to your questions. And anyway, to tell you properly, I'd have to start well before the war, before my time in England, and I can't do that. Perhaps the best I can do is to say that when I was seventeen, I fell in love with a distinguished Italian poet, and he with me. At this distance, it's hard to say who was more foolish. How hard it is, she said, looking away, as if entranced by the voluptuous arrangement of pale blue iris and ivy in a corner vase, how hard it is to put words to this, when one never has. I poured a little more coffee into her cup, though it was risky, my action, since she liked her coffee to be the way it was. Too distracted to notice, she raised her left hand. We were intoxicated by each other, absurdly so, and we actually ran off and spent three days together in Venezia . . . Her eyes closed for just a second, and the most curious expression crossed her face, one I'd never seen there before but recognized instantly. It was ecstasy. I tried to follow her into the emotion, but it was gone as swiftly as it came. My father, she said, found out, and put a stop to it . . . and he—the poet—permitted that. Her face hardened: I found that impossible to forgive. I still do. She sent out a brittle laugh: I suppose I'd rather hoped that he might die for me . . . something absurd like that . . . Instead, he was coerced by my family to break off the affair. They could have ruined his career, and he was a great light . . . so that was what he chose. I was sent to London . . . to recover myself. She picked up and then put down a petit four; it was iced in shiny pink, with a sugared violet on top. She studied it, picked it up again, and bit it in two. That's when I met your father, she said. All I could see was a sliver of her face. Anyway, she said softly, this poet, he was the love of my life. She lifted her dark brown eyes, and I noticed, as I always do, how wide the space between, and how thick and lush her hair. Her voice put on a little speed: How could he not be the love of my life—so much romance and then the tragedy of parting? Her voice was quick and clean: He was killed in the war. I was sent an obituary . . . that's why I was the way I was then . . . the time you asked me about . . . She looked up and dipped her head in the direction of our waiter . . . Surely it must be time for you to be getting back? I must have held you up . . . how late it is . . .

Mother, please, for heaven's sake . . . wait . . . I can stay as long as we like. She wouldn't. And these are the moments when I'd like to take a bat to her, because she turns to stone, and that's it. Like that moment in the rose garden when I begged her to tell me her opinion about Gareth's illness. I wanted her so badly to say that he would get well, that the shell shock would pass. She wouldn't. Just like the day the dog ran off into the woods with a leg of lamb that she'd marinated for two days, and she took one look at him and said: He must go. I won't have an animal behave that way. I begged and pleaded, and no, she said, just no. Just as now she turned her back to me and was heading for the curtains that framed the dining room, weaving gracefully through the white-topped tables, the door to her interior slammed.

SHE WOULDN'T RETURN to that conversation, and I knew it was kinder to let it lie. It set me thinking, though, about Mother's ability to cut off and move on. And about her perfect English and the fact that she'd sort of kept her Italian blood rather dark, passing herself off as English. She had long links with Wales, of course—her grandfather had owned the mine that Pater took over, although it was a trinket; most of his real mining interests were in South Africa. She hadn't told me she'd come over as a young woman with a broken heart, but now her marriage to the Pater fell into place, and also the way they were with each other, so private, so separate. I wondered if he knew about the poet and how hard it would be for him if he did. He just adored Mother, though I'd always known it wasn't quite the same for her. How difficult it must have been for her, a foreign woman living in England, when it was clear war was coming. And how much more difficult when the war came and Italy at first took the wrong side. I felt tenderly toward her for braving that conversation with me, and I saw why she hadn't taken a high moral tone about my infidelity, because of course, though she hadn't said so, the poet must have been married.

As is the way with Mother, she put that moment of vulnerability and grief aside and returned to her robust self. And when she was certain that I wanted to stay in India, she worked unfailingly to make things secure for me, in ways that she's most effective. She sorted out the manager of the Imperial Bank and gave instructions about the house in Assam. She sent off money to the bank there and put it in my maiden name. She'd managed to wangle quite a lot of trust money for me, having told the trustees that the money was needed for a clinic for Indian children. The English are guilty about India at the moment, she said. She tried to persuade me to buy a small house in Delhi, just for the security, but when I wouldn't, she didn't press the matter. When I said she was doing too much, she said: You know what I believe, Isabel. A woman must have her own property. If you won't buy in Delhi, like a sensible person, then at least this house in Assam will be yours.

WHEN SHE WASN'T OFF SIGHTSEEING, Mother was reading up on everything about India. She'd deliver little lectures over the potted shrimp at Claridges or instruct me on Sikhism. She even started risking a little Indian food but tended to stick with tandoori and korma. At the weekends we'd hire a car from the Ritz, and I'd take her off to

see even more mosques and temples, mammoth forts and octagonal
Mughal tombs and shrines . . . and gardens galore . . . and as many
domes and monuments as we could possibly cram into a day. And it
was on our last such excursion, to Humayun's Tomb, a place of such
beauty and tranquillity that we barely spoke to each other, that we finally had our first serious conversation about Sam.

We'd walked around the high-walled garden, laid out in what
Mother said was the Islamic pattern. She pointed out the tomb
crowned with a double dome in white marble. The inner dome forms
the vaulted ceiling, and the outer shell creates a soaring effect, very
Oriental. Gorgeous, I said, suppressing a yawn, I'm glad we came.
Now can we please have lunch? I'm famished. Mother shook out a
rug on the grass. We were perched on a rise, where we could feel the
breeze, and all around us the spectacular setting of the gardens, all of it
perfect in its simplicity. Joseph had packed a delicious lunch of cold
chicken, deviled eggs, potato salad, cucumber in light aspic, soft let-
tuce doused in chives, and a small sponge cake filled with jam and
cream. Champagne, of course; Mother doesn't venture on a picnic
without.

She was talking very fast. I can certainly see why you find him so
desirable, she said. The kindness, the sophistication and breeding, and
yet that shy distance, very Etonian, but less remote, and without the
pretension and self-consciousness. What struck me most, though, was
his enormous courage. He's like a soldier in the Light Brigade, who
has decided to go in for the charge, knowing entirely the consequences.

Mother, I said, could you be a bit specific? I was feeling an odd
sense of exhilaration and fear; we were actually going to have a real
conversation about my situation with Sam, and I'd no idea where it
would lead us.

I could, she said, moving into shade. Her cheeks were flushed,
and her forehead wore a tiara of damp pearls. She swiped her straw
hat in front of her face. Our position was backed by tall trees strewn

with vines, filled with birdsong, and ahead of us lay a vista of ancient, timeless calm, which she gazed at a long while. I've thought about him a lot, she said. He was with us, you know, for several days, and I must say I rather missed him when he left. I liked him very, very much. I've always preferred dark men; they seem so much more attractive than blond or carroty types. Of course I keep your father separate from such things, looks being of no account in marriage. She suddenly grabbed my hand: For heaven's sake, let me carve the chicken; you're ripping it to pieces. Anyway, we spoke, Sam and I, about the future, or what he could see of it. I was impressed, she said, lifting long, thin slices of white meat and placing them on my plate, that he was so frank with me. Perhaps that's because like him, I'm an impostor. Though unlike him, I can't identify my own country with oppression; one has to remember that England was once a colony of the Roman Empire. I think, she said, the form of Sam's resistance is going to be very personal. He's not going to lead a double life with you, that's what I felt. That he will resist on a personal as much as a political level. He doesn't separate the two. That's the striking thing about him. She hooked a long tendril of dark hair that had slipped free of her chignon and, with her forefinger, coiled it back into the neat bun. And this, she said, is bold, reckless even, when things in India are in such an uproar: the religious terrorism, the bombings of police stations. It's all very disturbing, and my feeling is that it will get worse. War in Europe unsettled things here. All those Indians who left India to fight abroad and saw people who were not like the British in their regard of them—these things change everything. I have been reading up on it, articles in *The Times* and *The Scotsman*. There seems to be a feeling that we can't stop here for too much longer, that it wouldn't be right. Gandhi's noncooperation is moral as well as political. It's as if Indians need to purify themselves from the pollution of foreign rule by conducting themselves with rigor and restraint. It is clear that Sam will do this in his life, and it seems to have left him with remarkable optimism about your future.

She smiled: I believe Gandhi refers to the British as Satanic, and I must say you can see why we must seem diabolical to them with our insistence on power and force. Sam, she said, handing me a glass of champagne, has explained to me the brilliance of the nonviolence crusade: The more the British resort to brutality, the more civilized the native becomes. All this will cause a great rupture if it goes on. Europeans will not permit imperialist thuggery, not even in the colonies.

And then: Are you intending to meet his parents? I mean, we have met Sam now, and I was wondering about that.

It took me a moment to recover. It's too soon after his wife's death, I began. We intend to take things slowly.

Hardly, she said dryly.

I ignored that. Sam's father, I said, is vehemently anti-British. I'm not sure he'd approve of me one bit.

Well, Sam won't do anything to put you at risk, I'm certain of that. But, she said sternly, whether you admit it or not, you are at risk. You are married to a man in the British Army. How can you and Sam live openly together? She shook out a starched napkin and dabbed the corner of her mouth. Sam's very sensitive to your situation. I saw this when I asked him how much your standing in society, here, would deteriorate through your connection with him. It was when my language—how shall I say?—deteriorated to the street, when I wondered how you would be perceived, what kind of woman—and I used an unfortunate, an ugly Italian word to convey my meaning—it was at this precise moment that he chose to speak to me in Italian, in a formal, beautiful version of my own tongue . . . She stopped, moved. It was so like him to elevate the conversation, as if through it he showed me how deeply he repudiated what I was suggesting. He won't consider himself in terms that others try to impose, and he's the same way about you. She shuddered for a moment. I fear dreadfully, she said, this idealism he has, this notion he carries that he can vault above prejudice by refusing it. I admire it immensely, but I fear for him, for you both. It would be heartbreaking if he became a tragic figure in all this.

We ate in silence for a while. Just when my mouth was crammed full of sponge cake, she suddenly came out with: Have you forgotten that you have a husband? Do you imagine that he'll actually let you run off with an Indian? You can't escape him by vanishing from Ferozepore, any more than you can take up a life of medicine without people hearing about it. Do you think you've become invisible? She poured herself more champagne. I've thought and read about these things a great deal, and I think I have some idea what you're up against. I admire your courage as much as his, and you must remember this in the time ahead. And then she went quiet. Her voice, when it came, was serious and sweet: When you insisted on marrying Neville, I should have forbidden it. It was wrong of me not to have done so. Without that, perhaps none of these difficulties would have occurred. Perhaps, even, if Gareth had not suffered so terribly from the war, and then died, well, perhaps . . . but what is the point of perhaps, ever, or what if? She stopped for the longest time. I found that I was hurling myself into the vista ahead of me for comfort, but now it had become dark, shadows hunched over lit grass, the radiance of the sun stalking the quiet water. I tried to speak, to explain to my mother, but she reached over and took my hand and pinned it down on the rug. Isabel, she breathed, I forbid this affair, I forbid it absolutely. You would be committing social suicide. You would be walking willingly into a public stoning. I must ask you to end it immediately.

Eighteen

After Mother left, my mood was somber and determined, but I was having none of her prohibitions and warnings. I was going to continue in spite of her, finishing my anatomy requirement, completing the papers and exams, and spending long hours in the library and lab. I'd made no close friendships since Gloria. I often felt guilty for not taking charge of her—as if I could have made a difference or altered her fate in some way. I kept myself apart, teaming up only when I had to, before moving back into solitary study. I was in a great rush to learn about medicine. Sometimes I'd wake at three in the morning and walk the streets for an hour, coming back to study, reading by the dismal light of a kerosene lamp. Often, on my early walks, I felt a shadowy presence walking the streets with me. As the streets slowly filled with people on their way to work, the sensation of being followed increased. If I turned quickly, I'd see a movement behind a wall or a shadow ducking into a crowd. I forced myself not to panic, but whoever was walking behind me knew exactly where I was at any given time of day and was tracking every move I made. Some days I walked alone, and then the whole perplexity of whether I was imagining it would begin again. I was certain that my follower was a man, tall and dark, wearing clothes of such anonymity that I couldn't tell whether he was Indian or European. I couldn't think about it, because I knew if I caved in, I'd see stalkers on every street corner and malice in every face. In all of this I noticed in myself a small piece of aberrant behavior. Mother had given me a lot of money, in nice clean notes, and I'd stashed them away in a shoebox at the bottom of my clothes cupboard. But every so often, I put more rupees in the box, until there was a large amount of money. I'd often count it, though I'd no idea why I was doing this. In case—in case of what?

SAM HAD CLOSED DOWN his connection with the mental institution in Ranchi, as well as his research on war trauma. He was now at the General Hospital at Lahore, and because of the great distance, we were separated again. Joseph was my only companion, and in my new determination to focus on the essential and eschew the ridiculous, I'd suggested we eat together, he and I, on those evenings when I didn't drag in too late. He'd agreed to this arrangement and even threw out little quips: Will mem now be using fingers? Eating off banana leaf? Could this be the end of bangers and mash? We sat at the kitchen table, which for the most part was covered in Joseph's manuals from the Calcutta Correspondence Course. He was studying what he called Superior English, so I asked him if he was thinking of joining the Civil Service. He spoke with deliberation: Mem, I am contented to feel that should that be my aim, it would not be entirely absurd. Good for you, I said, tucking into a plate of chicken makhani and snatching the last flap of paratha before he got it. Mem, he said, I need your opinion on a matter of some interest. I have just finished reading *Romeo and Juliet*. I had no understanding that the Feringhi had copied the caste system of India. This has been a great eye opener for me.

Once, when Joseph was weak with fever, it was I who started taking care of him. At first he was mortified, trying to jump to attention in his crumpled tunic in his high iron bed, not sure how to manage my presence in the alteration of things between us. When I took his pulse or temperature, he couldn't look at me, and for my part, I kept my eyes trained on wrist or thermometer and tried to ease his panic. Joseph, please stop imagining that you'll be dead in the morning. Pneumonia is perfectly manageable, as long as you remain in bed until after the fever breaks. This was one instruction he simply couldn't keep; when I came back from the hospital, he'd have tidied my papers, or settled the cushions and chairs, or concocted some tasty meal. I had to promise that I'd leave everything for him to get to when his strength returned, and I also threatened to lock him in his room. You are an incorrigible patient, I scolded. Only such patients, he shot back, will make of you a great doctor.

During his convalescence I was astonished at how much lighter his skin seemed to grow and remarked on it. He seemed delighted: No longer black as soot, mem. As fair now—he smiled shyly—as a Kashmiri. I did a little cooking for him because he'd grown thin, and since he adores quinces, I went to the bazaar and bought the plumpest and ripest I could find, peeled and cut up the barklike flesh, cooked and mashed it until it transformed itself from a rugged fruit into a creamy golden puree. I handed it to him in a small glass dish. He looked at it, picked up the spoon, and ate carefully around the edges; his eyes closed for a moment. It's so fragrant, he said, it is as if I am in heaven. When he had eaten it down to the last scrap, he said to me with deep feeling: It is a long time, mem, that a woman has cooked for me.

I took my meals with him in his quarters, since it's a miserable business to eat alone, especially when one's ill, and on one such occasion, he said to me: Mem, all my life I've had a longing for London.

Oh?

He looked bashful for a moment. The mission school when I was a boy had nuns that came from London to teach us how to pray. One of these nuns, I prayed for her incessantly, day and night, and while on my knees, my eyes and heart took up residence in her veil, and I could not untangle myself from her.

You loved a nun, Joseph?

As only eighteen can. He smoothed the napkin on his lap.

Did she love you back?

Perhaps mem can answer?

Oh, yes, I said. She loved you back. Of course she did.

He beamed with pleasure and then went quiet, his head down, his hands flat in front of him. One time, he said softly, I walked up to this nun when she was in the garden, on her knees, planting the soil, and when she looked up and saw me, I am certain, mem, that her eyes danced for me, and then they fell to the ground and hid under her robes where they lived their other life. She belonged to God, she was a bride of Christ, and it was very hard for me to remember this, though I knew that surely her beauty was not wasted on Him.

And she went away?

His eyes were black. There was a bridge over the river, he said, rolling a ball of rice with his fingers and dipping it, and when her train had gone—I could see it from the place in the church where the bell rings—when it crossed the water, I went to that bridge and thought to make an end to myself.

I put my hand over his, and he looked at me with an intensity I'd never seen. His skin seemed to catch fire. I moved my hand to his brow and then to his cheek. Your fever is breaking, Joseph, I said. I'm going to cover you with blankets to draw it out, so you can get better. He slept for a day and a half, and sometimes I woke him, to give him water through a straw or to sponge his face. When the fever had broken, there was a new tenderness between us.

It was only disturbed when the post arrived. He'd bring my letters to me on a silver tray, and I'd say: Is that all there was today, Joseph?

He'd catch the disappointment in my voice, and later he'd come back. I did not see these, mem, he'd say. They must have fallen in the dust.

SAM AND I wrote to each other every day, sometimes a few snatched words, other times reams, written at three in the morning or in an hour between lectures, but it was painfully inadequate. My body couldn't stand the absence of his. I'd lie sleepless in the dark and dream of him the way I used to at Ferozepore under the peepul tree. Just before falling asleep, when the mind rests at twilight, I'd think of his body, silt-colored and naked, as if he were lying on top of me, part of me, moving in a rhythm that only we two knew. It was as though we had embraced and were kissing, softly at first, and then passionately, and so complete was the connection that I could actually feel him inside me, and my body would orgasm. Later when I told him this, he smiled and said: You'll have to teach me how.

Often we sent wayward telegrams at moments of impatience: *Come at once, I can't wait another moment.* To which he'd reply: *I'll come on Saturday.* But since I knew that he'd have to go all the long hours back to Lahore in the morning, I'd wire back: *Stay where you are. Stick to the pact. Only seven weeks to go.* I tried to persuade myself that it was good for us to be apart, that we needed to pursue our own careers. I also knew that there was something about the process of internal change that was deepened by solitude. I told myself I could think more clearly without him, as I had when he was in London. My studies were going well. I was now managing the long hours better, but there were too many things we needed to talk about and too much emptiness that could only be filled by physical touch. So when a break in my studies came up, I asked Sam if we could meet in Peshawar. It was a deliberate choice of heart above reverie, body over mind, urgency over caution. He sent me a telegram with one word: *Yes.*

WE SAT AT THE EDGE of the bazaar section of Peshawar and drank green tea, with cardamom and lemon, called quwa. We said very little, sitting as close as we dared, our feet touching. Peshawar, which separates India from Afghanistan, China, and Russia, is a town of bazaars and fortifications, oddly surreal, the way frontier towns are. We were going to spend the weekend at a small house just outside the town; a friend of Sam's had offered it for the weekend. To get there, we needed to find some form of transportation, and it proved difficult since the place was humming with activity and intrigue. An aggressive breed of British frontier officer strolled the streets, and Russian officers, Anglophobic and disdainful, strutted among the Pathans, making deals, swapping information. There had been another incident, and reprisals were imminent. Every shop sold knives, machine guns and ammunition; opium was changing hands in stalls on the street; small boys ran errands for lawyers; horse dealers trotted Kabul horses and Abyssinian stallions down the shit-splattered street, urging quick sales. Shady characters smoked on corners. You got the sense that harsh justice and head lopping was the name of the game—all in close proximity to the Red Cross infirmary and the British fort. The British Army appeared to be running the place, but there was a sense that it was all a hoax, and things could change in a moment. The Afghan warriors moved through the streets in their black robes, beards, and turbans, eyes darkened with kohl—beautiful and posey as actors. I'd heard they could survive for days on end without food and water and could walk for weeks, only stopping to wash their hands and faces in the dust to purify themselves for prayer. Political agents and spies filled the bar of a run-down hotel called Dean's. On the lawn outside the front, tea was being served with cucumber sandwiches. Russian traders disputed with Indians, a man in a red cloak walked a dachshund on a gold chain, and the inevitable cows swayed down the street, as did the Baluchi nomads leading pack camels loaded with gorgeous carpets. There were no women, apart from two prostitutes in dusty burkas, who leaned in doorways, eyes glittering with fatigue, hunger, and sorrow. I thought of Gloria, and for one aching moment I thought I saw her crouched in the dirt near a rifle stand. I walked closer and caught a look in the woman's eyes so empty I thought she must be blind. She stirred and put up her hands for baksheesh, and in her lap was a dead baby. Sam gave her some money; his face looked tense. It was always zan-zar-zamin up here, he said: land, gold, and women. Now it's about war, terrorism, and land grabbing. Whoever's running the show, once the fighting's over and the locals are dead or maimed, everyone sits around waiting for money to rebuild the wreckage. It never comes.

I was having an attack of paranoia. I began to imagine Neville must be lurking close by—among that rowdy crowd of soldiers in a street café or in one of the side alleys? I knew he'd come to Peshawar during the third Afghan War a couple of years ago. When he'd left me at Ferozepore, he was heading to the southwest part of the frontier, around Quetta and Kandahar. But how could I know anything? So much time had passed. I'd no idea where he might be now.

Over the Jail Bridge we could see the parade grounds of the cantonment, with the regimental barracks, the messes and the club, and the green lawns and stately brick mansions—Anglo-Indian Gothic. Sikh guards marched to and fro in front of the iron gate; the Union Jack hung limp in the heat. This little England was so bizarre, perched on the edge of so much violence and squalor, the stinking bazaars and exotic trappings of a mad and magical town that led directly to hell. Up ahead stretched the granite folds of the Khyber Pass, and marching down the street came troops of nine-year-old war orphans, fair as Etonians, who'd been taken into military brotherhood, and were now heading up into the northern desert and on into the Hindu Kush to learn how to kill.

We walked to the far end of the town, before the road begins its dramatic wind toward Afghanistan and the desolation of the Central Asian plateaus, and stood there a moment at the Khyber Gate. It felt almost inhuman: the echoing of the great empty valleys beyond the town, the melancholy sound of an eagle, a burst of gunshot, the thunder of torrents racing through high gorges. Out there stretched a wasteland that had broken all ties with the lush, tropical floor of India.

We ate at a rough bar, with a collection of strange characters who reminded me of the espionage traders in Kipling's Great Game: a faded
Englishman, who spoke beautiful Urdu, reading Milton as he scoffed
down curry and rice; a Russian, whose blood had turned to vodka,
lying comatose on the floor. The food was delicious, chicken with
burned garlic and cardamom, lamb patties seasoned with 120 spices,
saffron-scented biryani, and small parathas cooked and served in a
black pan—so sweet, golden, and crisp they melted in the mouth. I
began to recover myself. Sam was edgy as a scorpion.

We paid an extortionate price for a horse and cart and were told
that most of the way was covered by a strategic road, built by the
British to connect Kabul, Peshawar, and Rawalpindi. The tall, bearded
trader was cold and disdainful when he described the road to Sam. In
excellent condition, sahib, defender of the poor, he said, with a trace
of contempt. I assure you, no craters, excellent for travel, no brigands
or thieves, nothing to bring disquiet to the sahib. We took the gharry,
which thank God had rubber tires, and had it loaded with supplies
and water bottles. What was all that about? I asked Sam. He seemed
almost to hate you. Sam threw his bag in the back and said with a
shrug: He does hate me. I'm Hindu. They consider us weak and ef-
feminate. Here either you're a man, or you aren't. Simple as that.

We set off, happy to be alone at last. I wanted to talk and fill in all
the things that letters couldn't say, but for a while just sitting next to
each other was more than enough. Being able to reach over and kiss
him or hold his hand was bliss. As we clipped along, I was reminded
of the long journey to Simla. It seemed like a lifetime ago. This road
was a single track leading into the mountains. A convoy of camels and
horse traders were heading east. In the small, scattered villages, water
buffaloes moved through bright paddy fields, and the smell of manure
and cooking fires made the cool air spicy. Boys played cricket on the
road; they hurtled out of our way at the last minute, just as they did in
Delhi. Then there was the open road, full of bends and potholes,
sometimes dangerous because of the instability of the cart, always

dusty and exhausting. I found it hard to concentrate; the horse was a stubborn brute, pulling to the left as if it wanted to turn back. But the land was lush and tender. Apple, apricot, and quince orchards bedded down in the reddish black soil, fields of grain in the valleys, and a long red flag among the green: opium poppies, vivid as cochineal. As we meandered through, Sam lounged back and smoked, reading the instructions to the house.

I both did and didn't want to tell him about Mother's visit. On the day she took the train to Bombay, we'd driven to the station in silence and, on the platform, stood and made the most absurd small talk: Will you give Pater the dressing gown I sent? And Mother: Now make sure you keep track of the money that goes to Assam, and always demand an accounting at the end of each quarter. She added: I'm so relieved that we never spoke of any of this to Neville. Me: Mama, will it be possible to at least write about things a bit when you get home? Her tossed head, and the train roaring and hissing as it came closer, then slowing down like a furious black serpent as we both cried, and she kissed me quickly on each cheek, once, twice, and turned on her heel to board the train, without—and how it broke my heart—without looking back at me and waving, which we always, *always* do. I wanted to call after her: Come back, come back. Don't be angry with me. And I thought with terror: Will I see her again? Will she ever forgive me? I stood on the platform, my arms clutched about me, and waited for her to appear at a window and wave. I waited until the train rounded the bend with a last rattle of its tail, and until the last carriage was out of sight, for just a glimpse of her face or just a wave of her kid-gloved hand. Rien. Niente. Kuch Nahi. I went home and bawled my eyes out.

I HADN'T WRITTEN to Sam about it because I knew it would hurt his feelings dreadfully, and worse, it would shatter his view of Mother. With Mother there are absolutes, and Sam's not good with those. I also didn't want to admit how isolated in the world we were, so I hid it away, along with my suspicions that someone in Delhi was stalking me. I just wanted to forget everything and love him, but after being with him for a few hours, I began to realize that there were things he wasn't telling me either. Of course there was nothing to point to and say: You're hiding something from me; it was more as if he'd done an inventory of his soul, and there were things he wasn't able to talk about yet. He said he wanted me to meet his parents. He'd spent some time with his father, somewhere outside the town of Jammu, but he wouldn't tell me where. His insistence that I meet his parents alarmed me. Perhaps the experience with Mother had shaken me more than I realized. I was expecting rejection, a courteous but articulate cross-cultural cold shoulder.

I found myself thinking obsessively about how his mother would react to me. I imagined that she'd had a close relationship with Sam's wife, even though I'd heard this wasn't so. I imagined that she'd disapprove of my having a career, even though she was a doctor herself. I thought she'd scrutinize my clothes, my skin, my hair. She'd check on my class, status, and education and ask about my parents. She'd look to see if I was sufficiently severe with the servants and could keep up with the half-Hindi, half-English gallop of their speech. And she'd talk about her grandson to see how I reacted. She wouldn't believe that we'd met by chance in Simla, and she'd certainly know we were lovers.

I'd promised myself from the start that I'd risk anything rather than live in a place of half-truths with Sam, but I wanted him to go first. I wanted to know how much he'd tell me about his first meeting with his father after the train burning at Pindi. I reached across and put my free hand on his knee: You've been rattled ever since you mentioned your father. What happened? He began to search around, as he always does at these moments, for a cigarette. I took it out of his mouth and handed it to him. He laughed and, grabbing the reins from me, pulled up the horse and kissed me on the mouth, and then in that shivery valley between neck and shoulder, and then all over my wet forehead. The horse wandered off the road into the shade, but already my head had turned to mush and my legs to water. He said: Why don't we stop and have a little reunion? He was already reaching over the seat. I'll get my coat, and throw it down for you to lie on. I looked around me. The cedars and spruces were surrounded by long grass full of serpents, wild beasts, and killing insects. I could imagine a tiger leaping out of the foliage at any moment. I'm not really the outdoor type, I said, and I'd like to get where we're going intact. We settled down in the gharry and resumed the last part of our journey, and just like an old, married couple, we bumped down the dusty road to our house by the river's edge.

Of course he wouldn't give me a blow-by-blow account of what had happened with his father. When I want details, I don't get them, and when I'd be more than happy with an overview, he'll give me every nuance of Gandhi's decision to align himself with the Khilafat movement, or drag me through the precise meanings of jihad, political and spiritual, or make the entire case for martyrdom. But eventually I did get some sense of what had happened, through casual questions, thrown in over a cup of tea or while we lay in bed and looked at the moon. And then one night, very late, he began to take me through a pivotal conversation he'd had with his father, as if by so doing, he were giving me an update of where he stood with India. From the minute I got to the ashram, he said, we were at each other's throats. Of course my father hates any kind of primitive living, and the only reason he was there was that the police were watching his houses. He wanted to get further south, but it wasn't safe to move because of the roadblocks. Kashmir and Jammu are seething, a hotbed of sedition, according to the British, as bad as Calcutta once was. Not— he laughed—that he was living in discomfort, exactly. I noticed that his Mercedes was parked in a shed out of sight of the sadhu, who was praying under a tree, and he certainly wasn't eating unbuttered rice. But he seemed to feel rather trapped. It upset me, because he's aged a lot in the last year, and the patch over his ruined eye makes him look less like a pirate than a man without an eye. Anyway, he was in a foul mood, and he's utterly disillusioned with Gandhi and wouldn't stop going on about it: This rubbish he has been spouting about paralyzing British rule in India is useless. Nothing has coaxed Indian policemen and soldiers out of the grip of the British. They're still marching to work as dutifully as ever; this pathetic loyalty to the crown is beyond my comprehension. We need to blow the roofs off over their heads. The antiliquor campaign is a disaster, it's had a most terrible effect on revenues, and Gandhi's toadying to the other side will end in us all being slaughtered by the Muslims. And—this is my real contention—Congress is *still* an organization of the elite and the educated, not the masses. India is moving to anarchy, not freedom, and I won't be part of the hand spinning; it's nothing but bloody rubbish and will be the ruin of us.

My father, Sam said ruefully, is such a mess of a man; he despises the making of money, but he views his own commercial life as being above all that. He has the intellectual arrogance of high-caste Indians, which can be so offensive. The man's never been in a peasant village in his life, but there he is sitting in the muck of the ashram, spouting away about Indians' being a theoretical people, not given to manual labor, putting out of mind all the millions that are and never will be anything more than peasants. The future is with the mills, he says; large textile manufacturing, this is what needs development now. The British, he'd rant, have given us democracy, an independent judiciary, canals, roads, railways, and lavatories that flush, but the Raj is economically incompetent. The British came to plunder, stayed to trade, but still cannot grasp the necessity of educating the mass of the people.

I sat with him, Sam said wearily, in a musty hut, while he and his cronies talked and argued all night. From time to time my father would look around him in complete bewilderment: Why are we not as rich as we were in the days of the Mughul Empire? Why do we fall behind? It's not because we've financed Britain's Industrial Revolution; it's not because it's too hot; it's not because we're a nation of lazy bastards. So what stops India from regaining her glory? No one could give him an answer, which meant that we were then subjected to his own history. From the time I was fifteen, he said with complacency, I would not consolidate my business with the great business houses of India—the Birlas, the Tatas. Instead, I began to break the English monopolies on cotton and jute, quietly, steadily, making deals with the maharajas on the side. And then, when fortunes quadrupled with war demands for textiles, I made another fortune and used it to buy guns. Cotton into arms. And for God's sake, our cotton is better than any other; it transformed the clothing of Europe decades ago. They were walking around in scratchy, stiff, lumpy pantaloons till Indian cotton brought in beauty, color, and suppleness. We were great manufacturers then; everyone wanted Indian cloth. So what in God's name has happened that most of our people are wearing cotton made in Manchester? At this point, when he was all riled up, someone would infuriate him by saying: Believe me, Hari, making money in India will never become respectable. And let us please remember that in the days of the Mughals there were still skeletons from coast to coast. Hand spinning is definitely not the answer. We need spanking new machines and local dyes, not chemical dyes coming from Germany. We need to look to Japan; they are finding ways of redefining their merchant classes. It is they, not the British, who will push us out of the water, mark my word. And at the threat from Japan, my father would retreat into silence, sucking on a cheroot.

Then he turned his attack on me: And what have you to say, sitting there, listening to us old men, without sticking your neck out—always in the middle, on the fence?

When he begins to attack me, the old men get uncomfortable and begin to retreat, and pretty soon it was just the two of us with the wind howling outside. He has a way of becoming unpleasantly personal, moving from politics to personal conduct, and he brings up all the things that make me furious. That night he cut rather quickly to the chase. Your association, he said bitterly, with Colonel Pendleton almost cost me my reputation.

I have no association with Colonel Pendleton.

Your visit to him after the burning of the train was a tactical error on the highest level.

I went to see Pendleton because he asked it. I was somewhat compromised, and I didn't want to refuse.

How can you be so blind to reality? He began to splutter: The fact that you go at all, at a time like that, after what had happened, it is beyond reproach.

I'd no notion of what had happened at Rawalpindi when I went.

In spite of that, going to the British, who wanted information out of you, about me, created a very bad impression.

I gave them no information. But don't let us forget that your activities killed a lot of people. I didn't know it at the time, but you were involved in the reprisals, and you were directly responsible for that man being murdered in that grotesque way in the chili field.

I was not involved in that incident.

You were involved in the whole damn thing. It has your marks all over it.

I resent that. Nothing has been pinned on me. They got what was coming to them, all of them. It disgusts me that your own sense of honor would not make you see that reprisals were necessary.

Revenge disgusts me.

Cowardice disgusts me. Your chum Pendleton didn't tie you to a tree or pull out your fingernails, but he wanted information—about me and whom I was involved with. That meeting with him sealed your fate and mine. He knows that he can't get you to take the British side anymore. You've lost your safety, and so have I, but God knows where you really stand in all this.

I know where I stand, and he knows I'm not involved in your activities.

He also knows that you won't collude with the British against us.

Don't you see where that leaves you? You have no choice but to change sides.

I've never taken sides, so there's no changing to be done. Crossing over, or pretending to, is an old game of yours—loving the English, imitating them, and then being disillusioned, playing both sides off the middle. My life has given me two sides. I never did have your illusions. I lost them at Eton. I won't collude with you, with them, or with Gandhi. His pacifism is creating religious violence, which the British are exploiting under our noses. I won't be part of any of it, but as I see it, refusing activism that is violent doesn't make me a coward.

Neutrality is cowardice. Look at what is happening in the Punjab: agitations and brutalities. Muslims committing outrages, killing and rioting, forcing conversions on Hindus. Soon the British will order martial law all over India, and then the real barbarities will begin. And where, may I ask, will you stand?

I reminded him that once he'd wanted above all else that I should be an Englishman, and now, at the drop of a hat, he wanted me to knife the British in the back. I want them to go, I said, and I'll find a part to play in that, but blowing up police stations full of Punjabis isn't going to do it, and setting fire to men wearing khaki uniforms to encourage them to come over to your side doesn't strike me as being particularly noble.

The part you will play, he said sadly, has already been assigned to you. You did believe in those ideals of civilization, and you thought you could live them out. Well, they gave you a chance to rat on your people, and you refused them. You won't get away with that. You're for or against them, but either way you'll always be a monkey in a suit—a pinstripe suit or a white coat—makes no difference. I see by your smile that you have no illusions about that. The British are beginning to show their true colors in India. They know how to make a man, but they know better how to break one. There are hundreds of us, right now, in prisons and basements, being tortured in particularly

English ways. They have that icy disgust for a brown body, that notion that darkness is subhuman; that deft and precise cruelty when torturing a wog that leaves off all humanity. Jail going is quite the thing, I heard an officer say, and we'll give them a run for their money while we thrash the living daylights out of them. It's too late, Samresh, to choose a side; it's been chosen for you because you are my son.

Talking to my father, Sam said softly, or rather, listening to him, is the most exhausting thing in the world. I end up feeling I've had ten rounds in a ring. What I tell him means nothing to him. And in the end I stoop to personal insult and tell him that the way he has chosen to use his own power, to brutalize with it, makes him more of an Englishman than I am. And then he turns on me. Ha, he said, this is the way you speak to me now. Educated as you are beyond my reach. Have you no shame? This is the way you turn against me when I ask you to honor me, even as I honored your wife? It was I who was the one to avenge her death, while you stood at the hospital beds, stitching up Muslims.

I COULD SEE THE DARK RIDGES of his vertebrae. I rested my cheek against his spine and felt him shudder. Without turning he said: He infuriates me, my father, his aggression and mania. I've never been able to deal with him. And I can't now. It's why I wanted you to meet him, know him a bit, before it's too late. He's going to get arrested, or hung up with the other corpses on the road to Amritsar, or blown from a cannon, as the British did in the old days. He knows all this. He won't stop. He's intent on maiming an evil empire that he once admired above all else. He just doesn't see that the harder he hates, the more he remains under their boot.

I rubbed his back: Why would you want me to go with you to see him when he feels the way he does?

I suppose it does seem ridiculous. I think it is a way of trying to confound him, making him see that I can take my own road. But you're right, not a good time to be round him at all. He can't separate the racial issue from the moral one. In this way he's particularly British.

I'd listened without saying much, but I was thinking that the change that began with Nalini's death was becoming more marked. His time with Pendleton, which he didn't speak about, had moved him over to the Indian side, but he resisted the direction. He stayed up all night, walking, smoking, and in the morning was very tender with me. You help me, he said, to get out of my head. I think too much. In the intimacy of those days, always so short and indescribably poignant, I decided to tell him everything too, and when I described what had happened with Mother, I watched his face and saw a small contraction around his eyes. He said nothing, but I knew he felt betrayed by her. I saw it differently. I think she'd genuinely tried to accept what we were doing but couldn't.

When I told him about the stalker, he was sitting at the table, grinding peppercorns. You haven't told me all of it, he said quietly.

There's nothing more to tell. Sometimes I think I'm imagining it. It's not that I've seen anyone, exactly. It's more a sense of someone following me. I shouldn't have told you.

He was quiet a long time. It's Neville, he said.

No, it isn't. I'm certain of that because he can't get back from the frontier. He's not allowed furlough for a year. The army won't let him leave. And anyhow, I'd recognize Neville.

He looked up. Well, it's not about Gloria. He pushed his hair back with his hand, his shoulders were relaxed, and his hand just kept grinding the pepper in the marble, turning the hard berries into fine powder. He laid out a line of green chilies and seeded and sliced them, then chopped the garlic in his expert, surgical way. He smiled at me, then reached across and kissed the top of my head: We should get someone to look into this, don't you think? His voice was full and warm, loving, the way it is when he's free of tension, and I saw that I was wrong to be apprehensive about telling him things or of trying to shield him. His use of the word *we* was precise. He was sensitive to the idea of taking charge, imposing a solution, or trying to be unilateral in anyone else's affairs. What was to be done about the stalker would ultimately be my decision, and I liked that immensely.

EARLY ONE MORNING we walked into the deep fringe of trees that edged the hills and came across something resembling a path and, after walking for almost an hour, found a ruined temple, gloriously broken and wild, surrounded by banyan trees. Giant roots had forced their way through the outer walls and taken up residence in the center of the temple; the walls were overrun with lichen and weeds; the pillars had been smashed or had caved in under the weight of the tree's gleaming, marbled roots. The friezes of celestial dancers had been stripped away, and the embankment had sunk into the dark earth, stone crumbling into sand. One beautiful honeycomb tower remained untouched by time and invasion, each stone laid out as it had been, centuries ago, perfect in its symmetry. There was something in us both that loved a ruin, and we sat there for hours, in silence, listening to the past in the whistling of the wind.

A thick fog was creeping in, and we headed back to the river, where we like to sit, or swim. It's quiet here, no bathers, no women hitting clothes on the rocks, no children throwing stones. I'd thought I'd always prefer the sea at Porthcawl to any other body of water, but the great rivers keep the sea in some ancient memory. It's there in their width and breadth and in the quiet beauty of the life they hatch around them. They're the arteries keeping the land green, the tributaries and irrigation channels that feed a nation always on the brink of drought and starvation. Orchids and hibiscus smother the black tropical floor of the valley, waterfowl swoop, parrots and doves gossip in the mulberry trees, and flocks of cormorants make waves through the glistening air. We like to sit near a small shrine and watch the gaudy red flowers bobbing on the brown water; a stork with a black neck tiptoes through the reeds; a boatman in blue trousers raises his hand and then poles on. And although our few days of being together are nearly over, the day is peaceful as heaven.

Nineteen

It was quiet, the way it is, even in Delhi, at two in the morning. At first I thought rain was falling or, perhaps, that the English schoolmarm was up, walking above me on the second floor, making a cup of tea, or talking to the cat. There was a wind blowing, and I heard a soft, rubbing sound. It bothered me because we'd had mice when the days had first grown cold. A couple of hours before, I'd heard voices on the street below; the schoolteacher had been out to dinner, or to the theater, and was chatting to her friends. In the distance the last trams were returning to the depot, and the sound of the wind came in waves, washing up against the bricks, hitting the windowpanes with thuds. And then complete silence that stretched on and on. I couldn't sleep. I thought of doing some work. I'd taken a course on infectious diseases, and there was so much to learn, books from England and Europe and from the medical centers in India, and more lab work yet to come; I was overwhelmed by it all.

As I lay in bed, for one clear moment, my isolation hit me. Here in this room, with so little trace of anyone but me, my life was shorn of human connection, dedicated only to study, and to reverie—about what was past, and what might be—and this only conjured up when I dared to think backward or forward. I tried not to. I just kept on working, keeping my schedule full, adding a demanding course, and then another lab requirement, attending more lectures, and spending more time with cadavers. I was exhausted, but I couldn't sleep, so I got out of bed and, utterly without warning, I walked straight into him.

A hand reached out and grabbed me by the hair. I started to run, leaving some of my hair in his fist. His other hand caught my upper arm and twisted it behind my back the way bullies do. If I could get to the roof and down the small passageway that runs the length of Queen's Mansions and out to Lancaster Road or perhaps to the wall between my quarters and Joseph's and bang on it? There's no chance of moving an inch. I refuse to scream. I try to bite the hand that pulls my head all the way to my left shoulder, but the arm moves, and the hand tightens its grip. I try to use my legs, but he anticipates the attempt and kicks in the back of my knees.

I still can't see his face. He stands behind me, not saying a word, not seeming to breathe. I know in my gut that this is not the same person who watched me in the garden on Delaware Street, but I do know he's a soldier, a man who knows how to creep up on other men, track them in jungles infested with leeches, disease, and wild beasts, and kill without batting an eyelid. A man who could shove a bayonet into a chest as easily as hack off a cobra's head, break a woman's back, or set fire to a hut full of children. He follows orders because it licenses him. Neville's words come back to me with the vividness of the smell of the ocean on the day they were uttered: I like to kill and I'm good at it. I've been doing it since I was sixteen and ran away to join the Royal Artillery as a trumpeter. My ancestors have all been soldiers, men with blood on their hands, professional killers . . .

He brings his face close to my cheek: You might as well give in.

I've got you now, and you won't get away. I can feel the warmth of his breath, and the intimacy is revolting. I screw up my eyes and block my senses. He twists his grip in my hair, and I'm forced to move where his hand pulls me—out of the study and back into the bedroom. I look at the sheets spilling over the sides of the tall bed, the sheen on the crimson and black-stitched Kashmiri quilt, the small red rug on the floor, where my feet had landed but a moment ago, and I wonder if I'll ever see them again, or whether this view of my room in all its silence and simplicity, its loneliness and quiet, will vanish with the plunge of his knife into my heart. The hand releases my hair and hurls me across the room. My hip crashes against the cast-iron leg of the bed, and the rest of me slumps to the floor. He moves across the room slowly, and now I see him all right, my soldier husband, my lover of the voyage out, my ticket to India. He bends his knees and crouches like a native in front of me, feet bare, body tipped backward. Why did you marry me? When you despised me, you and your mother, both.

I didn't know you to despise you, I say, but I do now. It's madness to provoke him, but part of me doesn't care, wants this done with, as if at this particular moment I can't think of any other solution. He tilts forward a little. I think you could be persuaded to love me again, don't you? He smiles: Even though you've been filthied? The glow from the lamp travels over the bed and swirls at our feet, and there's something about his face that's terrifying. It's gaunt and sharp, lidded and dark, and it's suffused with a calm hatred that was honed long before he ever knew me.

Sometimes, he says, on the North-West Frontier, we capture women, not Pathan women or Afridis—that would cost us our balls—but other tribal women, the less protected ones. Sometimes we fuck them, to taste the dark meat, the breasts and purple nipples, the rough hair, part the legs, the cunt, shove in—just for the curiosity of it. He smiles: But you know all about that, don't you? He looks at me with disgust. But unlike you, we can't ride roughshod over the women up there, too dangerous, you see, because a Pathan will do anything to avenge the slightest disrespect to his woman: a glance, a man lingering at the edge of a field, turning his head, looking . . . They have an ancient system, better than our laws, just clean, rough revenge. When it applies to a woman's honor, they call it tor—means black. He smirks: Now isn't that something? Only blood, you see, wipes out shame. The payment of shaam namah wipes out woman shame. He doesn't shift his position an inch and keeps his eyes trained on my face. They're protective, you see, very, of the women they cherish. He takes out a narrow knife and unfolds it slowly till the blade stands up in his hand. They don't tolerate disrespect. He brings the blade close to my face, to my cheek, and then turns it on its side, resting the steel against the skin under my eye, just below my eyelashes. I'm not going to do to you what they do, he whispers. I'm not a savage, and anyway, their way you'd need to be killed by your nearest male relative, your father or your brother, Jack, but they're not here, so that's not convenient, now is it? He holds open my eyelids and brings the tip of the knife right up to my eye.

Perhaps I've gone mad with terror, but I have to speak, anything to distract myself from the steel approaching my eyeball, and I blurt out: I remember you telling me how much your father, the major, admired the Afridis; seems you do too. It startles him, this tug back into our past, into the night conversations on the voyage out, the deck under moonlight, the train ride into the mofussil when he brushed my hair. He moves back, and my breath returns. There are Pathans, he says wistfully, who fought for us in the war. Only men like that could smile at Passchendale or Gallipoli; only men like that could come back and laugh about it: that ten thousand Feringhis could die for a few measly feet of land. It amused them no end. The savage man has got it straight, all right. Army's gone soft. Blood money—he smiles, slashing the blade across his arm—blood money is about honor. His blood is pouring down his arm, and I move instinctively and grab the sheet, ripping it to make a tourniquet to stop the blood drenching his hand and the floor, but he doesn't even glance at it.

Quite the doctor, he says, you could heal my wounds, no doubt. It's touching that you should think of it at this moment, but it's your blood we're interested in—yours and his. The army will take care of his, no problem there, and since his old man put his head in a noose, it's only you left now. He leans right into my face, grins as I jerk my head to one side, and whispers seductively: How could you have done it? Betrayed me that way? I'd have given you more freedom than most, been out of your hair, but you don't understand, do you? You think you can have your own life, do as you please. I feel the cold edge of the blade's flat tip just beneath my eye, and madness returns. I hear myself say: How is it that you can do as you please with a young Muslim woman and compromise her honor, her very life, and think it's different for you? I see his moment of shock, followed by a fury that flushes his face, narrows his jaw, and makes his chin leap out from his neck in a grotesque jerk. I say: She came to see me. They'd cut her hands off.

Stupid cow.

I panic and start sweating. I look at the knife, long and ruthlessly sharp, but it couldn't, could it—cut through muscle and bone? I'm shivering . . . about to pass out, remembering how his father, like the Pathans, enjoyed taking their time about it, leisurely cutting through a limb, separating a bone from its muscle and tendons in small, slow stages. An image of the wrist comes up; I see the placement of the bones, and I'm deranged with terror. Divining my thought, he smiles, saying softly: My bearer, who is just outside, could oblige with a more suitable weapon . . . I scramble up from the floor, but he's up, and before I can steady myself, he reaches back his arm and punches me in the jaw as if I were a man.

LATER, WHEN I COME ROUND, he's still here, crouching on the floor, the knife open. I can't look. I put my hands under my armpits to stop them shaking. He's thrown some water over me, and it mingles with his blood on the floor. The sheet has been tossed over the pool, turning the white pink. I've been waiting a long time, he says softly, to see you again. There's an old Pathan saying: Revenge is a dish which tastes better cold. Well, I've been cooling my lead, having you followed till I knew every step you'd taken since you got to Delhi. Did you think a change of clothes could hide you? Did you never suspect that someone was breathing down your neck and watching you wherever you went? Think back a little. That scene at the station with the two soldiers? Remember that? And the romantic houseboat on Lake Dal—all that time you thought you were alone, locked in a dark embrace? All those nights when you thought you were lost to the world, remember that? Well, your cries could be heard coming over the lake by a Pathan sitting in the dark listening to your rutting, smiling as he smoked. He tracked you day and night. When you rode up the hill, sat by the river, walked in your garden on Delaware Street, strolled down the street in Peshawar, walked to and fro to the hospital, ran around with that trollop in hijab, his eyes followed you everywhere. He's loyal that way. He'd die for me. As I might for him. So you see, I was with you wherever you went, I never left you, and, at any moment, if I'd given the word, he'd have reached out and snapped your pretty neck or slit your darky lover's throat as he lay sleeping by your side. You remember him, don't you? My bearer? You two never hit it off, now did you?

I remember he used to dress you in the morning.

He moves closer, inch by inch. Then he leans back and looks at me. He brings the knife to my face again and studies it, then slides it slowly up, as if shaving my cheek. He stops just below my right eye. And with a stroke, like a lick of fire, the blade slices right across and through. A warm spurt of blood fills my eye, blinding me, pouring down my cheek, landing in scarlet splats on my white nightdress. I haven't finished with you yet, he tossed casually over his shoulder before slamming the door.

IN THE MORNING, when Joseph brings in my morning tea, I'm sitting up in bed. He looks at me once and almost drops the tray. He stands there, shaking, and then manages to get himself and the tray to the table and puts it down with a crash. He rushes up to me, wringing his hands, moaning in a strange, garbled way, his body bowed over. I put my hand on the bed and pat where he should sit. He can't, just trembles there beside me, tears running down his face, looking, not looking, looking. Then his eyes dart to the sheet on the floor and the pool of blood. He whispers: What happened, mem? Who has done this? I look at him. His eyes widen with knowledge. He moves closer to the bed, picks up my hand and puts it under the quilt, and draws the quilt tenderly around me, tucking me in until I'm covered. I stop shaking. I sit, he stands, neither of us saying a word.

THERE'S A THICK square piece of gauze on my cheek, below my right eye, which has caught the flow of blood. It's saturated, drying into black patches. Very carefully, he lifts the edge of the gauze, breathing out with a gasp. He sucks in his breath and stands up: Permit me to go to hospital, mem. My hand grips his: On no account. My voice sounds as if it were coming from the bottom of a well. We can't go anywhere. His bloodhound is right outside. He looks closely at my face and then away, touching my cheek, his lip trembling. Mem, he says, my heart is broken.

He comes back with a cup of milky tea, and putting his right hand at the back of my neck, with his left steady as a rock, he brings the cup gently to my mouth, and I sip like a communicant. Just a little, mem, he says quickly; swallow on left side where mouth is not broken. And all the while as I sip, he murmurs sorrowfully: How could I be sleeping? How not wake? How could this be? Leaving the room to compose himself, he comes back with a bowl of warm water and some cotton wool. He begins gently to wash and clean my cheek, keeping well away from the eye, which is jammed. I can barely breathe as the cotton wool touches the skin around my cheekbones. As he washes my face, he takes my hands out from under the quilt to wash them also. At first, I won't open my fist. I don't know why, but

I won't. Slowly he prizes my fingers open. Inside are my eyelashes, all in a row, like a centipede that has dropped from a tree.

WHEN IT WAS GETTING DARK, he came back and helped me to eat, spooning soup into my broken mouth, dabbing the edges carefully, handing me small soldiers of soft white bread. When he'd set the tray aside, I said: Sit down, Joseph. He perched on the edge of the bed and then changed his mind and sat on the rug on the floor instead, looking up at me, his face perilously close to white. My voice was calm: Let's think this through, Joseph. His Pathan is watching the house. If you look out the window, you'll see him on the right, under the trees. I can't go to the police. He's my husband, he can do as he pleases, according to him, and he's probably right. I can't go to hospital or even try to get an ambulance. In fact, I can't go anywhere. My face is black and blue, and I can't clean it because the gauze will come off and there'll be another bleed. I have the burka to hide in, but I can't walk around alone, even if I could get out of here. He knows everything. He's been watching me since we first got here.

I'd been running through every option all night, and I went through them again with him: We could get out through the passage at the back. He probably came over the back wall and then up the fire stairs, but he'll have seen there's a way out through the alley. We could go down the fire escape, but the Pathan could trap us in the alleyway at the bottom. It's impossible, I wailed, unable even to cry.

I could go out the front door, mem, and he would follow. You could get away at the back?

We have to leave together, because I have to wear the burka and will need you to come with me to the station; then we'll separate. We'll take different trains, and both vanish for a while.

Outside, I could hear the mourning doves, the sound of peace and safety, taking me back to daybreak in the Welsh hills, waking to gentle winds, waiting for Milly to bring my tea and drag off my eiderdown and nudge me toward breakfast. The smell of Mother's lilac drifting in from the outside, the soft green of the low hills, the railway line winding through the valley, streams of silver-bellied trout, sheep in the meadows, and the miners' boots on cobbles, stopping in at the Miner's Arms to flush away the dust from their throats before heading home to supper and sleep.

And then Joseph waking me in the pitch black: Mem, the Pathan is sleeping. Get up at once. *Run.*

Twenty

I'm trying to read an article in the Delhi *Times*, which the conductor has brought to my compartment, but I keep reading the same paragraph over and over, something about a bomb exploding in the opera house at Lahore and the Viceroy barely escaping with his life, emergency powers following a bloodbath between Hindus and Muslims, mass arrests for sedition . . . I just can't retain any of it . . . my hands shake, and I keep expecting someone to be standing under the platform lights or in the shadows below the clock. I imagine a dark, hooded face staring through my window or a knife hurtling toward my eye. I clutch my dark robes and try to talk myself off this precipice, but I can't . . . When Joseph and I bolted from Queen's Mansions and headed for the railway station, I grabbed the first train out of Delhi, and it happened to be going to Madras. I know nothing about Madras except that it's at the other end of India, and that's where I want to be. Joseph is taking a train back to the Punjab. I was sobbing behind my burka, not wanting to leave him. He was looking at me in agony, not saying a word, until finally he gave me a push and said: Go, memsahib, now, before my heart rebreaks.

I pull the blinds down tightly and lock the door. I'm in excruciating pain, and my mind's scrambled. I hear Neville's voice, a sibilant echo in my brain, insinuating itself into every thought: I haven't finished with you. My fingers shake like a girl's. My teeth chatter in my head, and my legs are so weak I'll fall if I stand. As the train pulls out and the commotion dies down, I try to leave my fear behind me in Delhi. I try to believe in Joseph's wisdom—that it's over and done with and that Neville won't come near me again, that I've become untouchable to him—but the fear is overwhelming, and I can't shake it. I need to hide, to get so far away from here that his breath will leave my cheek. I feel my way through the hours, knowing my mind's cracked. I go through my valise and think of swallowing the chloral, which would vanish me into sleep and oblivion. I consider veronal, or the foxglove potion, or a bottle of distilled Chinese herbs; all these would calm me. But I can't. If I'm not on guard, every second, a hand might thrust itself through glass, a blade flick open, blood erupt from my eye . . . Am I blind? I don't seem to remember what the knife did. But then, without reason, my mind clears, and my body seems to fill with light. My fear goes in an instant, startling me beyond thought or comprehension. At this moment I know I could be mad, but what might seem like madness to others is perhaps no more than some chronic febrile condition akin to tuberculosis, or the return of malaria, when temperatures soar and the mind is so free of itself that stars fall through sunlight and the moon sleeps on the shadow of the earth. Memory whisks me up to the silver roof of the Himalayas and from there to the little caverns where Allah's warriors dream of the virgins of paradise who'll bear them away when the body is turned to light. Only a glimpse of this, before the edge of the curtain is pulled back and velvet night descends. But that's all we ever get, don't you think: glimpses?

I put myself in the corner, my bag a barricade, my basket of provisions, bought by Joseph from vendors on the platform at Delhi, waiting for a time when I might eat again. When the conductor knocks, I thrust my collection of tickets at him, muttering that there are no other passengers. I pull my robes ever more tightly about me and retreat further into the corner. He barely glances at me in my endless black. All night I barely move or sleep. I feel as though both my eyes were wide open, though both are snapped shut and one may never see again. Perhaps it's become a phantom eye, because blind or not, images dart back and forth behind it like bats at twilight: Neville's face, a blade clenched between knuckles, his arm breaking into blood, my face slathered in it . . .

IN THE MORNING the light is searing. A journey south through dead heat, balanced on steel tracks, searing hot, frantic with speed. The pain on the right side of my face is beyond endurance. I'm trying to make it part of my body rather than a wound throbbing in isolation. The train jerks and sways, it makes me nauseated, as does the thick smell of soot, but I'm alone, and I'm breathing. I don't look out of the window the way I used to when I first came, any more than I think of India as I did when it first called out to me with its slapping staccato sounds In-dee-ah. Now it's become my own adopted Ay-shee-ah, slow, sleepy sounds—a lullaby, a return to a Welsh rhythm, a kind of peace. The train moves slowly, gliding through heat. The paddy fields flash green and gold; a drowned lake holds up bowls of lotus flowers. As the train brakes before plunging into a tunnel, I stare ahead with only a snatched view of the train rushing on and on, dragging rivers, forests and marigolds behind it. *There was a time when meadow, grove, and stream, / The earth, and every common sight, / To me did seem / Appareled in celestial light* . . . Another endless train journey, after the exquisite days in Simla; after Sam had gone, after they knew. Where is he now? Don't think about it. He's sleeping in his bed or walking through the wards, holding someone's arm, putting his hand on a forehead . . . Joseph will have sent my letter. Don't think about it.

Things are made bearable by the kindness of an Anglo-Indian conductor with flame red hair and green eyes. He's curious, of course, seeing what appears to be a Muslim woman in an empty carriage, all the blinds drawn tightly, day and night; a woman who barely speaks, or moves, or even looks up each time he comes rapping. He enters with his own key: Just checking that everything's all right, miss. He smiles: So you speak a bit of English, then? He spots a bloodstained dressing, and I watch his face from behind the grille, but thankfully he lingers only a minute. Later he comes in with a basket of fruit and some clean towels: Courtesy of the railways, miss. I refuse all newspapers, but I do keep the first one, with the news of the bomb in Lahore. I'd like to read it properly, not now; constant pain uses up all my strength. A preoccupation with blindness keeps me in a state where the smallest sounds make me jump out of my skin, as if the terror of being blind had amplified my hearing.

The conductor hauls in a block of ice, which he sets at my feet: It's hotting up out there. Tell me if you need anything at the next stop. He brings in sheets and offers to have someone make up the bed at night. His presence is unnerving, but it's also comforting because sometimes in here, alone for hours on end, or a whole day, sitting on the slippery seat, I feel that my soul has lost its bearings and I might just wander off into some internal twilight with no return. Today, as he leaves the compartment, he says: Would you like me to bring you another pillow? I shake my head and he leaves. I pull my hands out from under my thighs.

I'm trying to put everything out of mind, just the way once I'd put Neville out of mind, even though Joseph repeatedly warned me: Bad penny, mem, not to be underestimated. Just as Mother cautioned me: Have you forgotten that you have a husband? The putting out of mind started with the war. I could shut out absolutely everything then. I'd last used it on the road to Simla when, for days on end, I'd been able utterly to forget the Muslim girl. Of course I knew it wasn't a good thing. I'd done my stretch of Freud and read Janet, in particular, *L'État mental des hystériques*. I'd even come to see, from a brief time in the emergency room after an atrocity, that what women and children suffer in the wake of trauma is identical to the experience of soldiers broken by war. I knew those symptoms and defenses, I'd seen them in Gareth, and now recognized them in myself. I could live in a trance state for days, barely using my senses, aslant from my body, not even feeling it, and then reality would break through like a mortar shell.

ON THE SECOND MORNING, as soon as the sun rose, I opened one of the blinds, lifted the burka, and took out my mirror. My right eye was black and blue, blood clotted into a line of black stitches. I put the newspaper on the seat beside me, with a towel and an enamel kidney dish on top. Out of my medical valise I took small balls of cotton wool, which I soaked in saline water. Bracing myself, I placed a strip of cotton wool on the livid skin below my eye. I left it there and studied the rest of my face. My jaw was considerably better. I'd reduced the swelling by pressing a handkerchief of shaved ice against my jawline. I'd also been using the ointment Sam had given me for my bruised thigh after the station incident; the violet and bilberry extracts were clearing away the black and purple marks quickly, leaving behind a more pleasant shade of gray. I knew that once I opened my eye, it would have to heal unshut, and I wouldn't be able to sleep. The pain was deep, like the severing of muscles, tendons, and ligaments. I tried to see my eye as a diagram—all the way from the optic nerve through the crystalline lens to the cornea. I was terrified of damage. As I let the swab loosen the black blood, I remembered how we'd treated a man with an ulcerated eye by clamping his eye open and putting a needle through his cheek and up into his eye, leaving it there for several minutes. Every week, as he endured this treatment, he calmed himself, holding his pain at bay with his breathing. When I asked him how he was able to do it, he whispered: I am talking to God.

Could I do the same? I applied the wet cotton wool to the sealed lid, gently swabbing at the crusted blood, trying to separate my top eyelid from the bloody trench below. I had to snap my teeth on a nail file to keep from screaming. I kept loosening the top eyelid with the swab until it began to open. It took two hours, with a lot of deep breathing in between, before the two layers completely separated. I had no lower eyelid. It had been sliced off. My tear duct was gone. There was a long, deep, open wound that was oozing blood again. But I could see. I could see. I covered the other eye to make certain. I began to breathe again. I laughed out loud. The pain, which had been excruciating, left me, and for the first time I wasn't tempted by the morphine.

It was a night when strange images came and went, of past pain, physical and emotional, of darkness followed by flashes of light, and of deep thought and new understanding. When dawn came, I sponged my face and watched the sun rise out of the sleeping earth. And for some reason, I retrieved the copy of the *Delhi Times*, somewhat splattered by my use of it as a surgical table, and went back to the article about the bombing of the opera house at Lahore. This time I read it in its entirety. Close to the end was a list of suspects arrested for sedition in connection to the bombing. Sam's name was on it.

MY FIRST REACTION was a fear so strong I thought I couldn't survive it. I began to shiver in the heat, so much so that I thought the malaria had returned. I stayed this way for what seemed an eternity, and then I seemed to hear a voice telling me to get off the train and go back to Rawalpindi. At first I took it literally and thought I was being asked to pull the emergency cord and get off the train there and then. Instead, I waited for the next stop, Nagpur, where I very calmly got off. None of this required any thought at all; it was automatic, like walking. I bought a ticket to go all the way back past Delhi and Lahore to Rawalpindi. I didn't panic. My fear had gone, and in its place was a quiet certainty. I was focused only on getting where I needed to be. I had to find Sam's mother. I knew she worked at the purdah hospital at Pindi, and I was pretty sure I could find it. It would take several days to get from Nagpur to Pindi. My eye would have healed by then, and the bruising on my face almost gone. I was wearing a sari, one that I love, pale pink cotton with a border of scarlet. I've worn it so much that if there weren't all these folds, you'd see right through it. Sitting on the floor on the red rug, he said: You in your wet dress with your breasts on display, even on the first day, you saw right through me. I kept the veil close to my face and chucked the burka out of the window. It danced through the air like a ghost and vanished in the smoke.

My mind had broken out of its cage. And now I forced myself to remember everything Neville had said to me about Sam that night in Delhi: We'll get him, and we'll throw him into prison. Not a political prison, nothing fancy; he's going where the murderers and thieves go. He'll eat dirty rice like everyone else, and drink river water, crap in the fetid yard, and break rocks in the quarry with the other wogs. Even as he was torturing me the way women are tortured, he was describing to me precisely how men were tortured, but is there any difference in the level of suffering, in the sorrow between us?

It was on my way back north, not far from Delhi, when the train pulled into some scruffy tin pot station, that I stopped being careful. I wanted to walk. My injuries were healing, and the veil was sufficient cover, so I left my compartment and strolled on the platform for a while. I asked for some tea from a man in a bright green turban, and as I sipped it, I saw out of the corner of my eye a dark, bearded figure who was watching me from the other side of the platform. I dropped the cup and headed back to the train. It couldn't, absolutely couldn't be. I'd been too careful, not moving from my compartment all this time. I couldn't have been followed. The Pathan had been sleeping when we left. But my mind was ajar again, rattling, and the images were back. I tried to undo my actions to see if that might have altered my fate. I should have kept going south. It was madness to take a train north again. What had I been thinking? There was no escape now. It was the Pathan. Even though I'd barely caught sight of him, I knew it was he. And then it hit me: I'd been followed from the time we'd escaped from the flat. He'd been tracking me every minute of the way. Just like before. He'd allowed us to escape and was just biding his time. I felt so foolish I could have wept.

I was determined to shake him off. The next stop was Delhi, and the train was making up for lost time, lurching around bends and approaching bridges with terrifying haste. He knew precisely which compartment I was in, no question about that. I thought about jumping. From the train when it slowed before a tunnel. From the roof into the paddy field. From an open door into the river. In the end the only, pathetic thing I could do was to change into European clothing, make my way to first class, and wait to jump off the minute we reached Delhi.

Twenty-one

I saw an ambulance, two orderlies, and a nurse dressed in white. I thought about running, but it was pointless because already the orderlies were making their way toward me. My mind stopped in its tracks, and I saw myself back on the blood-splattered floor, with Neville crouching in front of me. I remembered the precise nature of his threats, as if hearing them for the first time: I'll have you put away, no trouble at all. There's a place for women who don't know how to behave. It's called Ranchi. Perhaps you'll have heard about it from lover boy, though he's not there now, is he? Too bad. Ranchi's in the most miserable province on earth, in a dump called Bihar, nothing but dust and flies, flat huts, and ugly people who survive by eating rats and locusts. Moving closer to me, he'd whispered: All it takes to have you put away for good is one signature from the doc—military chappie, so no problem there. He's a friend of mind, the name's Lawson. Treated me for the clap a couple of times. He puts down his signature to say you're up the gonga, I put my signature next to his, and that's it: You're in with the lunatics, and the door slams shut, end of story.

I told him it wasn't possible without evidence. He smiled: But we've got our evidence, haven't we? All Lawson needs is to hear about a little bit of lunacy or violence from you, and that'll do it. You're looking confused. Not as bright as you'd have us believe, are you? He said, almost coyly: See this slash here on my arm, you did it, right? Very nasty. And—he almost crooned—anything that I choose to do to you tonight I can say you did to yourself, can't I? Who'd believe you? A woman out of her mind? Not a soul, believe you me, not a soul, and certainly not Lawson.

Even though I knew that the ambulance and the medics were there for me, coming straight for me, even when it happened, I was in no way prepared. In no way expecting the two medics to walk up to me, put their hands on me, one on either side, holding me by my elbows. I stared at them, dazed, as they marched me down the platform, and when I came to and began to thrash and struggle, they almost picked me up off the ground and dragged me to the ambulance. The doors were open, and the nurse was standing by. And it was then that I began screaming and fighting like a woman gone clean out of her mind.

THE DOCTOR SMILED MOURNFULLY when he handed my husband the signed paper, glancing sideways at me: I regret, madam, that you have left us no alternative. And my husband, adding his signature with a flourish, said with a smirk: No more gadding about for you, Isabel. Those days are done. One last train journey and then the lockup. He put on a small charade, a little sniff of regret, a hand to his mouth in a gesture of distress. I seem to recall telling you quite distinctly, Isabel, that women do not go gallivanting all over India unchaperoned, telling no one where they're going and what they're doing . . . and as for the rest of it—he gave a theatrical shudder—it's too disgusting to contemplate. The doctor, ignoring me as though I were a servant, turned to the nurse and said I should be put under sedation for a day, and then, when I was calmer, I could be escorted to my destination.

A JOURNEY EAST. My mind empty as a snail's shell, brittle with hopelessness. And that woman across from me, sitting tight as a purse, pretending not to be on guard, not even wearing her uniform because the starch is in her soul. She's taking me under orders. Calm as a stone I must be. I imagine too much, and because of it, I can already see the corridor with the locked door, a single glass square through which an eye stares. Bouncing walls and belligerents trussed like turkeys, arms locked across chests, hands behind ears, and the white jacket knotted at the back. No trouble to anyone, not anymore, not I. And I can't help thinking that if I'd not been interrupted at the hospital, I'd have had a month in the psych ward, learning about, not being, a lunatic. How can one not become lunatic when surrounded by it?

Crab Apple Annie—her real name is Ginny—is always polite: It's time for luncheon, Mrs. Webb. Would you care for a bite? We could get off at the next stop and go down to the restaurant car.

Go, by all means, I say. I'm very content where I am. Her mouth droops, and her brown, laced shoes click like a tongue. Mrs. Webb, she ventures, it is quite bad for the circulation to be sitting so much on the hands.

Very true, I say, knowing this is a problem I do have, the hands, I mean. She keeps the blinds tightly down so that people don't think she's traveling with an Indian. She fidgets endlessly in her corset and stockings, and this, in heat over a hundred degrees, does not seem lunatic to her. Her hair is drawn back so no strand gets away from the chignon with its glossy coil. Her hair is lovely, thick and brown. At night she brings it down, but after the brushing, she shoves it under a cap. My hair is unbound, in the manner of mourning, and it's the way I feel, heading east when somewhere north of here Sam is undergoing his own form of incarceration.

My nurse is uncomfortable each time she looks at me. My sari bothers her. It's the one thing I have left to remind me of who I used to be. They took all my things, bar one ugly gray dress. The sari had been tossed in a wastebasket, but I managed to get it out before anyone saw me. So this is what I amount to now: one sari, one frock, and a velvet bag. It amuses me that Nursey is so infuriated by the sari; every time she looks at it she turns her head away. I wanted to see if I could help her over this strange obsession she has with what people should or shouldn't wear, so I told her that according to my readings of the lives of Englishwomen in India in the seventeenth century, it was quite customary to wear a sari, even to marry in one: How beautiful the countess looked in her white, pearl-scattered sari, and Lord W. in full military regalia, his medals winking in the sunlight. The heat boomed like a drum, but everyone in the wedding party was cool and languid, some reclining on the grass of the Viceroy's garden, others holding silk parasols over their veils, others sipping champagne, while small native boys waved ostrich fans and laughed at the scarlet-uniformed band sweating under the tent. The portrait is in Delhi. I urge Nurse Briggs to visit the university and see it. You do tell such outrageous stories, she sighs.

Of course I'd certainly go for lunch if I thought I could make a break for it, push through the motley crowd, dodge the sweet and fruit sellers, the hobbling beggars, and race into the first rickshaw. But when we last walked together along the platform at Mathura, she made me wear a wristband covered in leather, which locks me to her side as intimately as a chastity belt. If I make a dash for it, she comes with me. She's apologetic: I just don't think it wise, Mrs. Webb, to put you on your honor, not when you've been so feverish and upset. And you do see—don't you?—that I can't have you charging off. I'm responsible for getting you to Ranchi, and that's a long way off. I'll unlock you the minute we reach the table. I don't give her any trouble because I feel for her. One look into those dull, tired eyes, and it would be hard to be cruel to her, the woman so young and already in aspic. What would happen to her if I didn't get to Ranchi? And why should I give a damn anyway? I can't quite reach a point of indifference about her fate, not yet. I'm attached, in spite of myself, by feelings of affection. I appreciate one brave gesture of hers when that fool of a doctor was advocating the usual cure for a high fever and was all for directing me to the dentist's chair. Nurse Briggs came to my rescue: If I may suggest, Doctor, let us try something else first. I've always felt a strong repugnance for tooth extraction, worse even than leeches, and often it fails to reduce the fever. He got out the hypodermic instead. I owe her my teeth.

And of course, being women, we began to talk. I wanted so much to tell her my fears about Sam, but of course I couldn't. I told her instead about the Muslim girl, and in so doing, I of course gave her a great deal of information about my husband. Mrs. Webb, she said, let us see if we can cure you of your tendency to sit on your hands. Perhaps I can point out to you each time you do it? I believe, in this way, we can dislodge the phobia and diminish the traumatic effect of the sight of the amputated hands. Of course, she murmured, there must be some other, perhaps closer reason why you would identify so strongly with this young woman's plight. She looked at me, but I didn't fall for it.

I certainly had some questions about her, too. I'd noticed, whenever she spoke about the doctor who'd both committed me and engaged her to accompany me to Ranchi that she spoke with an odd little echo in her voice, something lonely and aching. She liked during the journey to smock, when it wasn't too hot for either of us to move. Taking up the front yoke of a child's dress, gathering the white lawn into small triangles and tucks, with small, tight stitches layered with pink roses, she told me the dress was for a distant relative, living in Hyderabad. I liked to watch her sew because with her head lowered, I could see the perfect white line of her parted hair and the smooth dark brown nut of her head. And when her head was down, she was able to answer some of the questions I'd send her way, and in this manner we made small forays into the silent continent of her past, where no explorers had gone before.

I've been in India a great while, she said. I was born here; my family settled in Amritsar in about 1785. My grandfather was wounded at the time of the Mutiny—not as a soldier; he in fact held a senior post with the East India Company—but he took part in the English atrocities which followed that event. She looked severe for a moment. I regret the part played, the whole debacle, our own revenge desires; the Mutiny was a shocking affair, and it changed everything in India. Of course the company lost power afterward and the crown took over. My grandfather went into the clove trade and became rather prosperous. His daughter, my mother, married the Resident of Amritsar and was part of court society, while my grandfather rather went to the dogs—whiskey, you know—and he could not stop until it had poisoned his entire system. So bad was this that on one occasion, shaking with the DTs and raving like a madman, he was found in the harem of a Mughal nobleman and very nearly cut to pieces. This caused an incident between the Muslims and ourselves and would have had awful repercussions but for some silent moving of hands behind the scenes, and as can happen, the only incident that did occur turned out to be a Muslim Hindu dispute that the British Army was obliged to put down.

She looked up and smiled: You may have noticed, Mrs. Webb, that I am startled sometimes by your insistence on Indian dress, but I shouldn't be. Not really. My grandfather and my mother spoke fluent Hindustani with each other, and my mother was very attached to her religious idols. In fact, once or twice she wore a sari herself and would even take a turn in the park in it. But things changed, as they inevitably will. When I was seven, my mother returned to England with my father, and I was left behind, even though my younger brother was not. Later he took up the family estates in Devonshire and married the daughter of a French general. She bit the end of her thread. You will perhaps wonder why I did not go with them and how I have ended up as a psychiatric nurse in the practice of an army doctor?

While she sewed, I felt I had to be engaged in some kind of activity, and since embroidery wasn't my strong point, I found myself doing sketches of her on the backs of the dinner menus. She had deep brown eyes and a good complexion but wasn't a beauty by any means. Her nose was too sharp, and her eyes too deeply set. She didn't mind my drawing her, and it helped her talk if I wasn't looking at her directly. She went back to the subject of her grandfather. I suppose, she said, if we take the Freudian point of view, it is natural that I should have taken up this kind of nursing, my grandfather having ended up in the asylum at Ranchi. She looked quickly at me, but when I made no response, she went on. And I too have had my brushes with intoxication, of one kind or another. I feel myself lucky to have been taken on by Dr. Lawson.

When, I asked, did you become his mistress? My question threw her into something approaching panic. The smocking was set aside, and she went to the window and opened it a fraction, but that only stepped up the heat, so she closed it again, leaving us to the greater mercies of the revolving fan. She sat but did not pick up her sewing again. Mrs. Webb, she said sternly, working as I have in asylum wards, I have often found that it is the strong-minded and bold of our sex who end up in these places. I have made something of a study of it, and it seems to me that unconventional women, women who cross the borders culturally or religiously or, for that matter, sexually are made to carry the burden of those transgressions. One of the simplest methods of dealing with them is to place them out of sight, so that those outside need never be reminded of such collisions and indiscretions. It's this kind of thing that has enabled India to stay so backward, cut off from the women's suffrage movement and all the agitation that eventually brought progress to England before the war.

I found myself feeling a chill, even though it was sweltering in the compartment, and since I've come to recognize this as a foreshad-owing of some kind, I paid close attention to Ginny's words. My grandfather, she said, was a rare case. European men are very rarely incarcerated—more normal for him to have been shipped off Home, as in the end he was, but there were other reasons . . . She hesitated, and then rushed on . . . As it happens, Dr. Lawson was in possession of some information about my grandfather. His father had been the physician who had arranged for my grandfather's commitment, and after his death Dr. Lawson the younger inherited all our family papers, and so when an auspicious moment came, he was able to advise me of certain things about which I had never speculated before. That was nine years ago, and since that time I have been, as you so bluntly put it, Dr. Lawson's mistress.

Is there a Mrs. Lawson?

She died four years ago.

Ah.

Ginny had gathered up her stitchery and was at work in a rather frantic manner, pricking her finger and having to stop and being obliged to talk to me without cover, which so much distressed her that she cut a new path through the jungle: Mrs. Webb, now that so much has passed between us on this journey, I feel I should tell you that your connection to Dr. Singh can only cause you the greatest suf-fering. I see that you are startled. Perhaps you weren't aware that I knew this? Perhaps you are not aware that I have a particular reason to caution you?

Ginny, I said, obviously, there's some connection between your situation and mine, and you need to tell me what it is because it seems to me, since I'm the one actually heading for the loony bin, that I could be carrying the can for quite a few people here, including, I might say, you.

My nurse was so upset that she broke into tears and sobbed as if her heart would break. She rushed out of the compartment and disap-peared for several hours. I became so worried about her that I started to search the train, even knocking on doors and rather making a fool of myself, but she was nowhere to be found. I didn't think she'd throw herself from the train, that didn't seem the kind of thing she'd do, and also I was sure the train would have come to a screeching halt if she had, but it was hours before she crept back in and sat in the gloom of the shuttered compartment with me.

She was pale and serious and had obviously been crying. Mrs. Webb . . .

Oh, for heaven's sake, can you just call me Isabel like a sensible person?

It's a professional courtesy.

Well, please drop it.

I will try.

I apologized for my roughness and urged her to continue, if she could. These things, she said sadly, are so difficult to speak of when they've been locked up so long. I cannot prove what I'm about to tell you, because I know that some of the darker details have been removed from the documents of the East India Company, and also from my grandfather's will, but for all of that, it is clear enough. She shook herself. What I am trying to tell you is that my decision to accompany you to your destination was based on the fact that however wretched your fate, and however wrong it is to have you put away, I believe that future generations might be better served by the intervention.

Ginny, I snapped, can you please tell me what the hell you're talking about?

I know. I am so sorry. She pushed the pile of sewing further away from her and looked out of the window for a moment. It is so very difficult, she whispered, for me to separate my past from your future. And then, still with her face averted, she mumbled: Put plainly, the facts are these. Dr. Lawson told me nine years ago that the reason I did not proceed to England with the rest of my family, to be married in the proper way, was due to the fact that my mother had a direct Indian ancestor. My grandfather had married a woman who was half

Hindu and half Russian. She looked defiantly at me. I might say that he was utterly devoted to her, and she to him, but the secret got out, and her life was made so miserable that she ran away and was never seen again. My grandfather, as I've implied, never recovered from the loss, and my own mother was shielded from this information until we were about to set sail for England. When she learned that we were of mixed blood, she made an instant decision. She left me behind. My brother, who was blond, went with her. Just before she left, she sat me down and impressed upon me that I should never on any account have children and that if I did, I would create a life of bitter sorrow both for myself and for my child.

She got up and walked closer to the window and gazed out of it, and when she had controlled her emotion, she went on. My grandfather's original will had made provision for his children and grandchildren, but after my mother left, the name of the Hindu wife and all mention of her issue was excised, and a new will was created in its place. The executor of both those wills was Dr. Lawson the elder. He took me in and, since I was destitute, made sure I was educated sufficiently to become a nurse, so that I would be able to fend for myself. And his son, having grown up with me, I think felt pity for me and, knowing I could never marry, has been kind to me, but through a misfortune . . . a mistake . . .

The train was approaching a bridge, and I couldn't hear or speak because the irregular rhythm of the train and the pounding of the wheels made it impossible for me to do anything but keep my eyes trained on Ginny as she stared wildly at the carriage door. I moved forward so I could grab her if she tried to run out, open it, and fly out into the river below. I was thinking that she had in some perverse way just delivered to *me* her mother's message to her, and in a spasm of pity, I reached across and took the hand that held the needle, and when the noise subsided, I said to her: You are referring, I think, Ginny, to the owner of that little dress . . . ? Your daughter, perhaps? Her lip trembled, and in a burst of rage and hopeless sorrow, she snatched together the white folds, with their soft flounces of skirt and their sweet, puffed sleeves, their inlays of smocking, tucks, and pink roses, and with her mouth torn with pain, she ran to the window, threw it up, and hurled the dress into the dark turbulence of the river below.

And then she turned to me and, with an admirable act of will, ran her hands back from her temples to the knot at the nape of her neck. She sat opposite me like a guard. Mrs. Webb, she said, you are sitting on your hands again.

We didn't speak much that night, Ginny and I, nor did we go to the restaurant car to dine. I ordered sandwiches, but neither of us touched them. I stayed up a great deal of the night and often thought of just getting off the train at the next station and leaving her on it. Her story frightened me, warned me, bothered me, but I couldn't think too closely about it. I had to concentrate. I had to find a way to get back to Pindi. Each mile on this wretched train was taking me farther away. So when first light came, I went over to Ginny's berth and shook her hard. She woke quickly, the way nurses do, and was immediately alert: What on earth is the matter, Mrs. Webb? Is the train on fire?

It is not, I said tersely, but I'm getting off at Allahabad, and I strongly suggest you do the same.

She lifted her face from the pillow and rested her cheek on her hand. I wondered how long it would take you to come to this decision, and I must say I'm flattered that you would think of including me in your plan. She smiled: I have thought, you know, about letting you escape, standing by while you vanished into the crowd on a crowded platform, that kind of thing. In fact, I'm surprised that you haven't. You seem the type, and I mean that as a compliment.

Oh, really? I asked, startled. You'd have let me shove off and disappear?

I'm not sure, not now anyway. The journey has changed my mind, and relating my story has made me see how vulnerable you are.

I'm not sure that you wouldn't be in more danger out there than in the close confines of Ranchi—however awful that sounds. I've spent the night, she said, tying back her hair, having nightmares about it all.

When, Ginny, I asked promptly, did you ever take a risk in your life?

I am not, she said, in a position to take risks. I have had to take care of myself since I was seven.

I know that, and it's part of the reason why I've not run out on you before.

You were concerned for my livelihood?

Of course, but I've been trying to see if there's some way that I can escape without getting you into hot water with Lawson. I don't want you to take responsibility for what I'm about to do.

She got out of bed in her white nightgown. There is no possibility of that, she said. If you escape, I'll be held responsible.

And you'll lose your job?

More than likely. Dr. Lawson is not disposed to show me any leniency—not after the birth of the child. He refused her utterly. I had thought—idiotic, it now seems—that I would be able to bring her up as an English child, somewhere, and that through her, I could seemingly be English myself, or if the worse came to the worst, I thought I could pose as her ayah and still remain with her. But one look at the child—she, poor soul, for some reason, turned out to be a lot darker than I am, and . . . well, arrangements were made. She was removed from me the minute Dr. Lawson saw her. It took me months to locate her; she's living with an Indian couple in Bareilly who are paid for her keep. I was thinking of going there, to at least see if she was being taken care of, but then this situation with you materialized. She stared down at her long, strong hands. What sad accommodations come out of these mixed relations, and yet we always hope that the child will come out fair and will receive the world's blessing rather than its boot. The best I have been able to do was to make the dress, which—she smiled sadly—is now at the bottom of the river.

Ginny, I said, feeling the heat stoking up every piece of steel that encased us as it boomed down on the black roofed carriage and sent heat waves through the window, Ginny, can we look at it another way? Here we are. You're a nurse, I'm on my way to becoming a doctor, we have Dr. Singh, or we will have Dr. Singh—we could start a clinic. We have what we need: money, expertise, youth . . . We're not trapped; we can *do* something. You can get your child back. Anything is possible . . .

She looked at me steadily and picked up her hairbrush. We are all prisoners of the Raj, one way or another, she said. Don't deceive yourself.

I suddenly felt myself tip and grabbed the seat to steady myself. She got up quickly and came over to me: What's the matter, Isabel? What is it? You look as white as a ghost.

I just felt faint. It's nothing. I forced a smile: D'you know, Ginny, that's the first time you've called me by my name?

It's the first time you have shown a scrap of vulnerability, if I may say so. Now, do you think you should tell me what you're going to do—or not—in case, for some reason, I am apprehended and asked questions?

I think it better not to tell you where I'm going. But I would like to know if you're going back to Lawson or not.

She thought a long time. I'm not sure that I can, she said, though the thought of starting all over again, well, it seems terrifying. I have in some way been protected from the time I was seven and to be out there, alone, who is to say how well I can manage? I think I could pass myself off well enough as European, as I always have, but that was within the sanctuary of a family, people who took my Englishness for granted.

You do have your qualification as a nurse.

And I have some money saved. I think I will manage. After all, she said softly, I have nothing to lose. You, what you have, or will have, is so infinitely to be desired. I too would risk my life for that.

We've come a long way, Ginny, don't you think?

Indeed we have, she said softly. I can barely believe that I've told you what I have. She leaned toward me: But in spite of the sorrow, I cannot say that I regret breaking my mother's prohibition. If I have had a moment of real love in my life, it was when I first saw my daughter's sweet face and held her in my arms. You, Isabel, are stronger than I am, more determined, so you will succeed where I have not. You must try not to lose heart. Perhaps you are more afraid of the asylum than you need be. The doors of Ranchi can be unlocked, you know; new papers can come into being. Dr. Singh has a high reputation at Ranchi. I am sure he will be able to help you. Surely this must have occurred to you?

Dr. Singh is no longer at Ranchi, I said.

I was not aware of that, she said.

Dr. Singh, I said, is in jail. He was arrested after the bomb went off at the opera house in Lahore.

She was quiet a long time. My dear Isabel, she whispered, you do know, don't you, that if that is so, there is very little likelihood that he is still alive?

Twenty-two

I wouldn't believe what Ginny had said about Sam, though I went with great agitation to Rawalpindi, gnawing at my nails and nerves, almost in a rage when the train stopped too long at a station, or there was a delay on the line, or passengers took too long boarding. I was beside myself with worry by the time I got to Pindi, and when I was led into Sam's mother's office at the purdah hospital, I blurted out: Sam's alive, isn't he? Tell me he's alive. She smiled at me and said quietly: Yes, he is. I wondered when you'd get here. She gestured to a chair, and I sat, keeping the folds of my sari tight across my knees, feeling, for a moment, as still and contained as the Muslim girl had once been with me. I looked at the woman opposite me. Here she was at last, Sam's mother, the woman in the wedding painting, the person who'd been striding around in my mind, grilling and rebuking me, telling me that I wouldn't do, that our situation was hopeless, that it would all end in tears and tragedy. Now that I was with her, all the rehearsals on the long train ride dissolved, and I was able to see her as she was—a gentle woman, tall and elegant, wearing a white coat over a cream sari; it had a border of blue, in which gold geometrical designs stood out in sharp relief.

Suddenly feeling rather young and inept, I blurted out: I'm sorry to have spoken that way. I've been mad with worry.

Of course, she said.

So he's all right?

Her smile faded . . . there is every reason to believe he is, but unfortunately, we have so little information. There's a crackdown all over this part of India, and everyone is frightened. My son has been moved from one obscure jail to another, and usually we hear something after he has left, so it is all very frustrating. She pressed her knuckles together. You must try not to worry. We have many forces at our disposal. Samresh himself is extraordinarily good at adaptation. The hardships he is enduring will not touch him the way it might another man. He was very small when he was first put into the hands of the British. I winced. She immediately leaned forward and touched my knee. I'm so sorry, she said, that was clumsy. She shook her head. I am not doing well today, but please, for a moment, let us be personal. My son was frank with me about his feelings for you, and I respect what has happened between the two of you. It must be right or it would not have occurred. I regard it as his way of reunifying what is broken in him, and I imagine it is the same for you. It pleases me, so much, she said softly, that you wear Indian clothing, that you are bending into our culture rather than away from it. She looked directly at me, and in that moment I saw the shadow of Sam in her smile: I want you to know that I don't hold you responsible for my son's incarceration, not in any way. I believe his arrest occurred for reasons to do with his father's political activities. Things are changing in India, and that's a dangerous moment. She reached her hand across and placed it on mine for a moment. Try not to let yourself fall into panic or despair.

She left to make us some tea in an adjoining room and brought in a small tray with honey cake and a plate of Turkish delight. She picked up the pot and said: I'll be Mum, shall I? It's hard, she said quietly, all the English connections, all the little phrases and gestures which have become so much a part of us, to know which is us, which is not us. It's hard to know if we did right having Sam educated in England. These questions come up at a time like this. I fear he will suffer more now, not less, because of his close affiliations with England, and to me that feels so inhuman. After all, she said, the British have made him the man that he is, and now he will pay for it. But, she said, letting her hands drop down on either side of her chair in a gesture more of serenity than hopelessness, how could I have known what to do with so gifted a child? England seemed best for him, but now I see my husband becoming so confused and twisted about it all that he attacks his own son for being implicated in British oppression. Hate has entered his life, and he's put all his authority behind it, so much so that I fear it will destroy him. But, she said, we must be grateful that Samresh is not confused. He was never that. His mind is a clear, honest vessel. He is, as I'm sure you know, very aware of your predicament, more concerned about it than his own ordeal, and he will worry about not being able to take care of you. She looked at me and said: May I ask you what happened to your eye? Would you like someone to look at it for you here? We have excellent surgeons. I shook my head. It's healing, I whispered, but thank you. She waited a moment and, seeing that I was on the point of tears, carefully directed us back to Sam: Our lawyers have been thrown into the streets; civil liberties have come to an end, so we can't proceed that way. She gave a small, ironic smile: Even I, because of my husband, am under suspicion. But, she said, moving her chair closer to mine, we do have information because my husband has informers in all the locations we are tracking, so let me tell you exactly what we know.

Sam was arrested in the emergency room at the hospital at Lahore the night the bomb went off at the opera house. His arrest took no more than a few minutes, and by the time the medical staff understood what was happening, he'd been handcuffed and taken away. No one had time to come to his assistance. He was taking care of the wounded at the time; many schoolboys had been maimed and blinded by the bomb, as well as several members of the viceregal guard. She got up and closed the door to her office. My husband, I should add, she said, has had Samresh watched ever since the Rawalpindi disaster. So from the moment he was arrested, we've had him followed every step of the way. We know he spent the first night in a prison on the outskirts of Lahore. She looked at me: Do you want to know the details, because I can easily leave them out?

Please tell me everything.

She nodded and then, in a way achingly similar to Sam, leaned forward in her chair and let her hands drop between her knees. It's an old prison, she said dully, from the early days of the Raj, but the methods they use are standard. Prisoners are stripped and left naked in a single cell without a window in a fetid basement with a dirt floor. There are no lights. She kept glancing at me to see how I was doing, but I listened intently, noticing how her voice became increasingly clinical and precise as she went on: The prisoners are not fed for several days since the point is to confuse them and break the routine, the continuity of time, which is the thing that keeps us sane. We have no precise details of what he endured there . . . but . . . it is a place of torture and humiliation—as I said, the old ways of the Raj. He stayed there two days and then was blindfolded and put onto a truck with some other prisoners, about ten, I think—doctors, politicians, lawyers, the kind of people who make up the bulk of Gandhi's revolution, people suspected of sedition. They were driven into the countryside, where the prisoners were taken off the truck and made to walk for several days. A few of my husband's men followed them through the backcountry. He himself would have had no idea of where he was being taken. There are no distinguishing roads or villages out there, just a monotonous, hilly landscape. At night the guards confiscate the prisoners' clothing and bind their hands and feet. It is bitterly cold at night, and—she shuddered—he hates the cold . . . Her voice tightened: The body, in extremis, becomes riddled with nervous spasms and muscular tensions, and contractions settle in the brain, creating a restlessness bordering on hysteria. She looked at me, and her gaze moved to my damaged eye. I feel, she said, that you may be intuitively aware of these states, perhaps even have some experience of them? I was too distressed to answer her.

Please tell me, she said, if anything disturbs you in what I tell you, and I will stop immediately.

No, I said, please keep going.

You are like me, she said; you prefer the facts.

The facts help me not to go too far in my mind.

I understand, she said. From what I heard, they walked through forests for several days and then through a village where a Hindu reprisal against Muslims had just taken place; these things are terrible to see, not that he has not seen terrible things, in all sorts of ways. She stopped for a while. From there, he was taken further north, to a new prison that we didn't know existed. It's hidden away in the middle of nowhere, set back in the hills. The buildings are brand-new; there's a lookout with a tower and a locked gate in a high, spiked wall. The officers there all speak Urdu, and the Indian soldiers have been carefully trained in intelligence work. There is a building for political prisoners, but all the prisoners, we're told, are emaciated and ill, so anyone coming in from the outside enters an area of contagion. There is no infirmary. Disease is rife. Those who succumb die. On the upper level of the complex are the isolation cells, where Samresh was placed. Sam, she said, her voice becoming maternal, would immediately have measured the room and checked out every detail and all possibilities of escape. He would have instantly demanded to see the British intelligence officer—and paid for that impertinence. We're told that the isolation rooms contain a bed against a wall, no mattress or pillow, no pot, no water. There is a hook in the ceiling from which a rope hangs, but it's too high for suicidal purposes. There's a single bulb which never goes off. Prisoners are shackled, and their arms tied at the elbows, day and night, causing constant pain and, in time, permanent damage. One of my husband's men managed to get taken on as a guard; he has given us most of this information. We were told that they began immediately to interrogate Sam, beating him with bamboo poles several times a day and . . . well, I do not know the details; my own reticence prevented me from asking . . . Her face was becoming increasingly drawn and white, and I asked her if it was too hard for her to continue. No, no. She swatted it aside and went on: A shrill sound breaks the silence of the cell at ten-minute intervals, so that sleep is impossible. Later, of course, the brain finds a way to let the body sleep in spite of the siren and the bright light. But there's no way to measure the passing of time; there is nothing in the isolation cells to mark a wall or the floor, no implement at all. Sam would have spent hours trying to solve this problem, but by the time he got there, his brain, without food and sleep, would have grown lax and jittery. No sleep and no food takes us to hell or nirvana; the choice is God's. Sometimes, suddenly, the light will be switched off from the central grid, and darkness adds another element of disturbance. There are no sounds except for the siren, no birdsong, day and night are identical, and since the cell is either freezing cold or boiling hot, the prisoners become increasingly disorientated and afraid—isolated and suspended, outside time or space. Every attempt is made to disrupt routine. Sometimes the bowl is pushed through the opening in the door at midnight, sometimes at noon; sometimes the bowl is full, other times empty. When the guards stop patrolling, there must be an oceanic sense of desolation . . .

A nurse knocked, put her face through the door, and said: Dr. Singh, you are wanted in the emergency room. Sam's mother got up at once. Wait for me here, she said, while I get someone to handle this. When she came back, she was pale and shocked. She said: I'm afraid there is very bad news. She sat down in a rush. I don't have details, but something grave has happened. Samresh is alive—she got up and walked around in agitation—but the information is not clear, and I am unable to speak directly to my husband; he's disappeared into the hills, and I'm dreadfully afraid that he'll take matters into his own hands. I picked up her terror in an instant and now felt it coursing through my body. I went over to her and begged her: I'll do anything, anything at all to help. Just please don't leave me out of it, please tell me anything you know. I can bear anything, as long as I know. It was, I said, my voice breaking, the way we were together. He seemed, you know, sometimes so much older, as if he knew things, as if his life were preparing him for something he'd understood long ago . . . dark birds flew by in the twilight so fast and so randomly that I thought they were swarming and would at any moment dive into us and then crash through the windows and take over the room. I was feeling faint and a little giddy, and she came close to me, her hand reaching for my wrist, the cool, ringed fingers touching my pulse and then my forehead: Are you all night? I can get a bed made up for you while we decide what to do. She sat down opposite me. I think probably it would be safer for you to leave here. Things feel very precarious. There are rumors of some kind of terrorist attack; you'll be safer away from here.

I stared at her in dismay and covered my face in my hands. I'm pregnant, I said, and burst into tears.

Twenty-three

I left Rawalpindi immediately and took a train to Simla. My fear of Neville seemed ludicrous in light of Sam's predicament, and my worries about Ginny were dwindling. Now it was time for me to put the veil aside. I needed to read the papers, mingle with my own kind, and take the temperature of the times. I wanted to understand what the bombings and the rioting were about and whether we were indeed approaching the end of British rule in India. I knew I was about to move into a new phase of my life, and if India was on the move, I wanted to be part of it. And then, in a moment, I realized I was no longer in love with India, with the crimson, heart-shaped continent that had once so dazzled and intoxicated me. Instead, I'd come to love it, even to feel it loved me back; I wanted India to teach me how to live and love and how to bring up children, whatever their shade, in a place of safety. Above all, I wanted to be of some service to India, to finish my degree and do some useful work, since it seemed that we English had no right to be in India if not for this.

I'd decided on the Albert Hotel in Simla. The small hotels were dicey, and the bed-and-breakfasts out of the question; anonymity was guaranteed at the Albert. It was the grandest hotel in India, the Ritz of the hill stations. It had come out like a debutante, with a full display of fireworks and the best of banquets and balls, and there it was, lording it over the mansions up and down the Mall, a place of glamour and excitement, doors opening and closing on dowagers, millionaires and princes—the Chota Vilayat, the little England of India.

I strode in and then right out again. Its splendor was offensive; its glamour and finery were flippant and obscene. How had I even considered it? I stood looking down at the polished tiles of the veranda, not sure what to do or where to go, but in fact, I'd no choice about it: I'd told Sam's mother I'd be staying at the Albert, and so at the Albert I must stay. I walked back in and got myself the simplest and smallest room available. The manager was haughty and rude, intent on humiliating me. My room was on the ground floor, close to the basement, and there was barely enough space for a small bed and a chest of drawers. A window looked out on the back garden, with a chicken house to one side and a vast vegetable garden surrounded by high walls on the other. As the days passed, I began to love the room. It was a nun's cell, white all over, with muslin curtains and an iron bed. It had no connection with the rest of the hotel and was more like a small island shut off from the mainland. My days were spent in isolation, with a routine that helped regulate my anxiety and fear. I rose with the sun and walked the entire length of the grounds, down to the blue enameled lake and back up to the terraces, where I took tea and toast before anyone came down to breakfast.

I spoke to no one, and in the solitude and emptiness of my mind, reaching through absence and darkness, I tried to connect with Sam. When I lay on the floor, in a block of sunlight, I'd close my eyes and have a deep awareness both of his suffering and of his endurance. At night I had images of him in a cell in the darkness, waiting to be flooded with light, woken by a screech of siren, or a devastating rise or dip in temperature. I tried to stay awake, to be in tune with him; at first I was unable to, but after a few days, I began to spend most of the night talking to him in my mind, communicating with some part of myself that was wiser than I was about our future. At times, in a trancelike state, I would seem actually to be transported to a prison cell, and if I thought of him being beaten or tortured, I began to feel pain. At night I might wake up sweating, or freezing cold, and it seemed to me that this was less a disturbance of hormones than a telepathic communication. I tried to dismiss it, but odd experiences kept happening, and I remembered Sam's mother's remark that deprivation created altered states: hell or nirvana. Once or twice I'd find myself ravenous with hunger, and I'd rush to the dining room and eat in a most peculiar way, shoving food into my mouth as if I hadn't eaten for days. The behavior was so bizarre that I realized I was in some strange way trying to save Sam from starvation by my own gorging. But for all the food I crammed into my mouth, and in spite of my pregnancy, I wasn't filling out. I was again, as I'd been when he was in England, grieving the loss of him by becoming lean and strong, preparing myself again.

I spent so much time alone, and so deep in thought, that it felt like prayer. I returned to the things that Sam's mother had said about the physiological stress he was enduring, and I tried to consider how he'd bear it. I was thankful that his body was strong and that he was so disciplined and alert. One night, in a half-dream state, I visited the village where Hindus had massacred Muslims. I seemed to see it at the edge of the forest, as his mother had described it, but then I found myself entering a clearing, where I saw the charred remains of a village. There were no bodies. Barely a trace of human life remained: a broken pot, a hand, a shattered loom, the blackened carcass of a sheep, a door on which the Aryan Hindu sign had been painted in blood. The blackened leaves of a Koran flipped in the breeze that covered the trunks of the trees with ash. I thought I would hear the sound of lamentation and despair, but instead I seemed to see the dead going about their daily rituals as the earth turned on its wheel. When the rains came and flooded the land, the remains of the dead would be folded back to nourish another planting, and life would begin again. I saw Sam look at me and smile. It's only an illusion, he whispered, all of it, even the suffering, even the beauty.

I turned inward, moving around the contours of our child. I imagined a face and a smile, a voice, a color sweet as caramel. Life was brimming within me, putting on shape and form, making fingers and toes, eyelashes and nails, a nervous system, organs, and arteries—pathways to the heart and brain. I remembered that my heart would actually move over, making space for an infant even as it expanded with love. I wondered if Sam somehow knew that he was going to be a father again; would it be unbearable for him to think of that? Or of me? In the disorientation of solitary confinement, could he return to memories that were tender or ecstatic, or would they devastate him? Would he forget me as he'd had to forget his mother at Eton?

One night, waking from a dream, I experienced a sudden, horrific descent into a void. It was like being sucked into a vortex, spinning through darkness deep as hell. In the midst of it, I found myself flung back across the room at Queen's Mansions, watching the knife approach my eye, and this time, instead of freezing into numbness, I entered a homicidal rage. My skin was burning, my heart speeding to such a pitch of fury and hate that I thought it would leap out of my chest cavity. I had an image of tying Neville to the bed and cutting out his eyes, one by one. This image wouldn't leave me, simply would not go—however hard I tried to banish it. It horrified me so much that I plunged further into the dark, where I reached such a rim of self-loathing and despair that it reduced me to palsy. I tried to get out of bed and couldn't. My legs wouldn't hold me up, nor gravity chain me to the floor. I seemed to float, and if I touched my body, it seemed not to be there. This went on till dawn, and no amount of self-entreaty could rise me up out of the dark night, and no appeal to the safety of the child within me could release me from the lurching sea. When, finally, the madness gave way, my fury and grief led me directly into a sense of my own powerlessness. How could I have stayed in this room and done nothing while Sam was suffering? How could I let British thugs brutalize him and not intervene? Shouldn't I be blowing this hotel to smithereens rather than taking breakfast and lunch on its verandas? What was the matter with me that I'd not taken up arms on his behalf or joined his father and become part of the reprisals? I persisted in this violent manner until I realized I'd reached parity with Neville. That cleared my head. My body began to cool. I came up with some startling conclusions. For one, my behavior toward Neville had been vile, and even if we took into account an unholy alliance, a use of the other which resulted in downright misuse of the other, I'd certainly played a full part in it. And surely, by associating with Sam, by entering his life at all, I'd put him at risk the way Neville's recklessness had led the Muslim girl to her death. This last was so appalling that I knew I'd have to acquire some sort of faith or rip myself to pieces with the force of my emotions.

Remorse brought me to my knees and saved me. As dawn slid into day, I dragged up each and every transgression of my life, every betrayal and cruelty, each selfish and violent word or deed, each lie and self-deception, until I was buried in my own dirt. Who was I to judge Neville? Why had I seen him only as a soldier and a thug? Why hadn't I found the compassion to see him as a man who'd been brutalized by the system as much as he used it to brutalize others? Or as a motherless boy left to the cruelty and neglect of servants while his father rode roughshod over him? I'd seen him purely to despise him, and in this way I hadn't seen him at all. I'd gone on to humiliate him in terms that could lead only to murder or mutilation, his or mine.

SOMETIMES, as I walked through the arched garden gate into the intoxication of roses, there was a sense of panic, a return of violent images, and I felt I was coming undone again. I'd move quickly indoors to the sanctuary of my rooms and crawl into bed, pull the sheet over me, and stay there until my teeth stopped clattering. Late one night I found myself staring at the face of a woman who I realized was Sam's wife, the woman he'd married when she was no more than a child. For the first time, I saw my actions as reprehensible. I'd broken into the sanctity of a marriage, and at no point had I checked my own desires or motives or felt a single pang of remorse or guilt. It was days before I ventured out. When I did, it was in a sober and chastened mood. Something had shifted within me, and in turn it affected the way people regarded me. No one had approached me at all during my time at the hotel, but now, as I walked the gardens in the late afternoon, one or two women tried to draw me into conversation or asked me to join them for coffee. I began to pay more attention to the other guests and even ate when other people were eating—and not like a barbarian—and smiled and exchanged a harmless pleasantry or two. I saw officers gathering at the bar, or playing tennis, or taking tiffin out on the veranda. I listened to conversations and read the newspapers from top to bottom. I didn't directly engage with my own kind for long, but I watched them. They watched me too and respected my reserve. I knew that they were thinking I might have suffered some misfortune—a tragic romance, a husband killed on the frontier or in the recent trouble in the cities—something like that. I played the invalid, shrouding my face with frothy veils and low, shielding brims, and walked on the edges of lawns as others strode the center.

In spite of my fears for Sam, I continued to believe that everything would be all right, that he'd come back and life would resume again. Pregnancy was now making me buoyant, and I felt fully alive. This hatching soul was moving into its space, snug within my womb, and because of it, I was being granted a state of grace in spite of my transgressions. My back curved into a cradle, my hips became a shielding wall, and my face a mirror that my baby would smile into. I was deeply curious and excited about the color of the child, and I wondered if I could become Indian by living with an Indian man and having a child who was half Indian. Wouldn't that make me Indian

too? Surely, as we walked in the hills, no one would stop and stare at
us? I was finding a sense of peace, of belonging, and through it I began to reshape my old dream of vanishing into the immensity of India.
I wanted to locate a place where we could all be safe together. I spent
hours at the Simla library, gathering information, working out a plan.
I put all my faith into believing that it would come to be. I decided to
find out how I could legally be divorced from Neville, and I hoped
that at some point Sammy would come home and be with us.

A WEEK LATER, late at night, a note from Sam's mother was slipped
under my door. I snatched it up and read it without breathing: *Please
be ready at five A.M. tomorrow. Walk to the Mall and wait on the bench outside the jewelers, and someone will collect you from there.* The long days of
suspension were over. The fear and dread gone in a blink. I collapsed
into a heap of tears. I wrote two letters, one to the PO box in Delhi
for Joseph and one to Mother. And after writing a check to the hotel,
I packed my essentials in my battered velvet bag and waited for dawn.
When I left the hotel, dawn was breaking, and I sat on the bench and
watched the sky turn gold. Mist swirled at the base of the hills and got
caught in the pine trees; the Himalayas were tinged with the first pink
and gold of morning. The doves and parrots were calling, and the
sweepers came up the Mall in a single line, their brooms draped across
their shoulders like milkmaids all in a row. I sat and watched and
waited, my heart filling with a love that seemed to include all that I
saw, and remembered, and had ever known.

Above me on the ridge, with ancient pines lined up to protect it
from the mockery of the great mountains, was Christ Church, and
from the open windows of a house I could hear the tinkling sounds of
a piano and the competent sound of a woman's voice singing "Danny
Boy." I looked around me, as if for the last time, and it felt to me that
I was saying goodbye to England. It was cold, and I pulled my long
black shawl around me and waited. Finally a tonga came along and
stopped in front of me. I got in, and we moved swiftly, winding down

and down into the lower reaches of the crumpled town and out to where the path collides with the main road. A black Mercedes was waiting. Sam was not in it. I did not see him until hours later, when we got to an overgrown back road outside Chandigarh, where I was asked to get out by a driver who, until that moment, had said not a single word to me. Far off, from the shelter of the trees, a truck slid slowly out of the shadows onto the road, and a bearded man was helped off the back of it. He stood quite still on the white road for a minute, and looked about him, and then up at the sky, before he caught sight of me and began to walk toward me, his feet shuffling in the dirt road, one arm held stiffly at his side, white shirt flapping in the breeze. And I began to run. But oh, when I saw him led out of the back of that vehicle in its camouflage of branches, when I saw them help him down and how he almost stumbled, I stood there in the middle of the road, my knuckles pressed into my teeth and my heart stone cold, and I remembered how he'd walked across the compound at Ferozepore in his pale silk suit with his hair soft and curly, walking like a man who knew his place in the world, and who believed life was as simple as this: If you see in front of you someone who is suffering and you have the skills to alleviate it, you do so with all the means at your disposal.

Twenty-four

It was as if I'd dreamed it, or known the place from long ago, because when we reached the tea hills I was home. It wasn't like Wales, not in the slightest, but the air was sharp and clear the way it is in the Black Mountains. And I could breathe. We'd arrived at some other place, cooler, higher, and filled with light. We'd escaped the trains, and the beastly, torrid lower reaches, with their dust and pestilence, and were making our way up into the high plateaus of the tea hills of Assam. Up here, the Brahmaputra River and the high Himalayas separate us from China. We're part of a small tuck between two landmasses: the red heart of India to the left, Burma and Siam to the right, and Calcutta down on the coastline, where the many mouths of the Ganges open into the Bay of Bengal. Sam was sitting close beside me, his head resting on my shoulder. The covered tonga, chosen for its thick red velvet seats, was taking us up and up into the mountain meadows and high-altitude pastures, where cows move slowly and elephants bathe in lakes cluttered with water lilies.

In a bought room in the middle of nowhere, I'd begged him to take off his shirt. The doctor had given him a large supply of morphine and put a splint on his arm, but Sam hadn't let anyone touch his back. I tried again: Let me cut the shirt away, and then I can wet and ease the rest of the cloth off. You'll need to lie on your front. Come on. We have to do this. It's infected. When I moved toward him, his hand slammed down on my wrist. No, he said. No. Why can't anyone get it into their head? I rocked back on my haunches. I'd been trying for days to clean the wounds on his back, but nothing could separate him from his shirt, his stinking, bloodstained, once-white shirt. To distract him, I tried to take him away from his memories and back into our life. Above all, I wanted to tell him that I was pregnant, but his mood was so distant and strange that there was never a right moment. I decided to risk it: Do you remember that night when you were accusing me of knowing nothing about dengue fever, and I got you down on the floor, and we were laughing and we made love, do you remember? And he looked up and I saw that his remoteness had reached as far as the moon. I moved closer to his knees and took his hands and looked at him, and I said: Sam, I'm pregnant. His head jerked up, and then his face fell forward into his hands as his shoulders shook with sobbing. I watched him, wounded, uncomprehending, and left him. I went out and stood in the corridor, smoking, looking out of the window at the timber trees shooting into a fathomless night sky, at jungles full of man-eating beasts and spiders that paralyze in a second.

I thought he'd have known. And how could he not, when he can read a body simply by touch, divine a sick lung or a congested heart by moving his hands across an unopened chest or predict a malignancy without benefit of scalpel? I fought a desire to retreat inside my own body and further away from him. I shook myself. I remembered the scars on his back. I remembered how he howled in the night and sometimes sat upright in his sleep, gasping for breath. I thought about the night he came back to me and how his eyes never closed because he'd learned how to sleep with them open. In broad daylight a night-mare would roll him into walls, screaming into his fists. At times he'd crash to the floor and curl up, hands covering his head, knees in his face. And throughout it all, he never took off the white cotton shirt, which he'd been wearing under his surgical coat the day they came to arrest him.

I remembered that I loved him. I remembered also how he'd looked in the bright sunshine on the white road as he'd limped toward me. How his eyes had fastened on my right eye with its red and livid scar. He'd sent out one loud, piercing scream, which echoed through the hills. His head dropped, and I lifted it and held his face in my hands and kissed him all over his emaciated face, and then held him against me, feeling his heart bang up loudly against mine, and for a moment we were one again. I knew then that I had a choice: I could crouch down in the dirt with him, sit with him in the desolation of experience and mourn, and let it go on and on, the sorrow, the bitterness. But I wouldn't. I wanted to get up and stand beside him. I wanted to go forward into a place where the outrages of the body had no power or place, where memory held no knife and where our injuries were merely scars.

He still hadn't told me what had happened to him, except to say that he'd played chess in his mind and heard organ music and remembered all the words of the Easter hymns. He said it all calmly, but I remembered how, when he got out of the truck that first day and came toward me, his graceful coordination was gone, the light in his body was gone, his unruffled beauty was gone. He shuffled, and his left arm hung oddly, and when I reached him he stumbled on the dusty road, and I saw that his shirt was covered in long dark stains, the blue of old welts and the red of new wounds making a Union Jack on the white of his shirt.

I went back in and tried again. Sam, I said, I won't cut the shirt. I'll just loosen the cloth so I can get it off. Please lie on your front and let me help you. And he nodded. It took a long time, but I was, after the eye, quite an expert in this work, and I was able to avoid the blood flowing again. When finally the shirt lay on the floor, he reached over and took my hand, and gently kissed it, front and back, till it was speckled with his tears. I'm so sorry, he said, everything overwhelms me, it seems. I picked up the shirt, and inside the collar the label said: *Handmade, by Coles of London.* I wanted to hurl it out of the window, but instead I washed it in the tin sink and let the water run and run until it was white again. I hung it in the window for the sun to bleach. In the afternoon the sun moved back into our room and covered him where he lay on his stomach, one arm dangling on the floor, and the rays fell on the deep welts on his back and began to mend them. I let him sleep, day and night, night and day, and sometimes I'd close his eyes for him.

When he seemed stronger, I said: Can you tell me what happened? Would you be able to? Looking out of the window, for a long while he said nothing. It's not that I've been trying to exclude you. It's just that I don't want to make an attachment to it. It took everything out of me to stop being afraid, and I don't want to go back to that. I can only take small things, only focus on a bit at a time. When they first let me out into the sunshine, sound was excruciating. A horse neighing, a bricklayer slapping cement on a wall, the wind in the trees—any simple sound was unbearable. I could only look at what was right in front of me: small brown birds, a dragonfly hovering over a pail of water, pebbles . . . things were overflowing with feeling, and I couldn't take it. I thought I would fall to pieces. When they brought me out of the cell for the first time, if a bee touched my arm, I shivered; if a man groaned, I felt my heart would break. I'd get a glimpse of your hand running down my spine, or a sudden memory of your smile, or your body curled into mine, and I had to stop thinking. I simply had to forget everything except the moment I was in—nothing else.

He took a cigarette out of the packet and held it in his hand, unlit. The one thing I could have done there was to be a doctor, but they wouldn't countenance that. The prisoners were desperately ill. I asked why no one was being treated, and when I persisted, orders were given to torture me again, but in a different way. The match flared, and he lit the end of his cigarette but didn't smoke it. A Parsi, he said softly, a small, slack-bellied man with a kind face, came to take me into the courtyard. It had a paved circle in the middle where a square stake stood facing the midday sun. I remember how nice the Parsi was, and how talkative. I have been chosen for this work, he said, because I am blessed with a year's medical training in Bombay. I know how to bind the limbs of a man to assure maximum suffering without death. This is a gift, no? He stepped fastidiously to one side of a pool of dried blood. This, he said, is our place of execution. Yesterday was the decapitation of a high-ranking terrorist—face-down, head to one side, single blow to neck, spade more effective than sword. He shook his head disdainfully: That is not my work. I bind. It is the only thing for which I am famous.

Sam's voice was detached. I was hung, he said, on that stake by my arms. It was midday. I tried to keep my head up at first, but it was impossible, and when my head flopped, I had less air in my lungs, and without air I felt the pain more vividly. I managed to shift the angle of my arms to get a fraction more space in my chest, but the effort was too much. After five hours or so, sounds began to recede and then faded out altogether. When I approached suffocation, I passed out. I came to when a bucket of water was thrown over me. It was cold and dark by then, and a crowd of soldiers were sitting around a fire. They were eating and drinking, lighting cheroots and passing them around. When a sergeant came strolling by, the sepoys jumped to attention, and a little later one of the British soldiers walked over to the fire to ask why the prisoner was wearing a striped tie. We were told, a sepoy said, that this man was a pukka sahib, so we are honoring him. I realized then that I was hanging there not to terrorize the other prisoners, but to entertain the troops. I'd become a spectacle. It made me so angry that my mind cleared and the pain lifted. The officer who'd ordered this was exhibiting me as a specimen: a colonized creature, perhaps, or a white wog. I wondered if they were going to kill me. The minute I thought this, my body began to rally. My heart pumped blood in a frenzy, my lungs opened, my pressure rose, and a surge of adrenaline flushed away the pain faster than morphine. I was floating, looking down at them from a great height, and I knew they couldn't touch me. I heard an English voice, and I looked down at an officer with a hard-chiseled and furious face, who snapped out a single line: Get him down immediately.

Later, when I was taken to the interrogation room, he was waiting for me. He didn't tell me his name, but I thought of him as Latimer because he reminded me of a boy with that name at Oxford. The minute I was back in that room, I couldn't contain my rage.

He said one word: Sit.

I need my shackles removed, I snapped. When he heard my voice, his eyes widened. He nodded to the guard at the door, who came over to unlock my arms and legs. He offered his regret that I'd received what he called some rather harsh treatment, and he spoke, without irony, about the different degrees of persuasion, as if since I was an educated chap with a posh accent, I might appreciate the nuances. He ordered the guard to bring me some food and left the room while I wolfed it down. I refused his offer of a cigarette but managed to inhale as much of his smoke as I could. When he'd read my file, he told me that I needed to be more forthcoming. You have, he said, given us no information about the terrorists involved in the opera house bombing, and we are aware that you know at least two of them personally.

Your information is incorrect. I'm a physician. I have no connection with terrorism.

He lifted an eyebrow and told me dryly that my father had been a terrorist, of one sort or another, for nearly twenty years.

During which time I have mostly lived abroad.

I am referring to the present, he said, when your life has undergone—he paused—certain changes.

My purpose is to save life, not squander it.

Your life is irregular in several ways, which makes you a risk for this government. He then looked at me directly: You must be aware that someone in your father's organization has managed to develop an extremely lethal bomb, which is being used against His Majesty's forces in several cities? When he told me I was suspected of being involved in both the Lahore and the Rawalpindi incidents, I wanted to laugh: These are the charges against me? How could I be implicated in these events when on both occasions, I was enlisted as a physician caring for the wounded?

He asked me what my feelings were about the British. I think, I said, you are asking what I feel about you. I felt utterly calm. You've become involved in obtaining human intelligence by inhuman means, I said. This camp is run in a way that violates simple human decencies. The prisoners have chronic malaria and tuberculosis. They are half starved and exhausted, and your methods of inquiry are on a par with those used by the Inquisition or the sultans.

He went pale, but his voice was level. We are, he said stiffly, at a disorientating moment in history.

You are speaking about the end of the empire, I presume?

I am speaking about the religious wars we are trying to prevent in India.

Oh? I said. But surely yours is a Christian war against both Hinduism and Islam?

We are trying to stem the tide of anarchy, assassination, torture, and terrorism in India. We are responsible for this country; without our administration it will come apart.

Let it come apart, I said. Your government has become lethal and must leave.

He snapped: It's diabolical to suggest that the British should be above the methods of other state bodies; all governments resort to the same methods to separate a man from his information.

You think torture can be justified?

Torture can always be justified. Without it, many more people will die.

You would seem, I said, to have no sense of the unimaginable harm you have done us. I'm not a militant, I never was a militant, but I think you could imagine that I might leave this place a militant. I reached over and took one of his cigarettes: I'd be obliged if you'd light it . . .

He lit the cigarette. His tone shifted. I've just arrived here, he said. It is a brand-new camp . . .

May I suggest, then, a few things that require your immediate attention? Men cannot sleep with their arms shackled behind them, or they will end up permanently disabled. Disease is rife. You need an infirmary and a great deal of quinine, and the sick prisoners must be separated from the ones who are not sick. These are the basics of care.

I make the decisions here, Latimer said tightly. And one of them is to decide what to do with you.

Perhaps, I suggested, it is simply time for the old order to pass away.

I do not believe, Latimer said slowly, that you have any information that would be of use to us. He flipped through to the end of the papers. We do, however, have some information on file here which could be used against you. Your son, he said, looking down with a flush, his whereabouts are known to us, but the information is not on file anywhere else. He looked at me: I intend to destroy it. Your involvement with the Englishwoman is also known. She was last seen in Delhi but has since disappeared. I imagine that will be a relief to you. Then, Sam said, he rose and put out his hand, and I shook it. As I got up to go, he said: It might interest you to know that plans are being made to have Gandhi arrested for sedition in the near future. The country will quieten down once he's in jail, and things will get back to normal.

It was that night, when I was back in my cell, waiting for the guard to come and tie my arms behind my back that the first bomb went off, killing all the guards in their billets and making a huge crater in the courtyard. The barbed-wire fence flew sky high, and bits of it caught in the trees. A second explosion sent off a ripple of white light as an ammunition bunker was hit. Windows were blown out of walls; projectiles flew in all directions, looping back and coming to earth with a shriek. In the chaos, and under cover of the heavy smoke, one of the guards got me out of my cell, led me out of the camp, and onto the debris-sprayed road, where my father's black Mercedes pulled out of the shadows and drove me to safety and to you.

Twenty-five

The high hedges of the hill roads are tangled up with blue. Honey-suckle and morning glory coil into blackberry bushes, the cool mountains are draped in tea bushes, and the terraced hills glisten with rice. Rosy-cheeked hill women shove the bushes aside with their breasts, moving quickly, nipping off the tender tips and reaching over their shoulders to drop them into cone-shaped baskets high on their backs. Bullocks and elephants trudge the English roads, shaded by hedges crammed with red currants, hibiscus, and wild orchids. A Hindu temple appears on a rise and then vanishes at the next dip. The narrow road meanders into a forest of rain trees, then out into brilliant sunshine; pathways around the perimeters of the villages open into patches of vegetables and neat orchards. And then, lo and behold, there's a formal botanical garden, and next to it a small sanitarium and several elegant residences perched on the hillside. Children rush up from the ditches to offer sprays of canna lilies or little bunches of wildflowers; a sadhu sits upright by a roadside shrine, his eyes trained on God.

As we got closer to Jalpaiguri, I thought I should tell Sam a few things. I'm not quite sure, I began, how exactly I'm going to find this house of ours. Did I mention that?

You did not, he said, but I'm glad to know.

Well, I said, the Pater only talked about it once or twice.

He looked back calmly. We'll find it, he said, if it's there to find.

I'm now wondering, I muttered, if I'm being a complete idiot to imagine it will still be there, after all this time. Mother did communicate while she was here with a bank manager, not the original one who first managed the property but someone who knew about it at least, but we've probably been told a pack of lies.

They're a contented lot here, Sam said, looking out at a hairpin bend, and they've not had much to do with the British. I doubt it would have been blown up.

Perhaps the bank manager will have pocketed the cash, or maybe the dampness of the hills will have rotted the house, or maybe the tea gardens have simply kept on spreading so that now the house is no more than a hill of tea?

Maybe, he said, mildly, looking down a collapsed shoulder at pine trees a hundred feet below. But I'm more interested to find out what medicinal plants they have around here. Soldiers have been recuperating at places like this for centuries. Just the air is a tonic. He smoked his cigarette down to the stub, frowning a little. They're bound to have cinchona, so that will take care of malaria. He turned to me and smiled: The climate's rather Italian, in its way, don't you think?

Slowly, the road widens its girth, and the hills are less verdant. Tea grows from here to eternity, and they harvest it with urgency. Women fill and unload their baskets, passing them to men who run down the narrow tracks of the tea gardens to warehouses and factories. If you look at it from above, the tea gardens are like a maze of pale paths leading in and out of dense lines of trim, contoured bushes, with women in bright veils moving quickly in the heat. And somewhere in all this activity was a family house called, of all things, Sorrel Cottage, the place where Pater was born and spent his first years. I'd found the name of the village on a detail map, but that was the full extent of my knowledge. There were people to ask, who were courteous and friendly, though shy, and so it came about that at the post office we were directed to a strange wreck of a man, who was the plantation manager in the village. He sat on his veranda, smoking, watching as we got out of the tonga. He didn't get up, but I walked up to him, pushed back my veil, and put out my hand, and then he rose and said: Miss Herbert? I've been expecting you. I introduced Sam, and we sat down on battered cane chairs while he looked us over. His stare was wonderfully frank. You're not quite what I expected, he said. I thought that his nearest relative must be a praying mantis; when he walked, he had that rocking motion, though he wasn't a bit drunk. He stretched out his legs, which were as thin as a beggar's. Peters, at the bank, he said, advised me to get the house sorted out in case we had a visit. Your mother gave him his marching orders, I gather. I looked him over. His face was covered in dark freckles, and his hair, once obviously a mop of curls, was now standing on end. His skin was etched like the knees of an elephant, his eyes were the color of smoke, and he'd probably not had a decent conversation in twenty years.

I wasn't sure, I said, whether the house would still be standing.

Did you think it would be overrun by locals? In my experience, it's the Saxon race that has the tendency to seize the possessions of others. Your house is in good order, though I must say someone might have thought to come out and take a look at it once in a while.

Has it been used at all? I asked.

Well, it's not part of the plantation, or the estate, which I manage for the Fergusons. They, I might add, come out regularly to make sure there's enough money to run the place properly. I do take the liberty of using Sorrel when we run out of warehouse space; we store the tea in there, and, sometimes—he looked around him—when this place goes underwater, which it does from time to time, I move in and wait for the rains to go down.

Sam looked across at him and said with a smile: We hope you will continue to do so. The manager, who'd not bothered to introduce himself, looked startled for a moment. Sam breezed on, charming as ever: We have no plans to disturb things here—for you or anyone else.

There were things the manager wanted to ask, you could tell, and he became a little more chatty. I started, he said, in Ceylon, tried coffee, but it didn't work, too low on the coast. Did better up in the hills round Kandy, but I never liked coffee. Tea's the brew for me. Never drink it myself, but I love to watch it grow. It's the speed of the processing I like. Good workforce here, peaceful, just as smart as the Tamils, but better natured. We have no bombings in these parts. Shut off from the rest of the world. That's why I stay. Want to take a look round? I'll get the cart. The cart had thick rubber tires and a strong wooden construction with benches on both sides.

You didn't give us your name, I said, sitting opposite him in the cart.

It's Stanley, he said.

Just Stanley, or Stanley something?

Just Stanley, he snapped, one name's more than enough.

I knew then that we'd be pals. Call me Isabel, I said, and this is Sam.

Just coming for a holiday? Stanley asked.

No, Sam said.

Ah. Stanley nodded. This here, he said, pointing, is one of the warehouses, running out of steam rather, but works well enough.

It sat, long and flat, on a small hill surrounded by acres of tea, with a narrow, winding dirt road leading into the plantation. Over there, he said, those line cottages belong to the tea pickers' families; they each have a good plot for growing veggies, and they share the cows and goats. But let's go up to Upper Lake, and I'll give you a tour of the factories. We drove past the post office, and a small shop, which I hoped was a place to buy things other than tea and rice, and then went onto a dirt road that took us up into the mountains. The tea factory was perched on top of a hill, and once we got there, it was possible to see all the way down to the main road. I found it comforting to know that we'd always be able to see who might be coming up that road at any moment. The factory was a bit like a barn, but more substantial, with clean, straight exterior lines. It had rows of tall, regularly spaced windows, drawing in light and mountain breezes from all sides. Grass loped up to the front door, and several large apple trees made a stout, cheerful wall. Stanley took us into a central atrium. Hot air was being pumped from dryers to the upper lofts; wide fans kept the air moving. Tea must be withered first, he yelled above the din, not dried. When it comes down from the withering lofts, it goes on these racks to dry; then we crush the leaves, and let 'em ferment for an hour or so before they go in those big machines to get completely dried, then sifted and graded and packed. Quick operation; whole thing takes no more than nineteen hours. At night, he said, you could hear a pin drop here: utter silence, thick mists, but warm as toast inside.

Sam turned to him: If you turned the withering lofts into small rooms, how many would you have?

Sixty or seventy, perhaps.

Excellent, Sam said.

What's on your mind? Stanley asked.

A hospital, Sam said. We thought we might start one here.

Stanley smiled grimly: More absurd notions have floated around here, but there's plenty of disease—malaria by the jungleful and all the other regulars, with an emphasis on intestinal problems. All we have is an ancient infirmary with an inebriated Scot in charge and the TB sanitarium—probably saw it on your way up.

I imagine, Sam said, that you must do the doctoring round here?

I'm not bad. We can get supplies and equipment easily enough from Dhaka and Calcutta—good train service and the road's not bad when it's not raining.

All three of us looked up at the tea factory, each doing a private calculation.

And that's how it all began.

OUR HOUSE stands back from a dirt road, with a forest behind and a lake at its feet. It's an early Victorian gem, square and white, with a slender veranda all the way around. The garden slopes in terraces until you reach a wall of round stones, over which ivy and honeysuckle clamber. The dark earth below is covered with tufts of violets and petunias. Inside the house the walls are the palest green, and the floors are scuffed mahogany. There's a strong fruity smell of tea and the darker aroma of woodsmoke. Sometimes at night, approaching it, I see it as just one perfect oblong of light, the faintest shape of a house beneath an eyelash of moonlight. When we first arrived, it had been cooped up for months, and no one had opened the windows. Barely a stick of furniture on the ground floor, only a charpoy bed covered in a bright orange print, which we imagined Stanley slept in when the rains flooded his bungalow. The only signs of life were two paraffin lamps and a woodstove and a kitchen with two saucepans neatly washed and dried. Not quite up to our standards, I said, but it looks like someone has worked hard to clean it. Of the four bedrooms upstairs, all were stark naked, except for one which had a handsome solid teak bed in the middle of it and a wardrobe. They must have been put together where they stood, since there was no possibility of either leaving the premises. It was airy and light on the first floor when the windows were open. The main bedroom had a high ceiling with a central rosette and a frieze of lotus blossoms around the edges. Windows are new, Sam said, and we should be grateful the bed's made. He sat down on it, and I saw how exhausted he was. When I looked closely at his face, which was white and spent, I had the image of someone who was in the last stages of malaria. He took off his sandals, and I saw that they were sticky with blood. He turned his back to me when he began to take off his salwar kameez. I wanted to help him, because of his arm, but knew he would ward me off, so I let him struggle with it.

In the bathroom there was a sink, and taps that were dry, but someone had brought up some buckets of water. There was a white enamel basin and a steel bathtub, a stack of clean white towels and a chunk of soap. I splashed water on my face; it tasted sweet, mountain water, pure as air. When I came back, he was lying on the bed, with a sheet over him. His eyes were closed, and when I spoke, I wasn't sure he heard me. I sat down next to him. Twilight had entered the room, and he shivered a little when I touched his cheek. I went over to the fireplace, which was laid with wood, took his box of matches and waited as the kindling leaped into flames. In the bathroom I sat in the tub and threw water over my head to wash the dust off. I pulled my faded old rag of a pink dress out of my velvet bag and shook out its creases. A button was missing. Was it still in the pocket of his suit? I wanted to cry, for so many reasons, but instead I pulled the dress over my head and let the water from my hair drip down my shoulders, pooling beneath my breasts, radiating across my fat belly. Filling the enamel bowl with water, I soaked a small towel and went back into the bedroom. He was watching me carry the water without spilling it, and he had that mysterious smile, but it seemed sad to me.

I sat on the edge of the bed and raised his head to put a towel beneath him. I began to wash his face, softly pushing his hair back from his forehead so that it looked sleek and elegant, the way it had at the station when he'd come back from London, wearing the three-piece suit, jaunty as could be. His eyes were the color of shallow seawater, and it was painful to look too deeply into them. I washed his neck and shoulders, and the arm in its splint, and moved down the other arm. I washed his hands; the wrists were mangled and bruised, and I let cool water spill over them. He didn't flinch. I moved the cloth gently across his chest, down his belly, and over his ribs and was careful around the edges of his hips where lash marks curled around to the front. Looking closely at his body, at its emaciation and bruising, I was faint with sorrow. I closed my eyes with the pain of remembrance . . . how he'd moved the silk up and over my head . . . how he'd washed me in all my rage and fever and filth and had cared for me with more tenderness than any man had ever shown me. The absence between our bodies was deep and lonely; the memories etched in our flesh full of pain. I moved down the curve of his ribs; they stood out so clearly that it was like looking at one of those beautiful wood engravings in *Anatomy, Descriptive and Surgical*, by Henry Gray. The words came back to me: *Elastic arches of bone, which form the chief part of the thoracic walls; the true and false ribs, the last two being free at their anterior extremities; they are termed floating ribs.* The clear language of the 1870 edition flooded over me, and my hands began to shake. His eyes opened. I stooped to dip the towel in the water, rinsed and wrung it, and slowly came back to his body, but his eyes had trapped me. I was afraid without knowing why. I reached for the sheet that covered the lower part of his body and started to lift it. His hand tied mine to the sheet, fast, and I looked at the bones of his fingers and whispered like a chant: Semilunar, scaphoid, carpus, metacarpus, phalanges . . . I saw the cigarette burns. My body contracted into a fist. I began to wail. His hand rested lightly on my brow, my cheek, the side of my throat, and I grabbed and kissed it. I heard a sharp intake of breath. He moved and curled himself around me, tight as a tourniquet. It's all right, he whispered, it will all heal. I unclenched myself and looked at him. All his remoteness was gone.

He undid the little buttons down my front, one, two, three, and pulled the dress over my head. Let me look at you, he said, setting loose the strands of small pink pearls that were tangled in my hair. He ran his hand lightly over my belly, and I shivered, and so did he. Then he got off the bed and knelt in front of me and put his cheek against my belly, listening. I put my hands on his head and smoothed his hair, and he smiled at me, and now it was as if we were so close that he'd slid under my skin. He spoke in a voice that was warm and deep. Everything, he said, that happens to us, we do to ourselves, one way or another. I've been torturing myself all my life, the physical side attacking the mental, the Indian fighting the English, the endless quarrel with who I am. I opened the door to torture long ago, and now it's done.

If that's true, I whispered, it means that one side of me is going blind, or will be blind one day, this eye drying out with the absence of tears. He smiled with such sweetness: You were always blind; it's what I love about you. You don't see things as they are or life as it is. You barge on blindly, and that way you see more than the rest of us. Before you, I saw nothing at all. I was just so furious and afraid. You brought me to life. What's a little torture compared to that? Here, come on now, don't cry. Come and lie beside me. We can watch the sun go down. He kissed me again and again, and pulling me in under the sheet, he said: Do you think you can be happy with an Indian doctor all covered with scars?

ON OUR FIRST DAY, three people came and sat under the cedar trees in the garden. There was a woman carrying a small, flushed child, a skeletal old man with ulcers on his legs, and a boy with a filthy bandage covered in caked blood. We'd just come into the kitchen, and I heard Sam sigh as he looked through the window. The minute they saw us, the woman walked up to the back steps and, standing close to the edge of the open door, almost out of sight, reached in her hand to knock. Sam moved across from the sink to speak to her. She inclined her head to the boy's cheek, but he barely stirred. Sam touched his forehead and lifted the boy's eyelid. He looked quickly at me. I was standing by the door, watching them. Sam put out his cigarette, and after running the taps hard and scrubbing his hands beneath them, he took the woman and child into the front room.

I began to panic because he no longer had his brown doctor's bag with its compendium of healing. We had nothing apart from the scraps I had in my bag—some morphine, some bandages and painkillers—nothing to treat anyone. I looked out of the door. The old man sat under the cedar, knees up, chewing. The boy leaned against it, one leg bent against the trunk. Sam came back without the woman and child. I'm keeping them here, he said. It's typhoid. The other two will have to go to the infirmary until we have supplies. I went outside, and I saw him sitting under the trees, knees up, smoking. He put up his hands in a gesture of emptiness, and the old man laughed, and settled his back into the trunk of the tree. I could hear Sam's voice, speaking slowly, easily, taking his time. He explained that we'd have to get medicine and that they must come back in a few days. The old man and the boy looked at him and didn't move. He shrugged, smiled, and walked back inside. He draped an arm around me and gave a toppled grin: We'd better get cracking. Where did Stanley say the nearest infirmary is?

On the second morning, when I went to open the back door, there were ten more people squatting under the cedar. I looked at Sam, who was making a rapid assessment of our patients. He was divining what ailed them from where he stood, and then he walked outside and sat for a moment under the trees. He explained that our medical supplies were limited and that no more than ten could come tomorrow. When he came back in, he grinned and said: We'll have fifty by the end of the week. I turned the flame down on the Primus stoves, where needles and scalpels were bubbling away, and went back to laying out a row of enamel dishes. The rest of the equipment was in boxes, which we were trying to organize: bandages and ointments, surgical instruments, and a tall chemist's dispensary cupboard made up of square drawers, also a box full of books on Ayurvedic medicine that he'd found God knows where and a list we were putting together to get supplies from Calcutta. He touched my arm. I'll take the women and children, I said. The women sat clustered under a tree at a distance from the men. They'd established a queue and smiled patiently as I walked up, looking at my belly, putting their hands together and smiling. I took the first mother who came forward with a baby. The men had established no order, so Sam took a boy who was bleeding heavily from a wound in his thigh.

In the evening, as we strolled in the cool air, talking about the day's work, I looked around me at the immensity of the land and remarked that since we were so remote, how could anyone possibly know we were here? It takes one person, he said, and every sick person for miles begins walking. The next morning, as I took an early stroll up the hill, I came out of the trees and got a view of our slanting valley. A line of figures came walking across a field of yellow and green, with towering, terraced hills behind them and a wall of snow mountains beyond: a woman enclosed in a scarlet chador, a child in gray, with a smaller child hanging off her hip, two men in dust-colored turbans and baggy trousers, two women and a small child, two old women with bundles on their heads. They walked steadily. Tiny they seemed, surrounded by rice paddies, long slabs of blue irrigation water, plots of vegetables, and a cloudless sky. The figures stood out so clearly, walking in and out of shadow, making their way down the valley. It would be hours before they got to us. There were ten of them.

THIS AFTERNOON, as I was hanging some blue curtains, I saw a circle of red far off down the winding road that leads to our village. I kept stopping to look. It was a woman, I decided, who was carrying a red bundle on her head. She was the only walker on the road, and behind her were banks of rhododendrons, and behind them the brown shafts of the timber trees rising up the hills. Her littleness was framed by the blue-white peaks of mountains that blocked out the sky. You only caught glimpses, no more than that, of the mountains, the whispering trees, the smoke rising languidly, and the solitary figure. Then a hedge or a curve took them away. I missed the red when it was gone. I'd become transfixed by the color and stood there waiting for it to come back, and whenever there was no sight of the traveler on the road I began to panic. There was a bend shaded by tall poplars, and perhaps it blocked the view, but to me standing there waiting, it seemed as though the figure had fallen off the rim of the world. I got down off my stool, which I'd no business being on anyway, since I'm a barge now, moving through my own quiet space, enclosed in a kind of rapture that makes me whisper all day long: I love you, I love you—to you, to them, to everyone. Carrying a child makes the heart so elastic that it can take in the world with all its beauty and grief and wonder. And around the bend came the person walking. I saw that it wasn't a woman carrying a bundle on her head. It was a man with a face as black as a boot, wearing a scarlet turban. It was the turban Joseph had worn when he'd followed me up the Kasauli hills to Simla. And when he saw me waving my arms back and forth, he lifted his hand straight up in the air in salutation.